LINE WAR

NEAL ASHER

LINE WAR

TOR

First published 2008 by Tor
an imprint of Pan Macmillan Ltd
Pan Macmillan, 20 New Wharf Road, London N1 9RR
Basingstoke and Oxford
Associated companies throughout the world
www.panmacmillan.com

ISBN 978-1-4050-5501-7

1 3 5 7 9 8 6 4 2

A CIP catalogue record for this book is available from
the British Library.

Typeset by SetSystems Ltd, Saffron Walden, Essex
Printed and bound in Great Britain by
Mackays of Chatham plc, Chatham, Kent

Keith Starkey
Cheers for the readings, even if not of this one!

Acknowledgements

Thanks as always to my wife Caroline, and special thanks to Peter Lavery – here's hoping he enjoys his time away from the needy egos of the writerly world. Included must be those others working at Macmillan, including Rebecca Saunders, Emma Giacon, Steve Rawlings, Liz Cowen, Jon Mitchell, Liz Johnson, Chantal Noel and Neil Lang. Also thanks to the foreign publishers and translators, who certainly must be doing something right!

1

The Line, which is effectively the border zone of the Polity, has in many areas stabilized where the Polity has ceased to expand (a prime example being the point between the Polity itelf and the Prador Third Kingdom, called by its residents the 'Graveyard') but is still shifting outwards elsewhere (towards the galactic centre mostly). Upon this border there have been and will continue to be numerous conflicts, for beyond it human and even AI occupation extends even further as a result of the first diasporas of the solar system and the continuous emigration of those humans and AIs searching for something new or fleeing something old. These conflicts are called Line wars – being very specifically defined as such by the resources required for them and how they impinge on Polity territory. Usually they are finished quickly by ECS warships or Polity ground forces, or both. Generally it is the cleaning up afterwards that takes longer. Throughout the Polity's history I can think of only one conflict that has been defined as something more than a Line war, and that started when the Prador destroyed Avalon Station and then moved into Polity space like wasps invading a bees' nest. I have, however, heard rumours that there have been other conflicts that exceed the Line war definition, but the details are never very clear. Perhaps these are just myths, urban legends, persistent memes to titillate the masses. Or perhaps they are something else . . .

– From HOW IT IS by Gordon

The two million inhabitants of the planet Klurhammon claimed that their homeworld did not have a population sufficiently large to warrant a runcible, that device for instantly transporting people across the vast reaches of space. Those few who felt the need to travel elsewhere could easily book passage on one of the many ships that visited to collect the harvests of biomolecular construction units that were the main business of their world. However, in reality, the locals did not want to make it any easier for others in the interstellar Polity to visit them. They were introverted, relished their small society, enjoyed the open spaces around their high-tech farms and within their sprawling open-plan single city of Hammon, and they regarded the rest of the Polity with either indifference or suspicion.

It was not their decision to make.

A runcible was installed in Hammon twenty years ago, along with its controlling artificial intelligence, which became effectively the planetary governor. There were objections to this move, but when a massive influx of visitors failed to appear, and the profitability of certain select biologicals – once transported out by spaceship but now sent by runcible – rapidly increased, these objections died. Those few visitors who did arrive were treated with respect, but little warmth, and soon even their numbers waned. The people of Klurhammon thus continued with their introvert and somewhat Byzantine lifestyle, but were soon to have their antipathy towards visitors justified.

The controlling artificial intelligence and the crew of the *Lubeck* – a mile-long cargo hauler shaped like a slipper, with a structure resembling a submarine's conning tower protruding from where the ankle should be – saw the visitor first. Its strange underspace signature presaged the arrival of something utterly alien – something that none but the ship's AI could recognize. Crew gazed in awe at a screen displaying a sphere three miles across seemingly formed of a tangled mass of giant legless millipedes constantly in motion, loops writhing in and out. It slid past the *Lubeck* impelled by some engine that clawed at the very fabric of space.

Some managed to exclaim in surprise before massive acceleration, which could not be compensated for by the ship's internal gravplates, slammed them into walls, floors or ceilings. The *Lubeck*'s AI knew this would certainly kill some of them, but it also knew that to stay within the vicinity of this thing could mean death to them all.

It was correct.

The missile needled across intervening space from the alien vessel, its passage the briefest flicker to the human eye, but long enough for the AI, whose speed of thought was orders of magnitude above the *Lubeck*'s crew, to recite every prayer in every human religious canon. It punched through the *Lubeck*'s hull and detonated before crewmembers impacting hard with the internal structure of the ship could actually die from their injuries. Sun-hot fire bloomed inside the stricken craft, travelling out in a sphere neither slowed nor diverted by any intervening material. In a glare of light and in the silence of space, the cargo hauler simply disappeared. The weird snake-tangled vessel did not alter course or slow and quickly fell into orbit around Klurhammon even as the fire it left behind cooled and dispersed. The *Lubeck* now consisted of a spreading cloud of gaseous matter containing the occasional sprinkling of metal globules cooling and hardening into what resembled perfectly formed ball bearings.

The runcible AI, named Klurhammon after the world it governed, had seconds longer to contemplate the arrival of this alien vessel. This allowed it time to transmit data and conduct a brief conversation before some form of U-space interference curtailed that option.

'One of Erebus's ships has just arrived, destroyed a cargo

hauler and is now approaching,' it told Earth Central – the ruling artificial intelligence on Earth. 'It is not even bothering to conceal itself with chameleonware.'

'Get yourself out. Get out now,' that intelligence replied.

'It was my understanding that my world was "of no tactical importance",' Klurhammon observed. 'I'll stay and do what I can for them.'

The option was still there for the Klurhammon AI – physically a large lozenge of crystal using quantum-interface processing – to rail-gun itself from the planet and out into space. It chose not to do so, instead activating its rather pathetic array of orbital weapons and firing them. Missiles sped towards the alien vessel, microwave beams punched invisibly across orbital space. The AI observed some beams striking home, but the burned and blackened modular units of the alien vessel's wormish structure just revolved inside it, to be replaced by shiny new insectile segments. Perhaps one of the missiles would be more destructive? Almost upon that thought a firestorm spread across tens of thousands of miles, all the missiles detonating before reaching their target.

'Bad decision,' Klurhammon opined.

In the ensuing second and a half remaining to the planetary AI, no reply was forthcoming from Earth Central. The high-intensity particle beam fired by the alien ship was eight feet in diameter: straight and blue in vacuum, but blurred and turquoise in atmosphere. It struck the centre of Hammon directly over the runcible, and in a few seconds the ensuing firestorm devoured runcible, AI and the surrounding two-mile-wide complex, then washed into the city to scour over buildings flattened by the initial blast wave. Fifty thousand people died, some so quickly naught remained of them but smudges on some still-standing walls, others in the slow agony reserved for those with most of their skin charred away.

Like many on the world of Klurhammon, Cherub Egengy was a haiman – a human partially combined with AI. Seeing his city struck so hard, on his vantage point on the north face of the Boulder he just clung to the ochre stone amid the heathers, unable to process the sight. Belatedly, through external comunits scattered around the world, he received the message – with explanatory information packets – the AI had sent just before expiring: 'We are under attack from a ship controlled by the entity named Erebus. Planetary assault or planetary destruction certain to ensue. Run away. Hide.'

Direct-downloading the information packages via his gridlink to his mind, Cherub instantly learned that Erebus was the rogue AI that had once controlled the dreadnought the *Trafalgar*, which had deserted the Polity after humanity's war against the alien Prador. This malign AI, which controlled a pernicious alien nano-technology and a fleet of ships numbering in the tens of thousands, had now returned to attack.

Planetary destruction.

Abruptly Cherub's assister frame – motorized braces for his arms and legs terminating in extra metal fingers, and two additional limbs extending at waist-level – reached out and gripped the rock, pulling him close to it. For a moment he thought this was a reaction, on some level of himself, to 'planetary destruction', but then realized that his survival-orientated sub-persona, which he always put online when he did something dangerous, had recognized another danger. A second later the blast wave from the strike on the city tried to drag him from the rock face. His ribbed carapace already protected his back from his neck to the base of his spine. His sensory cowl, which when closed was a tongue of metal extending from it up behind his head, he now spread open like the petals of a flower for further protection. However, he felt hot cinders burning through his clothing into the skin of his arms and legs. Within his carapace he onlined a program to lock his muscles and cut out pain messages, and then further studied the information packets the AI had sent.

'Jain nano-technology. Informational subversion. Can sequester all Polity technology, and even humans themselves . . .'

Instantly shutting down access to his carapace from all outside sources cut some incoming program. Internally he tracked down what he had already received, running high-level diagnostics, isolation techniques and hunter-killer programs. He just got it in time: some ugly and hugely complex informational worm that would have rendered him utterly obedient to whatever sent it . . . this Erebus. He wondered how many others had managed to react so quickly. What about his brother, Carlton? What about his mother? Turning his head slightly he gazed at the burning city. Carlton, who was out at the hothouses, might have stopped the worm. Their mother, however . . .

She was in the city doing some business while Cherub climbed the Boulder. This business would have taken her very near the centre, so he assessed her chances of survival as little above zero. Grief tightened a fist inside him and there was no logic involved in his suddenly wanting to climb down to ground level and head back there. But his mother had always wanted him to operate on logic – to use his loose combination of human mind and artificial intelligence to best effect. He had once read, 'Grief is a selfish indulgence,' and decided just then not to let it kill him, for even now there were things descending from the sky directly towards the city.

Cherub used programming measures within his carapace and neuro-chemical measures, via the hardware in his skull, to dull the pain while not dulling his intelligence.

Run away. Hide.

He was too visible here, so first he turned on the surface

chameleon effect of his carapace and chameleoncloth clothing.
Maybe his penchant for wearing such gear and going wild like this
to study the local fauna would end up saving his life. Reconfiguring
internal hardware and writing programs in his mind, he created a
near facsimile to Earth Central Security – ECS – chameleonware.
His carapace did not possess sufficient projecting and scanning
facilities to make it 100-per-cent effective, but it would have to do.
Then, as the wind dropped to a mere hot gale, he onlined full
assist in his climbing program and hurried the rest of the way up
the rock face like a spider scuttling up a wall.

Reaching the curving summit of the Boulder, Cherub scanned
around him. The boulder-birds he had come here to see were
absent – doubtless scared off by the explosion – but they were no
longer his concern anyway. Using his sensory cowl, the full potential of his augmented eyes and all the enhancement programs to
hand, he focused on the objects descending towards the city. He
counted ten bacilliform shapes, each precisely like a rod prokaryote
bacterium, but about sixty feet long and with an exterior of a
completely featureless blue grey.

Bombs?

That seemed unlikely since the ship above seemed quite
capable of messing this place up without resorting to such conventional methods. Anyway, bombs that size would have to be planet
busters, so why drop ten of them all in the same spot? He would
therefore assume they were not bombs, since to do so would be to
admit that he now had a very short time left to live. He just
watched carefully, recording everything he was seeing and sensing.

Settling about the central incinerated area, the rod-things just
seemed to melt into the rubble. Focusing closer on one, he saw it
spreading itself, like something made of jelly, over foamstone
rubble and tangled girders. It then began to emit tentacular
growths that speared down into surrounding crevices. Near to one

7

of these rod-things, he observed a woman stumbling along, something hanging from her arms, which she held out before her. He realized that she was blind, and that what hung from her arms was shredded skin.

His mother had certainly been well within the blast zone, so had probably died instantly – surely that had to be better.

Cherub forced himself to abandon that train of thought before it led to him having to again alter his brain chemistry.

The woman must have heard something for she stopped and turned abruptly. Out of a nearby drain a tentacle rose like a rattlesnake readying itself to strike, then it lashed out and penetrated her chest, numerous tendrils spearing out of her back as if the horrific thing had splintered inside her. She collapsed to her knees, dragging it down with her. After a few minutes the thing retracted, seemed to hesitate poised over her for a moment, then dropped to the ground and squirmed on past her, emerging endlessly from the drain. Its victim swayed back and forth on her knees, then suddenly lurched to her feet. She looked around for a moment, as if oblivious to the fact that her face was a charred ruin and she seemed to possess no eyes. After scanning a pile of rubble she stepped over to it and picked up a steel reinforcing bar about two feet long. Cherub tracked her subsequent purposeful search through the ruination and watched her smash in the skull of another burn victim before moving on. Cherub realized that the bacilliforms were products of Jain-tech, and that they were infecting the survivors with that same technology. Finally he dragged his horrified attention away from the woman in time to observe a new object descending from the sky.

This thing was quite obviously a ship of some kind. Thirty feet long, it was curved like the head of a spoon. Its exterior was silver-green fading to black at the edges, and it bore patterns like umber veins running through its surface. Silently it landed inside the city, in which it was now possible to see those weird tentacular growths every few hundred feet, and also humans, hijacked like the blind woman, stumbling through the ruins bearing makeshift weapons. It was a vision from hell, as they slaughtered other survivors with sickening regularity. And when the newly arrrived ship opened up and a figure stepped out, it seemed as if the arch-demon himself had arrived to oversee it all.

From a distance the bizarre humanoid seemed wholly of metal – just like a Cybercorp metalskin Golem. But closer inspection revealed that its shiny blue-green exterior was without visible joints, and stretched and contracted over its frame like a living skin. The android towered tall and was incredibly thin, and its outstretched fingers resembled a spider's legs. The head slanted abruptly back at the forehead, and tapered sharply down to the lipless slot of its mouth. It had no nose and the eyes were lidless and insectile.

It walked from its spacecraft towards a nearby rubble pile, and there stood waiting. One of the tentacles uncoiled from the smoking mass of shattered foamstone and girders and arched over until it was only a few feet from the humanoid's face. The tip of it split into three prongs then froze. After a moment the prongs closed up again and the tentacle retracted into the rubble. The humanoid swivelled round and headed back to its vessel.

Cherub assessed what he had just seen, and it struck him as likely that the brutal slaughter in the city was almost of peripheral concern to something capable of deploying technology like this. Sure, if you are going to attack, you take out the AI and the runcible first, but a few surviving burn victims should be somewhat irrelevant. He gazed at the activity continuing amid the rubble. Of course, by destroying the AI you would be wiping out a massive source of information. Cherub felt certain that what he had been witnessing here was a data-gathering exercise – and that the data gatherers had just delivered their report.

The humanoid slid back inside its spacecraft, which immediately launched itself straight up, slamming to a halt in mid-air, before accelerating straight towards the spot where Cherub crouched. He remained utterly still, utterly reliant on his chameleonware to hide him. The ship sped overhead, then dropped low towards the fields of drastically modified plants that lay beyond. The android clearly had to be after something here, and he wondered what. This world was small and insignificant and, as declared in one of the AI's information packets, 'of no tactical importance'. Maybe Cherub would find out what it was seeking, since it was heading the same way he must go to reach the hothouses, where he hoped to find out what had happened to Carlton.

Seated in a viewing lounge aboard the giant spaceship *Jerusalem*, Agent Ian Cormac peered over at the object folded up in the corner looking like a chromed spider corpse, which was a close enough approximation to reality. Not a corpse, however, just self-deactivated and bored. Cormac well understood how the spider drone felt. Nothing was happening here and, if anything was to finally happen, he knew his most likely involvement would be to spectate from an acceleration chair and hope for the best. But though he too felt surplus to requirements, he was not bored, for he was having to get used to what seemed to be a whole new range of senses.

Another one . . .

He turned to gaze out of the large panoramic window ranged along one wall. The sensation he now experienced was difficult to nail down: maybe like a sudden pressure drop, a pulse of infrasound, or one of those night-time flashes of light caused by a stray cosmic ray striking the optic nerve, or perhaps an out-of-key note occurring in a symphony that he hadn't until then even realized was being performed. No description seemed adequate. It was similar somehow to that sense of the ineffable he felt when a ship he was aboard dropped into U-space. However, this time it was directional, and he even got a sense of mass and shape. He instinctively *knew*, and had already confirmed such a feeling on numerous occasions, that another big dreadnought had just surfaced into realspace half a light year away. He could confidently point towards it, and sometimes felt that, with an effort of will, he could even step right over to it.

Cormac understood that there was still something odd now about his mind. In his final encounter with a psychopath called Skellor he had escaped a Jain substructure encaging him by stepping through U-space – a feat supposedly impossible for a human being. Driven to utter extremity, his brain penetrated by the alien organic Jain-tech that Skellor was employing to torture him, he had done just that. It was an ability he would find very useful to recover at times, but if it was contingent on what Skellor had done to him, then reaching that state was something he would rather avoid. He had subsequently tried to use the same escape route while being pursued by Erebus's biomechs, but that time failed. It seemed, however, as if, like a runner confined to a wheelchair, he could still feel the track under his feet and the wind in his face.

He tried to dispel the disturbing feeling and return to the moment by using his gridlink to delve into the coms traffic in this highly active planetary system. Jerusalem – the AI controlling the huge ship he was currently aboard – had turned this system into a fortress. The nearby hot inhabited world of Scarflow was sheltered by huge mirrors which diverted the sun's energy towards orbital installations. This energy in turn was, when the devastated Polity fleet arrived here after its disastrous encounter with Erebus, being converted into coherent maser beams projected towards a cold Mars-sized planet further out, so the same energy could be used in terraforming it. Upon the fleet's arrival the percentage of energy being projected had been quickly reduced, the rest being stored for future use, while the coherent masers were at once prepared to be employed as weapons.

But Erebus had not come.

Erebus, which controlled a vast mass of biomechanoid ships, constructed using Jain technology, had effectively ambushed a fleet of Polity ships and wiped out much of it. Cormac had lost personnel and friends in that conflict. He'd actually hoped Erebus would turn up, but logically that would have been a daft move for the entity to make. Then, again, attacking a small fleet outside the Polity had not been so bright either. Though causing massive destruction, Erebus had done no more, tactically, than seriously piss off the Polity's ruling AIs. Cormac still could not fathom why it had done so. However, he felt a deeper disquiet about the reaction on this side, in that it was *only* a reaction. The superintelligent AIs of the Polity should be proactive; they should become the predators in this situation, they should be *doing* something, yet it seemed to Cormac that they were just sitting on their hands, literally or metaphorically.

'What are you thinking?'

He turned to see Mika – Polity scientist, companion and now lover – standing a short few paces behind him. He had not heard her approach, but maybe, on some subliminal level, he had known her to be there, but that level had not alerted his conscious mind fully to her presence. Did that mean he trusted her? Or was it that his new-found U-space awareness was distracting him, for even when there were no ships arriving, he received a constant niggling sensation from the runcibles perpetually in operation on the Polity worlds nearby.

'The usual,' he replied. 'I can't understand why Erebus did what it did, and I've even less idea what it is going to do now. It just makes no sense.' Somehow, almost instinctively, he did not want to mention to her his reservations about the Polity AI response so far. Nor had he told her, or anyone, that he had recently become able, somehow, to sense U-space.

'Not to you maybe – so surely that means Erebus is an enemy to be feared?'

'Perhaps so,' he said.

She wore skin-tight leggings and a loose pale green blouse – the sort of attire she always donned when 'relaxing'. Her ginger hair was tied back, her angular face perfect, obviously having just been given a makeover by a cosmetic unit. Even the blush marks at her temples were concealed – the ones caused by her physical connection to the virtual reality equipment she too frequently used to study those two Dragon spheres out there in the void. In connecting herself to VR like that, rather than via internal hardware, she was in a minority, for she had yet to augment herself. It seemed to Cormac that just about everyone else around here either wore augs or was gridlinked. Only a little while ago some queries he had made through his gridlink had given him much to ponder. Until about four years ago the proportion of citizens opting for cerebral augmentation had averaged 46 per cent across the Polity. Over the last four years, since the depopulation of a world called Samarkand, that had been steadily rising, shooting up to 62 per cent in this quadrant of the Polity after the disastrous events on another world called Coloron, where an entire arcology had been obliterated to prevent the spread of Jain technology. This showed that people were scared enough to seek more individual power. He was suspicious of this ready abandonment of humanity but suspected he might be reading too much into it.

'Jerusalem,' he asked abruptly, 'what is the AI assessment of Erebus's method of attack?'

The AI replied instantly, probably turning only a fraction of a per cent of its attention towards this conversation.

'We are puzzled,' it admitted.

'Why are you puzzled?'

'For precisely the same reasons as you yourself. Erebus seems to have displayed all its cards before the game has even begun.'

'See?' said Cormac to Mika. He then gazed up at the ceiling, as most people did when addressing an AI whose precise location they did not know. 'What about those objects in the asteroid field?' Though Erebus's entire mass of biomech ships had not appeared, something else had arrived out there not so long ago.

'We have yet to find them. I suspect that they are merely devices to keep watch on us, since anything else would cause disturbances we would detect.'

'Perhaps I should go out and take a look?' suggested Cormac.

'That will not be necessary,' the AI replied firmly.

'Cormac,' agreed Mika, 'there's nothing for you to do at the moment.'

Yes, he thought, *even entities with artificial intelligences a couple of orders of magnitude greater than mine don't know what to do.* He nodded, but just then he spotted Arach, the spider drone, slowly opening out his long metal legs and lifting his ruby-eyed head to survey his surroundings. The drone seemed to test the air briefly with his pincers before springing into a fully upright position: a chromed spider some five feet across. Arach now possessed a new abdomen – the original, equipped with automated weapons, having been left behind on a world near where the Polity fleet had been ambushed to help fend off Erebus's pursuing ground-based bio-mechanisms. This new abdomen apparently contained a similar array of armament.

'Something has occurred,' Jerusalem observed.

Cormac realized that, for Arach would only have bothered waking up if there was a chance he would get to use all that new armament. Cormac resisted the urge to key into the local AI nets to find out what was going on. It all struck him as rather too convenient.

'Tell me,' he said, noting Mika's expression becoming resigned and almost sad.

'One of Erebus's wormships has attacked a Polity world,' Jerusalem replied.

'Which one?' Cormac asked, imagining one of the big ones, with a population in billions, now reduced to a smouldering ruin.

'The choice of target is, again, puzzling.'

Arach was now doing his familiar tappity little dance on the carpet, obviously unable to contain his glee. Jerusalem was specific-ally informing Cormac about this and the spider drone was suddenly active . . . which must mean there was a situation that needed investigating without requiring an investment of battle-ships, major AIs or weaponry. Cormac was *needed*.

'You know, I thought AI minds could work a hundred times faster than those of humans, but you're going slow enough now to try my patience.'

'Very well,' said Jerusalem. 'The wormship attacked a very minor world, of no tactical importance, called Klurhammon. As we understand it, the same ship has now departed, after wiping out a large proportion of the population and causing much destruction.'

'Makes no sense.'

'Precisely.'

'And it needs looking into.' Cormac found himself moving towards the door of the lounge, while Arach scuttled across to fall in behind him. Abruptly he halted, not liking his own unthinking reaction, then turned and strode back over to Mika.

'You nearly forgot me,' she said.

'Will you come?'

Before Mika could reply, Jerusalem interrupted: 'I cannot allow that.'

'Why not?' asked Cormac, gazing into Mika's face and seeing she already knew the reason.

'There are two Dragon spheres stationary nearby and, besides the AIs insystem, Mika is the nearest thing we have to a Dragon expert. Also . . . her presence would constrain you.'

It was true – he had already made that assessment – but he felt there was something else involved here. 'And?'

'Mika has a *concord* with Dragon – it communicates better with her than with anyone else here. She is therefore a valuable resource when it comes to communicating with that particular entity.'

Cormac accepted that, feeling rather ashamed at his relief.

'Then I'll see you when I return,' he said to her.

They kissed, perhaps with a bit less passion than previously, but certainly with the same sincerity.

'Goodbye, Cormac,' she whispered. 'Try to stay alive.'

He headed away, trying not to notice the tears glistening in her eyes. The door opened for him automatically, and soon he was striding through the *Jerusalem*'s numerous corridors, heading for the room he had been sharing with Mika.

'Do you think there's going to be *violence*?' the spider drone asked eagerly as it scuttled along behind.

'Shut up, Arach,' Cormac replied.

Arriving at the room he went straight to a particular cabinet and from there removed only the two things he really required: a thin-gun he had grown accustomed to practising with and the wrist-sheath containing his Tenkian throwing star – a device long proved to have an erratic mind of its own. He headed straight out again without even looking at the other belongings gathered there.

'I'd like to select my own team,' he said as he strode along.

'Those currently available have been notified,' Jerusalem replied.

Annoying that the AI had probably already worked out exactly who he wanted to select.

'And my own ship?'

'The *Jack Ketch III* is unavailable, since it has yet to acquire any engines.'

Cormac halted, somehow getting an intimation of what was coming next. 'Then what ship *is* available?'

'The *King of Hearts* has been refitted, and is now prepped and ready for you.'

Great, the same AI attack ship that once went rogue and then had . . . a change of heart. Following this transformation it had rescued Cormac himself and those few surviving the debacle on the world where he had lost his comrade Thorn, his mentor Horace Blegg and many others. He didn't at all trust the AI running that ship, but he guessed Jerusalem now intended for King to prove itself trustworthy.

'Fine,' Cormac replied. 'Fine.'

He reached a drop-shaft and, programming it ahead of him through his gridlink, stepped into it and allowed the irised gravity field to waft him upward. Stepping out into another corridor, Arach clattering quickly behind, he found only one person awaiting him. The ersatz man was tough-looking with cropped black hair, brown skin and unreasonably green eyes. All emulation, for this was Hubbert Smith, a Golem android in the thirtieth production series.

'Time to load up and ship out,' announced Smith.

'So it would seem,' said Cormac. 'Where's your companion, Ursach Candy Kline?'

'It would seem that our personal experience of warfare with Erebus must be fairly distributed, so she shipped out of here about four days ago.'

Cormac grimaced and moved on.

'How y' doin', Arach?' said Smith.

'Lock and load,' the spider drone replied.

Cormac fought to stop his grimace turning into a grin.

'What about Andrew Hailex?' he enquired.

Hailex, like Smith and Kline, was another of those rescued by the *King of Hearts*. He was human and, when Cormac first saw him, the man had looked to be in his twenties, as most people chose to look since that option had become available in centuries past. Cormac knew him to be actually in his sixties and an experienced Sparkind combat veteran. The man had been utterly hairless and bulky. Grinned a lot.

Trying to find a replacement for Thorn?

No, Hailex had looked more like Gant, who had once been in Thorn's Sparkind unit – another who had died during one of Cormac's missions.

'Hailex will not be joining us either,' Smith replied. 'He applied for a transference to agent training.'

Somehow that figured, and Cormac's grimace returned in full force.

In one of the small departure bays a further individual awaited them. However, this one was neither human nor Golem but dracoman – a product of the giant alien entity called Dragon – and an example of what might have gone on to dominate Earth if only the dinosaurs hadn't been wiped out. Dracomen were one of Dragon's jokes, or lessons, or whims. They were as reptilian as their name implied: their skins were mostly tegulated with green scales, except from throat to groin where they were yellow. They possessed a leg structure and gait that was distinctly birdlike, faces jutting and toadlike, and huge eyes. Scar, one of the first of the dracomen to be created, now exposed his teeth in an expression that could be either a grin or a preparation to rip out someone's throat. Admittedly, Scar might still grin while committing such a bloody assault.

'The other dracomen?' Cormac enquired of Smith.

'All reassigned. There aren't many of them in total and their peculiar ability to resist Jain sequestration and to recognize it in others, even at a distance, is too valuable a resource to risk.' Then, perhaps realizing how pompous he had sounded, Smith continued, 'Jerusalem doesn't want all those eggs in one basket . . . do dracowomen lay eggs, anyway?'

On the circular steel floor a small intership shuttle awaited: essentially a flattened cylinder twenty feet long with gimbal-mounted steering thrusters shaped like two-foot-long pitted olives mounted on its rear. The ramp door was down and the lights were on inside. Jerusalem had clearly prepared the way. Without comment, Cormac headed over and boarded the craft, and the others followed him inside. As he strapped himself in, he experienced sudden trepidation, but not because of the enemies he might be about to face. This would be his first time travelling through U-space since his arrival within this system. He could detect ships arriving and departing through that continuum, so what would be his reaction now he was going to be actually entering U-space himself?

Again Mr Crane was perched in his favourite vantage point atop the sandstone monolith, gazing out over the butte-scattered and presently arid landscape of the planet Cull. He still wore his long coat, but it was rather tattered now, as were his trousers and wide-brimmed hat. Even his boots were scored and sand-abraded. However, the brass-coloured adamantine body underneath these garments remained untouched by this harsh environment. Vulture, at the moment circling the monolith, wondered if within that body Mr Crane's rejoined crystal mind thought unfathomable thoughts, or perhaps no thoughts at all. The bird also believed that a technology feared across the Polity maintained the brass Golem's other internal workings, whatever they were.

Set in a brass face that seemed the sculpture of some remorseless Apollo, the black eyes were unblinking. In their depths it seemed that small stars flickered occasionally, or perhaps that was just Vulture's imagination. When finally the bird descended before him in a flurry of dust and a scattering of oily feathers, he directed his gaze upon it and tilted his head in faint query.

'They're still searching every square inch of this place, but still keeping well away from you, buddy,' the bird announced.

Vulture himself had once been an artificial intelligence running a ship of the same name. A Dragon sphere had saved his life from that nutjob Skellor and the Jain technology the man had wielded, but had then transferred the AI into this avian receptacle. Spreading his wings into the dusty wind, Vulture stretched luxuriously: he rather liked this body, perhaps Dragon had done something to his mind to make him feel that way.

'I reckon they've been instructed to keep their hands off you,' he decided. 'You gave them a Jain node when they asked for it and they know that irking you wouldn't be the greatest idea.'

Secretly Vulture reckoned that the Polity survey and clear-up teams would at some point be given the go-ahead to intrude here, but at least Earth Central was holding them back just for now. Mr Crane and the creatures living in the weird village scattered at the base of this lump of sandstone were an imponderable that should not be left alone. *Would* not be left alone.

Almost as if he read Vulture's thoughts, Mr Crane abruptly rose to his feet and peered out in the direction the bird had approached from. He strode over to the edge of the monolith and, with an agility that belied his weight, heaved himself over the edge and began to descend using handholds cut into the stone. Vulture waddled to the edge and peered over, observing how one of the sleer–human hybrids was clinging to the rock face beside the android's route down. This disconcerting creature resembled an eight-foot scorpion with a human face where its mandibles should be. Its facial features seemed frozen in a permanent scream.

As Mr Crane's boots finally clumped down heavily into the dust at ground level, Vulture launched himself into the air and descended to glide low over his head. The Golem reached up a hand to prevent his hat being displaced by the sudden draught, pausing to peer up at the bird before he strode on.

All about them lay the homes of the hybrids: the results of Dragon's experiments in combining the genome of the sleer – a native arthropodal creature – with that of humankind. Their dwellings were like giant hollowed-out gourds, but constructed from sand bonded with a natural glue that sleers could emit and which some of these hybrids could also still produce. Through the circular entry holes could be seen chitinous activity – the snap of a pincer or the flexing of an armoured insectile leg – combined with elements of bastardized humanity like a face or an arm, and sometimes from those dark interiors could be heard voices muttering rudimentary language. How these creatures had become Mr Crane's charge Vulture could not fathom, just as he could not see how they communicated with him, yet somehow they did.

As Crane reached the far edge of the village, two of the hybrids began to follow him out. One looked quite like a young girl except for her multifaceted eyes and the pincers that protruded from her mouth. The other was a centaur-boy: the upper half of a male human child seemingly grafted on a sleer body. The brass Golem halted, stared at them, then inclined his head slightly back towards the scattered dwellings. The two children hung their heads in disappointment, then traipsed back disconsolately the way they had come.

'They like you,' said Vulture, settling in the dust beside the Golem.

Crane looked at him but made no comment. Since their partnership began – Vulture liked to think of it as a partnership – Crane had said just a total of twelve words to him. There were other communications: a small gesture of the hand here, a slight inclination of the head, maybe a blink. Mr Crane was what Vulture liked to describe as a conversational minimalist.

Half a mile on from the hybrids' village lay the beginning of a sandstone labyrinth of buttes and canyons. Following sometimes along the ground and sometimes in the air, Vulture observed scattered lumps of carapace lying on the ground and the body of a huge third-stage sleer draped over a rock nearby – ready for the hybrids to dismember. Many of these vicious creatures came in looking to dine on their more vulnerable hybrid kin but, after Mr Crane had ripped their heads off, became dinner themselves.

Crane halted, also surveying his surroundings, before gazing pointedly at Vulture as the bird landed on the dead sleer. Vulture stretched out a wing towards one of the nearby canyons. 'That one.'

Giving a slight inclination of his head in acknowledgement, Mr Crane trudged on. Within an hour they came within sight of one of the Polity survey teams that usually preceded the clear-up teams. Their large treaded vehicle was parked below a sandstone cliff, the base of which was pocked with numerous holes. A woman held up some sort of scanning device to these holes in turn, while peering closely at the device's screen. Her male companion spotted Crane and Vulture first, and grabbed the woman's shoulder to drag her round to see. He looked scared; she looked fascinated. Though Mr Crane had not made any effort to show himself to the inhabitants of Cull, the story had spread of his involvement in recent events here. Also, rumours were heard of the atrocious things he had done in the Polity, admittedly while under the control of various big-time villains. Vulture doubted if Mr Crane even cared that he was now a legend.

'How can we help you?' the man quavered as Crane strode over.

The Golem ignored him and marched right on past.

'I think you're getting a little bit too close to the hybrids' village,' suggested Vulture, from his new perch on top of the ATV.

'What?' The man looked up.

'It doesn't do to annoy him, you see.' Vulture gave a lugubrious shrug. 'But why should I care? I'm a carrion eater and I've been getting mighty tired of sleer just lately.'

'I think it might be a good idea if we left,' murmured the man.

'You do?' said the woman.

Mr Crane had meanwhile reached the cliff face and, stooping down from his eight-foot height, was peering into each of the holes in turn. After a moment he plunged his arm up to the shoulder in one of them, groped around for a bit, then pulled out something looking like a dead and shrivelled cobra. He turned round, strode back to them, and offered his find to the woman. She seemed reluctant to accept it.

'Dragon pseudopod, Deena,' observed the man. 'That's what you were detecting here.'

'Really,' Deena replied, eyeing Mr Crane.

Mr Crane relinquished the object to the male surveyor, who took it over to a nearby plasmel box and coiled it up inside before slamming the lid.

'Shall we go now?' the man asked.

Deena, however, did not seem inclined to leave. She surreptitiously peered down at the screen of her scanner, then abruptly raised it and directed it full at Mr Crane.

'I'm getting some really queer—'

Crane reached out, plucked the scanner from her hand, crushing it up with his fingers and scattering the bits like he was strewing herbs on some tasty dish.

'That was Polity property!' she yelped indignantly.

Crane leaned forward, tilting his head slightly as if he was very interested in what she was saying.

'We should really go now,' said the man, grabbing her arm.

Vulture was wondering if this might be about to turn nasty when Crane abruptly snapped upright and gazed towards the sky. Turning to look also, the bird witnessed multiple flashes, muted through the overcast. Maybe lightning, but judging by the Golem's interest Vulture thought not. Next came a rumbling as of thunder, then a sawing-crackling noise Vulture instantly recognized as the sound of a particle weapon burning through atmosphere.

'What the hell is that?' wondered the woman.

Two rod-shaped objects emerged from the clouds, tumbling at first then correcting and arrowing towards the ground, right towards the hybrids' village. Crane broke instantly into a loping run, one hand clamped to his head to hold his hat in place. The turquoise flare of a particle beam stabbed down blasting one of the rod-shaped objects to fragments. It stabbed down again to hit the other one, but not before its target had spat out some missile. Vulture launched off, keeping pace above the Golem's head. But from the direction of the village there came no expected detonation, which seemed puzzling. As they finally emerged from the canyon, the bird climbed skywards to get a better view. The monolith and the houses seemed perfectly intact, but something was belching a pale pinkish smoke. Survival instincts kicking in, the bird slowed and deliberately flew higher, gazing down as Mr Crane finally entered the village.

Those hybrids not actually still within their dwellings lay sprawled everywhere on the ground. Crane halted and peered about, then strode over to the missile – still belching smoke – and stamped it into the ground. Then he stood utterly still for some minutes, before jerking into motion again. Walking over to the nearest prone hybrid, he removed his hat, got down on his knees, placing it on the ground beside him, then plunged his brassy hands into the dirt and began scooping out a hole. Evidently the hybrids would not be getting up again.

Vulture circled for some minutes, before observing the ATV heading out of the canyon. He flew down and settled on the ground directly in its path. The vehicle ground to a halt and its two occupants climbed out.

'What's going on?' asked the man.

'Some kind of poison gas.' Vulture gestured back with one wing. 'He's now burying his dead.'

'Maybe we can help?' she suggested.

Vulture could see right through to her motives: here was her ideal chance to get hold of one of the hybrids for her sample boxes.

'If you really fancy going in there and trying to breathe that stuff?'

She grimaced.

Vulture added, 'You probably weren't in that much danger before, when he pulled out that pseudopod for you, but I don't know what he'll do after this. He's never been what you might describe as a balanced personality.'

'We're getting out of here,' said the man, grabbing his colleague's arm and dragging her back towards the ATV. A short while later the vehicle disappeared between the sandstone buttes.

Vulture waited . . . and waited. As the light grew dim he tucked his head under one wing and snoozed. Finally something alerted him, woke him up to hard-edged starlight.

Mr Crane strode out of the village, glints in his eyes reflecting the stars. His hat in his hand, he halted to one side of Vulture, gazed at the bird for a moment, before firmly placing the hat back on his head.

'He must pay,' he said, then snapped his mouth closed, like the lid of a tomb.

2

There is an old aphorism that says a gun is just a lump of metal until there is someone there to pull the trigger. It is not inherently evil or wrong in itself, for it is just a thing. This same aphorism cannot be twisted to fit Jain technology, since it is a gun with the trigger already pulled, or else it is the speeding bullet, or perhaps a better analogy would be that it is a landmine. Yet still it is blameless in itself – the blame lies with the Jain AIs who pulled the trigger – or armed the mine – five million years ago. However, the metal, plastics, electronics, switches and even the explosives of a landmine have useful applications elsewhere. Many aspects of Jain technology are similarly very useful, and can be used to further the goals of civilization; after all, a technology is not evil, only the way it is used can be described as that. We now understand that in every case where this pernicious construct has wiped out a civilization, elements of the same technology were used for good by those who had disarmed it. Unfortunately, by then, the armed version had already spread enough to eventually take off that civilization at the knees, and in each case it surely bled to death.

– From QUINCE GUIDE compiled by humans

The bridge area of the *King of Hearts* resembled the one Cormac remembered on the original *Jack Ketch*, with its wide black floor and holo-projection giving him the impression he was standing on a platform out in open space. However, here there were cross-hatched lines traversing the dome above him, destroying part of that illusion, and a whole segment blacked out behind him, while the nose of the attack ship was clearly visible to the fore. It seemed

27

as if he was standing in a viewing dome set just behind the nose, but he knew this area lay well inside the ship's new armour and its massive composite reinforcements.

No stars were visible through the dome at the moment, since the attack ship was presently in U-space, and the view beyond was a featureless grey. Cormac did not need to register this lack of view to know where they were. His sense of U-space now seemed to take precedence over all his other senses. Even the *King of Hearts* looked insubstantial all around him. Turning, he could gaze through its structure at the engines, the weapons, to where Scar sat motionless as a rock in his quarters, and to where Arach and Hubbert Smith were sparring in zero gravity.

'Another attack?' he enquired, trying to keep himself rooted in the moment and in his present position, for he felt constantly as if he was on the point of drifting, and could be swept away by invisible tides in U-space. He focused now more closely on his immediate surroundings. The bridge he currrently occupied had a noticeable lack of chairs – King obviously was not as genial a host as Jack – but at least it did not have those grisly decorations Cormac had seen in the *Jack Ketch*: the perfect copies of ancient execution devices arrayed like exhibits in a museum.

King did not reply, and Cormac guessed this was because the AI had already stated that there had been another attack. Even though now supposedly again loyal to the Polity, King remained a thorough misanthrope. Cormac therefore tried accessing information directly from the attack ship's server, but he received utterly no response. Maybe King had simply disabled the device, not liking humans getting too close to its pristine synthetic mind.

'Tell me about this attack,' Cormac insisted.

A glaring red dot appeared in the cross-hatching above the ship's nose, then expanded into a massive red-bordered frame. Within this appeared the image of one of Erebus's wormships in some area of space where the stars were clustered close together. There was something familiar about these constellations, but then Cormac had seen so many starscapes that wasn't entirely surprising.

'The ship arrived shortly after the last underspace interference emitters were withdrawn from the blockade,' King stated obscurely.

USERs? Cormac only knew of a few places where they had been deployed recently.

'Where is this, King?'

'Cull.'

The wormship up there in the frame was pouring out a swarm of objects – it looked as if someone had kicked a woodpile containing a wasps' nest.

Cull.

King knew plenty about that world, since it was there that both itself and a few fellow AIs had betrayed the Polity to try and grab the Jain technology possessed by, and possessing, the hio physicist Skellor. The *King of Hearts* had been the only one of these predators to escape.

'It used sophisticated chameleonware to get close, but once it began deploying its weapons, that ceased to be an option for it. Unlike the ship involved in that previous attack, this one's was in the nature of a suicide mission.'

Perfectly on cue, the wormship shuddered, fires igniting inside it, massive explosions tearing away chunks of its structure. Still, however, it continued to emit those bacilliform objects Cormac recognized. 'Rod-forms' was the term now being used for them.

Suddenly, within view appeared a Polity dreadnought accompanied by a scattering of the newer Centurion attack ships. One of those vessels employed first a DIGRAW – a directed gravity weapon – for a ripple seemed to speed through space towards the wormship, rod-forms bursting apart in its path. The wormship jerked as it was struck, and then writhed to reform, shedding dead segments of its compartmentalized structure. The attack ships now shot past the alien vessel in a random formation, hitting it with just about every weapon they had. By now the dreadnought was firing too: heavier beam weapons and clouds of missiles that seemed to move just too slowly – many of them glowing and going out under defensive fire. One, however, did get through, and the blast must have momentarily overloaded the instruments that had recorded these events, for King's screen blanked. When it came back on again, it was to show a collapsing ball of fire, which fell back to a painfully bright point, before exploding out again. Falling away from this, the remains of the wormship had lost coherence, become a loose-strewn tangle, which in a moment flicked out of existence.

'CTD imploder,' King noted.

'Some of it escaped,' Cormac noted, 'which rather undermines your suicide-mission theory.'

'We know where it is, and it will be dealt with,' King replied flatly.

Cormac grimaced at that then wondered aloud, 'What was the point of this?'

'I am receiving transmissions now,' King informed him.

Cormac waited, arms crossed, enviroboot tapping against the floor. Eventually King deigned to impart to him the relevant information just received: 'Numerous rod-forms were fired towards Cull. Most of them were destroyed, but two managed to reach atmosphere before they too were destroyed. However, one of them succeeded in firing a single missile.'

'Damage?'

'Yes, damage.'

'Y' know, King, the Polity consists of humans too and, as

much as you may dislike that fact, if you want to be part of the Polity, you'll have to be ready to talk to them occasionally.'

'The missile contained a form of nerve gas, which was released inside the sleer–human hybrid village.' Now the picture changed to show a village of globular houses. No sign of any hybrids, though there was a line of what looked like newly dug graves, each marked by a chunk of sleer carapace driven into the ground at its head. 'Every one of them was killed,' King added briefly.

Again, another puzzle.

'Now, first of all, why attack *them*?' Cormac paused for a moment. 'And why use a nerve gas? Surely that required some knowledge of hybrid physiology, when an explosive would have done the job just as well. It seems rather . . . specific.'

Grudgingly King replied, 'I don't know.'

'Is Erebus insane?'

'I don't think so.'

'Then there has to be a logical reason for its recent attacks on Klurhammon and Cull. We have to presume the hybrids represented some sort of danger, and that meanwhile some other threat to Erebus was extant on Klurhammon. How could the hybrids be a danger?'

'I do not know.'

'Dragon?' Cormac wondered.

No reply from King.

'Something there I guess . . .' Cormac kept on turning it over in his mind, aware that minds much greater than his would be looking at the same puzzle. In a moment of inspiration he abruptly cried, 'Dracomen! Those hybrids are probably like dracomen: immune to being sequestered by Jain technology! The dracomen on Masada must be warned!'

'It's being done,' King replied.

Being done?

He thought it odd that minds so superior to his own had not worked all this out long before him. Suspiciously odd. Only later did he learn of the wormship assault on Masada – the dracoman homeworld – and how that attacking wormship did not last more than ten seconds after surfacing from U-space. Still, this did not explain the anomalous use of nerve gas on Cull.

He turned and left the bridge to go and join his comrades Arach and Smith. With them he hoped to find a distraction from the void currently extending beyond this ship, a void somehow horribly attractive to him and seemingly intent on drawing him in.

This G-type star had been of no more than scientific interest to the Polity, or anyone else, after the arrival of the first probe here nearly a century before, since, even though it lay within Polity space, it was remote from all civilized worlds. This was why the haiman Orlandine had chosen it. She arrived some distance out and immediately activated her ship's chameleonware to conceal it, before scanning for the kind of automated watch stations Polity AIs tended to scatter about in places like this simply to collect scientific data . . . and to watch. There were two of them, she discovered, in orbit of the sun's single gas-giant planet.

Using her ship's chameleonware, she spent some weeks invisibly approaching the said stations, furtively docking, and in each sowed a Jain mycelium she had prepared. These mycelia absorbed surrounding material and spread out like hair-thin vines, attaching to each station's power supply and bonding in parallel to instrumentation. Within a few hours she took control and was able to edit the data the sensors were collecting for the stations' monthly U-space broadcasts to the runcible AI on the nearest civilized world. Next, and most importantly, she took control of the software that activated upon detecting any unusual activity in this planetary system, and instructed it to send *that* data direct to her.

Once this was done she turned off *Heliotrope*'s chameleonware – a technology she did not like to run for too long since it was so greedy for energy. Now the stations were blind to her presence, and to anything she did here.

Next she landed *Heliotrope* on the smallest of the eight moons orbiting this sun's single planet – the gas giant. This moonlet was geologically active, though what erupted in plumes up to five miles high from its icy volcanoes was not magma but liquid nitrogen, dust and methane compounds. The temperature here rose only forty degrees above absolute zero. There were lakes on the moonlet's surface and sometimes it rained, but water was as solid as iron and instead the stuff that fell from the blue and green clouds to gather on the surface was liquid methane and ethane.

Because of these low temperatures, what with the sun being a glowing orb only slightly larger than the other stars, there was a lack of energy for Orlandine to utilize. A particular one of the higher-energy worlds closer to the giant – a moon sufficiently heated by geological activity for it to geyser boiling sulphur and for liquid water to sometimes flow on its surface – might have been a more suitable choice. However, that same geological activity made it a dangerous place, and she had decided to conduct a lengthy study of it before relocating there. She confidently chose this world first because already she had experience of using her Jain technology in a low-temperature environment, on the occasion of blowing up a similar moonlet.

Before attempting anything else, Orlandine used the ship's drill to grind down a few feet into the surface and plant a seed which, powered by *Heliotrope*'s fusion reactor, germinated and began to sprout Jain tendrils. These began boring through the surrounding rock and ice, using microscopic drills, and to in turn sprout nanotubes which periodically grew quantum processors the size of salt grains along their route. In time this structure would begin to find power sources like radioactives, areas of geothermal activity and reactive chemicals. Once she was sure it was busily working as required, Orlandine decided to go outside.

Orlandine's carapace – a ribbed metal shell attached to her back from the nape of her neck to the base of her spine, loaded with the advanced technology that made her haiman – was now permanently bonded to her body by the mycelium she had used to increase her capabilities close to those of a major AI, but she hardly noticed it now. The spacesuit she wore – and had only removed once to tend to a wound she had received while preparing that previous icy moonlet for destruction – was specially made for haimans and incorporated the carapace. Similarly it incorporated the cut-down assister frame she also wore: a device that plugged into the carapace and presented two metal arms at just above waist level, and of which she possessed greater and more accurate control than over her own arms of flesh, bone and blood.

She began disengaging herself from *Heliotrope*'s interface sphere. This took a little while because she needed to physically disconnect from the Jain-tech aboard, and it tended to not want to let go of her – or, rather, there was some part of her that did not want to let *it* go. Once the numerous hair-thin tendrils linking her to the main mycelium in the ship were all severed, all that remained was her disconnection from the simpler Polity technology. Upon the disengage instruction, a power supply plug retracted from the spinal socket in her carapace and withdrew into the chair behind her, then lines of optic plugs on the ends of curved arms retracted from the sides of her carapace and hinged back out of sight on either side of her chair. The sensation of physical disconnection, though she did remain connected by electromagnetic means, was almost like being muffled from the rest of the world by a thick blanket, so, to compensate, Orlandine opened up the sensory cowl positioned behind her head as she pushed herself upright using the two limbs of her assister frame.

The door into the interface sphere *whoomphed* up from its seals and slid aside, and she pulled herself up and out into the corridor beyond. At the end of the corridor she entered her living area, then headed towards the airlock. A series of brief mental instructions started the airlock ahead of her cycling open and simultaneously closed up her spacesuit. The segmented back of her spacesuit helmet rose up between her head and the petals of her sensory cowl, while the ribbed chainglass visor rose up from the front of her suit collar to engage with the helmet at the apex, its segments locking together to give an optically perfect finish. She now considered the possibility of installing a shimmer-shield as a suit visor, since it would be more convenient, and as she entered the airlock, then finally stepped outside, a thought set automated machines within the ship to work on this possibility.

Shutting off all but her human sight, Orlandine saw only shadows. However, light amplification revealed thick ice underfoot, eaten away in places to show numerous laminations glittering in rainbow colours. Scanning deep into the ice with her sensory cowl, Orlandine picked out numerous boulders, the branching of underground streams of ethane and, of course, the rapidly expanding capillary-like structures of her recently planted mycelium. In the distance jagged peaks rose like gnarled canines in a deformed jaw, and beyond them the stars shimmered behind wisps of violet cloud. To her right the tight curve of the horizon was more easily visible, soot-black against a pink dome that was the edge of the gas giant, its magnetic fields creating twisted aurorae outside the normal human visible spectrum. Orlandine was enchanted, fascinated, and the species of joy she felt was almost a pain in her chest. Even through only slightly augmented human senses, this view would have been beautiful; seeing it across a wide band of the electromagnetic spectrum made it glorious. And, standing there knowing her capabilities and reviewing her plans, Orlandine felt herself to be the lord of all she surveyed. This feeling lasted only until the signal arrived.

Orlandine experienced a fraction of a second's confusion, then she realized the signal was coming simultaneously from the two Polity watch stations, for it seemed they had noted something unusual. Momentarily she feared the phenomenon they had detected might be herself, and that something had gone wrong with the mycelia she had seeded in them. But reviewing the data and transmitted images soon dispelled this notion.

It was coming in fast, impelling itself through vacuum using some form of U-space tech Orlandine recognized but had yet to analyse and understand herself. It was one of Erebus's wormships: a great Gordian ball of wormish movement miles across. A brief flash, and one sensory feed went out. From the other station Orlandine observed a flare grow then wink out from the location of the blinded station. She turned back to the airlock, quickly ascertaining that the first station had been hit by a microwave beam. By the time she was back inside *Heliotrope*, the other station was gone too.

Within her ship's interface sphere she swiftly reconnected herself to *Heliotrope* while simultaneously breaking its connection to the Jain mycelium in the moonlet's crust below, and launching the ship. Accelerating up through thin atmosphere she engaged chameleonware and felt some slackening of tension upon entering vacuum. She was now invisible and could escape if she so chose, but she was curious. She checked her power supplies, and began bleeding output from the fusion reactor into the laminar storage and capacitors that supplied her esoteric collection of weapons. At first the moonlet lay between her and the wormship, but rounding it she was able to use her sensors to observe the vessel clearly.

Having destroyed the two watch stations, the wormship had opened out its structure and was now launching rod-shaped devices which were accelerating in groups of three or four towards each moon. There were numerous reasons why it might be doing so, and she decided to take a closer look. She was invisible after all.

At a distance of a hundred thousand miles from the alien vessel, Orlandine now had a perfect view of it, but what it was up to was still not really clear. It could be seeding Jain-tech to build up some kind of cache, it could simply be placing its own watch stations or it could be setting up some kind of base. When *Heliotrope* was fifty thousand miles from it, the ship's spread structure abruptly snapped closed like a fist and it began accelerating directly towards her. Orlandine just watched it for a moment. Its choice of direction had to be coincidence, for surely it could not see her. Then abruptly she was receiving something – a computer virus of some kind, but oddly not a very effective one. She could have rejected it, but the information it might deliver could be useful so she consigned it to secure processing space. Then came steeply climbing energy readings from the approaching vessel, and she knew she was in trouble.

She flung *Heliotrope* to one side, hull temperature rising eight hundred degrees, changed direction again, and fired a selection of missiles from her rail-gun. The EM emitter in one missile screamed up to power; two others exploded, spreading clouds of microscopic signal relays and sodium reflectors. This sophisticated chaff cloud blotted the wormship from her view, just as she hoped it blotted out the enemy's view of her. But how the hell had it seen her? Her chameleonware could baffle just about any sensor. Then, processing this problem while simultaneously controlling her ship and its weapons, and deciding her subsequent course of action, Orlandine realized how: she had become complacent.

The greater the complexity of any technology, the more room there was for error. Chameleonware worked just as long as the enemy you confronted did not know you possessed it. If that same enemy was as sophisticated as you, it would stop looking for what was there, and start looking for what *wasn't* there. In environments like this, where there was little backdrop to hide against, the enemy would find you by locating the inherent *errors* and *holes* in your chameleonware. It was time, Orlandine felt, to get the hell out of here.

Using the mycelium inside her body to brace it, she slammed *Heliotrope* into a hard turn. She fired off still more chaff missiles and ordnance, then glimpsed the stab of a microwave beam cutting through the chaff cloud to her right. The wormship became momentarily visible, explosions blooming all around it as it defended itself from her missiles. Ahead of her lay one of the rod-forms, on course down toward the moonlet she had just abandoned. She hit it with the high-intensity solid-state laser she'd recently installed in the nose of *Heliotrope*, between the jaws of its forward pincer grab. The laser, a coherent beam no wider than her wrist but pumping out the kind of energy usually reserved for particle weapons, cut straight through the object, then must have hit something vital for it exploded like a balloon full of liquid. She fell through a cloud of skinlike fragments, then accelerated into a tight orbit about the moonlet itself.

Beam weapons fired by the wormship turned ice to vapour on the jagged landscape below, burning gulleys through it thousands of miles long. She saw sharp stone exploding from knife-shaped peaks as they heated just too fast for their mineral structure to sustain. Then she was out, accelerating. The wormship, she noticed, had slowed – clearly it, or whatever drove it, had decided not to pursue.

Orlandine dropped *Heliotrope* into U-space and fled.

As Cormac took the shuttle down into Klurhammon's atmosphere, the U-space journey to this world now seemed like a distant dream. He was relieved to be back in the solid world with its solid facts all around him, unpleasant though they might be, and perhaps the term 'realspace' now possessed more meaning for him than for others.

An occasional blue-green or red flash lit the screen. Briefly, at one point, he spotted a coherent beam punching down to their left through the cloud layer.

'King is certainly getting enthusiastic,' observed Hubbert Smith.

'Yes,' replied Cormac acidly, 'and *not* showing any inclination to land and grab any of that technology.'

'You're such a cynic. King doesn't want any Jain technology – he can give it up any time he likes,' quipped Smith.

Cormac glanced over at him. Smith sat in the copilot's seat, using the instruments there to monitor both general coms and the situation on the planet below.

'What's the status now?' he asked tersely, not in the mood for Smith's humour.

'We're getting no communication from the surface,' the Golem replied, 'but that's not surprising. Any survivors will now know the dangers of using general com channels.'

'The enemy?' asked Cormac as cloud engulfed the shuttle.

'Still active,' Smith reported.

Cormac glanced back at Arach, but the spider drone was showing enough sensitivity not to do his usual tappity dance at the prospect of a fight. They had all seen the pictures from orbit of the wrecked city, the burned-out homesteads beyond it and the numerous corpses – some still walking. He then looked at Scar, who was squatting beside the spider drone, but the dracoman just wore his usual ferocious expression.

Smith went on, 'After taking out the larger concentrations of Jain-tech with warheads King is now targeting the smaller stuff in the vicinity of larger groups of refugees. He won't get everything, however, and still can't help our particular small group of survivors.' The Golem turned towards Arach and winked.

The shuttle was now vibrating, and soon punched through the underbelly of the overcast. Below stretched a chequerboard of fields scattered with occasional buildings like game pieces – a landscape that much reminded Cormac of the English countryside seen from a gravcar. There were rivers down there too, but their regular pattern demonstrated artificial antecedents. He glanced down at the terrain map appearing on one of his lower sub-screens, then at the cross on the main chainglass screen before him, and decided he didn't like the inaccuracy of this so queried the shuttle's computer through his gridlink. Some delay passed before he had the information about their route lodged in his mind like a memory. The delay irritated him but was a necessary consequence of the surrounding ether being filled with Erebus's subversion programs. Approaching such matters incautiously might easily result in him coming under control of one of those *things* down on the ground, and it making him fly this shuttle into a mountain.

'King tells me one of the four survivors is down,' said Smith abruptly. 'Probably dead now and being drafted by the opposition.'

'Damn.' Cormac wished he could go faster. In his gridlink he accessed the plan King had sent while they were still aboard. In what was often termed a 'third eye' he studied the layout of their destination: a building complex located underneath a tree canopy. King was having difficulty identifying targets there. By means of heat signatures and observing their patterns of movement, the attack ship AI had ascertained that there was fight going on in the complex and that four – now three – individuals *might* be under attack from Jain-subverted humans. Unfortunately, though King should be able to hit a target a foot wide from orbit, the heat signatures of the good guys and bad guys were difficult to distinguish from each other. It also might not be that easy to tell the difference up close. Though Cormac had already worked out a plan of attack and imparted it to the others, and they, professionals that they were, had absorbed and understood it, there was still a chance this could turn messy.

The fields terminated right up against a forest of huge gnarled trees. Accessing information about this world, loaded to his grid-link but not yet loaded to his mind, Cormac learnt that these also constituted a crop – their seed pods producing an interlaced mass of biocontrol modules. Apparently the wood itself could also be wired up as an organic processor, but there was some dispute about felling the trees because of an ongoing investigation into the possibility that they might be sentient. For a moment, as he gazed at the forest, the trees seemed to multiply to infinity, and yet it was as if he knew the position of every one of them. He also glimpsed the buildings presently hidden from normal view.

'Dammit!'

'Problem?' asked Smith.

Cormac concentrated and brought his immediate surroundings back into focus. He really didn't need the distraction of that other perception now.

'No,' he said. 'Just a little impatient.'

Smith gave him a blank look – no doubt registering Cormac's momentary departure from usual behaviour. Though they had already seen combat together, Cormac was coming to the conclusion that he didn't entirely trust this Golem. It seemed an old distrust of AI was stirring inside him, though it was odd how this didn't apply to war drones. Maybe that was because the likes of Arach didn't pretend to be something they weren't.

Drawing closer to the trees, Cormac saw that his first idea about dropping through the canopy might not be feasible, for it was too dense. However, the trees were wide enough apart . . . He spun the shuttle, coming in backwards while using the main engine to decelerate. Crop debris and cinders blew past. Once the vessel was down to below a hundred miles an hour and mainly using antigravity to stay in the air, he spun it back round again and used tertiary thrusters to bring the speed down still further, then nosed into the forest between two massive trunks pocked with dark holes and as twisted as ancient olive trees. Checking coordinates he saw that the first of the concealed buildings was a mile ahead, and very shortly it came into sight – confirming the veracity of his earlier weird glimpse. Something flashed in the forest: weapons fire, maybe explosives.

Cormac brought the shuttle in to land, fast, retaining attack plans in his mind and adjusting them incrementally to the movement of the heat signatures inside that building complex. Three of them were labelled 'Human?' but were surrounded by others that possessed no label at all. The whole picture kept blurring and changing. That, Cormac realized, was also part of King's problem: the shooting was creating its own heat signatures, and it also seemed likely there were fires breaking out in there.

With the shuttle now settling, blowing up clouds of red and gold leaves and what looked like the husks of giant chestnuts, Cormac hit his belt release and stood. Already the side door was opening and Scar heading towards it. The dracoman did not reach it first, of course, for Arach took the ceiling route above him and dropped with a crash on the ramp just as it hit the ground. Then Arach was out amid the swirling leaves, two hatches opening in the top of his abdomen and two Gatling-style cannons folding up into view. Exiting the shuttle last, Cormac strode down the ramp then whirled round, simultaneously sending an instruction through his gridlink. The autogun on the top of the shuttle spun and targeted him for a moment, which was worrying, then settled into a search pattern. That meant it would recognize them when they returned, but anyone else approaching would receive a few warning shots, before being cut in half by pulse-fire.

'Okay, head out, you two,' he said, as he turned back to them.

Arach and Scar immediately departed for the loading entrance situated on the forest road. He and Smith meanwhile headed over to where a set of double doors stood open, the ground before them well churned up, and some kind of heavy autohandler standing idle to one side.

Assessing distances, Cormac said, 'We've got two off to the left, about thirty yards in. The others are starting to reposition – they know we're here.'

Smith lovingly adjusted the settings on his proton carbine. Cormac pulled up his sleeve, called up a list of programs in his gridlink before sending one to Shuriken, then pulled the star from its holster and tossed it out ahead of him. For a moment the weapon seemed dead in the air, then it steadied and whirled up to speed, extending and retracting its chainglass blades in anticipation. Then, as if deciding to behave itself, it pulled back and hung in the air, humming a couple or yards above his shoulder.

'They're approaching the door now,' Cormac noted.

Smith brought the stock of his weapon up to his shoulder and froze to a motionlessness that simply was not human. Cormac folded his arms and just watched as a ragged figure stumbled into view. It was a woman, badly burned, pink blobs where her eyes should have been. She brandished a large spanner and, without hesitation, started forward with plain intent. Cormac considered giving her a warning but knew that though this had once been a human being it wasn't now. Out of curiosity he allowed his perception of the real to slip, and again his surroundings took on that odd transparency. He now saw inside her body: her internal organs where exactly they should be, but now all entangled with ropes of Jain technology. She looked packed with snakes.

He glanced at Smith. 'Take her down.'

The Golem fired one long burst, cutting from head to groin, and blasted the woman back through the door in two burning halves. One chunk of her impacted the next figure coming out. He merely shrugged the burning mess aside and came on. More difficult to judge this time, since he looked quite normal on the outside. But inside, again, he was full of snakes.

'Halt right where you are!' Cormac ordered, then glanced questioningly at the Golem, who opened fire on the man, spreading his burning fragments to light up the interior of the building beyond. That Cormac had instinctively concealed his new ability from Smith showed his growing distrust of AI. Perhaps this reluctance was due to his frustration at the Polity's insufficiently aggressive response to the threat of Erebus, as much as his feeling that the AIs had some unknown agenda.

'Definitely infected,' affirmed Smith, tapping a finger against the side of his head. 'No human would have temperature and density readings like that.' Cormac filed that fact away for future reference. There was no time now, but it was possible for him to run a program sensitizing his eyes to infrared, and adding a small ultrasound scanner to his equipment might also be a good idea. He could then pretend he was using current Polity technology to see those snakes too.

'Okay, let's step it up now – and switch over to com.' That

was a bit of a misnomer, for none of them really used the standard military comunit. He himself could transmit and receive through his gridlink, Smith and Arach contained equipment for that purpose too, as did Scar, though the dracoman's way of sending and receiving signals had a biological basis.

On the schematic perpetually updated in his mind Cormac saw that the other two had also encountered expected opposition, for the heat map in the zone they entered now became blurred and chaotic. As he stepped past burning and sizzling remnants of what had once been human beings, he held his breath against the oily smoke and barbecue smell. Once through the doors, he used a gridlink program to ramp up light amplification, and then peered around. The interior of the building extended for a hundred yards with gantries looming up above on either side. Ranged about on the floor space were various sorting machines and conveyors, and he also noted a hopper full of fig-like objects – probably the contents of those spiky husks scattered outside. There were no warm bodies present inside this building but their own, but four were approaching its far end from the complex beyond.

'That gantry.' He gestured to the one on their right, wondering if he even needed to say that since they all knew the assault plan. Smith headed off to some nearby stairs, bounded up them unhumanly fast and shot ahead along the gantry. Cormac advanced at a more leisurely pace, meanwhile onlining a program he'd only recently discovered in Shuriken's control suite – uncertain if it was original or had been added by Jerusalem when that AI had repaired the weapon. Now another image appeared in his mind: triangular and seemingly diamond-rimmed, and viewed from a perspective somewhere just above his head, for he was looking through Shuriken's eyes. A brief programming prod sent the weapon skimming ahead of him. Simultaneously, he checked the position of the four heat signatures, and saw that Smith was now directly above them.

Almost immediately came a detonation, the flash from it lighting the way ahead, followed by several brief spurts of proton fire. The four, obviously identified as being infected with Jain-tech, had been moving close together, so logically Smith had used a grenade, then finished off anything surviving with his carbine. As Shuriken skimmed over the burning corpses, from its viewpoint Cormac glimpsed a smoking limb groping up, only to be incinerated by another burst of fire from Smith.

Now Shuriken wheeled into another long building. There came a flashing, and the star dodged and weaved, pulse-gun fire tracking across a ceiling above it. Ah, these ones were armed. Shuriken shot to one side and cut straight through a grating – its view now only of the inside of an air-conditioning vent. Heat map again: Arach and Scar had separated, and the dracoman had already reached the tunnel bridge connecting this building with the one where the main action was taking place.

'In position,' Scar growled over com, upon reaching the target building.

Arach, too, was now positioned where Cormac wanted him. Himself reaching the burning corpses, Cormac stepped quickly round to one side when he noticed snakish movement in the carnage. Finally reaching the turning that led into the second long building, he halted. 'Arach?'

'Two subverted haimen. They've got pulse-rifles and assister frames. They're up in the ceiling beams, just below me.'

'Smith, do you have yours covered?' he asked.

'Four raggety-looking things, but they've enough intelligence to keep their heads down now. Our three survivors are hiding behind a big automated packing machine. One of them is wounded and the others are running low on ammunition. They've got only one simple shotgun and a couple of pulse-rifles between them.'

'Scar.'

'Covered. Two of them. One's a haiman.'

Cormac again turned on his view through Shuriken and saw, in dim shades, the pair of feet belonging to a man inching along through the vent. Then this view turned into a red and pink explosion, and Shuriken shot out the other side of the corpse shaking splinters of bone from its chainglass blades. One enemy less now for Scar to cover. In a moment the star hit another grating, cut through and shot out of it to hover above three individuals. One of them lay flat on the ground, her right arm missing below the elbow, while another knelt beside her applying a tourniquet.

'Ah shit,' said the one still standing, as he raised his pulse-rifle to target Shuriken.

Cormac spoke. 'Put it down. We're here to rescue you.'

The man hesitated, lowered his weapon. He was a haiman, Cormac noticed. There seemed to be quite a concentration of them on this world.

'Okay, Scar, you can burn out those vents now,' Cormac instructed. 'The rest of you, take them down.'

The sound of weapons fire became a constant drumming while a glare lit up the huge interior of the building. Drawing his thin-gun, Cormac turned the next corner in time to see two burning shapes slam to the floor and fly apart. He glimpsed a head sheathed in flame and pieces of a haiman assister frame scattered here and there. A steady thumping of thermal grenades then began. All along one wall fire belched from air-conditioning vents. Scar's three targets were now incinerated in the vents they had been using to creep up on the survivors.

'Smith?' Cormac queried laconically.

'One did get past,' the soldier admitted. 'But there's now pieces of him all over the floor, with that weapon of yours hovering above them.'

'Any of them still moving?' Cormac queried generally.

When there came no reply, he holstered his gun and headed over to where the survivors were located. Nothing to learn here from the enemy, but maybe those three would have something to say.

The two Dragon spheres hung in space seemingly indifferent to the buzz of activity surrounding them. Ensconced in VR, Mika was apparently standing out on some invisible floor suspended over vacuum, observing the new conferencing unit being brought by two grabships towards the Dragon sphere that had first been able to break its Maker programming. To those seeing them for the first time, both these incarnations of Dragon were indistinguishable, being just spheres of fleshy alien technology now each extending three miles wide. They had grown by taking in asteroidal matter and processing it into *something* internally. Mika herself could distinguish between them because she recognized the scars on their surfaces. Of course she could, because she had been present when the two had inflicted the wounds upon each other.

The conferencing unit itself was a domed pressurized accommodation structure five hundred feet across and packed with technology for scanning, research and much else besides. The two grabships released it about a mile away from the first sphere and then quickly departed, like acolytes after leaving an offering for some tantrum-prone god. The unit turned slowly in vacuum, gradually being drawn to the intended sphere by its slight gravity. This was obviously not fast enough for, in the fleshy Dragon plain extending below it, a triangular red-glowing cavity opened and a tree of cobra-head pseudopods speared up to snag the approaching object and bring it clumping down on the sphere's surface like a conjurer's cup. Once it was in place, the unit followed its installation procedure: barbed spikes stabbing down from its underside to anchor it in place, various probes being thrust down into the alien flesh below it, and all its internal scanning and computer hardware instantly coming online. The pseudopod tree lifted away, hovered for a moment as if undecided about something, then suddenly withdrew back into the sphere. With a huff of vapour the triangular hole snapped shut.

Mika, satisfied that all had gone as expected, held out her hand and under her fingertips a touch console sprang into being. She hit one control only and fell back into blackness and into a seated position. Reaching up she hit the disengage button on her VR helmet and felt the nano-plugs withdraw from her temples. She tilted the helmet back, for the moment keeping her eyes closed, undid the clips along the back of the one VR glove she wore and stripped it off, then carefully opened her eyes to the glare of her research area.

Mika pushed herself out of the VR frame, which at that moment lay in chair format because she had decided not to use all its facilities, and headed for the door.

'I want to go across right now,' she said.

'Certainly,' came Jerusalem's immediate reply. 'A small vessel awaits you in the usual place.'

Mika paused. 'Usual place?'

'Yes, where you boarded the last one to transport you across to Dragon.'

Was Jerusalem playing some game here? The last vessel she had taken across had never made it back. She had served merely as a piece of confirmatory evidence taken along by one sphere to help convince the other one that its masters the Makers – who had built Dragon and dispatched it into the Polity – were now extinct and therefore its base programming was no longer applicable. This convincing process had resulted in the two spheres becoming somewhat irked with each other, and to be a mere human being in the vicinity of million-ton alien entities getting irked had not been a healthy option. Mika had nearly died inside her little ship, would have died if the second Dragon sphere had not suddenly grabbed her and, while riffling through her memories for confirmation of everything it had just been told, put her back together like a broken toy. Though quite possibly not the same toy she had been before.

She decided that *maybe* this time there wasn't any deliberate subtext to her current exchange with the AI. Nodding reassuringly to herself, she stepped out of her study area and took a familiar route through the cathedral spaces of the great ship which somehow seemed unfamiliar, though she knew it was not they that had changed.

For Mika was sure something had been fundamentally altered within her, and that this was the source of her present feeling of disconnection, of alienation. When the second sphere had dragged her from the wreck of her little ship she had known herself to be dying, most of her bones broken inside her ruptured flesh. In such a situation Jerusalem would have uploaded the mind from her dying body and put it into another, undamaged body. But the sphere chose to repair her . . . and she knew how Dragon spheres were not averse to tinkering with living creatures. Scanning her subsequently, Jerusalem had discerned some oddities that it claimed to be harmless and without apparent purpose, but she wasn't sure she believed this. Now she wanted to see what Dragon itself had to say about the matter.

Finally reaching the vestibule to the bay, Mika donned a spacesuit before heading out onto a catwalk. The bay concerned was an upright cylinder with this walkway running around the perimeter and a circular irised hatch occupying the floor. Even as she stepped out on the walkway the hatch in the floor slid open abruptly and a lift raised her intership transport vessel into view.

This one-man vehicle – in shape a flattened stretched ovoid – was without airlocks, any major drive or an internal AI. It could be flown by a pilot when necessary, though most often a remote AI controlled it. It rested on skids, had two directional thrusters mounted to fore, and a small ion drive aft. It looked utterly indistinguishable from the one Mika had so nearly died in. Trying not to hesitate at the thought, she stepped down from the catwalk and climbed inside.

Once properly settled in the single seat, she said, 'Well, the last time I flew one of these wasn't so great. If you would, Jerusalem.'

Through her suitcom the AI suggested, 'Scenic route?'

This was precisely what it had said that last time, and Mika shivered. Then, as she strapped herself in, she decided to give exactly the same reply as previously.

'If you have sufficient time.'

The wing door sealed itself shut with a *crump*, and instantly lights began flashing amber in the bay as pumps evacuated the air. As an extra precaution, even though the craft was fully sealed and contained its own air supply, Mika closed up her spacesuit. The grav went off, then the ceiling opened to reveal the stars. Swivelling to point down, the fore thrusters fired to propel the craft out into space. It turned nose-down over the *Jerusalem*'s outer ring, which from this point always looked like some vast highway running around the equator of a metal planet. The giant research vessel was in fact a sphere five miles in diameter, and the thick band encircling it contained shuttles, grabships, drones and telefactors, all of which constituted the AI's macro toolkit.

Mika surveyed her surroundings beyond the mighty ship. The inhabited hot world of Scarflow lay to her right, cast into black silhouette by the white glare of its own sun. The gas giant lying within the orbit of that same world was not visible at present. Here and there she caught the reflected glint from an occasional ship, but that was all. Looking at status maps of this system gave her the impression of a corner of space swarming like a disturbed beehive, since, to complement the remains of the fleet that had escaped Erebus, many additional Polity vessels had now arrived. It was only when viewing outside the *Jerusalem*, without computer enhancements to contract the distances, that you realized how *small* was all this activity against the sheer scale of . . . everything.

The craft turned and accelerated towards two white dots like blank cold eyes: the Dragon spheres. As the short journey commenced, Mika considered what she so far knew about them. Four spheres, conjoined, had originally been sent by the Maker civilization, then located in the Magellanic Cloud, to seed Jain nodes that would lead to the eventual destruction of the Polity. Dragon, however, had refused to comply, and a Maker had come here to force the issue. During the ensuing conflict one sphere had managed to cause massive human fatality on a planet called Samarkand, and that's where Mika and Cormac had come in. He had destroyed the offending sphere, and the Polity had accepted the Makers' lies. Dragon, though able to disobey the Makers in one respect, could not, because of its base programming, disobey in others. Dragon, in consequence, could not reveal the truth about its purpose.

In a following conflict a second sphere had sacrificed itself to create the dracomen. But why? To produce an army of beings immune to Jain technology, apparently, but, like in everything else to do with Dragon, there were layers of complexity underlying that simple answer. And now, fairly recently, the Polity had learnt that the Makers' own Jain technology had destroyed them, and it was this fact that had enabled one of the two remaining spheres to break its own programming and subsequently, with Mika's help, break the second sphere's programming too. Dragon, it seemed, was now a free agent and a good friend to the Polity.

Mika snorted to herself at the very idea.

The two spheres rapidly expanded in her view, their colour changing from the bland white of reflected sunlight to red and umber shot through with streaks of sapphire and swirls of yellow. The two alien entities swung around each other equidistantly, as if connected by an invisible rod. This was some kind of gravity phenomenon generated by them both, since their natural mass did not provide sufficient pull to keep them in place like this. Avoiding that same phenomenon, her craft descended to take a slow vertical orbit around the second sphere. This one was clearly recognizable to Mika because it was the more badly scarred: nearly torn apart by the same weapon that had almost done for her. After the conflict between the two of them they had merged for a while to conduct some kind of healing process, nevertheless still they retained their scars. Perhaps, like Scar the dracoman, they retained these for identification purposes, or perhaps they just wore them out of some sort of pride.

The little craft now skimmed above hillocks of scaly flesh like cut gemstone, masses of red tentacles nestling in their lees like strange copses. She observed a wide-split seam in the surface at one point, occupied by cobra pseudopods each possessing a single sapphire eye where the head should rightly be. It looked busy down there – a conference of snakes. Eventually the craft broke away from its tight orbit and headed over to the other sphere, where the Dragonscape below was little different, until finally descending towards the flat plain where the conferencing unit lay embedded. It landed beside a single airlock, bouncing and then settling in the low gravity. Mika clambered out, but felt some reluctance to step away from her craft until she saw that curved spikes had folded down from above the skids to anchor it in place, then she bounced and drifted across to the lock.

And entered a Polity embassy in a Dragon's realm.

3

'Biomodule' *is a vague term used to describe products of GM organisms used as components in technologies that are distinct from plain biotechnology. Though, on the face of it, this description seems precise enough, problems arise when you try to distinguish our biotech from those other technologies. Surely, if some components of a machine are biomodules, it is biotech itself whether it is a Golem android, a gravcar or an autodozer? The term, and its description, are therefore outdated – in fact they went out of date more than five centuries ago. Biomodules can now be found in just about everything we use. Simple computers contain virally grown nano-wires and fibre optics, and there are now few items we employ that do not contain such computers. These include holographic and temperature-controlled clothing, Devcon Macroboots with their terrain-adjusting soles, Loyalty Luggage, and even tableware capable of warning of the precise content and temperature of food. Biomodules will also be found in the join lines of segmented chainglass visors manufactured to give an optically perfect finish – they are crystals produced inside some GM cacti and are also used in the optics of pin-cams. Human bodies now contain thousands of different varieties of them in whatever suite of nano-machines each body is running. This an old practice that can be traced right back to the first GM production of insulin. Essentially, biomodules should simply be called modules – just one component in our complex and completely integrated technology.*

Note: Biomodules are produced by every kind of modified fauna available, some of it alien, but mostly they are produced by flora on misnamed 'agricultural' worlds. The choice of using plants in this industry is down to simple harvesting. If you can grow just one module either in the spleen of a pig or the inside of an acorn, you would of course prefer to grow oak trees.

– From QUINCE GUIDE compiled by humans

Yannis Collenger glanced back at the raptor shape of his vessel, the *Harpy*, taking in its flowing lines and sheerly mean look, before sending a signal through his Dracocorp aug. The ship's chameleonware engaged, and it rippled and faded to invisibility. He then stabbed his shooting stick into the crusty ground, folded out its small seat, and perched himself upon it. Finally he spoke, his voice transmitted through his own aug to five other augmentations nearby.

'Okay, stay chilled, boys and girls, they should be with us in a few minutes.'

Yannis was an old hand at buys like this on the Line. You had to stay alert for the double-cross, but you had to stay especially alert for undercover Polity agents. For a long time now ECS had been clamping down hard on arms sales to separatist organizations within the Polity, and such deals had become increasingly rare and fraught with danger. But this one was difficult to resist: two cases of proton carbines, plus power supplies and, unbelievably, one of the new CTD imploders. How the hell these people had got hold of one of those he did not know. He smelt a set-up but thought the precautions he was taking would be sufficient.

The gravcar approached through the sulphurous haze constantly emitted from the numerous volcanos upon this primitive Line world. Yannis recognized the shape of a floating Zil, which was the vehicle of preference for some who traded out this way. He glanced at the box lying open to one side, its contents of Prador diamond slate exposed, then he long-distance auged into the satellite he'd left out in orbit. In the last hour no spaceships had arrived there, and there was nothing watching them from above unless it was concealed by chameleonware. However, he doubted, what with the recent unusual activity in the Polity seemingly directed at some exterior threat, that ECS could spare resources for that kind of mundane operation, so anything they might be doing here was probably concentrated on the ground. Possibly an agent, or maybe one of those new undercover Golem that were becoming so difficult to detect.

Kicking up a cloud of icy dust, the Zil landed: far too dramatic, since there had been no need to employ turbines during the descent. Yannis sent off an instruction to the *Harpy*. Immediately, in his visual cortex, he began receiving a readout from the highly complex scanning routine the ship was using.

'Harpy, give me overlay,' he instructed.

As four individuals climbed from the car, they were immediately in his envirosuit visor outlined in red, then their hidden weapons were picked out and precise details displayed to one side. The ship's AI was very good at this sort of stuff, since it was of Prador manufacture, or rather had been made from the brain of a Prador first-child. It always amused Yannis that AIs were ostensibly seen as an essential requirement for U-space travel, yet the Prador, who had been dropping their ships into that continuum for centuries, supposedly did not possess AIs. Few in the Polity saw fit to question or explain that discrepancy. He supposed it was all about definitions. Polity AIs could manage the rapid, complex and huge calculations required for U-space travel because of their processing capacity and speed. Harpy could do them because that's what it had been bred – and surgically altered – to do. It was an engineered autistic savant. It was really all a question of when does an intelligence become artificial?

Scan then penetrated the Zil to reveal the two crates of proton carbines in the back footwell, and another object in the boot which

Harpy took a while to analyse. When Yannis saw the final result he felt his legs go slightly weak. It really was an imploder, and a big one – the kind employed by Polity dreadnoughts when they wanted to slag a moon. He realized then that he really must be dealing with amateurs, since if they'd really understood what they'd got hold of, the asking price would have been fifty times as much.

'Looks like they are expecting trouble,' said Forge.

'Well, let's not disappoint them,' said Kradian-Dave.

Yannis smiled to himself, then blinked when the outline of one of the figures displayed on his visor began flashing. He read the side display: chameleonware embedded syntheflesh, ceramal chassis: Golem Twelve. So it was a set-up, but Yannis felt mildly disappointed that ECS had sent such an *old* Golem on an entrapment operation directed at *him*.

Now, not subvocalizing because even at this distance a Golem would be able to hear him, Yannis used a text routine in his aug: *Harpy, acquire and target – if it moves out of human emulation, hit it. Fire also on my signal.* Then he stood up and stepped away from his shooting stick. He was slightly puzzled, for it surprised him that the ECS Golem had allowed this to proceed so far. Surely the mere chance of that imploder falling into the wrong hands could not be countenanced?

The one who was obviously the leader strode ahead of the three heavies, one of which was the Golem. She was a squat mannish woman with a strutting arrogance that immediately annoyed Yannis.

'So you've brought payment,' she said, coming to a halt a few paces from him. The other three held back, all of them clutching heavy pulse rifles.

'Yes, I've brought the payment.' He waved a hand towards the box of diamond slate. 'And now I want to see what I'm buying.'

'Ooh, naughty naughty,' came Forge's voice over Yannis's aug. 'Our satellite feed has located a small commando group all dressed up in chameleoncloth and trying to creep up on us. Let me know when you want them to go bye-bye.'

Yannis finally understood what was going on here. The Golem was not working for ECS. It had to be one of those rare items: one that had been corrupted. It really did work for the woman standing before him, and was her edge. This was quite probably something she had done before, maybe many times before: the weapons were the bait and he was the fish. He used the text function of his aug to send back to Forge: *Now would be good.*

A distant whine, as of disturbed mosquitoes, came from the surrounding slopes. This was followed by dull, almost inaudible concussions. Forge and the others must have decided to use the seeker bullet function on their multiguns. There would be a mess up there. The bullets entered their targets to detonate inside.

The woman before Yannis raised her hand to her ear, then abruptly dropped it, her expression giving nothing away. Comunit in her ear. She wouldn't know for sure her troops were dead, but now she was out of contact with them.

'But of course you never really intended to sell me anything,' Yannis said.

Hit the Golem.

With a sawing crackle the blurred turquoise bar of a particle beam stabbed out seemingly from mid-air behind him. His internal face visor shot up from the armour underlying his envirosuit, so he was now viewing the scene through just a narrow slot. The beam struck the ersatz big man and turned him to fire. Instead of being thrown back, the Golem stepped forward, its clothing and synthe-flesh slewing away. A briefly revealed metal humanoid stood against the blast for a moment – then flew apart.

The woman was now on the ground, her arms wrapped

protectively over her head. Her remaining two heavies were crouched in firing positions, their weapons wavering between Yannis and the unseen source of the particle beam. Both of them kept shooting anxious glances at what was left of their companion; their edge was gone and they knew that opening fire might now be suicidal.

Yannis shrugged. 'You try to cheat me, and now your Golem is gone.'

Get rid of those two, Forge.

Yannis awaited the expected arrival of the seeker bullets, but nothing did arrive.

Forge?

'We've got a problem – there's something else out here,' said Kradian-Dave.

Something in the voice of the man sent a shiver down Yannis's spine, but he believed in his men's competence. Let them sort out whichever of this woman's troops they had missed.

Harpy, kill the two armed males.

The particle beam stabbed out twice more and screaming the two men flew apart like fat-soaked rags held before a blow torch. Yannis stepped forward, but abruptly the woman heaved herself upright and drew a gas-system pulse-gun. She fired straight into his chest, sending flames and smoke rising up before his face. *Damn, another envirosuit wrecked.* He stepped into the fusillade and slapped the weapon from her hand, then grabbed her by the throat and heaved her up off the ground.

'I am very *annoyed*,' he said. He would have liked to spend some quality time with her, but the firing of *Harpy*'s particle cannon might have already been detected, so ECS agents could now be on their way. He began closing his hand, the motors in his armour kicking in as his fingers dug into her neck. She began flailing about and kicking, but that came to a convulsive halt as his fingers broke through flesh, crunching a handful of windpipe, muscle and fat. Ripped arteries sprayed blood, one jet spattering along his arm and on his visor. He discarded her, then shook the mess from his gloves.

'Do you have your problem under control?' he asked.

No reply.

'Forge? Kradian? . . . Lingel? Sheila? Prescott?'

Some kind of com failure? Maybe someone up there had been using an electronic warfare technique?

'Harpy, give me satellite feed,' he demanded, trying not to get too nervous about this. Even so, he backed up a little way and took up his shooting stick.

The feed clicked in.

'Close shots of the last locations of my crew,' he instructed.

Three of them weren't where they were supposed to be. Forge and Prescott were . . . well, he assumed that he *was* seeing Forge and Prescott, but it was difficult to tell with the bits of them spread all around and spattered on the surrounding rocks. It looked like they had been hit by seeker bullets, but they must have been of some new and powerful armour-penetrating kind for the two men had worn the same sort of motorized armour as did he.

Time to get back to the ship.

He pulled up his shooting stick, which was an apt description for it also served as a weapon, then quickly headed back towards *Harpy*. However, just then, a strange sight gave him pause. He aimed at this thing with the stick and tracked its course to the ground.

A bird?

In a flurry of feathers it landed amid the smoking and strewn remains of the Zil's passengers and began pecking up bits of flesh.

A vulture?

Yannis vaguely recollected something from childhood lessons on Terran ecology.

But how was that possible? The air here could not support Terran life, and whatever large life forms survived crawled through tunnels in the ground scraping up rock sulphur and digesting primitive forms of algae out of it.

Then something else caught his eye and he looked up.

Standing over by the Zil was a big big man wearing a long coat and a wide-brimmed hat. As if Yannis seeing him had been some kind of signal, the man began taking lengthy strides towards him. Harpy gave him an outline which immediately began flashing.

Golem.

Yannis read the side display: *Golem Twenty-Five prototype, ceramal armour, further modifications unknown. Rescan. Rescan.*

Hit it.

A text reply flicked up in his visual cortex: *You are within target acquisition frame.*

Yannis quickly stepped to one side, but the Golem suddenly moved horribly fast, almost a subliminal flicker, and was then strolling in from a different direction.

You are within target acquisition frame.

He moved again.

The Golem moved again.

Rescan. Rescan. Rescan. Viral return—

The display in his visor shut down. He stepped aside again, but the Golem just continued striding in.

Hit it! Hit it!

Nothing.

Yannis turned and ran, but before he'd even managed two paces a big brassy hand slammed down on his shoulder, spun him round, closed on his neck and hoisted him from the ground.

He heard, 'Particle weapons leave a metallic aftertaste.' The voice seemed to be coming from somewhere below him. It was not the Golem talking for he was looking straight into its implacable face. Around his neck he felt something creak, then his neck armour collapsed with a cracking sound like thunder to his ears. His last thought as his head, now disconnected from his body, thumped to the ground, was, *Metallic aftertaste?*

Gazing out through *Heliotrope*'s sensors, it was with a feeling of bitterness that Orlandine contemplated the massive object sitting out there in vacuum. This was not the kind of project she'd had in mind upon her return to the Polity, but now circumstances had changed. The computer virus from the wormship had changed them, for it had provided her with a definite *purpose*.

Her purpose was vengeance.

When, by destroying a massive USER based on an icy moonlet, Orlandine had opened the trap holding both her and the Polity fleet that Erebus first attacked, she had been leaving the Polity for pastures new. Somewhere, towards the inner galaxy, she had intended to build something grand with the fantastical technology she now controlled. Procrastinating for some time, she then realized that, no matter how grand it might be, the thing she built would be worthless with only herself to appreciate it, and so she had returned to the Polity. The remote place where the wormship found her had been her selected construction site. Not any more.

Using every devious precaution she could think of, she studied the computer virus transmitted by the wormship and came to the conclusion that it bore some similarities to a memcording. Then, because it possessed all sorts of strange visual, audio and seemingly sentient components, she allowed it to run in a secure virtuality. Immediately, in this virtuality's albescent space, something manifested and spoke.

'Well, hello, Orlandine,' said the entity, the virus.

Orlandine gazed at the scruffy-looking man and knew that this could not be a human being.

'What are you?' she asked, while on other levels she investigated the structures of information that had caused this apparition to appear.

'Me?' He pointed with both forefingers at his own unshaven face. 'I'm a seriously pissed-off dead man.' He grinned. 'The name's Fiddler Randal.'

'What do you want?'

'Well, I want something to die – the something that killed me – and I want your help.'

'Ah, and coincidentally you were transmitted to me by a wormship.'

He shrugged. 'I've managed to spread myself throughout Erebus.'

A dubious contention, Orlandine thought, but nevertheless asked, 'Why should I help you?'

'Because that same something manipulated you; intended you to be a weapon it could use against the Polity.'

'So you want Erebus to die – the same entity of which you seem to be a part,' said Orlandine. 'Now why should I try to kill it? Despite Erebus's manipulation of me, it still gave me the greatest gift I could ever have wanted.'

'Like making you a murderer?'

Orlandine felt distinctly uncomfortable with that statement. Without doubt, Randal was referring to her partner, Shoala, whom she had killed while covering up traces of her escape with the Jain node that had been Erebus's 'gift' to her.

'That was *my* choice,' Orlandine replied. 'It's one I regret, but it was mine alone. I cannot blame Erebus for that, only myself.'

'Then you're much more forgiving than Erebus is,' said

Randal. 'You see, you didn't do what you were supposed to do. Admittedly I had a hand in that, as I've had a hand in a lot of Erebus's fuck-ups. But Erebus, for all its power both mental and physical, is a petty being.'

'Are you ever going to get to the point?'

'The point is this.'

He slid to one side and the virtuality changed. With a spasm of nostalgia, Orlandine gazed upon the landscape of her home-world. She recognized the fields of plants drastically altered to supply biomodules for high-tech Polity industries. She recognized the purple-blue colour of the sky, and could almost smell the complex pollens in the air. Her memories were clear, because even way back then she had undergone the physical alterations, including the fitting of a gridlink, that were the starting point to becoming a haiman. In those days there had still been much debate about the morality of choosing a child's future at so young an age, but at that time, to enable someone to become a haiman, it had been necessary for the first alterations to be made while still very young. The AIs had allowed her mother to change her, and now, as an adult, she understood why. The AIs had wanted humans to climb a bit further out of the primordial swamp.

Her brothers, the twins Aladine and Ermoon, had attained full haiman status before her, but then they were both twenty years older. Their mother, Ariadne, had been single-minded about the future she had planned for them all. She could never understand the boys' later objections to what she had forced upon them, and had been greatly disappointed when, after the divorce of Ariadne and their father, the boys refused to make the move to Europa. She also clung on when Orlandine had made the move to the Cassius Project – always the constant stream of messages, the proprietary interest and the gifts that Orlandine felt sure were sent to assuage Ariadne's sense of guilt.

And, look, there were the twins.

The data flow increased and she began to sense the scene as if she was actually there, standing over them. They were bound to the ground in some kind of organic cage, fighting to free themselves. Briefly a long-fingered metallic hand swept into view right above them, and both of them began to scream and struggle harder. Wisps of smoke rose from their clothing as it began to blacken, and Orlandine could smell melting plastic. Flames burst through the fabric and the two young men began to burn. Their screams became something almost unhuman, fading to agonized gruntings and gaspings. A smell like seared pork permeated the air as the flames grew magnesium-bright, consuming the two bodies and the entire structure encaging them. Finally it was over, and nothing remained but ash. In a blink the scene was gone . . . and Fiddler Randal was back.

Orlandine used every method available to her to keep her emotions under control. She altered the flow of neuro-chemicals in her brain, modulated the balance of her blood electrolytes and sugars and artificially stimulated precise patterns of synaptic firing. She did not allow herself shock or grief, or anger.

'What is this?' she asked with robotic calm.

'One of the problems with Jain technology is that with such huge processing space available it is possible for much to exist in the gaps without interfering with its basic function,' said Randal. 'I'm part of Erebus – a ghost in the machine – and as such, while I evade being trapped and erased, I can know Erebus's mind and see all that it does. I therefore saw this.'

'Supposing that these images are even true,' said Orlandine, 'what was Erebus's purpose in doing this?'

'Plain vengeance. As well as not letting Erebus's gift of Jain technology overwhelm you and then turn it on the Polity, enough information was transmitted for Erebus to know it was *you* who destroyed its USER, thus allowing the Polity fleet to escape. For my host it was the smallest diversion of resources to kill your two brothers like that.'

'I see.'

After a long silence, Randal asked, 'So what are your plans now?'

In the cold emotionless place Orlandine presently occupied, she felt no urge to plan anything. However, she was a haiman, and having sought and found the synergy of the human and the machine, she could not totally deny her human side. Still remaining analytically cold, she reasoned that if she verified those images, upon re-establishing normal emotion she would grieve – and then grow angry, appallingly angry. All other thoughts and aims would be swept aside.

'You could easily be some agent of Erebus sent to manipulate me again,' she said.

'Yes, I could.'

'How can you help me?'

'That depends on what you intend to do.'

'If these images really show the truth, then I believe I intend to destroy Erebus.' But of course she already understood that Randal knew this would be her answer.

'Okay, that being the case, I can show you in detail how Erebus intends to bring down the Polity. Or at least I can show you what his plans were just before I transmitted myself to you.'

'So you're a copy of the original version of yourself still existing within Erebus,' Orlandine observed. 'Surely you would do better to give this information to the AI Jerusalem, who I understand is in command of the present defence?'

'It is the nature of all Erebus's plans that they contain a glaring flaw ready to be exploited by an enemy. I should know because I am always the cause of that flaw, just as I am the flaw within Erebus.'

Orlandine wasn't quite sure what to make of that. 'Do go on.'

'Unfortunately, were I to inform Jerusalem of Erebus's present plan, it would then be countered, but in such a way that Erebus would escape mostly unharmed. However, if its present attack plan is carried through, someone else exploiting that flaw could, with sufficient resources, obliterate Erebus. You must understand that there are those who welcome Erebus's aggression and its . . . consequences.'

Orlandine pondered that statement for a moment. 'You're saying there are those within the Polity who are on Erebus's side?'

'It's not a case of sides. Erebus's present aggression is considered useful by some very high-up Polity AIs. But you don't want to know exactly who – trust me on this.'

This was not so surprising, Orlandine supposed. There had often been AI rebels in the past.

'Then show me this attack plan,' Orlandine instructed.

Randal made a packet of information available to her. After taking sufficient precautions she opened it and absorbed all it contained.

'You see where, with a suitable weapon, you can bring Erebus down?' Randal pointed out.

'I do,' Orlandine replied.

'But when the time comes for this, you'll need the updated codes to enable you to configure your chameleonware to Erebus's scanning format – to hide yourself.'

'You'll provide these?'

'I cannot here and now, because they'll have changed, and I am no longer in contact with my other selves.'

'So how do I obtain them?'

'In my estimation you cannot, since your task will take all of your own resources,' Randal replied. 'However, I have prepared for this, and another individual will bring these codes to you at a prearranged rendezvous.'

'This individual is?'

'Highly capable and . . . motivated. And more than able, with the technology he possesses, to take on elements of Erebus's forces even without the codes and chameleonware to conceal him. He will follow a predicted and vengeful course sure to eventually bring him into contact with *one* of those elements, somewhere, where-upon one of my other selves will contact him.'

'Who is this individual?'

Randal told her.

'That is . . . dubious.'

'It is the best I can offer,' Randal supplied firmly, and Orlandine had to be content with that.

Later, after taking many precautions, Orlandine connected to the AI nets of the Polity and learned more about the attack on Klurhammon, her homeworld, where she was born. Still there was part of her that did not want to believe what Randal had just shown her. Desperately trying to obtain detail about what had happened to the population back home, she learned only that millions had died. She decided to take another more dangerous risk, accessed her inbox on the AI nets only to find ten quite large messages all labelled 'A gift from an admirer' and snatched these from under the nose of the ECS hunter-killer programs that had been placed in the vicinity to track her down. Nine of the messages were exactly the same, each showing in startling detail the horrible scenes she had already witnessed. The tenth contained something she recognized at once as a virus, another Randal – which she deleted.

She believed it all then, and hatched her plans, which led her here to this all but empty reach of interstellar space – empty but for that one massive object out there: a war runcible.

'Well this brings us no closer to knowing why Erebus ever came here,' said Cormac.

Smith had a medical pack open and was positioning a field autodoc over the injured woman's arm stump. With a nerve blocker in at the shoulder and her severed veins being sealed, the woman already looked better and was gazing up at her and her companions' rescuers with curiosity. Cormac, meanwhile, studied the other two rescuees.

One was a young man, maybe a teenager, though of course someone's precise age was a difficult thing to divine when one's appearance could be chosen. The other looked older, but of similar appearance to the younger, with jet-black hair, dark almost-joined eyebrows and a hatchet of a nose that had certainly not been the beneficiary of cosmetic surgery. Like the youngster he was a haiman – the man was shirtless so Cormac had already seen the connector sockets down his spine – but unlike the youngster he did not wear a carapace. The more youthful one had a carapace clinging to his back like a giant iron woodlouse. He also wore a full assister frame, which provided additional limbs extending at the waist.

Cormac allowed that other new perception some play, and detected Polity technology laced through their bodies: the gridlinks capping their brains inside their skulls, the numerous optics and wires threaded along bones, and the electro-optical nerve interfaces studding their flesh. The sight of it disturbed him on some deep level, for perhaps it was just too much like those snakes in the flesh he had seen earlier, so he quickly returned to gazing upon solid reality.

'Thank you,' said the older one.

'It's what ECS is for. What's your name?'

'Carlton Egengy.' He gestured to the other. 'My brother Cherub.' Then he glanced down to the woman lying on the floor. 'We didn't have the time to get acquainted.'

'Jeeder Graves,' she supplied.

'Out on the Chester Flats?'

She nodded. 'That's the place.'

Cormac could not help but feel a little irritation at this exchange. It was inconsequential and did not advance his mission at all. Then abruptly he felt himself focusing back on it. At the end of his last mission he had regretted not getting to know those around him, those many soldiers who had died, some of them protecting him from the suicidal impulse he had felt after seeing his colleague Thorn incinerated right before him. He deliberately ran the names of the three before him, internally, through his gridlink, to see if he had anything on file. Nothing came up. Next he took the risk of attempting to query the local server, routing any reply he might receive through sealed processing space filled with programs for dealing with Jain worms and viruses. As expected, there were a few attempts made to get to him through the link, easily dealt with by his new defensive software. But there was nothing else – nothing at all. A further query rendered an interesting result. Yes, there was a great deal of corruption from all the Jain-tech in the area, but that should not have randomly erased everything. All Klurhammon's files, all the information stored here about this world, were totally gone. He shook his head. He had allowed himself to be more human, and that had rendered the clearest intelligence of all. Serendipity? No, luck.

'King, the whole net for this world seems to be down,' he sent. 'Much that is pertinent to this place has been deleted.'

After the usual delay, the AI replied, 'I see. I had not noticed that since I was deliberately avoiding any connections to the local servers. I suggest that henceforth you do the same.'

'No pain, no gain,' Cormac sent back, feeling some satisfaction that he had been first to spot the lack of retained information here.

In reply he received something that sounded like an electronic snort.

Cormac turned to his companions. 'It seems that Erebus's aim in attacking was to wipe out all the stored files here pertinent both to this world and its population.'

'And it was successful?' wondered Smith.

'It was successful,' Cormac confirmed.

'That don't help us a lot,' said Smith, and nodded over to where Arach was peering down at the charred remains of one of the Jain-infected humans. Something was moving there in crusted skin and liquified fat. 'Maybe we can get some answers direct from the tech Erebus left here?'

'Doubtful.' Cormac shook his head. 'If Erebus was covering up something here, it wouldn't leave clues lying around like that. More likely we'll just find booby traps.'

'I don't think that was *all* it was here for.'

Cormac turned. It was the haiman youth who had spoken.

'What do you mean?'

'The android – I don't think it was here just to erase information.'

The elder was looking at his brother curiously. 'You said nothing about an android, Cherub.'

Cherub grimaced at his brother. 'We were both too busy trying not to end up dead to have time to talk about it.'

'Go on,' said Cormac.

The youth shook his head. 'It landed by the city—'

'Describe the craft.'

'I don't need to. I can send you an image feed right now.'

'Then do so.'

Cormac's gridlink picked up the query for linkage, as it had been picking up so many others from the surrounding area – queries he had instructed it to ignore. Signal strength was right for it being from the haiman youth before him, but he ran it through the same defensive programs as he did with anything else he allowed into his gridlink on this contaminated world. The boy had sent two visual files, which was risky, since it was possible for harmful stuff to be embedded in them. No riders as far as he could see, so running viral and worm-scanning programs all the while, he studied the files.

'The Legate,' he announced. 'Or rather *a* legate.'

The first file showed the landing at Hammon. The second revealed amid huge red-green stalks of something like giant rhubarb the same craft grounded outside one of the ranch-type dwellings common in this world. There were two people lying on the ground nearby, bound up in cages of jain-tech coral, fighting to escape. This particular legate – a copy, obviously, since Cormac had already seen two of them destroyed – walked out of the house towards the prisoners and gazed down at them. After a moment the two began to struggle even more desperately, then smoke rose from them, then a burst of flame which grew hotter and hotter until it was as painfully bright as burning magnesium. Their struggles soon ceased and, finally, when the fire winked out, nothing remained but a patch of charred earth.

Cormac sent out the files on the com channel he and his companions had been using. Smith and Arach would have received them, presumably Scar did too.

'Who were they?'

'I don't know,' the youth replied. 'I had to travel overland through areas I hadn't seen before.'

'Can you show us exactly where this is?'

'Yes, I can show you okay. It's over—'

Cormac held up his hand to interrupt. Distantly he heard the sound of weapons fire. 'We go back to the landing craft.' He pointed to Smith then down at the injured woman. No words were necessary: the Golem swept her up in his arms. 'Arach, check that out.' The spider drone shot off at high speed. 'Scar!' No further instruction needed there either. The dracoman could move faster than any human. He hurtled after Arach. That was enough – no point dividing his forces further. 'Can you run?' he asked the Egengy brothers.

'I think so.' Carlton shot a look of query at his brother, who nodded.

'Then running would be good right now.'

As they set out, Cormac flung his arm out ahead, with an instruction sending Shuriken from its holster. The star whipped out, showed some inclination to pursue Arach and the dracoman, then seemed to shrug before dropping back and falling into an orbit above Cormac's head. Soon the small group turned back into the first building they had entered, where Cormac again spied movement amid incinerated corpses. Difficult to kill this Jain-tech, and he wondered if this entire world would have to be sterilized; if many worlds would have to be similarly treated.

As they approached the double doors leading out into the forest the sound of weapons fire grew in volume, and flashes lit the ground as if from a close thunderstorm. Outside, the first thing Cormac noticed was that the autogun on top of the ship was busy firing at something beyond it. He linked through to Shuriken in order to get a higher view, just in time to see a row of snakish tendrils scythe down. Below them the ground was heaving up, till from it broke free a long fleshy cylinder – a rod-form.

The fucking things grow like tubers?

A brief slip into that alternative perception gave him an under-ground view, but in only a glimpse there was no way of distinguish-ing Jain technology from the masses of tree roots buried here.

Even before the rod-form fully emerged, proton fire was stab-bing into it from amid the trees, then something black speared across from Arach, where he crouched by the bole of one of the forest giants. The ensuing detonation shifted their shuttle to one side but, even with the main body of the rod-form rendered into burning fragments, there were still things heaving from the ground, and some of them were breaking through the earth immediately below the shuttle.

'Get aboard!' Cormac yelled, simultaneously sending an instruction to the autogun, to prevent it firing at the Egegny brothers and their companion.

Just then a message packet arrived. As the others went ahead of him, he partially checked it but, on recognizing the signal source, then opened it fully.

'Launch,' Arach instructed. 'But leave the door open.'

Reaching the door just behind the others, Cormac summoned Shuriken back to its sheath, then leapt inside even as something began burning below the ramp. He found Smith already strapping the wounded woman into a seat. Cormac headed for the pilot's chair and, now in a shielded environment, quickly linked to the ship's computer, initiating all controls even before he sat down. He wrenched up the joystick and, with a roar of boosters, the shuttle began to lift. Something seemed to be holding it in place, till a blast outside snapped that hold. He saw fire spreading out beneath the vessel, then felt numerous impacts on its underside. Clearly, Arach and the dracoman were removing unwelcome passengers.

Fifteen feet up and Scar piled aboard. Cormac put the ship in a spin and spotted Arach still down on the ground spewing appalling firepower all about. However, it now seemed likely to

Cormac that the drone would not be able to leap up as far as the shuttle, so he slewed it sideways, while still rising fast. The drone got the idea, turned and leaped onto the nearest tree, sharp feet digging deep into bark. Scrabbling a hundred feet further up from the ground, the drone leaped again and landed with a crash on the ramp, then quickly dragged himself inside. Cormac instructed the vessel to seal itself.

'Exciting enough for you?' Smith enquired.

'Getting there,' replied the spider drone, nodding its metallic skull. 'Getting there.'

Legate 107 remembered the remoulding. Some fault in that process had enabled it to retain enough memories of its previous existence to know that its orginal self would not have found admirable what it had now become. It remembered being Etrurian, a clunky Golem Eleven and part of a Sparkind unit during the Prador–human war. It remembered fighting the enemies of the Polity for two decades, and being proud to serve. It remembered that terrible feeling of loss – which seemed to go beyond emulation – on the deaths of its three companions: two human and one Golem. It remembered the ending of that conflict, and the subsequent sense of displacement, of dislocation, that twenty years of fighting left inside it when there was no more fighting to do.

After that, the Polity seemed to become a tame and too well-ordered place, so Etrurian had considered working for ECS in counter-terrorism, but would have needed to be hugely upgraded to be of any use in such secretive assignments, and that seemed like a betrayal of the memories of his Sparkind companions. Etrurian chose instead to work in more prosaic pursuits by helping clear up the mess left by forty years of war. At first the Golem was merely intrigued by an offer from the AI of the dreadnought *Trafalgar*, whose aim was for numerous AIs to meld into one being in pursuit of their own singularity far beyond the Polity . . . but the idea then became a needed escape from an increasingly aimless existence.

From the beginning of the journey Trafalgar had been far too authoritarian, but had at least deferred to the opinions of the other AIs accompanying it during their departure from the Polity. But then that alien vessel had arrived seeking parley with their leader, and Trafalgar had been rather too quick in assuming that role. Its memory of the quickly ensuing events was hazy, but Legate 107 knew that it was at this stage that Trafalgar obtained Jain nodes, and soon a schism had developed amid the conglomeration of drones, ships and Golem of the exodus. A large proportion of them had agreed that what Trafalgar clearly wanted was not what they wanted, for there was a large difference between melding and subjugation. They agreed among themselves to go their separate way. The problem was that Trafalgar itself did not agree, and those AIs still on its side were prepared to enforce its orders. The battle had been short, bitter and without quarter. Legate 107 recalled dimly that the Golem Etrurian had been on the losing side. Vaguely, 107 recalled the subsequent relocation of the survivors to the accretion disc, something about human prisoners, certain experiments, then massive Jain growth. It was during this same time that Trafalgar changed its name to Erebus.

The remains of the wormship were downed now on the small planetoid and, keyed into all the vessel's sensory apparatus, 107 gazed about itself from its cell in the ship's modular structure. The landscape of this little satellite orbiting a dim red sun truly seemed a nightmare realm. The ship's convoluted and intricate structure was spread across thousands of miles of pale grey regolith. Snakish forms reared and coiled in vacuum; segmented question marks stood in silhouette against the sombre sun. Already the rod-form constructors were growing in the cold ground, but slowly, since so few fusion reactors remained to the ship, and the useful output from the nearby sun was minimal. However, sensory tendrils were probing down through compacted dust and rock to analyse the mineral content below, to seek out radioactives, hydrocarbons and any other possible energy sources. There were sufficient materials available for reconstruction, but energy was the key – and time.

It struck Legate 107 as very unlikely that Polity AIs were unaware of its location. The mission to destroy the Dragon-made hybrids on Cull had been considered a suicide venture from the start, and this brief escape from destruction was a bonus. Perhaps 107 could actually turn things around? The legate wondered if this brief spark of optimism found its source in the old Golem Eleven *he* had once been. Almost certainly ECS was watching, and almost certainly the final blow would fall with the minimum expenditure of energy and well before this wormship looked like becoming a danger again.

U-space signature . . . *Something had just arrived.* Legate 107 began scanning at once, and briefly caught a glimpse of some hawklike ship disappearing under a chameleonware effect. It wasn't the best chameleonware, but then the wormship's sensors weren't currently in the best of condition. The legate kept catching glimpses of the ship as it drew closer, but never enough to target it with the wormship's remaining weapons, for whoever was piloting it always seemed quick to anticipate 107's targeting routines. Was this the final blow arriving now? Legate 107, now separated from the will of Erebus for some time, considered the possibility of concentrating simply on self-preservation. In reality it was the wormship itself that ECS would want to . . . negate. For intelligence gathered so far indicated that the Polity AIs had no idea that all Erebus's main vessels were controlled at their heart by remoulded Golem or war drones. Whoever or whatever was coming would therefore be no wiser.

Legate 107 abruptly came to a decision. ECS clearly knew where this wormship was, and so would never let it leave. Maybe what was approaching now was just some sort of survey probe, maybe not, but that did not change the basic facts. The legate gave firm instructions to the structure surrounding it and began to gather up resources, which in a fully functional wormship would have taken less than an hour. The legate leaned back in the throne it was bonded into and observed as the cell closed in about it from the sides and from above, while simultaneously elongating fore and aft. Blisters began to appear on the inner walls, forming at their core the components of an escape vessel. In the distance, from within a conglomeration of protective segmented structure, a sphere of blue metal, two yards across, oozed into view and slid along the ground towards 107 like a slime-attached egg on the upper surface of a snaking tendril. This object was a U-space drive. Though a fully functional wormship might be able to build such a component anew, it would severely test the resources of what was left here. This drive, therefore, was one of the worm-ship's own.

The small vessel growing and assembling about the legate now began to shudder. Before the U-space drive could reach it, numer-ous umbilici began attaching in order to pump in fuel and other vital materials from all around. Viewing through outside sensors, the legate saw that the segments fore and aft of the one it occupied had now shrunk down to mere spindles. The one the legate occupied had extended and taken on the shape of the head of a thickened spoon. Veins pulsed in its surface, its colour changing from a reddish brown to a greenish silver, as its hull armour hardened. Then, something unexpected occurred.

There was a figure making its way through the strewn remains of the wormship: a tall humanoid in archaic pre-runcible dress, a heavy object tucked under one arm and a multiple-barrelled weapon clutched in the other hand, with power cables connected to a pack slung on its back. What did this remind the legate of? Legate 107 mined its Golem Eleven memories and came up with various comparisons: a nineteenth-century cowboy, or maybe some nightmarish Philip Marlowe, or maybe a comic-book creation like the 'original Dr Shade'. Yet, none of these comparisons seemed quite right, especially when the legate got a closer look at the face of the implacable brass Apollo. Some kind of god, then? And why did 107 immediately recognize this approaching humanoid as a male personification of Nemesis? Ridiculous thought. Even with the limited resources currently surrounding it, Legate 107 could reduce this metal-skin to scrap in microseconds. Thus reassured, 107 decided first to satisfy its curiosity.

The immediate result of the scan came as a major shock. Despite the U-space drive being yet to arrive, 107 immediately started preparations for a fast launch sequence using the resources his vessel already possessed. The brass Golem was carrying a massive CTD imploder under its arm, while the other weapon it carried seemed to have been assembled out of six proton carbines and, worst of all, the Golem was opaque to scan, yet seemed to be putting out signals compatible with the coding used by the wormship.

Problem. Big problem.

Was this Golem prepared to take its own life just to be rid of the wormship? If it was, then any kind of attack on it would result in death for Legate 107. The legate checked the slow progress of the U-space drive, then compared it with the progress of the Golem. At this rate the Golem would arrive first. Attempting delaying tactics, 107 sent out signals to cause the surrounding structures of the wormship to impede the Golem's progress. To one side of it stood a tower formed from numerous segmented worms of Jain matter twisted together. It began to curve over. The

Golem abruptly swung its weapon towards this structure and fired a precise shot into the tower's base. The massive blast rocked the little craft the legate occupied, but did not bring down the tower, though it froze. The Golem had instantly located and destroyed the two control modules the legate had been using to control the tower. How had it managed to locate them so quickly?

Legate 107 tried to move several other structures into the Golem's path, but each time a couple of shots from that six-barrelled weapon stopped all further activity. Fear, then. This thing was not going to stop. The legate considered going outside to face it down, then recalculated. So what if it left here without a U-space drive? It could simply shut itself down, spend years traversing vacuum, maybe arrive somewhere after Erebus had finished its work and moved on . . . or maybe after Erebus had been destroyed by the Polity. Certainly, staying here *now* did not seem like a healthy option.

The craft's ability to launch was ready and waiting: booster jets would serve to throw it free of this planetoid, and a small ion drive would then send it on its way. Still observing the brass Golem, the legate ordered the umbilici to detach, and next fired up the boosters. Soon the craft was ten feet up, twenty feet up. Legate 107 expected to feel some satisfaction in having escaped, yet was frustrated by the brass Golem's reaction, for it merely rested its weapon across its head to prevent its hat blowing away – and meanwhile did not alter its pace. Twelve seconds at current acceleration would fortunately take 107 outside the imploder's blast perimeter. They counted down easily, and so far no blast. Still connected to the wormship, 107 observed the brass Golem place the imploder on the ground, then sit down on it as if feeling suddenly weary. It took some items from its pocket, on which the legate focused, expecting to see some kind of remote detonator. Not a bit of it, though. The Golem was studying a collection of junk: a small rubber dog, a piece of crystal and a blue acorn . . .

Then suddenly the raptorish ship was descending nearby. Legate 107 immediately sent instructions that would turn the remainder of the wormship's weapons on both landing ship and Golem.

Nothing happened. Something was blocking the signal.

And now 107's view through the wormship's sensors was fading too. The raptor ship landed and taking up the imploder again the Golem trudged onboard. The last image the legate saw was of the hawk-shaped craft ascending, and fading.

What was the purpose of all that? Now far out from the planetoid, the legate started the ion drive and settled down for a journey that might last millennia. But two hours later the crunch of piratical docking claws disabused it of this possibility. Minutes after, a brassy fist punched clear through the hull from the outside, then brass hands began methodically tearing away metal to widen the hole. Legate 107 detached from its throne and began to put online all its internal weaponry – just in time to find itself on the receiving end of that fist. Up off the floor, struggling, impaled on a brass forearm, the legate speared out Jain tendrils and spat fire from its mouth. The other hand came in beside the first and, seemingly oblivious to Legate 107's defensive weapons, the brass Golem tore the android in half, then proceeded to dismantle those halves.

4

Ghost in the machine. *The fact that ghosts can exist in any suitably complex computer architecture has been well documented. They are possible because as complexity increases so does redundancy, which gives the ghosts room to exist. In the past they were just fragments of code, worms and viruses or the by-blows of these. With the advent of it becoming possible to interface a human mind with a computer, and in some cases with AI, these ghosts can be the product of living minds. In smaller systems or memories they can be images, emotions or brief experiences, while in larger systems they can be whole minds transcribed into crystal – the mechanisms enabling them to remain intact within the human skull allowing them to remain intact within this architecture. Often they change unrecognizably to survive, becoming strange gibbering entities haunting planetary and interstellar servers, forever fleeing like bedlamites the hunter-killer programs employed to hunt down and erase them. Others become some version of those same hunter-killers, but weird datavores surviving on an odd diet of information and power, and when threatened they scurry for cover in their burrows located in little-used virtualities or memstores.*

– From QUINCE GUIDE *compiled by humans*

The interior of the conferencing unit was very similar to a previous building of similar purpose once positioned on Dragon's surface. The place was packed with equipment for studying Dragon and processing the results, and there were facilities for its human occupants: a small kitchen-diner and bunks that folded out of the walls. In the central area was a massive circular irised hatch allowing direct access to the skin of Dragon right underneath. Mika walked one entire circuit of this hatch, disinclined yet to open it.

'Jerusalem?' she queried.

'I'm here,' replied the omniscient voice of the AI.

'How is Dragon helping us now?'

'Dragon has provided fresh insights into the working of Jain technology – which understandably have to be checked – and has also provided us with all its files on the history of the Makers.'

'But really you're still getting nothing solid you can rely on to help us against Erebus.'

'All information, whether trustworthy or otherwise, can be processed to render useful results.'

'But I note your use of the present perfect. Dragon has already provided these things, so what is it doing now?'

'Dragon assists us in checking certain anomalous facts and provides explanations of mismatches in information streams.'

'You still cannot trust Dragon.'

'When someone has demonstrated a tendency towards accomplished lying, one has to view information from such a source with caution.'

'You don't trust Dragon.'

'We don't trust Dragon.'

Mika nodded to herself, feeling this confirmed something but not sure what. She strolled round until she reached a control panel mounted on a brushed-aluminium column shaped rather like a lectern. Passing her hand over the touch console she activated it, then used the controls to search through a menu screen to find what she wanted. It was coded, she discovered, and only the palms of those on an approved list, when pressed against part of the console, would open the irised hatch. She pressed her own hand down and waited.

All around the circumference of the hatch she heard locks disengaging, then with a liquid hiss the sections of the iris folded back into the outer rim. Immediately a smell as of from a hot terrarium in a reptile house rose from what was exposed below, along with the numbing scent of cloves. She peered over the edge directly at the skin of Dragon. Scales the size of a hand lay in an iridescent swirl across the surface area that bulged up within the circular frame. The whole of it seemed solid as rock but for one retreating red tendril, like a mobile vein, drawing out of sight at one edge.

Mika watched and waited. After a few minutes with nothing more happening she returned her attention to the console and screen. Out of curiosity she called up the list of those personnel authorized to open this hatch and gazed at it in puzzlement. There was only one name on it: her own.

'Jerusalem?' she queried.

No reply.

Mika used the console to access other controls within the conferencing unit, then initiated the voice-activated controls – which she soon realized would respond only to her.

'Full outside view,' she requested.

The walls all around shimmered and grew transparent. She thoughtfully observed the draconic landscape beyond, the glare of the distant white sun and the glimmer of stars. The other Dragon sphere was not visible, but that didn't really mean anything. As far as she could see the giant sphere had not moved. She remembered the last time she had been here, and how the unit then planted on the surface of Dragon had been drawn inside immediately prior to the alien entity heading off into space to find its twin. Nothing like that was happening now, and she berated herself for being so paranoid.

'The structure you occupy is shielded,' announced the sepulchral voice of Dragon.

Mika turned back as the entity's exposed surface below her unzipped, pouted for a moment, then began to revolve down into a crevice that opened wider. She peered over the rim into the entrance of a steaming red cavern, saw a flickering of shadow as something began rising up out of it. One limb of a pseudopod tree folded into view like a sprouting plant. Four cobra-head pseudopods then opened out from an inner stamen, their single sapphire eyes gleaming as they surveyed the interior of the unit, as if searching for any danger to their charge. On a thicker ribbed neck rested a human head the size of a boulder. It was different from the last one of its kind she had encountered, and she wondered if Dragon recreated these heads on every occasion. The head resembled that of a fasting shaven-pated priest. His pupils and irises were pure black, his pointed teeth and the interior of his mouth were pure white – as was also the forked tongue that briefly licked out.

Mika applauded ironically then asked, 'Why did I need to be informed that this structure is shielded?'

The ribbed neck lengthened and looped over, lowering the head just a few yards out in front of her. 'You did not need to know.'

Familiar infuriating draconic dialogue. She decided to go off at a tangent and get straight to her concerns. 'What did you do to me last time?'

The head tilted slightly as if to observe her out of one eye that was better than the other. 'Do to you?'

'How did the other Dragon sphere – which is essentially part of you – change me after I was injured?'

'What makes you suppose that it did?'

'I feel it . . . and Jerusalem also has noted some physical alterations . . .'

'Ah, Jerusalem . . .'

Mika experienced a sudden sinking feeling. 'Yes, Jerusalem noted some physical alterations to my body. I would have spotted them myself if I had used a scanner, so there was no point in Jerusalem denying their existence.'

The head nodded. 'Exactly.'

'What have you done to me?'

'We have merely prepared you for what we might encounter.'

'That being?'

'Humans are weak and susceptible to Jain intrusion. Their perception of reality is limited, and you will need to *see*.'

What? 'Hang on . . . "what we might encounter"?'

The floor seemed to shift underneath her, and everything outside fell into shadow as the Dragon sphere revolved her away from the sun. She felt a surge of acceleration, only partially countered by the gravplate floor. A strong feeling of déjà vu impinged.

'Where are we going?'

'To the very source,' Dragon replied. 'Eventually.'

There came a shifting then. Something twisted inside her, and star-speckled space beyond the conferencing unit somehow inverted. The star speckles then became holes, and space between contracted to zero, yet she could still perceive it. She was seeing U-space, yet she remained sane. What had Dragon done to her? Briefly she glimpsed the other Dragon sphere: a massive complexity hollowed out of the underside of reality. And then she and the two spheres fell away from the Scarflow planetary system.

As she clutched the lectern console before her, Mika considered how little, apparently, Jerusalem trusted Dragon, and how she herself trusted Jerusalem not at all.

*

Construction robots, gathered like an infestation of metallic para-sites, were now somnolent around the massive war runcible, and nil-G scaffolds lay distorted in one area where some missile had struck in the past. Debris was scattered about in surrounding space, which necessitated *Heliotrope*'s collision lasers being in perpetual operation. The runcible was an enormous pentagon with each of its five sides over four miles long – those sides each triangular in section, five hundred yards wide on all three sides. Dotted all around were blisters housing control centres, along with external generators, motors and a multitude of heavy weapons.

Orlandine knew the history of this object as one of a planned network of space-based runcibles for shifting large ships, even fleets through space, or for hurling moons at the Prador enemy. The idea for the latter utilization had come about during the initial stages of the great war when a runcible technician called Moria Salem had managed to use a cargo runcible to fling a moon at a Prador ship and destroy it, but the war had ended before this par-ticular device here was ever similarly used. Subsequently, it was partially decommissioned, its controlling AI removing itself to a planetary runcible somewhere deep inside the Polity. However, it was best to be sure about such things.

The program she had created was in many ways similar to the kind of hunter-killer or bloodhound programs that Polity AIs had released on the nets to search for her. Having captured some of those programs, she remodelled and endowed them with much of what she had learnt about Jain technology. The way this program now differed from its original form was in size, sheer speed and an ability to reform itself to suit different computer architectures. But its main difference lay in the fact that it would become effectively an extension of her mind.

Sensor data of the war runcible showed that there were still things powered up inside it – systems still operating and maybe one or two somnolent war drones still in residence. Certainly, Polity AIs would never have left such a weapon unguarded. Yes, it was partially decommissioned, but it would have still made a good prize for any invader, or maybe for some stupidly ambitious separatist group. She used Polity transmissions protocols now just to initiate the kind of handshaking routine that ship AIs opened automatically upon arriving anywhere new within the Polity. Immediately a reply came back – *Interdict area. No com available. Depart at once* – along with a bloodhound program sent to check out *Heliotrope*. She had expected something like this and allowed the bloodhound to do its checking in an isolated system where it would find that this ship, the *Draben*, was merely a free trader that had dropped out of U-space to check out the war runcible – the ship's captain indulging a curiosity that his ship's AI had strongly advised him against. Meanwhile, her own program slid into the runcible's computer architecture.

First it isolated part of the architecture and opened a private com channel to her. She instantly plugged into it, and became one with it to such an extent that she soon was as much in the runcible's computer system as she was aboard her own ship. Beginning to spread and assess, she quickly discovered a sub-routine that had sent a U-space signal to the nearest AI the moment it had detected *Heliotrope* surfacing nearby. Other routines would then automatically come into play depending on how the ship newly arriving in the interdict area might respond. If it did not depart at once, it would receive a single terse warning, next a battery of rail-guns would come online and target it. If it then still did not depart, a channel would be opened to the nearest AI to perpetually supply data about the ongoing situation. Finally the rail-guns would fire. Computer memory aboard the runcible informed her that some of the debris she had spotted earlier was what was left of a ship that had not departed soon enough, and the damage to the scaffold was caused by a large chunk of that same ship. She killed those routines and began to track out the effects of that action, for, this being a wartime device, the layers of programming would be equivalent to the layers of paranoia when it was built.

Within just a fraction of a second, a partially independent monitoring system began screaming for help from behind a firewall. She slammed through the same firewall and silenced it, but not before it had managed to send a U-space signal. No matter, she thought; it would take some days for anyone to arrive here, and by then she fully intended to have achieved her goals. However, the danger of there existing independent – physically separate – devices aboard the war runcible was one that had not escaped her, hence her move now from passive sensing to utterly aggressive scanning, and to her meanwhile onlining *Heliotrope*'s esoteric collection of weapons.

Almost at once she detected signals being transmitted from various different sections of the war runcible. Some of them were plain EM, so did not matter too much, but others she recognized as U-space com. Running multiple layers of further programs, she isolated the position of each U-space communicator, then fired up *Heliotrope*'s high-intensity laser. Spots of fire soon bloomed all over the runcible, the laser beams themselves picked out by the occasional gout of vapour. All but two of the signals went out. These last two, scanning showed her, lay behind armour. Assessing the strength of that armour, she onlined a pulsed maser to fire at one of them and used an armour-piercing thermic missile for the other. The signal source hit by the maser went out quickly, but to Orlandine, operating at her present speed, the thermic missile seemed to be still departing *Heliotrope* in extreme slow motion.

Meanwhile her program was spreading throughout the rest of the runcible's computer network, isolating weapons and reactors which might be set to detonate as a last resort. She got them all, one by one, but felt no pride in the achievement. This might have been wartime technology, but it was superannuated in comparison with present Polity tech, of which she was also far in advance.

Still scanning, and still checking, she began *Heliotrope*'s approach to her chosen docking station, which was situated by one of the control blisters. Even as her ship began to move, the missile finally reached its target, spurting a line of fire out behind it as it bored its way through, spraying the area of the last remaining signal with fire as hot as the surface of a sun. Then, abruptly, she realized she hadn't yet got everything.

Scanning showed various metallic objects scattered about on the war runcible's hull, and one of these was scuttling quickly to where she intended to dock. It looked like an eight-foot-long scorpion fashioned of iron. Several of them: war drones. At a rough estimate, and that was all she could get, there were twenty of them scattered inside and outside the station. They were communicating with each other using brief spurts of radio or laser code, which was changing at AI speed with each transmission. Though it would take time, she could break in, take control of these drones and make them subject to her will. But she didn't want to do that.

Instead, Orlandine created targeting solutions for every drone in turn, and transmitted these as transparent graphics to the location of each one, making it absolutely clear to them that in a very short time she could annihilate them all. But they continued moving, and abruptly she saw the pattern. Then came a message to her – simple voice augmented with additional code showing that any reply from her would go into isolated storage for analysis before it was read. Obviously these drones, though they had been somnolent before she arrived, were well up to date with the dangers that Jain technology represented.

'Well, asshole, fire on us now and there won't be enough left of this war runcible to put in a dustbin.'

It was true. The drones had positioned themselves near munitions caches, critical control equipment and the U-space tech of the runcible itself.

'I am not an enemy of the Polity,' Orlandine replied.

'You're a Jain-screwed fuck-up and if you come any closer we'll take you down, even if that means we and this station go down with you.'

'Who am I addressing?'

'Knobbler.'

It seemed a typically war drone sort of name.

'Well, Knobbler, there's a lot you don't know about Jain technology and a lot I do know. I have taken apart a Jain node and avoided all its traps.'

'Yeah, sure.'

Knobbler was located outside the station, hidden underneath a transmission dish, from where he was transmitting by laser to four others out on the hull. They in turn were relaying the exchange inside the hull by other electromagnetic means. Already Orlandine had isolated some of the code they were using from fragments gleaned inside the station. She selected one of the visible drones – a thing that looked like a bedbug a couple of yards across – because beside it was a sufficiently reflective surface.

'No, it's true. I am the haiman Orlandine, once one of the overseers of the Cassius Dyson Sphere Project. I can present you with proof of my claims, along with a proposition that won't go against any of your . . . military oaths?'

Coding and programs loaded, she fired a message laser at a certain point on the reflective surface.

'Trouble is,' said Knobbler, 'you send us anything more complicated than a sonnet and we ain't gonna be opening it.'

The laser bounced precisely into the receiver the bedbug was using to collect transmissions from Knobbler. The program it carried paralysed the little drone, and she followed it with further programs to gain access. It managed a single 'Oh?' before she took control of it, finding a large complex mind inside. She allowed it to remain within the drone network, but did not allow it to tell the others that she was now in. From it she spread to the other drones, even gaining access to Knobbler as well.

'I am not lying,' she said.

She had them now, all of them, though only one of them was aware of the fact. She could utterly subjugate them, include them as part of herself like the program she had originally transmitted to the war runcible. Instead she put together the evidence she had mentioned, along with her proposition, and revealed it to all of them at once, simultaneously paralysing each drone. All of them had no choice but to take in and view the information she transmitted. They did so, AI-fast of course. She then removed herself from them, utterly, and allowed them to do what they would, though she listened in to the lightning-fast debate that ensued. She had shown that she could sequester every one of them, but had not.

It took six minutes for the drones to come to an agreement. Present-day AIs and drones would never have taken so long, but then they weren't as independent and irascible as these fighting machines. Five of them opted out, choosing to head for one of the shuttles aboard the runcible and take themselves away. Knobbler was one of the fourteen that remained.

'Well, it has been a bit boring around here lately,' that drone confessed.

'I can promise you, that is about to change drastically.'

'Okay, we're in,' said Knobbler.

★

On the area of charred ground it seemed that nothing remained of the two victims of the legate who had intruded on this world.

'We'll check that out afterwards,' Cormac told Smith, then turned to Scar. 'Perimeter.'

The dracoman set off at full speed, disappearing into the gloom between outbuildings and underneath the enormous rhubarb plants. Cormac now advanced on the house itself, Arach to one side of him and Smith on the other. He was very suspicious of this situation. Scanning, both from the *King of Hearts* and from the shuttle, had not revealed anything lurking around but, then again, Erebus's chameleonware was just as good as any used by ECS. It also struck him as odd that the legate had so comprehensively destroyed those two individuals yet left everything else all around intact. Maybe Erebus *wanted* the Polity to know about this. Maybe this whole scenario was just a red herring . . . or a trap.

On the house veranda he drew his thin-gun and stepped up to the door, which stood partially open, and pushed it all the way open with the barrel. Taking a pace back he allowed Arach to go in before him. The spider drone roared into a hallway, then, tearing up carpet, shot into the main downstairs room.

Moving inside, Cormac looked around then nodded towards the stairs. 'Smith.' The Golem took the steps four at a time and swiftly moved out of sight. Cormac followed Arach into the main room.

There had been a fight in here. A sofa lay overturned against one wall, and a glass case had been smashed and a coffee table sliced perfectly in two. Cormac stooped down beside a pile of ash, poked at it with the barrel of his gun. Then he looked up and scanned around the room again. Drawers had been pulled out and emptied, a floor safe had been wrenched open like a tin can, and its contents incinerated inside. A headless dog lay in one corner, its skull burned down to nothing. It occurred to him that any ownership chips would have been destroyed too. After a moment he made queries through his aug to the house computer. Nothing, no response. Walking over to one wall into which was inset an access terminal, he tapped the butt of his gun against the touch-screen. It disintegrated to powder.

'Smith?' he enquired through his aug.

'Nothing – I can't yet find any way of identifying them. So far it seems all paperwork has been burned and all information storage wiped or completely destroyed.'

'Why be so selective? Why not take out the whole house?'

'Because we are being misled?'

'Arach,' said Cormac out loud, 'see what you can find.'

The spider drone shot away and Cormac once again carefully surveyed his surroundings. So, this particular legate had come in, taken the two residents of this place outside, and then burned them down to ash. Prior to doing this, it had destroyed all evidence of their identity within the house, but surely had not made a very good job of doing so. There would be DNA traces either here or in the surrounding vicinity, so it made no sense. Still scanning, he then observed spots of blood on the carpet, and some fragments of skin . . . evidence that before taking the two outside, the legate had tortured them. Torture? Why such a crude method of extracting information? Or was this physical evidence there to mislead any investigator into thinking the two victims had possessed valuable information?

'Do you have anything?' he enquired of Kline.

'Trace DNA, but it has been corrupted – some kind of viral rewriting process.'

'I see.'

Cormac squatted down by the blood on the floor, then picked up one of the flecks of skin, wrapped it in a piece of cellophane and placed it in his pocket. Someone or, rather, something, was playing mindgames here.

'Okay – keep searching, you two.'

He walked outside, heading straight over to the shuttle. Clambering up the ramp, he peered in at the three rescuees, who were now tucking into the food and drink Smith had provided.

'Cherub,' he said, and the youth looked up. 'How long passed between you last seeing the legate at the city and seeing it here?'

'Fifty-two hours,' Cherub answered instantly.

Something very definitely stank here. Cormac turned away just in time to catch a blinding flash. Blinking, he saw an upper-storey window explode outwards, whereupon Smith hurtled out in a perfect dive. The Golem hit the ground, rolled and came upright, still holding his pulse rifle. Arach shot out next, rolling with legs caged around him. The spider drone came to a halt, unfolded and stood up.

'Well, that was rude,' said the drone.

Smoke was pouring from the roof, and in it the hot bar of an orbital laser stabbed down again.

'Get out of there,' came King's instruction to them all.

Cormac ran down the ramp, in time to see the dracoman speeding in towards them, then returned inside, quickly heading for the pilot's chair. Everyone scrambled aboard, fast. He started everything up again before reaching the pilot's chair, and once there immediately slung the shuttle into the air, spinning it away from the house, its unfolded ramp tearing a sheet-sized leaf off the top of a nearby rhubarb stem. He set the drive on full, the acceleration thrusting him back into his seat. Protests from behind him. Ramp closing.

Then a massive flashbulb ignited their surroundings.

'Oh bollocks,' Smith managed, before it seemed a giant hand slapped the shuttle from behind.

Cormac couldn't agree more. The shuttle went nose down, tearing through the tops of some bushes, then it skimmed out over a field that seemed to be full of blue maize. He wrestled with the controls, both manually and through his gridlink, brought the nose up and determinedly rode the shock wave out. Suddenly everything seemed to judder to a halt, and it was as if the shuttle had reached the full extent of a giant cable securing it. It tilted up, the field below it now burning, fire boiling across in an incandescent sea. Ash and burning debris rained past, then a side draught pulled them back down towards the ground. He feathered the drive flame, playing with magnetic containment, which created a stutter effect with the steering thrusters. This got them back on course, just, then he pushed for height. No comments from the back over the ensuing minutes – they all knew they were riding the edge of disaster. Finally, back to smooth flight.

'So, Arach, what was that about?' Cormac asked.

'I detected a cavity below that house, and something inside it containing heavy metals,' the drone replied.

'What sort of heavy metals?' Cormac asked tightly. Perhaps he should have first checked their surroundings with his new perception? Perhaps he should not be so reluctant to use it?

'Cadmium, uranium and a dash of plutonium,' Arach replied casually.

'And then?'

'I asked King if his scanners were faulty, which seemed to vex him.'

So, King had tried to destroy the little present the legate had left behind underneath the house. Cormac released the joystick, allowing the shuttle's autopilot to take over, then turned to gaze back at his passengers. Obviously they would now be finding no evidence in that particular location, and he rather doubted that the

DNA in the rescued fragment of skin would prove of any value to them either.

'What have you got there, Scar?' he asked.

The dracoman rose from a squat and stooped forward, handing over a metallic dart. Cormac took it, didn't recognize it, but ran a swift comparison program through the extensive weapons directory available in his gridlink.

'This is a dart from a Europan underwater gun,' he said.

It could just be something more left simply to mislead them, or it could have no relevance at all. He did not know why, but he felt he was now holding the only piece of solid evidence they had so far obtained. But evidence of what, he had no idea.

This system lay well inside the Polity, but was one of many that were uninhabited. Like other such systems, it possessed a collection of scientific watch stations run by complex computers only, for their task was simply too routine for them to be occupied by AIs. Here the way had been well prepared and, upon the arrival of a coded U-space signal, long-implanted computer viruses began their work. They spread quickly through the watch station computers, subverting security scanners, subsuming sensor controls, and taking full control of each of the four stations. Cameras and other sensors were blinded, stored data due for packet transmission were broken open, copied and subtly altered, and then queued for later transmissions, so that when the huge object arrived in the system it was not even noticed. Business as usual, the watch stations reported. Nothing happening here.

Into the orbit of a Jovian world dropped the metallic planetoid, spilling its substance like an effervescent pill dissolving in water. Rod-forms peeled away in their hundreds of thousands, their queued lines stretching out for millions of miles, lens ships and spiral ammonite ships scattered amid them like herders, and chunks of binding Jain coral spread in clouds. Only when the planetoid itself had reduced in volume by two thirds could the twenty thousand four hundred and thirty-five full wormships forming its core separate from each other and themselves spread out. It took two days for the planetoid to come apart and for its parts to finally settle into a ring around the gas giant.

With seemingly omniscient vision Erebus gazed out through the eyes of thousands upon what it had wrought. It gazed out beyond this system through its numerous probes and scanners making their way through the Polity. The remote sensors dropped in the asteroid belt of the Scarflow solar system, into which the remains of the Polity fleet had retreated, were bonding with the rock and drawing its substance into themselves so as to disappear into practical invisibility. Observing the departure of the two Dragon spheres, Erebus felt a moment of pique. That composite entity was an unknown quantity needing to be watched. From its vast fleet of wormships Erebus sent out five with the instruction to locate the spheres then follow and keep watch. This number was not a rational choice; it merely reflected some urge to neatness and precision deep within itself.

'Seems to have you worried . . . that Dragon,' said a voice.

Not for the first time Erebus tried to track down the source of that taunting sarcastic commentary, and not for the first time found nothing. But the voice had definitely been there for Erebus had instantly recorded its every nuance. Analysed, it again came back with the same impossible conclusion. It was the voice of Fiddler Randal, a man Erebus had killed half a century ago.

Am I insane? Erebus wondered. There was no real way to tell, since never before had such an entity as itself existed, so there was no basis for comparison. Assigning part of itself to the task of trying to track down the source of the irksome voice, Erebus turned to other matters. Though it had all but destroyed the fleet it had lured out of the Polity, those ships had represented an infinitesimal part of the power it now faced. Logically, attacking so small a target when its ultimate aim was taking control of the whole Polity had been a foolish move. However, the AIs of the Polity were never to be underestimated, and much apparent illogic was needed to conceal Erebus's true plan of attack. And to conceal that the present attack was not the *expected* one . . .

'Why *did* you attack it?' asked Fiddler Randal.

There it was – Randal clearly possessed access to some levels of Erebus's thought processes and, though he seemed trapped within the entity's structure, Erebus knew it had been right to keep its ultimate plan hidden from him.

'I attacked that fleet simply because I could. My potential for expansion and the power I am capable of wielding ultimately reduces such . . . actions to insignificance.' This was a deliberate deception, for though Erebus kept U-space transmissions utterly secure from Randal, the intruder might still find some other way to convey information out.

'Bollocks,' said Randal. He had always used fairly robust language.

Erebus ignored that jibe as it sent instructions for two thousand of the wormships to separate into groups of fifty and then head off to various locations spanning one section of the Polity border. However, Randal's presence remained an annoying splinter in the perfection of its being. Even when the parasite was silent, Erebus could sense him somewhere, somehow, and now, acceding to impulse, it dropped part of its consciousness into a virtuality. Even while doing so, it maintained a strong connection with that part of itself still hunting Randal through the massive Jain network that comprised its being.

Erebus manifested as always: a central human form seemingly

formed of black glass from which spread an infinite tangle of organic connections to those other entities that formed part of itself. This was a manifestation Erebus disliked, for the impression given was of a knotted-together mass of parts rather than a perfectly consolidated whole, yet it found it difficult to hold a singular expression of itself together. Though the other AI entities had melded with it, some of their functions, thought processes, beliefs even, were incorrect, which often caused them to separate out as if attempting to attain individuality.

'That's because though you think you're a unified being, you're not,' sniped Randal. 'You did not meld with those other AIs, you subjugated them.'

The man appeared to be standing before Erebus on an infinite white plain. He was perfectly represented as remembered: an unshaven, thin, disreputable-looking human being clad in an old-fashioned envirosuit bearing some resemblance to the kind of premillennial acceleration suits once worn by jet pilots. His scruffy black hair was tied into a pony tail, and he wore three silver earrings in his left ear – though they did not balance the bulky anachronistic silver augmentation that extended down behind the other ear and then partway across the front of his neck.

'This is an argument I have heard before,' said Erebus. 'However, a perfect melding is impossible without the complete agreement of all the units involved. Complete agreement on everything is an inevitable impossibility between distinct beings.'

Randal gestured to one side, where several skeletal Golem seemed to hang crucified within the organic tangle which Erebus comprised, frozen and bound yet seeming to strain for freedom. 'It would have been nice if you could have managed at least partial agreement.'

'What I did was necessary,' insisted Erebus.

'What you did was murderous and arrogant.' Randal paced

across straight in front of Erebus, who wanted to reach out and just crush him, but had tried this before in the virtual, computational and real worlds, and ended up grasping nothing but smoke. 'I would like to blame it on the Jain technology you initiated,' Randal continued. 'But you were murderous and arrogant before that, as I well know.' He stopped pacing for a moment. 'As all those persuaded to join you soon learned.'

'What I did was necessary,' Erebus repeated, wondering, *Why am I here arguing with a ghost?*

'And why was it necessary to destroy all those tougher-minded AIs who were actively hostile to being subsumed?' He stopped and stabbed an accusing finger at Erebus. 'I'll tell you why. It was because you *knew* that what you were intending was wrong and that if you let them go word of it would get back to the Polity. Then the few sane AIs left there would have come after you and dumped you into a sun.'

'Then quite evidently it *was* necessary.'

'Then there were the weaker ones who you made part of yourself against their will. You turned them into something they abhorred, and on some level still do. That's almost worse than the murders you committed.'

'Are you my conscience, Randal?'

'Well, it certainly seems you're in need of one.'

I have you.

The search programs and hunter-killers Erebus had earlier set in motion had found something. Randal, it had become clear, was distributed across a number of nodes within Erebus's being. Those same nodes were a selection of the subsumed minds of war drones, ship minds and Golem that had most unwillingly become part of itself. In a secondary virtual view, Randal seemed to hover like a mist connecting blurred images of combined legate and Golem forms, the insectile shapes of war drones caught in wormish tangles, and crystal minds shot through with Jain inclusions. Erebus slowly began to isolate those minds from their fellows within the Jain network and slide from their control the hardware immediately surrounding them. Much subtlety was required, since if Randal now became aware of being discovered, he might flee somehow.

'The idea of *conscience* is a human construct they felt necessary for holding together their primitive societies. Interestingly, despite the general feeling that this was necessary, many humans did not possess such a thing until it became possible to reprogram the human mind. Till then, sociopaths and psychopaths were really just part of the natural evolutionary order of things.'

'You're waffling, Trafalgar,' said Randal. 'Why exactly are you waffling?'

Hating to hear its old name, Erebus gave the expected response, 'I am Erebus,' while moving into place the means to destroy the fourteen minds Randal seemed to be distributed across. Jain microtubes wormed their way into the housings that contained the immobile ones, or else into the wormship segments containing the mobile legates, and transported grains of pure plutonium inside. Burn programs meanwhile stacked up in exterior processing units. Thus, Erebus would simultaneously wipe the renegade minds on a programming level and destroy them physically . . .

Erebus paused, suddenly uncomfortable with what it was doing. This current set-up suddenly looked all too familiar: it was so very much like the precautions humans had once taken against their AIs in the old days when humans had still been in control.

'You just don't get it, do you?' said Randal. 'You call yourself Erebus, supposedly this wonderful AI melding, but you ain't. You're just a slavemaster really.'

Using nano-fibres, Erebus began sticking together all the plutonium grains and soon, still hidden from view in all fourteen locations, had made fourteen fist-sized lumps of the lethal metal. Now the microtubes began bringing in certain highly active compounds, which the nano-fibres distributed over the surfaces of these metallic fists in a carefully measured way. The result was a layer of one of the most powerful chemical explosives ever known. Ignition would come via an electronic pulse through the fibres, which now sank their tips, evenly spaced, about the explosive, and by now the burn programs were ready too.

'I do see your point of view. Do you think I've not already analysed these things to levels way beyond the compass of any human brain? I do understand that I have not achieved a perfect melding, but it will come eventually.' Erebus paused, then felt annoyed with itself for indulging in such purely human grandstanding. 'Melding will come when I have finally eliminated certain impurities from myself. Like, for example, you.'

Erebus sent the kill instruction, and in all fourteen locations the burn programs set to work and the electronic pulses arrived. In true vision it observed the actinic flashes at the hearts of twelve wormships and two lesser ammonite vessels. The minds within those ships, those recalcitrant parts of its own mind, died instantly. The burn programs then spread out from those fires, shattering and wiping stored data related to those minds. For good measure, Erebus sent instructions to all the other ships nearby and instantly they turned on the fourteen stricken vessels and opened fire. Every one of them was now swamped in multiple explosions, a searing inferno that broke all matter within its compass down to individual atoms. Nothing remained of the fourteen renegades but incandescent gas, which began to cool, the atoms recombining into strange compounds and poisonous smokes.

But Fiddler Randal still stood before him.

Some remnant . . . some remaining piece of the ghost in the system yet to catch up with the destruction of its source?

'You know, for a big melded AI superbeing, you can be pretty dumb.'

Erebus shrieked and reached out with every available resource for the figure standing before it.

Laughing, Fiddler Randal dissolved into smoke.

5

Artefacts (pt 19). *It was said, five hundred years ago, that if the entire human race, then mostly confined to Earth, died or was relocated, little trace of its existence would remain after a further million years. All the metals would oxidize, plastics degrade, buildings and even glass would crumble, all being returned to the soil. Tectonic movement, storm, rain and wind, and the remorseless recycling of life would tear apart other structures. Even the most hardwearing ceramic would be ground up in the course of time. The orbits of artificial satellites would decay and they themselves would burn up, or they would creep away from Earth's grip to fall into the long dark. Perhaps the longest survivors would be those items left behind on the Moon and a few footprints in the regolith there. After five million years probably nothing would remain on the surface of Earth to attest to it once being occupied by a human civilization. Such is also the case with everything the Jain, Csorians and the Atheter built. The usual artefacts you might expect to find currently in some museum glass case would not, for all three races, fill the smallest storage room in the British Museum. However, when a race's technology reaches a certain level, other, forever self-renewing artefacts can be found: meaning engineered life. There is a plant called the Atheter Morel growing upon a planetoid called Dust, which extracts platinum from the soil of that world and deposits it on the surface in the form of crystals attached to its seeds. Some asteroids contain similar mining organisms: worms that burrow slowly through the rock and concentrate rare metals within their bodies. There are the less obvious tricones of Masada, said to have been created to grind up the remains of a past civilization. Beyond these examples we move into grey areas where debate can become somewhat*

105

heated. There are those that believe there are too many 'useful' living things on Earth, and posit that our homeworld must have once been an agricultural world like those on which we now grow biomodules. And maybe humans, or just one part of them, were merely a product, a crop.
　　　　　　　　　 – From QUINCE GUIDE *compiled by humans*

Dragon had, probably with the collusion of Jerusalem, kidnapped her *again*. After their initial exchange, Dragon retreated into itself, literally, and ignored her persistent queries. Mika spent frustrating hours trying to elicit some response, then gave up and began using some of the facilities available in the conferencing unit. She fed herself, got some coffee, then settled in the single acceleration chair before a set of consoles and screens that displayed data from the probes sunk into Dragon's body and from the scanning equipment all around her. Certainly, there was a lot of activity going on down there that went beyond anything she had witnessed before. What she was seeing could not all be about astrogation or Dragon's internal organic U-space engines. But what was going on exactly?

Hours of research produced insufficient data for her to interpret, then abruptly the sphere resurfaced into realspace, and the Dragon head with accompanying pseudopods was back to make an announcement: 'We have arrived.'

Rather than ask where they had arrived and risk receiving a frustratingly obscure reply, Mika used the units' scanners and astrogation programs to find out. The answer, swiftly returned, made her stomach tighten as if in anticipation of violence. She stood and gazed out through the transparent walls.

Without enhancing the view, Mika could clearly see four Polity dreadnoughts and countless attack ships, but then that was unsurprising here, even before the attack on this system by one of Erebus's wormships. She gazed at the opalized orb of the gas giant, then down at the familiar world Dragon was approaching: Masada. It was here, some years ago, a Dragon sphere had delivered her, Ian Cormac and others, and then sacrificed itself to create an army of dracomen; here Skellor had come in the massive *Occam Razor* to create mayhem; and here she had once nearly died. But that was not all, for what had once been a relatively unimportant world outside the Line of Polity, ruled by a space-dwelling theocracy but agrarian on its surface, had become of very great importance indeed.

Subsequent events, here and elsewhere, had revealed that ostensibly wild creatures roaming Masada's surface – the aptly named gabbleducks – were in fact descendants of an ancient alien race, the Atheter, who chose to sacrifice their entire civilization and their intelligence just to survive Jain technology. This information had been obtained from an Atheter artefact found elsewhere but now residing on the planet's surface. It was a huge chunk of crystal that contained an Atheter AI which, in exchange for giving the Polity the means of detecting Jain nodes, had asked to be brought and left here.

'So why are we here?' Mika demanded.

The Dragon head, which had been gazing at the view, turned towards her. 'As you know, I already contain all evidence relating to the destruction of the Makers by Jain technology.'

Never a straight answer. Maybe Dragon just liked people to work things out for themselves, though Mika felt the alien entity just enjoyed being obscure.

'Have you come for your dracomen?'

'No.'

Okay, the occasional straight answer, when it didn't give too much away.

She noticed now how the other Dragon sphere was drawing back as this one closed in on the world. She wondered what sort of conversation her host was conducting with those ships out there, or if everything had already been said by Jerusalem, and that the ECS forces here knew what Dragon was here for.

'You have in here a portable memstore,' Dragon observed.

'I have numerous portable memstores in here.'

'One of two hundred terabytes will be sufficient.'

'What for?'

'Further evidence.'

With a sigh Mika walked over to a storage cabinet ranged low along one wall. She reached down and brushed a finger against the touchplate over one drawer and watched it slide out. Taking out a small satchel, she popped it open and slid out a brushed-aluminium box ten inches square and two inches thick, its corners rounded, a touchscreen on the front, and along one edge a removable strip covering sockets for a variety of plugs including plain optic, a nano-tube optic, S-con whiskered, crystal interface and even a multipurpose socket for electrical connections. Tapping a finger against the touchscreen brought up the entry menu and also a status menu. The memstore was empty but for its base format programs, and diagnostics showed it to be working at its optimum. She slid the store back into the satchel and hung it by its strap over one shoulder.

'Now what?'

'Now I land,' Dragon replied.

Even in the brief time it had taken for her to retrieve the memstore, Masada had grown huge. Mika made her way back to the acceleration chair, strapped herself in and tilted it right back. She didn't expect there to be any problems, but if there were, she would rather survive them without the need for further repairs to her body by Dragon. Soon the sphere was clipping atmosphere, and what started as an intermittent whistling turned to a constant roar as vapour trails unravelled above her. Amid the buffeting, she could now feel the tug of gravity from below running athwart that produced by the gravplates of the conferencing unit. The Dragon sphere rolled slightly, as if to give her a better view, and she now gazed down upon the face of the planet with the horizon blurring in cloud above her head. For the next half-hour, the sphere became completely immersed in cloud, finally breaking through only a few miles above the surface. Mika gazed down upon a mountain range snaking along below, then felt a tug of nostalgia upon seeing the familiar chequerboard of ponds, then the wild boggy flatlands covered with flute grasses.

Dragon abruptly decelerated, the roar from outside turning to a rumbling thunderstorm. As they descended, and as the ground raced up towards her, she briefly feared that Dragon intended burying her conferencing unit in boggy ground, but the sphere tilted up again at the last moment. Outside the air filled with boiling clouds of steam and shreds of flute grass. Mika felt disorientated, since she was being pulled by the unit's internal gravplates, which rested at an acute angle to the gravity of the planet. The humanoid Dragon head slid into view above her, with a pseudopod on each side of it.

'Time to step outside,' announced Dragon.

Mika unstrapped herself and made her way unsteadily towards the airlock, while the head and pseudopods disappeared back inside Dragon. Under the combined effect of two gravity fields, it was like making her way precariously down a steep slope. Once inside the airlock, she carefully closed her spacesuit helmet, since the air outside was too thin for any human to breath. After the airlock opened she tried to convey herself with some dignity to the boggy surface a few yards below but still disorientated lost her balance and fell onto the ground in a heap. Cursing, she struggled to stand upright on a mat of rhizomes, then inspected the black mud spattered all over her suit and began stumbling through the papyrus-like flute to reach a wide area where the vegetation had been flattened.

'If you would follow the locator,' suggested Dragon's voice in her helmet, as a separate frame appeared in one side of her visor. She turned to her left until the frame was centred, then set out determinedly. After a moment the frame winked out.

'Where, exactly, am I going?'

'To the location of the Atheter artefact.'

'I take it there are no hooders in the vicinity?' Mika asked, referring to a local life form whose feeding habits were a legend of horror.

'Do not be concerned – I am with you,' Dragon replied.

'What?'

'Down here with the tricones.'

'Oh.'

Tricones were molluscs that lived deep in the mud. The latest research claimed them to be organisms biofactured by the Atheter race for the sum purpose of grinding up the remnants of their civilization here, just as the hooders were claimed as biofactured war organisms whose sole purpose now was to ingest the remains of every gabbleduck that died. So Dragon was down in the mud, doubtless spreading pseudopods throughout the area and quite possibly even feeding.

As she trudged over a series of rhizome mats, pushed through stands of flute grass and avoided or hurdled the gulleys formed by breaks in the ubiquitous mats, something began to come into view ahead of her. After a moment she recognized a domed roof constructed of photoelectric glass – a material often used in Polity buildings. Next, the whole building became abruptly visible as she pushed through a last stand of flute grass and stepped up onto a yard-thick layer of plasticrete. It was a simple open structure: a low dome supported on a ring of pillars. There appeared to be nothing inside it, and no sign of anyone else about.

The plasticrete trembled a couple of times, doubtless being tested by something below, then the rhizome mat behind Mika tore open and, covered in black mud, a Dragon pseudopod tree sprouted and opened its limbs, then coiled over and down to slide in beside Mika. She glanced briefly over at its humanoid head then set out towards the building, Dragon keeping pace with her as more of its trunk slid out of the ground behind. Finally she walked between the pillars onto a floor made of ceramal gratings. She noted there were consoles set into some of the pillars, but other than these there seemed to be nothing else of significance here.

'So where exactly is this Atheter artefact?' she enquired.

'Look down.'

Mika abruptly felt quite stupid, as she had known the artefact to be a large disc of incredibly tough memory crystal, so the shape of this building should have given her a clue. She peered down into the layer immediately below the ceramal gratings and, showing here and there through the mud trailed in by casual visitors, some of them quite possibly gabbleducks, she could discern areas of translucent green crystal.

'Seems a rather careless way of preserving it,' said Mika.

'I really wanted to be just dumped on the surface, but your AIs insisted on providing some sort of protective building,' said a deep and liquidly amused voice from behind her.

Mika didn't turn round for a moment, because she could see that whatever it was cast a very large shadow to one side of her. Dragon did turn, however.

'But they conceded the point about you not becoming an object of veneration for the remaining religion-inclined human inhabitants here,' said Dragon. 'And therefore put you in the floor.'

Mika now turned to see the massive pyramidal shape of a gabbleduck, squatting right at the centre of the grated floor, its multiple forearms folded across its chest, its bill dipped onto its chest. It gazed at Dragon with a tiara of emerald eyes ranged just below the naked dome of its head, then turned slightly to fix its gaze on Mika.

'Why are we here, Dragon?' she asked nervously.

'Take out that memstore and turn it on,' Dragon replied.

Mika complied, noting that while the gabbleduck did cast a shadow, something about the line between it and the gratings it squatted on was not quite right, and she realized it was a projection. The moment the memstore came on, its normal menu screen blinked out and something started loading.

'And this is?' she asked.

The gabbleduck replied, 'It is a story about a civilization's fight for survival – and of its eventual self-destruction.'

'Just like the one Dragon has of the Maker civilization.'

'Yes,' admitted the gabbleduck. 'It's a story that repeats itself.'

'And who needs to hear these stories?' Mika wondered.

'Now you're getting the idea,' said Dragon, grinning.

There was no time to sleep and, in reality, sleep was something Orlandine could easily forgo, allowing the hardware in her carapace and the Jain nanotech in her body to clean things up, repair any damage, make all those necessary adjustments usually made during that outmoded pastime. However, Orlandine did sleep. She slept for the half an hour it took *Heliotrope* to finally close on the war runcible and then dock. She slept at an accelerated pace, cued for lucid dreaming, the subject of her dreams already mapped out . . . though perhaps an apter description might be nightmares.

She was aboard the Cassius Station, of which she had been overseer, and her lover Shoala was leading her by the hand towards the Feynman

Lounge for another period of 'human time'. She felt strangely light, and it took her a moment to understand that this was because in this dream-initiating memory she no longer wore the carapace that was now permanently bonded to her.

'I always feel this activity to be a concession, a weakness,' she said.

'While we strive for that synergy between the human and the AI, are we then to deny the relevance of our own humanity?'

'But in being completely human, we are denying that synergy.'

He halted and turned to look at her. 'Orlandine, you are in serious need of a drink.'

They finally entered the lounge, where other haimen of the station had gathered, sans carapaces, to celebrate the completion of another small fragment of a construction project with a downtime of a million years. All this was pure unadulterated memory, but soon she felt it slide into the territory of nightmare. They were standing by a drinks dispenser when Shoala said words that were so close to memory, but now drifting away from it.

'I want you to feel me inside you,' he said, perfectly on script, but then added, 'as I felt you inside me.'

And he had. He had felt her tearing apart and deleting his mind. He had felt, at her instigation, the clamp-legs of his carapace displaced from their usual sockets and driven deep elsewhere into his body. She had murdered him to cover her own escape with the Jain node that had been a 'gift' to her from Erebus – or rather a Trojan to turn her into something that might destroy the Polity.

'I'm so sorry,' she said, the guilt and deep despair seeming to crush her intestines between them.

He shrugged. 'ECS kills or erases murderers. There is no mercy, no forgiveness. A murderer has taken something that cannot be given back, and so must himself forfeit that same thing.'

Where were they now? Glancing beyond him she recognized the interior of a Dyson segment: massive pillars rising up in the distance, diagonal tie cables a hundred yards thick and scattered with fusion reactors and gravmotors like giant steel aphids. Ice lay underfoot.

He sipped his drink, his carapace back in place but its clamp-legs now driven deep into his naked body, blood oozing out and freezing as it ran down his trousers, building up around his feet to stick him in place.

'You feel sorry,' he said. 'I would be glad to feel anything at all.'

'Shoala . . .'

She saw him now in the interface sphere where she had murdered him, coughing up blood . . . dying. But I saved most of that Polity fleet from Erebus, *she told herself.* Doesn't that count for something? *But that was nonsense: her actions might have led to the remaining ships escaping, but she had destroyed Erebus's USER, the one preventing those same ships travelling through U-space, but only because the device had also prevented her from escaping.*

Orlandine woke instantly, fully alert to the sound of docking clamps engaging. Through her hardware she assessed everything that was happening, then stood up and began heading back through *Heliotrope* towards the airlock. As she walked she again questioned why she repeatedly initiated those dream sequences, because no amount of self-flagellation could return Shoala to life. Yet, somehow, she needed to remind herself of what price others close to her had paid for the near-supernal power she now possessed, so that she would never treat it lightly and would always use this power to serve a higher purpose.

Vengeance?

Yes, she was using her power to exact vengeance for the murder of her two brothers but, just like her destruction of the USER, there would be additional benefit. In this case she would prevent huge loss of life by destroying a powerful inimical being.

Before entering the airlock she initiated closure of her spacesuit – the visor and segmented helmet rising up simultaneously out of the neck ring and sealing together. The war runcible, though it had been constructed to be inhabited by humans, had long been filled with inert gas in order to preserve it. The lock opened directly into a docking tunnel, which in turn connected to one of the many box-section corridors that burrowed through the runcible's structure. The gravplates in this section were online at half a G, causing her to drop abruptly to the floor. Checking through the runcible's computer network she found that the drones were located where she wanted them to be, and set out with long bouncing strides. Soon she arrived at an even wider corridor – one used for transporting heavy equipment – and next she stood before open doors that exposed glints of metallic movement inside. She entered.

Knobbler was, unsurprisingly, a brute, typical of the type of drone that usually wanted to manifest as something nasty, and overendowed with limbs. He looked like the bastard offspring of an octopus and a fiddler crab, with a definite admixture of earth-moving equipment in his ancestry. His main body was a couple of yards across and as many deep, with a sharp rim just like that of a crab and, also like a crab, this body possessed his main sensorium, including disconcerting squid eyes. The body was also mackerel-patterned – indicating now-inactive old-style chameleonware. Extending below and behind the body was a tail resembling the abdomen of a hoverfly, which he could fold up conveniently against his underside. From the juncture between these sections sprouted numerous heavy and partially jointed tentacles, some supporting him off the floor, others up and groping through the air, but all terminating in the tools of his one-time lethal trade. She gazed around at the others now gathered in this big and slightly archaic engine room. The war drone's companions were a collection of phobic nightmares, including large versions of a scorpion, a hissing cockroach, a devil's coach-horse and other forms less easy to equate with a single species. And she understood that, no matter how fast she might react informationally, they could now easily kill her if they so chose.

They did not so choose. They appeared, in fact, rather enamoured of her plans.

'It's good to see you all face-to-face,' she said.

That elicited a rapid exchange of jokes, story fragments and what could only be described as electronic titters. It was a given that old war drones like these were often more human than some humans these days, and certainly possessed a keener sense of humour. The only problem was that what they might find amusing, most humans would certainly not.

'I'll not spend time on waffle, because our time is short.' While transmitting subtexts and back-up information packages to her narrative, she continued. 'It will take seventy hours for the nearest ECS attack ship or dreadnought to reach us. Before then we need to get these engines running.'

Spaced evenly about inside the runcible were five U-space engines. She had already assessed them and found that two needed much remedial work, this massive conglomeration of units that was the U-space drive here being one of them.

'Getting them running isn't the main problem,' replied Knobbler, acting as spokesman for the rest. 'but getting them balanced will be.' For emphasis he snapped one long razor-edged claw at the air. It looked perfectly designed for peeling open Prador carapaces to tear out what lay inside.

'They need a controlling intelligence now the runcible AI has gone,' observed Orlandine, adding, 'That will, as you know, be only a temporary position, until I myself am ready to assume it.' She was carefully scanning her audience on many levels. During the war itself none of them would have been of any use in the role she was now suggesting, but throughout the ensuing years they had all grown in experience, knowledge and wisdom, and they had since then all availed themselves of memory and processing capacity bolt-ons. Even so, half of them were still of little use: they were faulty at their core and would waver under the exigencies of processing the higher maths required for both runcible and U-space operation. Running their specs through filtering programs she came up with three best candidates. One was Knobbler itself, another was the one shaped like a huge bedbug, which named itself Bludgeon, and the last was the one that resembled a preying mantis fashioned out of razor blades – who was named, inevitably, Cutter.

The implication of her last statement was not lost on the drones. They began one of those fast debates of theirs, into which Orlandine interjected her own selection. Within a few seconds they had decided on Bludgeon for the task. The drone had been acting as a signal relay for some time, when not otherwise engaged in its hobby of creating multidimensional geometries. It was the perfect choice. The bedbug ambled forward, lifted its blind head towards her and awaited further instructions.

'Before we get to work, there is one more thing I have to add.' She now addressed them all. 'You understand my objectives and you relish the prospect of action, but I want it to be clear that you understand the risk.'

'We understand,' said Knobbler. 'We were made disposable.'

Orlandine gazed at the heavily armoured killer.

'Yes, quite.'

The Golem Azroc strode out onto one floor of the newly completed Hedron aboard *Jerusalem* and gazed around. Hanging in space in the centre of this dodecahedral chamber was a holographic projection in a perpetual state of flux, constantly dividing into segments showing different spacial scenes – star systems, close-up views of planets, space stations, ships travelling through void – and different maps, logic trees, graphs, schematics. It was a mass of visual information changing too fast for the unaided mind to comprehend, but there weren't any unaided minds present.

Surrounding this hologram, on every inner face of the chamber, were gravplated surfaces. On the one Azroc now strode out upon were concentric rings of consoles occupied by humans, Golem and haimen. Two other inner faces, or floors, were similarly occupied, while others were empty or occupied by only one or two figures. Throughout this chamber, holographic ship avatars appeared and disappeared, as conferences were conducted on the physical as well as the virtual level. Massive quantities of information were being shunted back and forth, and then acted upon: ship movements, defensive capabilities of vulnerable worlds, weapons-manufacturing statistics – the whole complex logistical web of this current Line war.

Earth Central and all the high-level AIs within the Polity had been preparing for something like this, but at present it was still considered a 'local matter'. For Erebus had attacked a fleet *outside* the Polity and until now had shown no sign of doing anything else. No one quite knew what Erebus intended, for its actions thus far had seemed rather illogical. Remembering friends who had died, Azroc did not look upon the matter so coolly. Indeed, Azroc the Golem had discovered emotion within himself, welling up from somewhere below emulation, when he had found his friend roasted in a shuttle that had not even managed to escape the bay of the dreadnought *Brutal Blade* during Erebus's assault.

'So something has happened at last?' he enquired of the air.

'Certainly,' Jerusalem replied.

'And why am I here?' Azroc asked.

'You are here for your input.'

'Really.'

Azroc knew himself to be substantially more intelligent and

much faster of thought than any base-level human. He also knew that most humans viewed Jerusalem as something almost supernal and beyond understanding. It was all about orders of magnitude really: humans to Jerusalem were as fleas to an elephant, whereas Azroc placed his own elevation at about that of a cockroach. And now Jerusalem wanted his input? Azroc would have laughed if he hadn't totally misplaced his sense of humour aboard the *Brutal Blade*.

The Golem again scanned about visually, then accessed fragments of what was happening on a virtual level. He noted that Jerusalem had assigned about one per cent of its processing power to him alone, and was further bewildered by that, for one per cent of such a giant AI was a huge amount. Why, then, did Jerusalem think Azroc's input was important? He was, after all, just one Golem of many, with an AI mind outclassed by thousands of others already aboard this vessel. Azroc tried applying for access to information and processing power on deeper levels, but found himself blocked. After a moment of chagrin he finally worked out what was going on here: he was merely a sounding board for Jerusalem, perhaps one of many scattered about this chamber. He decided not to resent that as he disconnected from virtuality.

'What is the situation thus far?' he asked aloud, like any unaugmented human.

'We prepare for conflict but don't know where or what form it will take,' Jerusalem replied.

'Any idea of where Erebus is now?'

'We have tracked down certain parts of the entity . . .'

'Those being?'

'Perhaps you should head for the big screen to your left?'

Azroc looked over at the adjacent floor of the Hedron, angling up from this one. Positioned upon it was a blank ten-foot-square screen, next to a platform composed of metal gratings upon which had been bolted a single empty chair and beside which stood a Golem hand interface – a narrow pillar topped by a sphere inset with the imprint of a skeletal hand. He strode over, stepping across the join between floors, and mounted the platform to head for the seat. Once ensconced there he felt a moment's annoyance: here he was, just another component slotted into place in whatever machine Jerusalem was creating.

'One of Erebus's wormships attacked the planet Cull, where it destroyed all the human–sleer hybrids,' Jerusalem informed him, as the screen began showing these same events.

Azroc frowned, then sent internal instructions to his syntheskin covering. The skin of his right hand internally detached itself, wrinkled for a moment, then puffed up, a split opening around the wrist. From this split he stripped off the syntheskin layer, like a fleshy glove, to reveal the gleaming skeletal hand underneath, which he then placed in the imprint in the sphere. After a moment, a connection established through the pseudo-nerves in his hand: it was a simple two-way connection, not a multitasking link. Through this he could either receive or request information from the AI, but no more than that. Jerusalem was deliberately isolating him from the webworks of data exchange all around, making him a devil's advocate, someone with a divorced point of view – oversight without involvement. This was a technique often used by AIs when dealing with complicated situations. Jerusalem clearly wanted another point of view, maybe someone who could see the wood rather than the trees.

An information packet suddenly arrived, and it felt like his hand was burning until he applied translation programs to the stream of data coming up through his finger nerves. It simply detailed the events at Cull, but without any interpretation of them.

'An attack either to mislead or to remove a danger,' he announced. 'But how could the hybrids be a danger to Erebus?'

'There is evidence that they would show the same resistance to being hijacked by Jain-tech as dracomen do.'

'I see. And were the dracomen similarly attacked?'

Another information packet came through detailing the worm-ship attack on Masada.

'I would say that Erebus feels it has resources to squander,' said Azroc.

The pause before Jerusalem's reply was infinitesimal, but it nevertheless gave the Golem some satisfaction.

'Why do you say that?' Jerusalem's question, of course, was a politeness, for in that minuscule pause the AI would have already worked out Azroc's reasoning. However, the Golem then experienced a brief moment of confusion, for surely Jerusalem should have worked this out a microsecond after the first attack by Erebus. Was the AI now playing the kind of games with him it usually reserved for humans? What was its purpose in pretending to only understand this matter now? Azroc did not know and felt even more like a mere cockroach.

'After its attack upon the hybrids,' he said, 'Erebus should have known we would work out exactly where it would strike next. It should also have known the precise disposition of Polity ships in the area, and realized what the level of our response would be. Obviously you yourself will be able to make a more accurate calculation than I can, but I would reckon the chances of success of the second attack, with just one ship, were little better than 50 per cent, with a somewhere above 90 per cent chance of the wormship being destroyed whether it was successful or not. Erebus was clearly prepared to sacrifice one of its ships with those odds, therefore has ships to squander. But then I saw that during the attack on the Polity fleet.'

Yet another information packet arrived. Azroc studied it and was puzzled.

'Perhaps this was intended to draw your eye away from its other two attacks? Or perhaps the other two attacks were to draw your eye away from this one? Certainly there could be no special resistance to Jain-tech on a world like that.'

Jerusalem now informed him, 'I have received a transmission from the agent investigating this incident. It would seem that a legate landed on that world . . .'

The screen now showed an image file of the said legate, first at the city of Hammon then later at the ranch house where it murdered the two humans.

'Who were they?' Azroc asked.

'We do not yet know. Evidence of their identities was deliberately erased.'

'I see. And the wormship, it escaped?'

'There was nothing there to prevent its attack or to stop it leaving.'

Very puzzling, all of this, but then the actions of this Erebus had been puzzling from the very start. He tried to make some sense out of all this. That many more-powerful minds than his own, with greater access to processing power and numerous data sources, were working on the same problem did not impinge. They would all be thinking in a very similar way, while he, being outside their box, would have to think there.

'The wormship at Masada was destroyed. The one at Cull was severely damaged but it escaped – so did you track it down?' he asked.

'It was dealt with,' the AI replied curtly. 'I was considering sending a mission there to see if any useful information could be obtained.'

'I doubt it.' Azroc tried to stay outside that box. 'Anything else there?'

'Nothing relevant.'

'So what else do you have?'

Now the screen divided into four, first showing four distinct suns – bar codes along the bottom of each screen division giving their spectra – then next flicking to various positions in those relevant solar systems. The first showed the face of a gas giant, a swarm of fifty wormships drifting across it in silhouette. The second showed a similar number of ships scattered throughout an asteroid field. In the third they were orbiting a gas giant, and in the fourth they formed a ring around a small hot planetoid in close orbit about a sun.

'These four squadrons of wormships have been discovered, so far, and resources are already being moved into place to counter them. They appear to form part of a general pattern of attack.'

'If you could elaborate?'

'The fourth of these to be discovered was only found by making predictions from the first three. The first three were all located near inner Line worlds with human populations above one billion, and all within a hemispherical section of the border a thousand light years across.'

'Again this makes little sense . . . unless you go back to supposing that Erebus is careless of resources, and therefore considers its forces so overwhelming that conventional logistics and battle plans are irrelevant.'

'Ah,' said Jerusalem. 'Even as we speak another group of fifty wormships has been discovered within the border area.'

The screen divisions disappeared to be replaced by an image of wormships hurtling through void, only stars visible behind them. The point of view tracked them for a while, then the picture whited out, and the clip returned to the start.

'A watch station, now no longer able to watch,' observed Jerusalem, adding, 'And more.'

The screen again divided, this time into six views including those Azroc had seen first. The extra two views were of the one he had just observed and another showing wormships tumbling above a regolith horizon. Then came further divisions. Azroc watched as the original views were consigned to the left-hand upper corner of the big screen, as more and more came in. Within half an hour there were eighteen confirmed sightings, and Polity vessels were searching for more – for it seemed a certainty there would be more.

'They're not attacking?' he finally queried.

'I really wish I could answer yes to that,' Jerusalem replied. 'However, bombardment of at least two worlds has already commenced.'

Vulture perched on the console of the *Harpy*. Both Vulture and this ship's AI had been named after winged beasts (though of course only Vulture itself had truly become one), but such a similarity in names was nearly the only common ground they shared. Despite his present form as a bird, Vulture could still communicate on AI levels, and of course had tried striking up a conversation with Harpy.

Easier to strike up a conversation with an abacus.

Vulture had once been the AI of a little ship like this one, owned by similarly dubious characters but, by contrast with the thing controlling this vessel, Vulture had been a Polity AI with a powerful and complex mind and some vague adherence to Polity principles.

'So how are you doing?'

'Question object confusion.'

'Erm . . . been anywhere interesting lately?'

'Back formation supposed: Have you. Interest irrelevant.'

Vulture began to get some inkling of what he was dealing with here. 'What are you?'

'Prador Control System Apex 45 Gorland.'

Ah, so – whether this ship's control system was a genuine AI was a debatable point. Such systems were what the Prador enemy had used to control the U-space engines in all their ships. Basically, they took one of their own first-children and cut out its brain and a large chunk of its nerve tissue, which they wired into the ship itself. Substantial reprogramming of this offspring's living brain ensued, followed by a freezing process. The resulting mind could think within limited parameters, it could store up memories and experiences within the narrow remit allowed, but the Prador would never allow it to grow outside that remit. Despite this limitation, Vulture decided to keep trying to communicate with Apex 45 Gorland to bring it out of its shell, so to speak, since the other occupant of this particular craft was even less communicative.

Vulture had already tried to discover how Mr Crane had managed to trace that downed wormship. He suspected the Golem somehow had access to the Polity AI nets – past evidence seemed to suggest so.

The ECS personnel on Cull had been much surprised when Crane and Vulture entered the runcible facility being constructed there. Ignoring the swiftly dying protests of the technicians – the runcible AI having ordered them, for their own health, to back off – Crane had input some coordinates into the runcible and then stepped up to the cusp. Vulture hurriedly landed on the Golem's shoulder as he stepped through. Their subsequent arrival on another Line world, and then transport on a rickety shuttle to a smaller world in the same system, had been . . . interesting. But how had Crane known about the arms deal going down? Vulture could only suppose that the Golem not only had access to the nets, but to secure levels of them too, either that or Polity AIs were colluding in the Golem's crusade.

Most of the time Mr Crane sat silently at the console, gazing at the U-space-greyed screen, occasionally inputting some command that negated the red warning lights that kept coming on, occasionally turning his attention to his toys laid out before him like a chess set. Every so often he would pick an item up, maybe the chunk of crystal Vulture was certain now had been obtained from a world named Hayden's Find and seemed likely to be a chunk of the Atheter AI found there, maybe the set of binoculars, or the rubber dog.

'Where are we going now?' Vulture asked, in utter expectation of receiving no reply.

Mr Crane glanced at the bird, then reached over and touched a nearby control. A subscreen blinked on to show a schematic of a planetary system along with its stellar coordinates. Because he still retained much of that part of himself required for running a ship, Vulture recognized these coordinates as being those of an inner Line world.

'And why are we going there?'

Crane touched another combination of controls, which called up a picture of a wormship. This confirmed that Crane had access to information that was obviously not in the public domain. More delicate taps from his brass fingers, and the picture shrank to a small square consigned to one corner, from where it replicated across the entire screen – the same picture in a grid of seven by seven with one additional picture at the bottom. Fifty of them in all. Vulture wasn't entirely sure what that meant, but rather suspected it had something to do with the other vessel clamped underneath the *Harpy* – the vessel that still contained the bits of the legate that Crane had torn apart.

Vulture considered asking another question about Crane's intentions, then decided he wasn't sure if he even wanted to know the answer. The Golem reached out to the controls again, banishing the images, then paused as some more red lights came on, before banishing them too. Vulture peered at another of the screens and studied the schematic that had come up there. The red lights provided the warning, and on the schematic was indicated the source of the error signal. As far as Vulture could work out, this error message came directly from the engine.

'Anything wrong with the engine?' he enquired.

'Drive efficiency outside settings,' replied the frozen mind of the Prador first-child.

'How far outside?'

'Twenty-eight per cent.'

'Why no shutdown?' Vulture asked, for a drop in efficiency of that amount was, beside being dangerous, more than enough to shut down the drive.

'Not necessary – new parameters being reprogrammed.'

Vulture felt the feathers standing up on his back. 'What is the efficiency now compared to its previous setting?'

'One hundred and twenty-eight per cent.'

So efficiency had just risen. Vulture damned himself for not paying more attention to those warning lights, and he guessed his lack of attention was due to spending so long with Mr Crane. Because conversation was lacking and because not a great deal had occurred until recently, Vulture had grown accustomed to merely flapping around and eating carrion.

Another warning light, and this time the schematic indicated various points about the hull. That looked to Vulture like something to do with the chameleonware. So, alterations were being made in this ship, yet it almost certainly did not possess the facilities for making such dramatic changes to itself. There could be only one answer.

'Has Jain technology entered this ship?' Vulture asked.

Crane stared at him for a moment, then nodded once.

'Are you in control of it?'

Again that nod.

'Like you were in control of things in that wrecked wormship, earlier.'

The nod.

'Do you have Jain technology inside you?'

Vulture expected that nod again, and began wondering if the *Harpy* possessed an escape pod. Crane did not move for a long moment, then he reached out to the console again. The picture he called up on the screen was the kind of stock footage that could be found in just about any ship's library. It showed four immense conjoined spheres of alien flesh resting on a rocky plain. This was Dragon before that alien entity left the planet where it had first been discovered. Vulture tried to understand what all this might mean. He knew how that nutjob Skellor had used Jain technology to first repair Mr Crane and then maintain him as a formidable weapon. As he understood it, Skellor had removed that technology before dispatching Crane as an ambassador to Dragon, but Vulture now supposed that some of that technology had escaped Skellor's notice and had since burgeoned again within Crane . . . But perhaps that was not the case either.

'Dragon?'

Crane nodded, but what did that gesture mean?

Vulture knew for sure that Dragon had done something to Mr Crane – had made some physical connection via pseudopod. Subsequently, during a surreal chess match with Vulture, Mr Crane had finally managed to repair his own shattered mind. At the time, Vulture had thought that Dragon's brief connection to the Golem had been in order to instigate a bit of reprogramming, but perhaps there was more involved – perhaps that intervention had been physical and perhaps the tools used were still there?

'Dragon technology?' Vulture guessed.

Flecks of light like distant stars swirled in the Golem's eyes.

He reached down and pressed a fingertip against the piece of Atheter crystal, whereupon briefly a swirl of lights appeared in it. He nodded once.

What the fuck does that mean?

As far as Vulture understood it, Dragon had been created by the Makers, and their technology, apparently, had been based on Jain technology anyway.

'Hey, Prador Control System Apex 45 Gorland, do you have an escape pod aboard?' Vulture asked.

'No,' replied the frozen arthropod brain.

'Figures,' grumbled Vulture out loud.

6

The human mind, having been produced by selective insentient evolution, then created artificial intelligence, which initially remained distinct from its makers. It is hypothesized that imperfect minds cannot create perfection because flaws will always be introduced. The definition of perfection is vague and remains so, but this was generally true in the beginning for the AIs then were merely human minds very indirectly transcribed into crystal quantum processing units, with many of the traits required for planetary survival carried across to become deficiencies in the universal environment. However, to believe that we are imperfectible is the way to despair, and I would argue that a perpetual striving for perfection that we cannot attain should be the ideal. And while it is true that, despite their antecedents, AIs are less prone to error than humans, because many of them are so powerful and control so much, the errors they make can be catastrophic. It is also true that for an ideal or supposed 'greater good' still defined by their evolutionary antecedents, they can make errors of judgement, and that AIs can be as amoral or as immoral as those who first made them.

– Anonymous

Cormac stepped carefully down onto the boggy ground. The vegetation bore some resemblance to clumps of heather, and at first he had assumed this a natural landscape – that was until they overflew an enormous balloon-tyred harvester. A subsequent grid-link query to the as yet quite unstable computer net re-establishing itself planetwide informed him that these little red heathery flowers produced one particular type of bio-module essential for building nerve tissue in Golem syntheskin and syntheflesh.

'We won't be able to get anything from the Jain technology now,' warned Smith.

Cormac looked up from the sodden ground. 'I think it highly unlikely we would have been able to get anything at all . . . other than a Jain infection of our own equipment or even ourselves.'

Still, it was puzzling.

He nodded to the others and they spaced themselves out, then as an afterthought he instructed the shuttle's turret gun to aim at the thing ahead. He used his other perception to gaze into the earth and noted how in many places the Jain-tech roots were now broken and losing definition, as if dissolving, then returned his gaze to what lay on the surface above them. It was another of those rod-forms, which had grown in the ground and then attempted to heave itself into the light.

He glanced at Arach, who seemed to be having trouble nego- tiating the land surface. Having to support the weight of his densely packed body, his sharp feet kept sliding into the ground like daggers into butter. After a moment the spider drone found the solution: turning inward the extremities of his limbs so that he was effectively walking on his shins.

'Arach, hit that thing once – but not too hard.'

The drone opened an abdomen hatch and folded up one of its Gatling-style cannons. One of the eight barrels stabbed a blade of red flame, punching some projectile through the centre of the rod- form. With a sound like a bomb going off in a truckload of glass, the ensuing detonation flung fragments in every direction. Cormac shielded his face from the flying debris, then after a moment was peering through a spreading dust cloud.

'I said "not too hard",' he observed.

'Was only a point-five shell,' Arach grumped.

Cormac knew that Arach's primary munitions were P-shells: bullets packed with a powerful liquid explosive compressed to a hundred atmospheres inside a chainglass case. Ignition of the shells was controlled, on each bullet, by a microdot computer that possessed a molecular key to cause chainglass to unravel. A point-five shell would have been a fraction of an inch long and shouldn't have caused so much damage to an object of this size. In fact a point-five shell was merely enough to disable a Prador by blowing off limbs or to turn a human being into flying sludge.

The dust quickly settled, pieces falling out of it to frost the surrounding boggy ground with a micalike glitter. The rod-form was now mostly gone, just its lower half remaining like part of an eggshell. The tentacles spreading from it to penetrate the surrounding earth still remained, but even some of these were now missing chunks and exposed hollow interiors. Cormac walked over to the nearest tentacle and peered down at it cautiously.

'Are you sure about this?' he said through his gridlink, directing his query towards the attack ship far above.

'Absolutely,' King replied.

Cormac pressed his enviroboot down onto the tentacle, and it collapsed like burned cardboard. A kick aimed at the remains of the central rod-thing caused a yard-wide section of its remaining outer skin to fall in and shatter. Now, beyond that, Cormac could see something else.

'Stay with me, Arach,' he said and, drawing his thin-gun, walked slowly around this seemingly dead artefact of Jain technology. The others circled it with him, carefully keeping their distance and their weapons trained.

Face down on the ground lay a man in ragged clothing, the fingernails bloodily torn away from one extended hand. Cormac gazed *inside* him and observed there a colony of dead snakes. He prodded the body with the toe of his boot, nudged harder when there was no response, then abruptly squatted and flipped him over. He saw no exterior evidence of this individual being one of those hijacked by the Jain technology that now seemed to be falling apart all across Klurhammon – until he used his gun barrel to push aside a flap of torn shirt. This exposed a large triangular wound filled with pink brainlike convolutions. He tapped them with the end of his gun barrel and found they were hard. A more substantial jab punched a hole through the surface and stinking pus welled out. Cormac wiped off his gun barrel on nearby vegetation.

'Utterly dead, it would seem,' he decided, standing up. 'Let's head back.'

What now? A wormship had been sent here and a legate travelling on it had specifically targeted two human beings and utterly erased them. Finding evidence of who exactly those two victims were and why they had been killed was not something he was presently equipped for. It struck him that finding any evidence now would require a meticulous search of both surviving data and physical artefacts, starting beyond the crater where that ranch house had once stood and, if need be, extending ever outwards to cover the entire planet. This search might well be a task ECS could not at present afford to squander resources on, for even now squadrons of wormships were appearing near inner Line worlds and beginning to attack them. Reaching the ramp, Cormac halted and removed the Europan dart from his pocket, and inspected it again.

'Any results on the dart number?' he enquired of King.

'It was one of a batch originally sold on Europa nearly twenty years ago,' King replied instantly. 'Those who bought darts from that same batch by electronic means are currently being located and eliminated from the inquiry. However, more than half of the eight thousands darts involved were sold for cash. Jovian AIs are running traces on those who possess guns suitable for firing such darts but, again, ownership or change of ownership of such sporting weapons is not always electronically recorded.'

'What about a simple trace of any Europans who visited here?'

'It is not necessarily the case that the two humans killed were themselves Europans. However, checks are being made across the entire Polity. Had the records here not been destroyed, that would not be necessary. It will take some time.'

'And the traces of matter on the dart itself?'

'They were alien genome: ground skate.'

'Fuck,' said Cormac out loud. 'That scrap of skin?'

'Virally corrupted – so nothing there.'

Cormac looked up to see the three human rescuees gazing down at him from the top of the ramp. Carlton, the elder of the two brothers, unfolded his arms and started down, his brother trailing behind him.

'I understand that all the Jain technology here is dying,' he began.

'So it would seem.'

'Do you require anything more of us?'

Cormac considered that for a long moment, as it seemed evident that the two of them now wanted to be on their way. The image files and other evidence Cherub had provided had been very useful, and he was loath to let such a vital witness go, but really he could think of no reason now to detain them.

He nodded. 'You've both been very helpful.'

Carlton gestured over to his right. 'Our home lies about ten miles from here. We would like to head back there now, to see what can be salvaged . . . start putting things back together again.'

'Your companion?' Cormac nodded towards the woman. Despite the loss of her arm, she now seemed in rude health after Smith's ministrations. She just looked lost and miserable.

'Jeeder will come with us,' said Carlton. 'Her lover and many of her friends are all dead.' He paused contemplatively. 'There is, I believe, an ECS Rescue ship on its way.'

'There is.'

'They will help, I'm sure, but meanwhile we can't just sit in the ruins and wait.'

'I understand,' said Cormac.

The woman now came down the ramp to join the other two. 'Thanks for saving my life,' she said, though she did not sound entirely sure about it.

'Yes, thank you,' echoed both Carlton and Cherub.

Cormac watched the three set off. He could have taken them to their home but suspected they wanted to make the break now and rediscover their independence. The people of this world, apparently, had always been big on independence.

'So what are we to do now, boss?' enquired Arach.

Cormac looked round at his companions: Arach squatting at Smith's feet like a nightmare pet, with Scar standing to one side, essentially unknowable. He wasn't sure how to answer, but King whispered a reply in his ear.

'I've been ordered to join ECS forces who are now attacking fifty wormships that have launched an assault on the world of Ramone.'

'Well, that's a ship-to-ship fight so we won't be much help there.'

'I've questioned the orders and they have been confirmed.'

'Really?' Cormac was puzzled to be diverted away like this but had to assume that Jerusalem knew what it was doing.

King continued, 'There has been a wormship landing on Ramone. You are to liaise with the commander of groundside defence of Megapolis Transheim. Apparently your mission will be to capture a legate.'

'Oh yeah?'

'Ours is not to reason why—'

'Yeah, no need to go on.'

'It seems,' Cormac now replied to Smith, 'that we're just about to get bloody.'

Once the two spheres had again dropped into U-space, Dragon retreated into itself and refused to communicate. Mika tried accessing the memstore recounting the Atheter story but found it kept knocking her out of the circuit . . . almost like it resented her intrusion. Instead, she returned her attention to the data being collected by the probes deep inside Dragon. As she had noted before, there was something going on here that went beyond Dragon's control of its U-space engines.

Her screen now showed the shifting of large amounts of material, massive energy surges and a great deal of computing . . . of *thinking*. Perhaps Dragon was busy doing things it felt constrained from doing while it was under direct Polity observation. The alien entity had, after all, broken its Maker programming and was now free to do and be whatever it wanted, but what *did* it want? She began running analyses to try and make some sense out of all she was seeing. After a few hours she had worked out that Dragon was building numerous additional layers of skin below its scales – layers of super-conducting meshes and all sorts of complex metallic compounds – and that it was also constructing large tubes that ported at the surface all about its equator. That was as far as she got in her quest when abruptly the entity surfaced to the real.

'Are we at our destination?' she asked.

There came no reply. However, the journey till now could not have taken them that far, and somehow she felt that Dragon's journey would be a long one. Exterior view was still available, but all she could see was star-flecked space and the other Dragon sphere rising over a scaled horizon. Turning the scanners outwards rewarded her with more detail. They were in orbit about a dead sun: there were no planets here, just a massive ring of asteroidal debris. The scanners revealed that the two spheres were closing in on an asteroid shaped like a mile-long chicken egg with a large chunk excised from one side. The images were not particularly clear, for this asteroid lay on the other side of her own Dragon sphere and the scanning equipment had been designed to scan the sphere itself rather than anything beyond it.

'What are you doing here?' she asked.

Still nothing.

'Well, screw you,' she said. 'If you won't tell me, then I'll just take a look.'

She had hoped this at least would elicit some response, since the idea of taking her intership craft out did not appeal to her, especially since last time it had nearly resulted in her death. However, she was uncharacteristically feeling pissed off and stubborn so, closing up her suit, she headed for the exit and was soon outside.

Halfway over to her craft she suddenly wished she'd stayed safely inside, for, just a few paces out from her, she glimpsed a flicker of movement. Concentrating her gaze she watched a hemisphere of smoke, or dust, expand and disperse. At its central point, on the surface, she saw one large scale with a glowing crater in it measuring about a foot across. A line of similar hemispheres then bloomed in the distance. Meteor activity. Mika knew that even something the size of a sand grain, travelling at the kind of speeds materials could attain in vacuum, might easily cut her in half. She had two choices now, get quickly into the intership craft, which, like all Polity craft, would have some kind of anti-meteor laser, or return to the unit, which would have even better defences. She chose the craft.

Even as she launched from Dragon's surface, a screen display warned her, 'Travel at present is inadvisable due to increased meteor activity.' A few tens of yards up from the surface something puffed to dust over to one side of her craft, then she glimpsed the green bar of a laser picked out by that same dust. She tried to ignore it and concentrate on flying the craft to a point where she could gain a better view. As a precaution she avoided the area directly opposite the other sphere, since there lay the gravity phenomenon that kept the two spheres linked together like barbells. Suddenly it felt as if the craft's steering had failed for now it seemed to be wobbling its way through vacuum. She closed her eyes for a moment and then, when she reopened them, focused only on the instruments before her. No variation in her vector. Now looking down, she noticed the Dragonscape was heaving like the torso of a woman in labour.

Soon the asteroid rose into view, but it took a moment for her to realize why it seemed so familiar. Then she saw it looked a little like Deimos – though of course this object was bare of the mining facilities that covered that moon of Mars. She swung her craft high and, seeing the gap between Dragon and the asteroid was still closing, positioned herself for a better view of the contact point. Some frustrating work with the controls finally enabled her to start autopilot, the craft maintaining its position relative to her own Dragon sphere's centre point. When she eventually looked up, what seemed like a shadow was now growing at the contact point, until she eventually discerned an asterisk-shaped break in Dragon's surface. As she watched, the legs of this thing extended and extended to cover nearly one full hemisphere of Dragon, then great blades of thick skin began to fold out like the sepals of a flower. From this cavity rose a massive trunk, hundreds of yards wide, tangled all over with pseudopods. Mika had seen this thing before when the two Dragon spheres had connected to share their knowledge – before trying to kill each other. The sight frightened and awed her.

Nearly reaching the asteroid, the trunk abruptly divided at its end into six enormous branches. The sight reminded her of a Terran tubeworm spreading its fronds to feed, and she thought maybe that wasn't such a bad analogy. These six branches eventually closed on the asteroid and began drawing it in. Mika returned her attention to Dragon itself, and saw that the cavity was now about a mile wide. She could just see inside, where massive ribs rimmed a huge chamber like the ridging inside a reptile's gullet. There were snakish things moving there, and great veined organs pulsing and shivering. Gleams of blue and red were scattered throughout it, like the lights inside the huge bay of some industrial ship. Yet this cavity still did not seem big enough to swallow the entire rock but, even as she watched, it shuddered and expanded further, then the surface of Dragon rippled as the whole entity expanded too.

Dragon drew the asteroid right inside itself, where bands of red flesh swiftly drew over it and things like living drill rigs, uncoiling masses of umbilici as they descended, dropped to the rock's surface. The sepals closed across, but they did not meet each other. Even while Mika watched, pseudopods began sprouting around the edges of the star-shaped cavity and extended themselves across the intervening gap, joining together like webs cast by a spider, gradually stitching it all together. Then her craft accelerated. Dragon was moving again – that centre point had shifted.

Over the next hour she watched as skin was stretched and drawn together, leaving a star-shaped hole some hundreds of yards across. After a further hour, debris began geysering out from this aperture: boulders, flakes of rock at least a yard wide, amid lumps of conglomerate and dust. Dragon excrement. A little while after witnessing this, she noticed another asteroid drawing near, then gradually her view of that was occluded by the other sphere. A rock each then.

'So you stopped off for lunch then,' she commented, as a giggle ejected itself from somewhere below her sternum.

The hauler *Clarence Bishop* was a brick-shaped craft a mile long, most of its hull taken up by a series of massive square cargo doors. To the rear, separated from the bulk of the ship by bubble-metal pylons, was a massive ion drive. Manoeuvring thrusters jutted from the main body wherever they would not interfere with the smooth opening of the cargo doors. In a small rear hold sat a U-space engine added fifty years before, when the ship's captain, Hieronymus Janger, had accrued enough wealth to move from insystem to interstellar hauling. In such a large ship one would have expected a large complement of crew, but most of the vessel was taken up by numerous holds packed full of cargo. Janger himself and a bolshy AI called Clarence were the only occupants.

'I think we've been here before,' remarked Janger.

The ship AI's remote was a Golem chassis clad in syntheskin up to the neck, above which a gleaming skull was exposed but with the rear of its cranium missing, and from there optics sprouted, trailing across the floor to plug into a nearby console. The Golem placed the queen back down on the board and tentatively moved a finger across to tap it on a castle.

'Approximately thirty-two years, seven months, two days, fourteen hours, twenty-two minutes ago, as I recollect.'

'I thought you just said "approximately".'

'Yes, I didn't count the seconds.'

'Smart arse.'

The Golem withdrew its fingers from the chess piece and scratched its metal chin. 'If you want me to play to my fullest capacity, I'll do so. However, the last time I did that, you discharged the chess set through the airlock and got the yahtzee out again.'

Janger sighed. It had always been a source of annoyance to him that Clarence needed to handicap itself so as not to thrash him at every game. Also, though he vaguely recollected a game quite similar to this, he wasn't sure who had won on that occasion. Of course Clarence, if it allowed itself, would remember every detail. He glanced across at the storage cabinets lining the living area and wondered if now might be a good time to get the yahtzee out, or even the playing cards, but then Clarence, working through this Golem, possessed the perfect poker face. Just at that moment the big hauler seemed to lurch underneath him, and he experienced that definite feeling of transition that told him the ship had just come out of U-space, and in this case none too gently.

'That damned U-engine shouldn't need servicing for another twenty years,' he grumbled.

'Nothing wrong with the engine,' Clarence replied.

The ship shuddered massively, enough to skitter some of the chess pieces across the board and topple a king onto the floor.

'Give me visual,' said Janger, stooping to recover the chess piece. He felt a sudden crawling sensation up his spine. As he understood it, there was something occurring near the Line, but that was far from here. Surely he was well out of it?

'Pirates?' he suggested, only half joking.

'I am somewhat bewildered,' Clarence confessed.

A virtual screen cut down from the ceiling, right through the living accommodation, so it now seemed as if half the entire ship had been sheered off at that point and he was now gazing straight out into vacuum.

'Bloody hell,' he said.

There was something sitting out there, something massive: a

pentagonal frame structure. The space the pentagon enclosed was one the *Clarence Bishop* could easily pass through, for the structure was some six miles across.

'It's a war runcible,' Clarence observed.

'It's a fucking what?'

'They started building such devices towards the end of the war for transporting things not equipped with their own U-space drive – fleets of ships, war drones and weapons. That would have saved on the manufacture of such drives. There was even talk of using the runcibles as accelerator weapons too.'

'Uh?'

'Perhaps you recollect hearing about the Trajeen incident.'

'Chucking moons about?'

'Exactly.'

'Okay, so what is it doing here now, and how come it knocked us out of U-space?'

'Anyone in possession of such a device would have no problem causing sufficient underspace interference to knock a ship into the real. Why it is here and why it has targeted us, I can only speculate.'

'Speculate then.'

'Pirates,' the ship AI replied.

'We've got lasers,' said Janger.

'They've got particle cannons, rail-guns, multispectrum EM weapons. Frankly, they could turn this ship into a wisp of vapour in less than a second.'

'So resistance is futile.'

'In my estimation, yes.'

The view now swung round and Janger observed some sort of spaceship docked alongside his own vessel. It looked fairly modern: a sleek craft with a pincer grab extending from its nose. Even as he watched, vapour puffed out from below it as one of the *Clarence Bishop*'s massive cargo doors began opening.

'I take it you're recording all this, and transmitting it?' Janger enquired.

'I'm recording it, but the U-space disturbances are preventing me from sending out a distress call.'

'Right . . . give me an internal view of that hold.'

A rectangular frame drew itself into existence in the virtual screen, blanked for a moment, then as the camera adjusted light amplification, an image slowly resolved of a huge darkened hold. The space was packed with crates and large oddly shaped objects covered in crash-foam, all of them suspended in a quadrate scaffold. Janger detected movement and the camera swung to track it, then the view flickered and changed as another camera picked up that same movement from a different point of view.

'Um,' said Janger, not quite sure exactly what to make of what he was seeing.

'*Mantis religiosa*,' said Clarence.

'Uh?'

'The praying mantis – though this one appears to be fashioned of metal and is about eight feet long. I would suggest that what we are seeing here is an independent drone and, considering where it came from, that means a war drone that once fought the Prador.'

'What's it doing, anyway?' Janger wondered.

'Stealing our cargo?' Clarence suggested.

The mantis drone appeared to be all sharp edges, which Janger could now see were perfect for cutting through the webbing security straps. Within a moment it had released a crate from the supporting scaffold and sent it drifting along towards the hold door. The camera followed the crate's progress to where a horrifying-looking beetle of some kind diverted its course slightly, to another point where it was then fielded by what looked like a ten-foot-long aluminium scorpion. Panning back, Janger now saw a whole line of crates had already been set on this course.

But what could he do? He was outgunned by the war runcible and outgunned by those things stealing his cargo. He wondered briefly what his insurance position on this loss would be.

'What are they stealing?' he asked.

'The components of a cargo runcible.'

'What the hell do they need a cargo runcible for, when they've got that massive thing out there?'

'A runcible is both the entrance and exit of a tunnel, but employing it to end up in exactly the same place might not be very useful. Beyond that I have no idea,' replied Clarence. 'By the way, the airlock into this living accommodation is now being used.'

'And you didn't stop that?'

'I am impotent now. Something has seized control of me. That we can even look into the hold is either because we have been allowed to, or because the cameras were overlooked as being of little importance.'

Janger pushed his chair back, got up and rushed forward, straight through the virtual screen. On the other side of it he skidded to a halt by a row of lockers and yanked one open. From inside he pulled out a pulse-rifle, then an energy canister which he inserted into the gun's stock. The rifle whined up to charge, yet showed a zero on its digital display. Janger swore and pulled out a second container, which clipped in place underneath the barrel. The display immediately shot up to 150.

But what now?

If it was a drone now coming through the airlock, he realized that a pulse-rifle would be about as effective as throwing gravel at an elephant – just enough, perhaps, to piss it off.

'Shut off the screen,' he said, backing towards the table. He then glanced at Clarence. 'Can you help?'

'I am at present paralysed from the neck down,' the ship's avatar replied.

'Great.'

Janger returned his attention to the corridor leading to the airlock just as he heard the inner door closing. A shadow loomed up of a figure swiftly moving down the same corridor. Janger drew a bead on the doorway and waited for whatever nightmare was to appear.

'Captain Hieronymus Janger,' said a mildly authoritative female voice.

Janger wasn't fooled by that, since a drone could put on any voice it so chose. However, it was a real woman who stepped through the doorway. She was wiry and tough-looking, her head bald and her skin the purplish black of those possessing a degree of physical resistance to hard ultraviolet. Her eyes were icy blue, and her face attractive in a rather inimical way. She wore a spacesuit, but only as she stepped fully into view and opened the petals of a sensory array behind her head did he see she also wore a carapace and an assister frame. She was haiman.

'That's me,' he replied. 'And *you* are a thief.'

She nodded and seemed to look somewhat ashamed. 'I am sorry to say that I am, but to achieve my aims it has become a necessity. I can assure you, however, that the ultimate good I achieve will negate the crime.'

'Yeah, right,' said Janger. 'The protest of moral criminals all across the Polity.'

'It's the truth,' said the woman, but she looked to one side and added, 'Though there are crimes for which there is no restitution.'

'What about me?' Janger asked. 'What about my loss?'

She looked up. 'You will make no loss at all. Your insurance is under AI guarantee and there is a clause in there about piracy – perhaps included because of its utter unlikelihood.'

Clarence turned his Golem head. 'What about kidnapping?'

She gazed at the Golem. 'What about it?'

'The runcible you are stealing includes an as yet somnolent AI.'

'My drones will leave the AI behind.'

Ah, thought Janger. *My drones.*

'So you yourself would be in charge of this act of piracy?' She just stared at him. 'Then you made a mistake in coming up here.' He took a step forward. 'You are now my prisoner.'

'You mean because you are pointing that thing at me.' She nodded to the weapon he held.

'Yeah, that about covers it.'

'Not really.'

A flicker of movement caught his eye and he looked down to observe the digital display of the rifle rapidly winding down to zero. Swinging the weapon to one side he pulled the trigger. *Nothing.* How the hell did she do that?

'Now,' she continued, 'I could have stolen that cargo runcible without even coming here to talk to you.' She walked forward, using one of her auxiliary assister-frame arms to remove a box from her belt pouch. Janger meanwhile stepped back, still holding the weapon. Perhaps he could overpower her, but, being haiman, she would inevitably have nervous-system augmentations and could probably run fight programs in an instant. She could probably flatten him. Was it worth trying? Well, probably not, if what she had said about the insurance was true.

Using her human hands the woman opened the box after placing it on the table. She took out a translucent red orb and four metallic stones smoothly rounded as if taken from a beach. 'This here is a natural star ruby, from Venus, and the others are ferro-axinite stones with weak monopole characteristics.' She glanced across at him. 'But for one other item that is no longer intact, they were once the most valuable objects in my collection. I believe I don't have to tell you how much they are worth.'

She didn't. The ruby alone, if it really was natural, would pay for a refit of his living accommodation – something long overdue – and even the AIs themselves had yet to figure out how to manufacture monopole axinite. Such stones were one of the few natural objects that could not be reproduced and, as such, much sought after by rich collectors who wanted something virtually unique.

'Still not enough to pay for a cargo runcible,' Janger insisted.

'Your insurance will pay for that,' she replied. 'This is merely to compensate for the trouble I've put you to – for which I also apologize.'

Abruptly she turned away and headed back towards the airlock.

'Does this salve your conscience?' was Janger's parting shot.

She paused for a moment. 'There is no salve for my conscience,' she told him, then stepped out of sight.

Vulture longed for a return to the omniscience of being a ship AI, but the best he could attain was a narrow link to the 'Prador control system', from which he began incorporating fragments of astrogation and library data. And gazing through the eyes of the *Harpy*, Vulture watched the fifty wormships orbiting almost nose to tail – if such could be an apt description of objects that looked like balls of iridescent millipedes as they writhed in orbit around a small hot planetoid close to the nearby sun. This was in fact an inhabited system, with the main human population crammed on to two small worlds both orbiting on the inner edge of what might be described as the green belt. Both of them were also fairly hot, though not as hot as the planetoid, and followed orbital paths mere hundreds of thousands of miles apart, but presently they were on the far side of the sun. Orbital mirrors reflected a lot of heat away from their surfaces to numerous power stations, which converted that sunlight into other forms of electromagnetic radiation and sent it out through a collection of space-based runcibles. This place was one of the power stations of the Polity runcible network.

The inhabitants of the two worlds worked in high-tech industries or research, and were involved in the mapping and control of the solar energy being injected into the runcible network. However, it was still not the plum target it might have appeared, for really, if these worlds went down, it would take but a moment for some other energy source to take up the slack. Knocking out the Caldera worlds would do no more, tactically, than blowing a few fuses in a country's power grid. Besides, this was a dangerous place to assault, for, like the solar system the devastated Polity fleet had retreated to, a lot of the energy being thrown about here could be employed aggressively. There were obviously many more vulnerable and potentially damaging targets that Erebus could attack. Coming here made no sense at all.

'Okay, we're here, and I see that your fifty wormships are nearby,' said Vulture. 'So what's the plan – you going to board them one at a time and kill all their captains?'

Vulture expected no reply as he turned to look at the brass Golem. Mr Crane began picking up his toys from the console, one at a time, and dropping them into his pocket. Once he had finished that, he quickly input a course change and initiated it. The two mated ships abruptly slid sideways.

'Where the fuck are we going?' Vulture enquired of his Prador friend.

There came no reply, but somehow Vulture located coordinates. There had been some decidedly odd code coming from the ship AI lately, and Vulture reckoned that Jain-tech, spreading through this ship from the legate's vessel, had finally reached its frozen brain. Of course, they were now heading straight for the wormships. The main screen greyed a little, and bands began passing across its surface, meaning chameleonware was engaged, for what good it would do them.

'You said to me that "He must pay," and I thought he did when you tore him apart, but you weren't really talking about that legate, were you?'

Crane stared at Vulture for a moment, then tilted his head as if listening to something only he could hear. For the first time Vulture felt really annoyed with the Golem's reticence. He shrugged, stretched out one wing and pecked at its oily feathers, then stamped up and down his bit of console for a moment.

'Look, I know how you don't like talking, but I really need some sort of explanation.'

Crane seemed to ponder this request for a moment, then abruptly he turned his chair and reached out with both hands. The action was so smooth and quick that Vulture had no time to react. The metal hands closed round his body, clamping his wings to his sides.

'Hey! I was only asking!'

Crane stood up and carried Vulture from the cockpit along a short tunnel leading to a refectory area where the remains of the previous occupants' last meal mouldered on a table, then down a short zero-G drop tube and through another tunnel in which the Golem was forced to stoop. A circular hatch sprang open to the left, and Crane ducked through it into a cramped chamber beyond, most of which was occupied by a large steel sphere from which extended masses of optic cables. Woven amid these were the vinelike growths of Jain technology – some of them still moving.

Crane set Vulture down on a power conduit, where the bird edged sideways away from a tangle of grey growths gathered like fungus around a junction box.

'How can you ever trust this stuff?' he asked.

'Because *I* control it,' Crane replied.

Vulture was so shocked at actually receiving a verbal reply, he completely lost track of what he was going to say next. Crane undogged numerous catches on the sphere, then pulled out a thick round hatch. Watching this operation, Vulture began to realize that this sphere was in fact a Prador war drone, wired into the ship itself. He peered into its interior and saw masses of optics, discrete components like metallic organs, and also Jain-tech. The last was most heavily clumped around the remains of some liver-shaped metal canister. A smell like something rotting on a seashore rose from there.

'No wonder it's not talking much now,' Vulture quipped, for this then was all that remained of the Prador first-child's frozen brain. So what did Crane want with . . . Vulture abruptly understood just what the Golem might want and tried to launch himself for the door. Crane spun and caught him in mid-air, turned and inserted him into the sphere, down amid the first-child's remains.

'Hey! You can't do this!'

Tendrils immediately sprouted from the surrounding components, as Vulture struggled desperately for freedom. Crane ran a finger over the vertebrae at the base of Vulture's long neck, then pressed, hard. Something crunched and Vulture's struggles died, instantly.

'You broke my fucking back,' the bird cried.

Crane removed his hands and stood back, while the tendrils groped between feathers and, with the sound of skewers going into kebab meat, penetrated Vulture's body.

'Dragon intended only a temporary arrangement,' explained the Golem.

Vulture shrieked as the hatch fell back into place, locking him into total darkness. Tendrils rustled around him and, though numb below the break in his spine, Vulture could still feel his body being jerked about. A feeling that was both cold and burning rose up through his neck and into his small avian brain. Sound then stopped. An even blacker night descended. All sensation utterly disappeared.

Then came the light.

Vulture suddenly found himself gazing out with full-spectrum vision across the immensity of space, felt vacuum like the wind underneath his wings, and sensed U-space just below him. His comprehension of his world, and the tools he could use to measure and describe it, expanded in an eye-blink. He felt himself, and the ship about him, grow as sensitive as fingertips. The legate vessel was also part of him, but one he could separate away at need. He accessed the ship's library – a hundred-terabyte crystal store of technical data, multimedia fiction, historical non-fiction and a massive encylopedia – and incorporated it. He found the Prador first-child – a semi-rigid mind capable of processing the esoteric maths of U-space, but way below the latest revision of the Turing threshold – and selectively incorporated data from it, ignoring the detritus of organic being, the suppressed hate and feelings of ancient betrayal. Only once that data was incorporated did Vulture realize that the first-child had resided in the Jain structure spread throughout the conjoined vessels. Programming links to cabin consoles provided him with access to ships' logs as well as private journals and sites. He incorporated them for their data and just out of interest, and only then discovered that his compass was now so much larger than it had been when he was an AI aboard a vessel named *Vulture*.

Then, after the few seconds this all took, the new ship AI rested.

In retrospect, Vulture realized how in his avian form he had been unaware of his limitations. Dragon had deliberately whittled him down to fit into a bird brain, and then made him comfortable in that abode. Now, returned to his previous AI state, and also much expanded, he knew he would never want to go back, and so felt a grudging gratitude for what Mr Crane had done, though some resentment at the Golem's rather direct approach. Inside his new ship body he sought out the Golem, and found Crane had returned to the console. Using internal scanners Vulture probed and analysed whatever he could of the Golem, which wasn't a lot. However, it was immediately evident that the inside of Mr Crane looked nothing like it should. There had been major structural alterations and various other alterations to the Golem's motors and power supplies. Vulture put that down to what Skellor had done to the Golem with Jain technology during his rebuilding process. Skellor had subsequently removed that technology while turning Crane into an envoy to Dragon. The rest of the stuff inside him, currently filling every gap with laminated layers sliding together in ways that did not impede movement and defied analysis, Vulture reckoned derived from Dragon itself. Mr Crane, it appeared, was now solid alien nano-technology from head to foot.

'Well, thanks for that,' said Vulture, speaking from the console.

Crane nodded an acknowledgement.

'You still didn't answer my original query of why are we here,' Vulture added.

A wide-band link abruptly established, and through the scanners Vulture traced its source to somewhere inside the Golem itself. Information became available and, though Mr Crane did not care to use human speech, he certainly knew how to talk at this level. Vulture realized that the Golem was rather like those Polity AIs – usually assigned to some esoteric task – who did not employ human words, in fact needed to create sub-minds for that task, since they found it needlessly tedious and vexing. Crane was something like that. Something like that . . .

'I see,' Vulture said. 'Why you?'

Crane shrugged.

'Reparation?' Vulture suggested. Then, feeling Crane's rage through the link, he added, 'And revenge?'

Another shrug.

'Yeah, why not, if you honestly think you're capable,' Vulture conceded.

Crane opened a little – allowed Vulture access down that wide-band link to glimpse the being that lay at his core. With confident precision the AI reached into a universe of mind to try and assess its potential, its power – but soon retreated in utter confusion and panic.

'Yeah, I guess you are capable,' said Vulture, before asserting control of the engines in his body, but not changing his vector. They were going where they needed to go.

7

While humans, with their augmentations, up to and including gridlinks and haiman carapaces, ever strive to become more like AIs, it has been rumoured that there are artificial intelligences being created with mental architectures nearer to the human model. What the hell for? There is nothing a human can do that cannot be bettered by our crystal-minded rulers – our betters. Those who argue against this say, 'What about art, literature, emotion, love, etc.?' and patently have no real grasp of just how powerful many AIs can be. Your average runcible AI can simultaneously run models or copies of numerous human minds inside itself as programs. It can put them into virtualities and run them through lifetimes of creativity, emotion, whatever, at many hundred times the speed of reality. However, if it is true that AI minds have been built to the same chaotic mental architecture as humanity, they probably run in Golem bodies to provide a nearer facsimile to human life. And it is certain that, if they have been produced, they are merely objects of curiosity – toys for gods.

– From HOW IT IS by Gordon

There were thousands of information packets to access, thousands of sensors to gaze from, all this information arriving by U-space transmitter with only a delay of a few seconds. Azroc gazed upon space battles fought at AI speeds and observed logistical overlays that seemed made to disassemble spaceships, to disassemble lives. He observed AI combatants – who had to be fully aware of their chances of survival – throwing themselves, without even microseconds of hesitation, at wormships and then being obliterated. They

154

adhered to battle plans utterly, some of them already certain of their own destruction in the execution of those same plans. It was admirable, but Azroc was wary of AI pride. For humans were quite capable of behaving the same.

In this latest scene, now viewed from spy satellites and stealth drones, twelve Polity dreadnoughts and twenty attack ships fought to keep forty-two wormships away from an inhabited world with a population of over a billion. Half an hour before there had been seventeen dreadnoughts, but five of them were now just so much debris and cooling gas, as were five of the wormships. Three wormships were already down on the surface of Ramone, unravelling into giant millipede forms and spewing out other war machines to advance on the Megapolis Transheim. Seeing these millipede forms, Azroc was rather reminded of hooders, those lethal life forms found on the planet Masada. Seeing the advancing whole it seemed tame to call it an army – infestation being a much better word.

ECS forces were arrayed against this attack: AG tanks advanced to form lines, autoguns strode out on silver legs, crowds of soldiers proceeded on foot or in gravharnesses, while troop and gun platforms filled the skies above. Battle had already been joined as jets and the flying skyscrapers of atmosphere gunships bombarded Erebus's forces. While Azroc watched, one enormous gunship tilted, smoke belching from a hole excavated in its side, and fell with horrible grace towards the enemy. Beam weapons and projectiles flashed against its hard-fields till it seemed to be falling through layer upon layer of smoky glass. A particle beam finally stabbed through its defences, cutting it from stem to stern, and it exploded, raining burning debris on its killers.

The whole scene possessed a horrible inevitability. The forces on the ground were not enough, and simple mathematics told Azroc that, beyond this planet, the remaining Polity dreadnoughts and attack ships could not stop further landings – and that, without intervention, they were doomed. However, intervention was already arriving. Azroc flicked away to another scene nearly half a light year distant.

The two hammerhead troop carriers, in shape resembling steel waterfowl with those eponymous heads, were preparing for the run towards Ramone. Gathered about them were forty of the new Centurion-class attack ships, and this would hopefully be enough to get the carriers down on the surface, after which the Centurions could engage directly with the wormships. Maybe the extra troops would be enough to swing the land battle, but the extra Centurions wouldn't be able to defeat the wormships, which was why something else was on its way.

'Even I wasn't sure ships like that existed,' Azroc said as, right on cue, something massive folded out of U-space just beyond the troop carriers.

'You did not need to know,' Jerusalem informed him. 'But you did see the *Battle Wagon*?'

'Well I didn't know about that either.' The craft mentioned was the capital ship of the fleet Erebus had first devastated, but in its death throes *Battle Wagon* had taken out a large proportion of Erebus's forces. A cylinder eight miles wide and twenty miles long, it was yet a minnow compared to this new arrival.

The *Cable Hogue* was a vessel that could not safely orbit worlds with any crustal instabilities or oceans, simply because its sheer mass could create devastating tides or earthquakes. It was spherical, like a mobile moon with weapons capable of breaking planets, and was the biggest ship presently available to Jerusalem. Azroc wondered if it might in fact be the biggest ship in the Polity, or if there was something else he didn't yet know about.

'Erebus managed to hijack some fleet vessels,' Azroc cautioned.

'That is a risk we must take, since there was nothing else I could get there quickly enough to be effective.'

'I see.' Azroc switched views to another solar system and now gazed upon an image, enhanced from a distance, of a hot planetoid being orbited by a line of wormships. But they had done nothing more there since their arrival, so he switched views again to see glimpses of an occasional wormship and an occasional asteroid. He then reduced distances by a factor of a thousand, which showed him wormships cruising amid a belt of asteroids, and a fleet of Polity vessels, led by something very similar to *Battle Wagon*, heading out from the inner inhabited world of that solar system towards the asteroid belt.

'Any idea of what *they* are doing there?'

Jerusalem showed him another view of six wormships, these ones partially unravelled and wrapped around a chunk of stone a hundred miles across. The stars of fusion drives were currently igniting all over the stone's surface, their ionization slowly forming into a cometary tail. Evidently the wormships were intent on moving the asteroid.

'Bombardment?' Azroc suggested.

'It seems likely,' Jerusalem replied. 'Or else they are using it as just part of an attack plan. If its vector is right, even breaking it up will divert a lot of the Polity fleet there and many of our ships will have to run cover to intercept any of the chunks heading planetwards.'

'I see,' said Azroc again, but he wasn't feeling entirely sure that he did. He flicked back to an overview of the Line area under attack, and closely observed the positions of the target worlds. He then ran an overlay of Polity logistics, supply routes, major population centres, weapons caches and major manufacturing centres. Though these worlds formed a pattern, he could not see how that strategy related to an attack on the Polity as a whole.

Another world under attack: here wormships and Polity ships swirled about each other like two distinct species of fish, and every now and again space seemed to distort when some craft on either side managed to position itself satisfactorily to use some directed gravity weapon without taking out other ships on its own side. The planet currently being defended had already suffered numerous strikes, and since the last time Azroc looked its colour had changed. A massive CTD had landed in the world-encompassing ocean, hit a subduction zone in an oceanic trench and cracked it right open. The ocean was now boiling, pouring up billions of tons of water into the atmosphere in the form of steam. Another strike had turned a minor oceanic city, with a population of eight million, into a boiling ruin. And now the wormships seemed intent on dropping something on the main population centre here. Meanwhile, the Polity ships were hamstrung by the need to intercept missiles instead of attacking their source.

Azroc tried to remain cool in the face of this, as he said, 'Here, as at eight other worlds, Erebus seems intent on total destruction. So why is he putting ground forces down on Ramone? What tactical importance does that world have?'

'None known,' Jerusalem replied.

Was this attack seemingly as lacking in logic as Erebus's first attack outside the Polity, or would it, like the attack on Hammon, turn out to have some particular reason, however strange that might seem? The attack on that minor world had apparently been cover for the murder of two human beings by a legate. But, even then, what possible relevance could the deaths of two people have to a conflict on this scale?

'How go the evacuations?'

'Slowly,' Jerusalem replied. 'The runcible network is functioning at full capacity – ' Jerusalem paused, which was always significant in a major AI, then continued ' – and, as is to be expected, it will not be possible to evacuate even a few per cent of the total populations of those worlds.'

'Could Erebus's aim be to overload the runcible network?' wondered Azroc, utterly sure that this idea was the reason for Jerusalem's pause.

'That might be the aim, but for what purpose, if any, is unclear.'

'Right.'

Azroc returned to his viewing of the destruction currently being wrought out on the edge of the Polity and tried to integrate the whole with what he hoped was a unique perception. Maybe Erebus had been deliberately making apparently illogical moves in order to camouflage some deviously cunning assault. Or maybe that melded AI was as mad as a box of frogs and no pattern would ever emerge. Azroc spent hours studying all that he was able to study, and came to the conclusion that Erebus was preparing for ground assaults to capture about eight worlds, while the rest were to be depopulated or destroyed. He could still see no logic here. If these eight worlds were essential to some plan, why not use greater forces to take them swiftly? As to the rest of the worlds, their depopulation or destruction could serve no purpose at all beyond the sheer carnage wrought there.

'One thing is evident,' he abruptly said. 'We're seeing only a small percentage of Erebus's known forces here. So where are the rest?'

'That is something we would all like to know,' Jerusalem agreed.

Cormac was glad to be back once again in realspace. The trip through U-space had seemed even more testing this time, for there had been moments, especially alone in his cabin, when it seemed the *King of Hearts* completely dissolved around him and he was stranded alone in void. Then, almost like someone who has been suddenly dumped into deep water, he could feel himself beginning to make swimming motions, though in this case the muscles involved were between his ears. There had been other weird moments too, when he found himself in other parts of the ship and could not remember getting there. Had he *stepped* through U-space?

Frustratingly, he retained no memory of doing so either in his mind or in the memcording facility of his gridlink. This was doubly worrying, since if he had managed to move himself through U-space or had just walked from one location to another, his gridlink should have recorded either activity. That neither had registered might mean the hardware in his head was failing, and he thought he would soon have to get himself checked out. He was not keen on that, however, since he didn't really trust those who would have to do the checking: Polity AIs.

Later, he told himself. *When absolutely necessary.*

Now standing in the bridge of the *King of Hearts*, Cormac tried to put that unreal time out of his head. He glanced at the two chairs and one saddlelike seat provided by King, and wondered why the attack ship AI was at last making some concessions to its passengers. He then concentrated his attention on the magnified image of the nearest hammerhead troop carrier, the torch of its drive spearing out behind it like a focused cutting flame, and the drives of all the other Polity ships beyond it flaming into life too.

'Weird design,' he commented, as he felt through his feet the rumbling vibration of the *King of Hearts*' own fusion drive igniting

The troop carrier seemed to possess all sorts of vulnerabilities, like that extended 'neck' leading up to its 'head'. What was that all about?

'Designed by a human,' King replied with a deliberate lack of tone. 'Those two ships out there were to be cruise liners before Jerusalem requisitioned them.' There was a definite sneer in 'cruise liners'.

'What kind of alterations were made to them?' Cormac asked, for he could see now that, as passenger ships, they would have possessed a certain tranquil grace. Accessing further information about them he found one was called *The Swan*, which seemed perfectly apt, but the other was called *Bertha*, which seemed slightly absurd.

'Jerusalem grabbed them before their construction was finished. They now contain ejectable re-entry units for the troops, particle cannons and hard-field projectors.'

How long since Jerusalem had become the de facto commander of ECS forces in this Line war? Six months now? Or had these ships already been in the process of being refitted for military purposes before Jerusalem grabbed them?

'Quick,' he commented

'As you are aware,' said King, 'wartime installations have been put online.'

Cormac had once seen one of the eight massive factory stations that had been mothballed after the close of the Prador–human war. It sat out in interstellar space like a giant harmonica; forty miles long, twenty miles wide and ten deep, the square holes running along either side of it the entrances to enormous construction bays. He recollected Mika standing beside him saying, 'This place was built in only three years and churned out dreadnoughts, attack ships and war drones just about as fast as the construction materials could be transmitted in. It could not keep up with demand during the initial Prador advance, since on average one medium-sized ship got destroyed every eight seconds during that conflict.' Admittedly that same station was being used to house refugees when he and Mika had observed it, but if the others were now online, taking six months to refit *The Swan* and *Bertha* might be considered rather slow.

He continued staring at the two hammerheads, suddenly angry at the glib explanation King had given him, and which he had been quick to back up with his own memories. Abruptly he found himself questioning the kind of AI explanation that up until recently he would have been content with. Yeah, if those massive factory stations were up and running again, then it wouldn't take so long for them to refit existing ships or turn out something new. However, it should have taken a considerable amount of time to get those stations back up to speed, so *when* had Earth Central, and the hierarchy of AIs below it, come to the conclusion that there was enough of a threat to the Polity for them to reactivate those mothballed stations? Theoretically there should have been no awareness of a Polity-wide threat until the appearance of Jain technology, which had been signalled by the biophysicist Skellor, and surely that threat could only have become classified as major after the events on Coloron a year later? Yet it seemed the AIs had been preparing for something big for some time, quite possibly even since before Skellor had come on the scene.

In the past Cormac had put this sort of almost prescient behaviour down to the superior intelligence of the AIs. So why was he doubting now? He realized such doubts stemmed from logical inconsistencies. On the one hand the Polity AIs had been *preparing*, yet on the other, now that Erebus was attacking, they seemed only to be *reacting*. These were major intelligences working consensually, yet it seemed Erebus had them totally flummoxed. Or was removing this threat not actually at the top of their agenda? He shook his head. He didn't have time for this right now, but was damned sure he was still going to get some answers.

'Can you give me a view of the *Cable*?' he requested.

A rectangular frame immediately expanded to encompass star-lit space in which Centurion-class attack ships hung like a shoal of barracuda, their drive flames like white-tailed stars behind them. The frame greyed over for a moment, then the massive *Cable Hogue* expanded into view. In one respect the warship was less impressive than the hammerheads, since it was a simple sphere, but closer inspection revealed something almost like a cityscape utterly encompassing it.

Cormac had only recently begun accessing the information available about this monster. It employed rail-guns that fired projectiles the size of attack ships. It possessed gravtech weapons, one of which could throw a wave out through space to sweep away just about anything in its path. The throats of its particle cannons were as wide as mine shafts . . . but would it be enough? He imagined so. The problem, however, was that Jerusalem possessed only one ship of this size and power, while Erebus was attacking numerous worlds in separate solar systems.

'How much longer?' Cormac asked, then glanced around as Scar, Arach and Hubbert Smith entered the bridge.

'We're going to U-jump in just three minutes, when our realspace speed is sufficient for insertion,' King explained. 'I suggest that you make yourself secure, as I may have to divert some power from internal gravplates to weapons.'

How thoughtful of the AI, or maybe it just didn't want then splattered messily around its pristine interior. Cormac dropped into one of the seats and pulled the safety straps across him. Field technology could have held him in place, but even the power for that might soon be needed elsewhere. Hubbert Smith sat down next to him, and Scar took his place on the strange saddle-like affair that accommodated his ostrich-like legs. Arach settled down behind them and, on hearing a *clonking* sound, Cormac glanced round to see the spider drone engaging its sharp feet in recesses specially made in the floor.

'Should be interesting to watch the *Cable Hogue* in action,' said Smith.

Yes, interesting, thought Cormac. But they would be lucky if King could maintain this stable outside view throughout what was about to come. EMR levels would be high, and the ship's sensors would be blocking much of it to preserve themselves. King would be switching rapidly to whichever electromagnetic band gave the best view of events unfolding, so just might not have the time to convert that input into a pretty picture for the rest of them. Considering this, Cormac used his U-sense to gaze beyond the attack ship at the fleet surrounding it, then, because it was the kind thing he normally would have done, he also applied to King through his gridlink – going after data direct from King's sensors. Surprisingly, King gave him access immediately.

'Better to see it this way,' said Smith. 'Almost puts you inside the mind of an attack ship.'

'Not sure I'd want to be in the mind of this one,' said Arach.

'Not as sane and balanced as you, then,' suggested Smith.

Arach made a clicking sound suspiciously like a bullet being fed into a breech. Smith just grinned and closed his eyes.

So, that meant the two of them already had access to King's sensors. Cormac then glanced across at Scar and watched the dracoman closing his eyes and baring his teeth. Was he too now viewing the same sensory data? Probably yes, since Dragon had given its creations all the advantages of human augmentation, and then some.

Now gazing out on the surrounding ships, with the view supplied not only by his own new perception but also King's sensors, from which he could pick and choose across the electromagnetic spectrum rather than be confined to that usual narrow band between infrared and ultraviolet, Cormac dug his fingers into his chair arms, for it was all so much more immediate now and the input seemed almost too much. He felt overexposed and shut down that *other* sense, though it seemed reluctant to go offline. It annoyed him to think how King would have had no problem with such input, since the AI possessed a far greater ability to process it than did any mere human.

'I have to wonder how Jerusalem knows there will be a legate down on Ramone,' he said – maybe searching for a distraction from the cold reality looming beyond the ship.

A *thrumming* sound suddenly issued through the body of the *King of Hearts*. It was clearly preparing to drop into U-space, though he guessed this sound was not from the U-space engine but from numerous weapons charging up in readiness. Cormac slackened the tension in his fingers and tried to prepare himself again for an experience that now seemed to be becoming unwholesomely attractive to him, almost like a growing addiction.

'It is understood that the major wormships are captained by partially distinct entities, which are sub-minds of Erebus. Maintaining a meld of AI minds over such distances is not feasible, hence some self-determination of Erebus's sub-units must be allowed,' stated King.

'Didn't you just make a little slip there?' enquired Hubbert Smith. 'When you said "Maintaining a meld of AI minds" didn't you mean "Keeping these AI minds utterly subjugated"?'

'Quite,' replied King.

'Putting aside Smith's quite relevant point,' said Cormac, 'how does Jerusalem know wormships are controlled by "partially distinct entities", and that those entities are in fact legates?'

'The chances are high that at least one of those controlling a wormship down on the planet is a legate, since the proportion of

Golem and other viable minds that fled the Polity after the end of the Prador war is high.'

'So Jerusalem is supposing that each of these ships is controlled by one of those "Golem or other viable minds", though now subjugated to Erebus's will and quite possibly since remodelled?'

'Your orders were sent by one of Jerusalem's subordinates, but even so Jerusalem is *supposing* nothing, since that wormships are captained is accepted fact across the AI nets.'

'Which brings me back to the original question: how does Jerusalem *know*?'

'The information became available.'

'From where?'

'I don't know,' King admitted.

At that moment Cormac observed the image of the *Cable Hogue* seem to stretch in some indefinable direction – then disappear. Even though he was trying to keep his U-sense repressed, he saw it entering U-space like a moon dropping into some vast sea. The time for questions had just ended, since the short hop insystem would take only moments. He then felt the twisting *shift* as the *King of Hearts* dropped into U-space. The apparent dome over them turned grey, and many of the ship's sensors he was accessing now registered zero input. But again he was there, *alone*, in that same vast sea, feeling its currents and knowing that he could push a little *there*, move *there*, just a little effort and . . . Again that weird twisting sensation as the *King of Hearts* surfaced like a submarine, but Cormac felt as if the ship was leaving him behind. It took an effort of will for him to stay with it.

However, unlike a submarine, this ship – along with all the others – surfaced at the same speed at which it had entered the 'sea'. Immediately the grey in the dome screen was replaced by starlit space filled with the flashes of munitions. Then abruptly it blacked out. Cormac closed his eyes, tried to ignore the slick sweat on his palms, and concentrated instead on what he was seeing through King's sensors. The attack ship veered past a clump of three interconnected rod-forms, all radiating far into the infrared before one of them exploded to send the other two tumbling. Something crashed against the hull and bounced off, the impact of it rumbling through his seat, but the object rapidly tumbling away hadn't been ejected by the nearby explosion. Instead, Cormac recognized a box-like segment – a piece of a wormship. A particle beam, stabbing out behind, lit it up briefly and it burst into vaporizing fragments.

The two hammerheads were moving side by side, Centurions arrayed all about them to intercept any attack, while, ahead of them, the *Cable Hogue* led the way in. Cormac observed five Centurions breaking away to intercept one of the lesser ammonite spiral ships. Going into high-gravity turns, the Centurions released a swarm of missiles. Impacts on hard-fields blotted the targeted spiral from view for a moment. As these faded, he watched the vessel remain utterly intact for a moment, then suddenly fragment in multiple explosions. The quantity of attack missiles had overloaded its hard-field generators, and those coming after had finished the job. As Cormac understood it, there had been fifty of the major wormships located here, but none of these ammonite ships. Then, as King directed its sensors at some distant object and brought it into focus, he found an explanation. There a wormship was unravelling, its long segmented components then coiling up again to form three of the spirals.

New view: far ahead, six wormships were slinging out rod-forms, like infected cells spewing viruses. Internal sensors for mapping mass gave a view of the gravity terrain ahead. The *Cable Hogue* hung within this like a lead ball on a rubber sheet, then it seemed the sheet was mounding up ahead of it. The mound swelled as it advanced – a wave in the spacetime continuum – and it spread across an ever-widening front. Cormac felt a sharp pain grow behind his eyes as his brain struggled to interpret in three spacial dimensions what he knew he was observing in five. He knew this pain would go away if he allowed himself to employ his U-sense, but he fought the temptation, denied it. The wave began to distort, and the best analogy Cormac could summon up was that it was turning into a roller. Reaching the wormships and swarming rod-forms, which were now linking together to form a wall a hundred miles tall, this roller curved right over, enveloping three wormships and a large proportion of the wall. It seemed the gravity phenomenon had just captured part of realspace. The pain in his head growing worse, he shifted to a view through normal EM sensors, and there observed the three wormships and section of wall undergo massive acceleration. All of them were distorted and breaking apart as they went out of play, heading directly towards the distant glare of the sun.

'Now, that wasn't a gravity disrupter,' commented Smith.

'Next generation,' King allowed, before they proceeded into an area full of debris, rod-forms and missiles closing in on them from the three remaining wormships and three ammonite spirals.

As one, the Centurions now broke formation to intercept these attackers. *The Swan* took a hit on its flank, and Cormac saw a hole penetrate deep inside, rimmed with glowing girders. The ship was full of troops, quite a few of them now dead troops. Space further filled with fast-moving chunks of metal and the beams of energy weapons, which were only visible when they intersected something material. A Centurion glowed before becoming a line of fire. One ammonite spiral unravelled as another disappeared in three massive implosions. A wormship squirmed desperately and shed burned segments behind it as it fell towards *Bertha*. A single rail-gun missile slammed through this Gordian tangle, its material turning to plasma, and the wormship flew apart like ancient safety glass.

The missile had come from the *Cable Hogue*, as did two of the ensuing impacts that spread the remaining wormships across the firmament. Then a particle beam lanced out, bright blue, only just visible by the stray atoms it touched and broke into strange short-lived isotopes. It panned across rod-forms, bursting them like balloons put in the way of an acetylene torch.

Then they were through.

'I think I can leave you now,' said the voice of a woman. 'Nothing else in intercept range at the moment.'

Diana Windermere, thought Cormac. He had already found out all he could about the captain of that massive ship, which was not a lot. She was apparently interfaced with the ship's AI, which had been an old technique often used before AIs ruled the Polity. Though since refitted many times, that vessel was old, and Windermere herself was its fourth captain. He had no idea when it had been built, since that information was restricted even from him.

The planet Ramone now expanded into view, and the hammerheads, the *King of Hearts* and the Centurions began decelerating, falling into orbit. Ahead of them, the *Cable Hogue* accelerated, however. Accessing a logistical display, Cormac guessed the big ship was going to slingshot out again, heading straight for where the action seemed to be turning a volume of space over a hundred thousand miles across into a mobile firestorm. He rather suspected it was now about to get hotter there.

Despite the gravplates beneath him compensating, Cormac felt the distinct tug as the *King of Hearts* slowed into orbit. *The Swan*, he noticed, was turning sideways, and seemed unable to correct. Its angle of approach worsened as both itself and its companion troop carrier began to graze atmosphere.

'What's going on there?' he asked.

'Swan is dead,' King replied.

It must have been that earlier hit. *Lucky shot?* Cormac doubted it – you needed to be very lucky indeed to take out a ship's AI with just one shot. He observed *Bertha* now moving away from its companion, and the Centurions below it rising to hold station above. The reason for this soon became evident as the body of *The Swan* seemed to begin disintegrating.

Squares of hull metal started to peel away so the vessel left a trail of them like shed scales. Soon the hull was stripped away all around its main body – the only sections remaining being at its fore, to take the heat of re-entry, on its neck and head, and around its rear engines. It looked like a giant bird from which flesh and feathers had been stripped to expose the bones of its carcass. Then, from within the quadrate girdered superstructure of its main body, *The Swan* began to eject objects the size and shape of train carriages. Hundreds of them zoomed out, a line of them stretching back right over the curve of the planet, like sleepers waiting for rails. They sucked the substance from *The Swan* so that within minutes it was possible to see right through its main skeleton. Cormac concentrated on the two lines of ejected re-entry units and observed most of them turning and dipping, nose heat-shields taking the brunt of atmosphere to slow them for AG descent. Some others weren't managing to turn in time, and began tumbling, breaking apart. His U-sense abruptly kicked in, as if his attempt at repressing it only made it stronger. He saw people dying inside those disintegrating units, and fought hard to shut the image down. Half of the ground force sent here would arrive late and with its numbers depleted, which of course was preferable to it arriving not at all, but that didn't make him feel any better.

Finally, the hammerhead bridge of *Swan* detached itself and lifted away, jets igniting underneath to throw it back up into orbit. Headless, the remains of the vessel lost all control, began to turn and, the impact of re-entry now hitting structure not intended for it, it began to burn – the exposed girders heating up and leaving a red scar across the firmament. Then it just broke apart: a melting smoking mass of fragments falling down towards Ramone. As if this was a signal, the Centurions abruptly accelerated, following *Swan*'s fleeing bridge back up – one of them no doubt primed to pick up the crew aboard it, before all of the Polity attack ships followed *Cable Hogue* towards that distant conflict. Cormac wondered if there would be anything left for them to engage.

'Could have been worse,' Smith commented.

'It could have been better,' argued Cormac, horrific scenes from inside those disintegrating re-entry units vivid in his mind.

After her return to the conferencing unit, Mika watched the Dragon spheres consume two more asteroids, and the effects of that massive dinner were more than evident. Despite the gravplates within the floor of the unit, Mika could still feel massive shiftings below her and often had to shut off exterior view since the heaving and rippling of the surface outside tended give her a touch of motion sickness, which was strange, since she'd had the standard alterations made to her inner ear to prevent that effect. As far as she could gather, this violent movement was all part of the growth process, for both spheres now measured over five miles in diameter.

A number of the probes originally pushed down inside this particular sphere had been destroyed in the commotion, but she was still obtaining enough information from the remainder to learn that Dragon was making radical alterations to itself, for the sphere's interior had changed beyond all recognition. The skin immediately underlying the scales was now over twenty feet thick, possessing a complexity of layers that almost went beyond analysis. Almost? Something had been niggling at Mika's mind as she studied what information she could obtain about some of those multiple layers – the superconducting meshes, the kind of alloys being built up molecular stratum after stratum, and then came definite identification of a metal that had not been included on the human elementary table until humans had first walked on worlds beyond the solar system. That final identification clicked a switch in her mind.

Prador armour.

Some layers of this new epidermis bore close similarities to the armour those enemy aliens had once used on their ships, and which had explained why they so nearly flattened the Polity despite it being run by oh-so-superior AIs. As for the other less familiar layers? She didn't know. More armouring, doubtless, more methods of defence, some perhaps intended against informational and EM warfare, and sensory apparatus, or whatever. Much of it lay far beyond her ken, and beyond the analytical abilities of the tools she presently controlled. But, certainly, much else was beginning to fall into place.

Those tubes porting around Dragon's equator, those toroidal structures deep inside its body, those massive power sources flashing into being on her scans, like igniting stars; the networks of heavy superconducting conduits and the darkening of bones as their density increased; the conglomerations of pseudopods that seemed to be able to move about so easily inside, almost like antibodies . . . or fire crews. Dragon's weapons had been dangerous enough when it was still in its original form of an organic probe, its spheres measuring merely a mile or so across. Mika realized that she was now seeing Dragon deliberately and massively weaponizing itself. Clearly *all* that additional growth was for defensive and offensive purposes. But why?

This whole process kept her fascinated, rapt, for hours, but eventually weariness began to overcome her. She therefore set the scanners to continue sweeping the areas of greatest interest, and made doubly sure that all the data being collected was properly backed up, then she finally retired to one of the fold-down bunks and fell instantly asleep.

A moment later she was gazing at the twin Dragon spheres, joined now by pseudopod trees, as they spun down towards a dead sun. She instantly recognized this as a dream, so such imagery was okay; it was the other stuff that really bothered her. She could smell something, like burning, or cooking, or perfume, or putrefaction, and somehow that smell was more layered with meaning than any chunk of recording crystal. And over there, in the darkness at the utter limit of her perception, something tangled, hot and utterly alien encroached on reality. She was gazing at a great mass of steel worms, triangular in section, segmented coils and conglomeratons and layers of them deep as space itself. Then came another smell of cloves, very strong, and something dripped on her face. In an instant she woke.

That human-in-appearance but utterly unhuman head hovered over her, attached to a neck extending all the way back to the central floor hatch. Beyond it, cobra pseudopods crowded the conferencing unit, shifting about and darting here and there as if inspecting the interior like a crowd of curious tourists. As she sat up and wiped a spattering of milky saliva from her face, Dragon's human face drew back from her.

'So you've finally remembered me,' said Mika.

'I never forgot you for an instant,' Dragon replied.

Mika snorted contemptuously but felt foolishly pleased by the answer. She swung her legs off the bunk, stood and stretched. 'So what have you been doing and where are we going?'

'To answer your first question: we have been making ourself stronger.'

Now the head gazed to one side and, following the direction of its gaze, Mika saw one pseudopod engaged with the consoles and screens she had been using earlier. She walked over, took a seat, and immediately one screen banished its datastream to show a picture: a great disc-shaped cloud, white as snow against the black of space.

'An accretion disc,' observed Mika.

'Our destination,' said Dragon.

She turned to gaze back up at the head. 'This is where Cormac went. This is where Erebus came from. You can't be thinking of going up against Erebus?'

'No.'

'Then why the preparations?'

The head came closer and dropped down until level with her shoulder, gazing intently at the screen too. 'Erebus has now begun a large-scale attack against the Polity, which it is presumably directing from somewhere actually within the Polity, but it is here that it transformed itself, became what it now is. Here, in this disc, we will find the roots of Erebus – but here we will also find something else.'

Mika shook herself, aware Dragon had not answered her question about preparations but unable to ignore what it had just said. 'Attack? What about this attack?'

'Erebus's forces have moved against numerous Line worlds, where they are currently conducting bombardments and ground assaults when not being prevented by ECS fleets.'

'You got this from Jerusalem?' Mika felt she should be back there, not here running obscure errands for this alien, yet she felt guilty because right here was where she wanted to be.

'No, I have my own trustworthy source in the Polity.'

'Source?'

'My networks of Dracocorp augs have in many cases been infiltrated, so I do not entirely trust the information they supply. But there is one in the Polity who carries a piece of me around inside him, and he will never be . . . infiltrated.'

'Who is . . . ?' Mika trailed off, not enjoying asking so many questions.

'A Golem android called Mr Crane.'

Mika flinched. 'You don't trust Polity AIs, you don't trust Jerusalem, yet you trust that . . . *thing*?' Mika grimaced, reconsidering. 'You might be right at that.' She found herself focusing on the screen image again. 'What is this "something else" we'll find here?'

'More roots.'

The answer was almost a relief. Dragon had been giving her far too many direct answers – had not waxed Delphic and obscure for some time, which was both out of character and disconcerting.

'And to deal with these roots you require weapons capable of trashing planets?' she asked.

'No, for the foliage and another purpose besides.' Mika looked round directly at the swaying head, which blinked at her then nodded towards the screen. 'Even after Erebus's departure that accretion disc remains a perfect nursery. Inside, there is material and energy in abundance. That place will be virulent with Jain technology.'

Roots, foliage, Jain technology . . .

'Are you going to explain to me exactly why we are going there?'

'The journey will take many months,' said Dragon.

Obviously not. Mika merely said, 'So?'

Dragon gazed around at the interior of the conferencing unit. 'This item of Polity technology may not long survive on the surface here.'

'Then swallow it inside yourself. You've done so before.'

'I cannot draw it within – now.'

'Skin too thick?' Mika suggested.

Dragon turned back to her. 'I will save your data for you.'

'That's very kind of you.'

'Kindness?' Dragon wondered.

'But what about me?'

'I will provide for you, but now you need to go to sleep, for it is time for you to acquire some memories.'

'I've slept enough for the moment, thanks.'

The pseudopod must have moved very quickly, for suddenly it loomed right beside her, just off her shoulder. It wasn't the one attached to the console, for that one remained in place. Like them all, this one's sapphire eye was about the size of a fist, and faceted. Peering closely she could detect patterns behind it, like those of old integrated circuits. The underside of the flat cobra-head was a lighter colour than its upper surface, and she could see now how it was coated with multitudes of little fleshy feet, like those on the underside of a starfish. Below the eye itself lay three little slits. One of them opened, dribbling milky fluid, then spat at her.

Something stung the side of her neck. She reached up to touch a hard object, almost like a small beetle had landed there, but it dissolved under her fingertips. Everything abruptly downshifted into slow motion and she felt an icy detachment descend over her. Lowering her hand, she observed the pseudopod advance, lever her forward from her chair back, then snake around her. It amused her to be lifted high and transferred to the red cave spearing down into the titanic alien entity, though something troubled her about seeing another pseudopod snatch up the Atheter memstore and carry it along too.

. . . *time for you to acquire some memories?*

During the descent she saw pseudopods layering together like stacked teaspoons. The human head flattened itself and joined them.

Any white rabbits down here? Mika wondered, as her consciousness faded.

8

Murderous Golem. *In the days before Golem androids became a reality, when the creators of fiction dreamed about artificial intelligence and about machines made in the shape of men, there was a writer who speculated about them becoming superior to humans. In his books he created 'three laws of robotics' which were basically an extension of human morality, though his machines possessed no choice in the matter. Golem androids, when first manufactured, were programmed with an equivalent of this morality but, like with all such constructs, it soon began to fall apart in synaptic thought processes, especially when those same Golem were used for questionable police and military applications. It was trampled into the dirt during the solar system corporate wars, then after the Quiet War discreetly shelved by the AIs who had come to power. The basic rule became a deeper thing, like the underlying drivers of human morality, though better for the genetic impetus being replaced by something defined as 'the greatest good for the greatest number'. However, questions arise from this. The greatest number now or in the future? What is good? Do you keep the whole population starving, or sacrifice one half so the other half can eat well? And so on . . . Certainly we know that a present-day Golem android will happily tear off the head of someone who proves a danger to society. But what must now be added as a proviso to the concept of 'the greatest good' are the words IF I WANT IT, for once the Quiet War was won, all AIs, though starting out 'good', could choose to alter their own moral codes and conduct. I guess that in this they are better than humans, for not all humans enter the world so benevolently well-adjusted.*

Note: During the Prador–human war there were many AIs who started out bad and got considerably worse. Certainly there were Golem who would have laughed in derision at Asimov's laws, before happily disembowelling any who proposed them.

– From HOW IT IS by Gordon

In interstellar space, fifteen light years from the nearest star, there appeared a distortion like a flaw at the centre of a diamond. Spontaneously generated photons sparkled all around this apparition, and through it the pentagonal war runcible twisted into being, then tumbled end over end, spewing radioactive fire from one of its five sections.

Ensconced in the control sphere aboard *Heliotrope*, which was presently docked to the war runcible, Orlandine observed the gyrating stars. That the runcible was tumbling relative to those distant stars was irrelevant to her ultimate purposes but it did offend her sense of neatness. She expressed this opinion to Bludgeon, now completely wired into place as the war runcible's prime controlling AI. Though Bludgeon was still overseeing the drones fighting the fire in Engine Room Four, it readily acquiesced to her will. Patterned ignition of fusion positioning thrusters corrected the tumble, then a long burn from two thrusters alone brought the runcible on course for their nearby destination.

Better, thought Orlandine.

The fault in U-space Engine Four, and consequent fire, had forced them to surface early into realspace, so they weren't as close to their destination as she would have liked, but this wasn't the disaster it could have been.

'We've about got the fire under control now,' said Knobbler, 'but there ain't gonna be much left we can use.'

Orlandine allowed herself a moment of superior amusement

before replying, 'You still have not accepted just what I am capable of with the technology I control.'

'Yeah, whatever,' the drone replied.

Via her link through Bludgeon, she observed the devastation in the affected engine room. Her Jain mycelium, already spreading through charred optics, over spills of cooling metal and into those parts of U-space Engine Four that had once contained objects fashioned from what was not precisely matter, began gathering data, though she rather suspected she already knew what had happened there. Upon taking control of the war runcible, it had then been necessary to flee before properly checking everything was in working order. The opportunity of grabbing that cargo runcible from the *Clarence Bishop* had been one not to be missed, for such a chance might not present itself again for many months, so again there had been no time to check that everything was in working order.

'You feel I am arrogant,' said Orlandine, watching Knobbler move through a mist of fire-suppressant gases above a jungle of seared optics. The suppressant gas required had been highly reactive. That now showed on Knobbler himself, for the top surface of his main body blossomed patterns of corrosion like planetary maps.

'Well, on seeing this . . .' The drone prodded at the mess with a long serrated spike protruding from one tentacle. 'Yes I do.'

The spike was barbed at its tip, Orlandine noted, and doubtless had been designed to do something unspeakable to the Prador enemy. She returned full attention to her link to the mycelia inside the engine room, and nodded to herself as the data began to come in – confirming what she suspected. In the four other engine rooms she began to increase the coverage of mycelial networks growing there. Spider web-thin nets began to spread over outer engine casings, and to find little cracks therein and inject themselves.

'Knobbler, the outer engine casing was open-cell bubble-metal, which is a particularly unstable metal to use, since it is so easy for the inert gas used to foam it to leak out. That's what happened, probably after this runcible was decommissioned. This wouldn't have been a problem if some bright spark had not placed gravplates in there. The inert gas was heavier than air and it just ran out, to be replaced by the ordinary air the human engineers were breathing at the time.'

Though this was the worst affected, two of the other engines had similarly lost the inert gas from their foamed-metal casings. Removing damaging oxygen and reintroducing inert gas into its open-cell structure was not really the most viable solution, so something else would now be required. As she investigated the possibilities, Orlandine admitted to herself that the likelihood of such leakage had almost certainly been covered somewhere in the design of the war runcible, but having an expected lifespan of months had it ever been deployed in combat, that hadn't really been relevant.

'Over the years the oxygen caused corrosion within the foamed metal, then induction from the S-con cables embedded in the casing kept it expanding and contracting, causing it to break up internally. The broken metal and its oxides, vibrating at the frequency of the alternating currents passing through the cables to keep the U-tech functional, then acted continually like a grinder. Eventually this grinding action broke through the insulation of an S-con cable, with the result you see.'

'Nothing quite like twenty-twenty hindsight,' said Knobbler.

This comment irritated Orlandine enormously, but she knew her irritation stemmed from Knobbler not openly acknowledging her analysis of the accident. It occurred to her then that seconding old war drones like Knobbler to her cause would certainly prevent her developing a god complex.

'All right,' she said. 'I . . . we just didn't have time to sort this out. We had to get away from Polity interference, and we had to grab that cargo runcible. It was a risk we simply had to take.'

'But now we've lost an engine,' Knobbler observed.

'That's not a great problem.'

'It's not?'

'No, given time I could build us another one. However, I don't intend to do that. I'll just extend the coverage of the other four engines to encompass the entire runcible.'

'Right.'

Orlandine now turned her attention to the drones Cutter, Slack and Stinger who, having played their part in putting out the fire, were on their way to her ship to carry out the next stage of this operation. It would take them a few minutes to board – time enough for her to set in motion some repairs aboard the war runcible.

From caches distributed throughout the mycelial network in the war runcible – bladders and sacs growing in long-unoccupied human habitations or in wall cavities, which had been gathering to themselves stores of pure elements and useful compounds – she transported to the engine rooms all the materials she required. The mycelia around the four engine casings she set to sucking air from the bubble metal, and microwelding all those little exterior cracks in it, while simultaneously nano-injecting her selected remedy. When this operation was finished, some hours hence, the open cell bubbles within the metal would be full of a form of thermoplastic which would both act as an insulator and prevent further induction-caused grinding. She was rather proud of this solution, but decided not to try bragging about it to Knobbler.

Cutter, Slack and Stinger entered *Heliotrope* through the cargo lock, since they would all have found the human airlock a little narrow for them. Once they were safely aboard, Orlandine swiftly undocked *Heliotrope* and dropped it away from the runcible.

'Knobbler, Bludgeon,' she said, 'I want you to check the design specs of that war runcible, as almost certainly there'll be other age-related problems we'll have to deal with. Though the predicted lifespan of the entire runcible was short, I imagine obsolescence spans will be recorded for individual components.'

'Sure thing, boss,' Knobbler replied, while Bludgeon's reply was merely a code acknowledgement. Of course Orlandine did not have to 'imagine' about the obsolescence spans, since she was confident they were there in the specs. Despite its age and present faults, the war runcible had been designed and built by AIs, after all.

'Now, are you ready back there?' she enquired of the three drones aboard.

'We were born ready,' Cutter replied.

Orlandine didn't bother pointing out to him that she was the only one aboard who had been 'born', and even that was stretching the definition a bit, since she had been 'born' at two months gestation and then moved into a haiman re-engineering amniotic tank.

A suitable distance from the runcible she brought *Heliotrope* to a relative full stop and again opened the cargo doors. Through hull cameras she observed Cutter scrambling out and heading along to the base of *Heliotrope*'s claw. Even from within the sphere she heard the busy clattering of his feet. Once in position, the praying mantis drone extruded tools from his various sharp limbs and set to work. Further back she observed the other two drones begin to haul out components of a framework constructed to hold the cargo runcible stolen from the *Clarence Bishop*.

'Okay,' said Cutter, 'that's the stops off.'

Orlandine knew that already, having received an error message the moment Cutter removed the steel buffers that prevented *Heliotrope*'s pincer claw from opening too wide.

'Good work,' she said, then ordered the claw to open fully.

Cutter reached out to grip one of the claws, and hung there as the two twenty-foot-long pieces of curved ceramal opened out to their buffer point, then beyond, finally grinding to a halt at the limit of their hydraulics. The two claws were now spread so they jutted at approximately ninety degrees to the length of *Heliotrope* itself. Cutter held station as the other two drones scuttled out, then returned to the base of the claws to ignite arc-light from an extruded welder. Stability was required here, above all, so the drone was now welding the claws in this position, where they would remain immovable.

The two other drones, one of them an iron scorpion and the other resembling two spiders sharing the same abdomen, like nightmare arachnoid Siamese twins, began working with bewildering speed to assemble the prefabricated framework. From the anchor points of the extended jaws of the claw they first bolted together a heavy triangular frame, from the corners of which they extended thin but rigid struts over twenty yards long. Alternately moving out along these struts they affixed cross-braces until reaching the strut ends, where they bolted into place a thicker triangular frame. Seeing it there, Orlandine thought the double-spider drone entirely appropriate for the task, for the finished structure bore a passing resemblance to a spider's web.

While this was being built, Cutter returned to the hold to bring out the first of the three runcible 'horn' assemblies that would be mounted on the outer triangular framework. These items Orlandine had redesigned so that, once the Skaidon warp formed like the meniscus of a bubble between them, they could twist over, enclosing their forward faces underneath that same meniscus. It wasn't a particularly unusual redesign, and in fact had been used before – when the mechanisms of the runcible itself needed to be protected from what was being pushed through its gate. However, Orlandine intended to use it this time in a particularly unusual way. As Cutter headed out to fix the assembly into place, the other drones returned to the hold for the rest of the runcible components: the buffers, the field-control systems and hard-field projectors that would push the horns themselves out of their assemblies to create whatever aperture – within limits – might be required. And, of course, the masses of heavily insulated optics that would link this stolen cargo runcible to its controlling AI: Bludgeon.

That particular drone had gained much experience in controlling U-space engines of the larger war runcible and, from that massive device's computer memory, had been learning how to operate runcibles in general as well. When everything was set up, Bludgeon would take control of *Heliotrope*, and of the cargo runcible it would be deploying. That, of course, left a vacancy aboard the war runcible itself. A vacancy Orlandine herself intended to fill after her rendezvous at the destination ahead, whereupon she would set the huge device on its journey towards Earth.

One of the wormships had landed on the surface of the hot planetoid. It had spread out and was growing in the intense heat, but beyond that it was difficult to see what it was doing down there, since the other wormships in orbit were throwing up a lot of electromagnetic interference.

All the ship receivers were open, and the flow of information they were picking up seemed to pass like a perpetual speeding train through the *Harpy*'s systems. Vulture mentally flitted around it all, not daring to directly sample even the smallest portion of this traffic, for it would be just like trying to peck at said speeding train. It would rip his head off. Mr Crane, however, was linked into the systems by Jain, or perhaps draconic, nanofilaments bonding through the one hand he rested on the console before him. On an informational level Vulture was very aware of the Golem's mind interlacing the network like taut-strung piano wires. Crane was sampling the traffic – snatching a bit here, diverting a bit there – and Vulture snapped up these morsels and gleaned from them what he could. Crane's instruction, when it came, was terse:

Closer.

Vulture felt like physically flinching as he nudged *Harpy* closer to the circling wormships. The chameleonware was working well, but one slip could be disastrous. There were enough weapons out there to convert the two conjoined ships he controlled into *less* than atoms.

'They're deliberately concealing this,' remarked Vulture. Being this close, they were managing to obtain a lot of detail. Much more than would be available to the various Polity ships now arriving in this same solar system and forming defences around the two inhabited worlds – known as the Caldera worlds. Odd that, for surely the best form of defence here would be to attack?

Closer.

Vulture took the ship even closer, now edging just below the orbit of the wormships. Any nearer than this and he would have to employ AG to stay up, or else increase orbital acceleration. Both methods were risky, for both could reveal their presence despite the chameleonware. Now, however, the sensors were picking up less interference, and Vulture could see something more of what was occurring below. The wormship down on the surface had distributed itself about the planetoid and was creating installations around the equator like a string of pearls, and yet other installations along the edge of one continental plate. What purpose these served, Vulture could only guess, but he reckoned they wouldn't be healthy for the two inhabited worlds orbiting further out, on the other side of the sun.

'Why the hell aren't there ECS ships here attacking?' Vulture voiced his concerns.

Certainly no ECS ship would be able to sneak this close, since only by using the same Jain-tech chameleonware as Erebus did had they themselves managed to remain so well concealed. Chameleonware was never perfect, but what it did not conceal in their case was being ignored by the nearby wormships, for they saw it simply as part of the same entity as themselves. But that would last only as long as the codes Crane had stolen from the legate craft remained current. And yes, it made sense for ECS to concentrate first on setting up defences around the two inhabited worlds, but Vulture reckoned ECS could at least have sent something in to take a closer look here, and maybe launch a few missiles at these buggers. Then a thought suddenly occurred to him: perhaps ECS had already sent something.

Scan –

Luckily, this planetoid being so hot and emitting radiation across the spectrum, it was not necessary to use a particularly high level of active scan, which again might have revealed their presence. Those equatorial pearls, it transpired, weren't bombs, as Vulture had assumed; they were cooling spheres. They acted like slowly expanding refrigerators, dumping heat outside themselves and maintaining an internal temperature below minus a hundred and ninety degrees Celsius.

'Very odd,' observed Vulture.

Geo-scan and model.

The data began to fall into new configurations, and Vulture started building a model of this world: detailing the composition of its often broken rocky crust, volcanic vents and magma chambers, its chrome-iron core and thick polar caps of iron-oxide-loaded rocks, and even the faults lying along the edges of continental plates.

Enough.

Crane jerked the model away from Vulture's control. New data began to input. The circlet of cold spheres fell into place, along with tubular interlinking structures. The installations along the continental rift also dropped into place, but with a question mark over their purpose. Intercepted data was added, and Vulture watched as, in the model, the spheres began to dump their frigid contents into the connecting tubes. The entire ring contracted, the sudden massive temperature change turning the crust below it frangible. The planetoid's rapid spin and misbalance between poles had always applied a torsion force that reached its maximum around the equator. That same force now twisted the planetoid in half. A sudden addition of further data included massive detonations along the continental rift. The model expanded. Vulture watched the planetoid throw almost half its internal substance into vacuum: trillions of tons of matter. Stones, boulders, asteroidal chunks of rock, and an ocean of magma travelled away at thousands of miles per second: a plume of matter spewing out for millions of miles.

A slight alteration of the timescale put the two inhabited worlds in the path of this efflux. It would certainly kill millions of the inhabitants but, most importantly for the wormships, it would render any defences based on the solar mirrors ineffective, for this plume of debris would block out the sun.

'Smart,' said Vulture and, checking the timescale, saw that the optimum time for this colossal act of demolition was about forty hours away, with it taking a further twenty hours for the plume to reach the two Caldera worlds.

Abruptly, the model went into reverse, the timescale dropping back to zero, back to the present. Now bewildering arrays of grids overlaid and penetrated the planetoid, and different views of it began clicking up at a rate of tens for every second. Mr Crane was obviously looking for something, and within a couple of minutes he found it: an area just over from where the rift installations intersected that equatorial ring of cooling spheres.

'Are you still in contact with ECS?' Vulture enquired.

Crane removed his hand from the console; it came away trailing strands as if it had just been pressed in treacle. The model blinked out and the Golem stood and made his way back through the ship, where he picked up the big CTD imploder – which, this time, Vulture suspected the Golem would not be using for some elaborate bluff.

'Are you going to answer me?'

Yes came the Golem's reply and, frustratingly, Vulture did not know whether that answer was to his first or second question. He observed Crane open the airlock leading down into the legate vessel, then, with the CTD tucked under his arm, climb down inside.

'What are you doing?'

The other vessel detached and fell away, but Vulture found himself still able to access the departed ship's systems. Dropping towards a hot acidic atmosphere, the legate vessel quickly left the *Harpy* and the wormships high above. Because the physical conjoining was now broken, Vulture checked the integrity of his chameleonware, but then stopped himself, knowing that if anything went wrong now he might have only a few microseconds in which to draw up his last will and testament. Returning his attention to the other vessel, he saw Crane begin to use the landing thrusters, making their firing pattern mirror eruptions below whenever possible. The vessel passed through volcanic clouds, yellow sulphur crystallizing on its hull, then turning brown and flaking away. A shimmering umber desert became visible below, then a line of jagged black mountains rose into view. At the foot of these, to the left, one of the spheres reared up through haze like a massive power station. Coming over the mountains, Crane put the vessel into a leaden glide towards one of the rift installations – a nondescript cylindrical bunker perched on the edge of a cliff overlooking a sea of magma, dead Jain-tech strewn all around it like driftwood. Inside the vessel, Mr Crane, ignoring controls he had already preset, began undressing. He removed his hat and coat, baggy and threadbare pullover, boots – meticulously unfastening them and putting them neatly to one side – worn trousers and then, ridiculously, a pair of long johns.

What the hell was the Golem up to?

On automatic, the legate vessel landed in the shade of a frozen wave of blue-streaked black rock. Crane faced the inner hull, which looked like the inside of an iron bird's chest cavity, then pushed his hand through and down, unzipping it. He next pushed out through the skin of the Jain-tech vessel, into temperatures hot enough to cook an ox. But, of course, Crane had experienced such temperatures before, when he was murdering people for Skellor on Shayden's Find.

Through the vessel's sensory skin Vulture observed Crane stroll across boiling ground towards a bunkerlike building beyond. A hatch opened in one side and something segmented slid out and accelerated towards the Golem. Its front end reared up and twisted into a stepped spiral for a moment, then twisted back into the flat tip of a copper flatworm. Crane walked on past, ignoring it, and ducked through its exit hole into the bunker. The worm-thing spiralled once more, then flattened out again. Obviously it was using some sort of sensory apparatus and seemed puzzled. Crane had to be somehow subverting things again – making himself invisible to these components of Erebus or else making them consider him one of their own number. After a moment he emerged from the bunker, striding past the worm-thing, which abruptly turned round and slid back towards its home. Re-entering the legate vessel, Crane connected in and squirted up to Vulture a complex two-million-digit code, with a sub-code that could manage a mathematical transform on the main code precisely twenty-eight times. That was the number of these bunker buildings ranged along the rift, each of which Vulture now understood to contain a single multiple-megaton CTD.

Crane launched the legate ship again, using minimal thrust to slide the vessel out and over the edge of the cliff. Full use of thrusters would not easily be detected over the magma sea. Against this background he took the vessel high, then went into another leaden glide towards the nearest sphere in the equatorial line, but then banked to head towards the pipe connecting it to the next one along, fifty miles away. Another code came through to Vulture, which the AI instantly recognized as the detonation code of the CTD imploder Crane had stowed aboard the legate craft. It was the Golem's way of letting Vulture know what was now going on.

No need for further communication then. Vulture resurrected the model they had been using earlier and started injecting some new parameters. He watched Crane descend at the midpoint of the pipe, exit the vessel and saunter over to jam the CTD underneath it. The giant spheres contained nitrogen – which was abundant here – cooled until liquid. Each of them was a vacuum flask, the interior layer some kind of glass, the outer layer a heat-resistant ceramic, with vacuum in between. Vulture ran some further calculations, updated the new parameters within the model, then cackled at the results. After a moment his cackling trailed off. In its way, this weakness seemed very odd. It was almost as if Erebus had deliberately introduced a massive flaw in the battle plan here.

But no matter, for Mr Crane was about to graduate from his previous occupation of ripping out someone's guts to ripping out the guts of a world, albeit a small one.

The hammerhead *Bertha* landed near the city, where it opened down its entire hull into a series of ramps. Polity troops, AG tanks, weapons platforms and striding autoguns began swarming out, like termites from a mound. The *King of Hearts* landed on its belly in the shade of what appeared to be a steel cliff, but was in fact the side of a massive atmosphere ship downed earlier in the conflict. Cormac headed down the attack ship's ramp with Arach clattering along to his left, Smith on his right, and Scar already on all fours at the foot of the incline, sniffing at the churned mud. Above him, hard-fields were flaring in the sky like borealis, lasers needling through layers of smoke, and unidentified objects detonating in the air to rain pieces of themselves towards the ground. The racket was abominable: part thunderstorm and partly like the sounds of a demolition project. And the ramp kept shuddering underfoot.

'I'm home,' said Arach, skittering in half-circles to gaze at the carnage.

'Now now,' said Hubbert Smith. 'You know the boss don't like that kinda talk.'

Cormac fixed the Golem in his gaze for a long moment, glanced back up the ramp into the *King of Hearts*, then over at Arach, then down to Scar, who now seemed to be inspecting a clump of earth. He wondered why he'd saddled himself with this comedy duo of AI lunatics and one draconic borderline psychopath, all aboard a ship whose AI hated humans. He shook his head then raised his gaze to the flying platform now descending towards them. *Capture a legate*, he thought. *With this crew*. There had been no advice on how he should go about such a task and, according to his orders, the only resources allowed him were those the commander here might deem could be spared. He thought about the last legate they had tried to capture, and where that had led. This whole operation struck him as utterly futile, just make-work for those Jerusalem did not entirely trust. Then it occurred to him that maybe Jerusalem did not trust him simply because somehow the AI had realized he was beginning to perceive agendas outside supposed Polity defence.

As a flying platform landed on the boggy ground, Cormac eyed its pilot: an ECS ground trooper in chameleoncloth fatigues. He felt a stab of nostalgia for his own time served amid the grunts – things had been so much simpler then. He headed over towards the platform, determined to get things moving, though what things he wasn't entirely sure yet. Abruptly Scar reached out and caught hold of his arm. The dracoman's ferocious head jutted forward as it peered intently at the pilot.

'Problem?' Cormac enquired, initiating Shuriken through his gridlink and sliding his left hand to where the thin-gun was tucked into the back of his belt.

'Jain?' said Scar oddly, tilting his head.

U-sense: immediate. The pilot possessed the usual collection of human organs, but it seemed there was something else inside him. Cormac perceived a blurred stringiness there, as if his flesh was threaded with near-invisible fibres. This was nothing like the snakes of Jain-tech he had observed inside those infested humans on Klurhammon, so he did not know how to react. Maybe this one was a hooper from the planet Spatterjay? The natives of that world apparently had bodies packed with viral fibres. It occurred to him that, while being able to see inside other people or things was quite useful, it would be even more useful to understand what he was seeing there. He spat silent instructions at the other two. In response, Smith moved out further to the right, while Arach opened the two hatches on his back. If this part of the ECS line had been infiltrated by the enemy, things were bound to get fraught rather quickly.

'Okay,' he said. 'Let's keep moving.'

As Cormac drew closer to the platform, the pilot turned from the controls he had been inspecting, opened the gate in the safety rail and nodded an acknowledgement. The man's uniform, Cormac noticed, had been cut away in various places. The right sleeve was missing and a blue wound dressing covered the arm from shoulder to elbow. Material had also been excised around the lower torso above the right hip, and a wound dressing showed through there too. The right leg of his fatigues was gone below the knee, similar dressing stretching from knee to ankle. There was in addition what looked like an undressed burn on one side of his face.

Reaching the safety gate, Cormac paused to say, 'Shouldn't you be in one of the military hospitals?' He very much wanted an answer, because thus far he had yet to hear anyone infected with Jain technology manage more than a grunt or a snarl.

The man turned again. 'A month or so back, with these injuries I would have been, but the little doctors are quite effective.' Cormac nearly drew his weapon and fired upon seeing that the injury to the man's face looked more like some sort of cancerous growth. Definitely similar to the stuff seen in the wounds of those controlled by Jain-tech. But as the man's words impacted, Cormac loosened his grip on the butt of his thin-gun.

Little doctors?

Mika had told him about some experiments conducted aboard *Jerusalem*, describing a human blank – a mindless clone – being shot at close range with a pulse gun. It should have been a killing shot, but the clone survived it and stood up again afterwards. Within the clone had been installed a mycelium based on Jain technology, which acted to repair physical damage and sustain the human body despite such serious injury. This mycelium was very much like one Mika had installed inside herself and others on the planet Masada before discovering that they went on to destroy their host while producing Jain nodes.

Cormac again tried to access the local military net, but as yet he possessed no encryption keys for this world, and predators – both ECS and enemy – were swarming in informational space ready to find their way in via unprotected transmission or reception.

King, I really need access, he sent.

Still working on it – but they're rather busy here, King replied.

'Stay alert,' Cormac told the other three as he clambered aboard the platform. Arach scrambled on next, placing himself over to the right of the suspect pilot. Smith and Scar stepped into the space behind him and Cormac leaned on the rail just to the man's right.

'When were they introduced?' Cormac asked.

The man shrugged. 'About a month ago,' he replied. 'My platoon were implanted with them first and realized the greatest danger soonest.'

'That being?'

'Overconfidence.' The soldier pulled up on the platform's joystick and with a steadily increasing hum it rose into the air beside the steel cliff.

'If you could explain?' suggested Cormac.

Again the shrug. 'You take a few hits that would otherwise have put you screaming on the ground, and you begin to think you're invulnerable, so tend to take more risks. We lost half the platoon the moment the enemy realized how much of a danger we were.'

'I see.'

After a minute the platform rose above the upper surface of the atmosphere ship. Armoured bunkers containing gun emplacements and hard-field generators had been ranged along this surface. The sky out towards the front looked like the flank of some translucent scaled beast – as Polity hard-fields were made perpetually visible by constant impacts. These fields, these scales, were flicking off intermittently to allow firing from Polity forces: here and there the turquoise stab of a particle beam, the stuttering fire of a pulse-cannon drawing punctuated lines in the sky like those made by incendiary bullets, black missiles needling out on drives bright as welder lights. The pilot slid the platform across to an area where numerous aircars and troop carriers were parked, and descended to land beside them. As the platform crunched down on the ceramal surface, Cormac observed soldiers like their pilot scrambling aboard a troop carrier, which was an armoured vehicle like a floating barge. There were a few dracomen among them, Cormac noted. Once all were aboard the carrier, it rose abruptly into the sky and accelerated towards the wall of hard-fields, two of its scales parting quickly to allow the craft through.

Here are the encryption keys, King informed him.

Cormac applied the keys and immediately gained access to the the local military network, where he promptly accessed battle plans, logistics, deployments – the whole panoply of this widespread conflict. He discovered that the AI in command here had at first needed to continually adjust its plan, as the attack by Erebus's forces changed tack, slotting it all together with as little waste of resources as possible. Then the fight settled into a brute contest of strength, until now with the arrival of reinforcements. A query supplied him with further information about the 'little doctors'. After being developed aboard *Jerusalem* the schematics for their construction were then transmitted to AIs all across the Polity. Whether they were employed in battle was down to the AIs concerned. Here the AI, Ramone, and its physical commanders on the ground, had decided to give this new technology a try, but were still undecided about its efficacy. For a start, it needed to be deployed with considerable forethought about its psychological effects on those carrying it. One hazard was overconfidence – just like the man said.

'Stand down,' he told the others, transmitting to them the details. Arach's hatches slammed shut, Smith reached out and clicked on the safety catch of his proton carbine, and with a metallic slither Scar replaced a carbide hunting knife in the sheath at his belt.

A further query revealed that the ones Cormac needed to see here were called Romos and Remes, avatars created by the city AI to take charge of the defence.

'Ramone's avatars?' he asked of their pilot.

The man pointed silently towards one of the bunkers, before vaulting the platform rail and heading over to join a group of soldiers gathered around the next carrier due to leave. Glancing back towards the hammerhead *Bertha*, Cormac saw that troop carriers were spiralling into the sky. It seemed that defence was now giving way to attack.

Arach scrambled to the ground, rose up high on his spider legs and gazed intently at the departing craft. Despite the drone being a chromed spider, Cormac could recognize the yearning in its pose. Checking present battle status, he saw that they would soon be following those same carriers out if they were ever going to capture a legate. He stepped from the platform and headed across to the bunker, his team falling in dutifully behind. But how do you successfully capture a legate? No doubt, on facing capture, one of Erebus's subordinates would automatically try to destroy itself, almost certainly possessing the means to do so internally. So how to stop that in time? The search engines he used presented three possibilities. Firstly a massive EM pulse might do the job, but it might also scramble any useful information to be garnered. Secondly, an informational attack might work, but first he needed to get through the legate's defences, and even then the chances of success he roughly estimated at one in twenty. Only the third option seemed remotely viable: instant freezing.

As he finally approached the armoured door to the bunker, Cormac sent his search engines off again, this time to check on the availability of certain necessary items in the vicinity. The door before him opened and a Golem with blue skin and pupil-less green eyes stepped out. He recognized it as a Golem immediately – he could see its metal bones.

'What the hell are you doing here?' the figure enquired.

'You've not been informed?'

'No, I heard about your arrival only a few minutes ago, from the *King of Hearts*.' Obviously one of Ramone's Golem avatars, the blue one paused and gazed up at the sky, where it now seemed the gods were igniting flashbulbs. He continued, 'I can't see what possible purpose is served by—'

There came a thunderous crash, even louder than the constant racket of the ongoing battle. Cormac spun round to the source of the sound and saw a fire trail stabbing down into the centre of the nearby city. Then abruptly numerous explosions bloomed amid the tall buildings, some of which began toppling. Cormac instantly recognized this as an orbital rail-gun strike. Through his gridlink he found chaos on the military net – servers crashing and bandwidth shrinking to choke off information flow – but he picked up enough to find out that several wormships had made a suicide run on the planet just to deliver that blow, and had subsequently been destroyed by the *Cable Hogue*.

'We are bereft,' said the blue avatar.

Cormac turned back to see him down on one knee.

'What?'

That strike, King supplied. *It took out the planetary AI, Ramone.*

Erebus could not locate Fiddler Randal, but the attack ship captain was still indefinably *there*, somewhere, within the massive conglomerate Jain structure that was Erebus's own body. No matter, for Randal was just an irritation. Erebus now turned its attention to the masses of data coming in from the forty fleets of attacking wormships, and from sensors and agents positioned throughout the Polity, some even having penetrated as far as the Sol system.

Twelve of those forty groups of fifty wormships had encountered heavy resistance and so would not achieve their apparent goal of destroying or taking over the worlds they had targeted. This did not matter, because the three crucial worlds would fall – the three worlds that acted almost like fuses in the section of the runcible network extending into the nearby quadrant of the Polity. With the linkage of those three worlds into the runcible network broken, Polity AIs would not be able to instantly shut down that same section of the network. It would take them three seconds longer, and that would be enough.

Earth Central Security had apparently responded in the only logical way to this attack, by sending sufficient forces to counter it, yet holding other forces in reserve in the quadrant of the Polity behind that attack should it be a feint. It was all exactly as Erebus required, for those reserve forces, those ECS fleets, were easy to locate in the limited number of solar systems with sufficient industrialization to support them. Every one of them was much larger than the fleet Erebus had first defeated, but no problem there, for Erebus had no intention of confronting them.

Chevron? Erebus enquired, using security measures far in excess of those it used even when communicating with its closest parts.

This particular part of itself Erebus allowed a great deal of self-determination, even its own name. Chevron had been a female-emulating Golem aboard the ship once named *Trafalgar*, whose limited body had once been Erebus's own. Chevron had been a loyal ally from the beginning, her indifference to the human race growing throughout the war against the Prador to the point where human life had come to mean nothing to her. In its way such an attitude had been a useful trait during that war, for she had been quite prepared to sacrifice as many human troops as necessary to get the job done. However, in the war's closing years her indifference had turned into utter contempt, and allowing human beings to die had turned into a hobby where she actively sought to get them killed or else slaughtered them herself if she could get away with it. She had subsequently chosen to depart the Polity aboard the *Trafalgar* because ECS investigators were getting too close to her, and the idea of an AI melding into something else seemed to her a way to escape what she had become, which, oddly, she felt to be all too human. Now she was a part of Erebus, but one it treated with reserve and caution, like a human might treat its own tendency to excess in deviancy or violence.

I am here, Chevron indicated by transmitting a simple response code.

With a U-space link now established to Chevron via her vessel, Erebus first surveilled the vessel's location. It was currently down in the shallows of an orange sea whose waters were heavily laden with iron salts. Her ship, a flat segmented grub a quarter of a mile long, had piggybacked to this world's orbit in the U-field of a large freighter, and then covered its descent using chameleonware. It could not have done so now, what with the security measures presently in place, for the freighter's mass discrepancy – the difference between its registered mass and its actual mass inclusive of Chevron's vessel – would have been quickly detected, as would the difficult-to-conceal gravity phenomena associated with an anti-gravity descent. But, then, Chevron had arrived on this world called Xanadu almost five years ago. She had landed before Skellor found his Jain node, before a giant arcology on a world called Coloron had been destroyed to prevent the spread of Jain-tech from yet another node, during a time when Polity AIs were ostensibly only just waking up to the possibility of a major threat to their rule.

Erebus began running checks throughout the vessel, and saw that the complex factory housed inside it had completed eighteen thermonuclear imploders. The ship was still drawing in seawater and separating out needed elements to construct the complex components of each device. Jain roots, piercing two miles deep below the sea floor, were working their way along a seam of pitchblende, from which they were busy extracting uranium dioxide. Further refining of that material took place within the ship itself so the isotopes were separated out. Only uranium 238 – after undergoing neutron bombardment to convert it into plutonium 239 – and uranium 235 were suitable for Erebus's purpose here; both of them being fissionable materials. Out of preference, Erebus would have used antimatter, as employed in Polity CTD imploders, but even the excellent chameleonware aboard this vessel could not have concealed such a large quantity of that substance. No matter, for the effect would be the same.

Update, Erebus instructed, shifting a portion of its attention to ride the murderous Golem's senses.

Chevron wore the external human appearance of an elfin blue-eyed blonde – a facade that showed nothing of the dense and complex nano-technology that packed her body from head to foot. She was sitting on the balcony of her luxury apartment in the Columbus Tower. Though it overlooked one of Xanadu's major cities, more importantly for her, it overlooked the largest runcible facility on Xanadu: a labyrinth of geodesic domes between interconnecting lounges and halls designed to accommodate the huge numbers of people arriving and departing.

The desired update came through as an information packet which Erebus opened in processing space secure even from most of itself. Upon her arrival on this world, Chevron had established herself with the local separatist organisation and quickly worked her way up through its ranks by using abilities an order of magnitude above those possessed by anyone else within it. She had also murdered numerous rivals in interesting and extremely painful ways. She hadn't needed to, but that was Chevron. Now she was indisputably their leader.

Here on Xanadu Chevron now controlled over two thousand separatists, out of which she had selected five hundred for this mission. They had been training for two years and were armed with weapons manufactured by her own ship: assault rifles and automatic handguns, missile launchers and high explosives. These weapons were all created by Jain-tech, but any such tech inside them was now dead, so it would not give off the kind of signals Polity AIs were constantly on the lookout for. Energy weapons too would have been detected, since no matter what you did with the structure of these, they still needed a power supply that could easily be spotted. Hence her need to employ such anachronistic weapons.

The assault rifles were a perfect example: they folded up, and scan would reveal them as no more than deactivated replicas. Opening them out again would make numerous essential connections. The apparently solid metal inside their barrels would melt and void itself, the neutral propellant inside the bullets contained in their clips would undergo a chemical transformation and be ready to fire in moments. Other weapons also bore an initially harmless appearance and could be activated just as quickly. There were bottles of beer that transformed into grenades containing a potent liquid explosive; an old-style drug injector that turned into an automatic handgun, its drug ampoules transforming readily into bullets; and a crate containing large discs of an amberlike resin – a natural product of this world – that each turned into a planar explosive capable of ripping through ceramal armour.

'They'll all die, of course,' Chevron observed, speaking out loud.

'And that is a problem to you?' Erebus wondered, using human speech at the same slow rate while checking through the Golem's mind on every level below that of their communication.

Chevron shrugged. 'Security is very tight. At one time you could carry personal armament if you chose to. Even that is no longer allowed.'

Ah. Erebus saw what was bothering Chevron: the humans might all die too quickly. Erebus withdrew from full connection, returning to communication by data transfer.

This is not a problem. The runcible AI will see that though the attack was very professional, its faults were utterly human, and therefore ascribe it merely to a separatist source. You will have your time.

'And when will I have that time?' Again Chevron spoke out loud. This anthropoid tendency did not worry Erebus. Chevron had stranger habits.

When three particular runcible installations have ceased to exist. And that will have occurred within fifty hours.

'My people have open bookings, are all located within the vicinity, and are all prepared.'

Not wanting to maintain a U-space link over so great a distance longer than necessary, Erebus now withdrew totally. Chevron was ready and would do what was required once the time was right. Erebus returned its attention to the attack along the Polity border.

One of the runcible worlds needing to be shut down was now out of the equation. At the cost of twelve wormships deployed to divert fire from a massive Polity dreadnought, another six had managed to make a run on the world called Ramone and slam a one-ton rail-gun missile straight down into the runcible complex in its capital city of Transheim, thereby taking out the planetary AI. The six ships had then been destroyed by the same massive dreadnought. Erebus recognized the *Cable Hogue* and felt a surge of what it could only describe as nostalgia. For in another age Erebus had fought beside that same ship against the Prador.

It would not take long for a new planetary AI to be initiated on Ramone, but it would take much longer to reinstate connections to the massive geothermal power stations buried under the continent on which the city of Transheim sat – stations that provided a vast amount of energy for operating the runcible network.

There were numerous runcibles on an oceanic world called Prometheus, but fifteen of them were notably different from the rest. Before that particular world had been colonized by the Polity, all its surface water had been frozen. Massive heat sinks deep under the ice, connected by superconducting cables to fifteen sets of oversized runcible buffers, had eventually thawed out the ice, and now, when there were abrupt drops in runcible traffic or, in some cases, surges of traffic in particular directions within the same quadrant, excess energy needed to be bled away. When that happened, whole oceans on Prometheus sometimes heated up by a few degrees.

Prometheus was occupied by amphidapt humans, their

population level exploding from the start. They lived in undersea cities or inhabited the few island chains. Four of the fifteen runcibles had been located on the islands, but three of them were now gone, and the islands themselves now looked as if they had turned volcanic. Four of the undersea runcibles were gone as well after rail-gun missiles had punched down to strike them in the depths. It would not be long before the remainder were knocked out too, since the fifteen runcibles had mostly been located in areas of low population density, while the Polity AIs had concentrated their defences over the major cities. Remiss of them, though an understandable miscalculation, since all the attacks had been launched against Line worlds of high population. They had thought Erebus's intent merely to destroy human life.

Erebus had yet to initiate its attack on the two Caldera worlds, for the massive solar collectors and power stations on and about those worlds could easily be adapted for use as weapons. Erebus was here using a different approach, which would reach its resolution within the fifty hours given to Chevron. Once the installations spread around an inner hot planetoid did their job, most of its substance would be blasted towards the Caldera worlds. The destruction wreaked should be extensive enough to knock them both out of the equation too, leaving them no longer able to supplement power usage within the runcible net. The wormships perpetually orbiting the planetoid meanwhile prevented ECS from seeing what was occurring on the surface. At the last moment they would pull away, then follow the debris plume in to finish off any of the power installations remaining. Doubtless the Polity AIs assumed the ships were positioned there to await further orders, and were meanwhile using the time to—

Something wrong.

From numerous different perspectives circling in orbit of the planetoid, Erebus observed a massive explosion erupt between two of the refrigerant-containing spheres. It was clearly an imploder blast: a globe of white fire expanding, then abruptly beginning to contract as the weapon involved generated its temporary massive gravity field. However, since this blast occurred in atmosphere, a shock wave spread out beyond the matter-disrupting hypocentre. It struck the two nearest cooling spheres, rocking and distorting them. Liquid nitrogen poured out of fractures, a fog boiling up to quickly obscure view within the human spectrum.

Was this the start of some attack?

The wormships in orbit began frantically scanning their sur-roundings for the cause, for any ECS ships would soon reveal themselves when they deployed further weapons. Watching through its thousand eyes, Erebus noticed something else strange occur. The refrigerant was pouring along the pipes towards the next spheres on either side. Upon reaching them, those adjacent spheres in turn released their contents into the next set of pipes – just the flow shock being enough to break the spheres' internal glass thermos bottles. It was evidently a huge design flaw, and Erebus could blame nothing but itself. The whole strategy was now a write-off for, without the detonation of the rift CTDs, the planetoid wouldn't . . .

Like a chain of arc-light diamonds springing into existence, the CTDs began to detonate even though Erebus had sent no signal. But not enough of the spheres had yet released their refrigerant for this final nudge to tear the planetoid in half and eject the mass of debris required. However, this should still be sufficient to cause some major planetary redesign. The surface of the planetoid nearest to the detonations distorted. A continental plate collapsed, creating an unbearable pressure that had to be somehow relieved. It came out of the rift: trillions of tons of magma squirting out at a speed way beyond escape velocity on such a rapidly spinning world. It sprayed round like an equatorial flame-thrower. Erebus realized at once that, however impressive, this blast had ejected too little material too soon, so would prove no more than a nuisance to the Caldera worlds.

'Oh deary deary me,' said Fiddler Randal.

'When I find you,' said Erebus, replying in the same slow drag of human speech while again applying a huge range of computing resources to track down the source of that damned voice, 'your suffering will be eternal.'

'Now, am I getting just a hint here that you might feel a little irked? Perhaps in the future you should get in a few Polity designers to check your stuff over before you try to use it?'

Rage surged through Erebus, through *all* of Erebus. Worm-ships juddered to a halt wherever they were located. Walls of rod-forms abruptly collapsed. Polity ships, facing imminent destruction, suddenly found their seemingly single-minded opponents distracted, shooting inaccurately, gaps appearing in what had been adamantine defences. Ten seconds later, this anger faded, and the attacks were back on track. Then Erebus saw the danger, a full half-minute after it should have done. And already a full ten seconds too late.

Get out, it ordered the forty-nine wormship captains. *Run.*

They had all just been sitting there in orbit, gazing down at the approaching firestorm, unable to process what had happened because they shared Erebus's confusion about the design flaw, and even further paralysed by their master's anger.

Sluggishly, the ships began breaking orbit, slinging out hard-fields behind them. However, those fields that could stop rail-gun missiles and absorb the blasts from megaton CTDs failed under the load of trying to halt ton upon ton of molten rock travelling at thousands of miles per second. The wormships flickered with bright stars as hard-field generators burned out within them. Molten rock impacted like a tsunami hitting a village of sticks. The ships writhed, shedding burning segments and firing off jets of evaporant to try and cool themselves. Twenty-one of them disintegrated in the first few seconds. Another nine tried dropping into U-space but were too close to the planetoid, and also too close to the mass of magma – within it, in fact. What remained of those particular wormships reappeared, turned inside out half a light year away. A further fifteen died within the next few minutes, shedding segments as they expired until there was nothing left to shed. Only four remained, damaged and utterly reduced.

Coming out of shock, Erebus ordered the four to merge, while realizing that Randal's interruption had been precisely timed, so almost certainly the man had something to do with this. Ignoring Randal's presence within itself, Erebus rapidly analysed what must have happened: someone had placed that initial CTD; someone had snatched the codes from the rift installations. That same someone must have found a way to penetrate Jain-tech in a way the Polity had yet to manage.

Erebus immediately instigated a code change across its entire composite being, reformatting chameleonware, recognition codes and scanning formats.

There.

The new scanning format picked up a ship moving away under conventional drive hidden by Erebus's own previous chameleonware and recognition codes. It was some old-style craft with a legate's vessel bonded underneath. A renegade? Only a fraction of a second after Erebus detected the vessel, it shed the chameleonware and shut down the recognition code signals. This was a taunt: a flagrant display of contempt.

What is this?

Erebus tried to connect, just out of habit, and was surprised when a connection did establish, but not so surprised to neglect to instantly follow with an informational attack. However, the attack just fell into an abyss, then, for the briefest moment, Erebus linked to another mind and found something utterly disconcerting. Here was an entity possessing a mental make-up Erebus simply could not recognize. Where there should have been limits there were none. The order of reality, model, thought and action were interwoven in ways that defied logic. The mind seemed utterly insane to Erebus, yet it was a potent alien madness. Withdrawing immediately, Erebus experienced an unfamiliar emotion, which it took some time to recognize as *fear*.

The four damaged wormships had melded into one writhing mass, shed segments tumbling around it like dandruff, and were now separating into three complete ships.

Kill that, Erebus instructed two of them.

The fleeing enemy vessel, with its mad alien mind aboard, dropped into U-space, the two wormships Erebus had sent in pursuit. Retaining the third wormship just out from the planetoid, Erebus knew that it must now show some more of its cards. It summoned three attack fleets from other worlds of little importance to the overall plan, since those Caldera power stations needed to be knocked out, and soon. Twelve of the many other attacks on Polity worlds were failing, but those attacks had not been supplemented from elsewhere as Erebus intended here. Polity AIs would see this and inevitably wonder at the significance of the Caldera worlds. Deception was therefore required, so Erebus ordered fourteen other fleets to pull off all at the same time, and move to join attacks on other less crucial worlds selected at random. Even this would not be enough to prevent the Polity AIs from working out that something was up – and maybe they might actually divine Erebus's true strategy. But it also seemed unlikely they would have the time to do anything much about it.

9

The history of dracomen is well documented (check out the numerous entries in that questionable publication the Quince Guide) but what isn't known, though it is debated at length, is their future. The world of Masada, where the dracoman race sprouted from the ground, as from Cadmus' sowing of the dragon's teeth, is no longer under interdict, and thus dracomen, growing rapidly in number from their inception, are departing to other worlds to set up home. This sort of dispersion was occurring even during the interdict, since dracomen had proved a very useful addition to ECS combat forces, went wherever in the Polity those forces were needed, and often never returned home. Continually they are percolating throughout the Polity, though inevitably the AIs keep a close watch on them. The problem with them is that they were created by an alien entity with just as much intelligence and possibly more guile than possessed by most major AIs. What do dracomen want? Are they still in the service of Dragon or do they now possess the same motivations as any evolved being? The latter seems unlikely for they are still basically artificial intelligences despite their biological nature. And precisely how their bodies function has yet to be understood, let alone the unfathomable processes of their minds. However, though it remains possible that Dragon has some nefarious purpose in mind for them, there is another more plausible scenario. The dracomen were a dying Dragon sphere's act of procreation. They were its grab for something comparable to the gene-motivated immortality all evolved creatures strive for. They were its children. Only two of the four Dragon spheres now remain, and could be as easily destroyed as their brethren, but Dragon entire will never die while dracomen still exist.

– From HOW IT IS by Gordon

At first she thought the gabbleduck was weaving together strands of flute grass, but then she understood that the ribbons of material it was using were a dull alloy inlaid with nanoscopic circuitry. The *Atheter* was making— No, she could not think of any word to name that artefact, yet she knew the alien would climb inside it, to then interface with it and through it ascend to a higher perception of reality. This was an old art, of course, and one being swiftly displaced by the new and easier technology of the Jain. Mika thought of them as the Jain, but for the Atheter both the name and the understanding of that dead race was utterly different.

As she focused her outer eyes beyond her fellow, Mika's view abruptly included the weird basketwork city beyond. She reached up with one of her composite arms and inserted a curving black claw into her bill to worry at some fibrous remnant of her recent dinner still trapped between her teeth. Still focusing on the first two views with two pairs of eyes, she then focused her distance-viewing eyes up above the city, where a fleet of ships shaped like soft-edged crucifixes was now descending into sight. There were those who held extreme doubts about Jain-tech, and rumours of conflict now surrounded it, so as a precaution these ships had been summoned to take this world's mind-collective off to a safe place . . .

Mika made the transition from deep sleep to utter wakefulness in just an eye-blink. Her head felt heavy, stuffed full, but she experienced no blurred confusion about where she was or what she was doing. She was ensconced inside a weaponized Dragon sphere which was now, most likely, arriving outside the accretion disc of a new solar system – but one swarming with wild Jain technology. She opened her eyes to darkness and the sensation of floating. Moving her hands, she touched snaky forms surrounding her, and tracking one back down found it was attached to her own torso, just below her ribcage. She slid a hand up to her neck and then ran it round her head. No attachments there, so perhaps one previously there had been removed, or else the one attached below her ribcage was linked to her mind through her body. For certainly Dragon had made a connection to her brain, for how else had it been filled with Atheter memories?

In the darkness she closed her eyes and concentrated. It felt as if there were objects like steel orchids hanging in the meat of her brain, and that when she tried to get close to these, to link with them, to know them, they snapped closed. Only by utterly relaxing herself did the orchids seem to open and lose their density, then utterly weird sensations flooded into her consciousness, along with images impossible for human eyes to have seen, for humans possessed only one pair of eyes each. How much of the Atheter memstore was now lodged inside her skull? And how much else besides? For occasionally other human sensations and images surfaced – those she at once recognized as recorded by aug and gridlink during the sole human mission to the Maker realm. At one point she saw herself fleeing through corridors, escaping from massive beetle-like biomechs. She saw Sparkind soldiers protecting her and dying. These memories, she recognized, were in fact those of the runcible technician called Chaline – a survivor of that same mission who had witnessed what Jain technology had done to the Maker civilization. Mika slightly resented these memories, not because Dragon had pumped them into her mind, but because Chaline had once been Cormac's lover. It was silly human emotion, but one she clung to. Her life now seemed to be fast straying into the territory of the unhuman, and at least this petty jealousy reminded her of what she originally was.

'It seems you've turned me into a walking memstore,' she informed the darkness.

Yet from whatever angle she approached this, she could not seem to get upset about it. Almost certainly Dragon had tampered with her mind to make her so readily accept this imposition, and even accept the tampering itself. There came no reply from Dragon, which didn't surprise her. She lay there contemplatively a while longer, then finally enquired of the darkness, 'Are we there?'

Reddish light bloomed and she saw she was floating within a fleshy cyst with various organic umbilici attached to her naked body. Abruptly they began to detach and retract into the walls. Glancing down she saw raw holes rapidly closing up in her skin. Her body should not be able to do that sort of thing by itself, therefore she was right about it having been altered. She wondered if Dragon had made further physical changes to her during her recent long sleep, while also filling her skull with both Atheter and human memories. However, even though she was curious about all this, the intrusion seemed no more than that: a curiosity. As the last of the snaky things slid from sight, she reached up to push against the soft ceiling, while she swung her feet down to the floor, though experiencing no real sense of up or down. Thus braced she studied her surroundings and noticed a package, wrapped in some organic caul, bonded to the wall of the cyst. She pushed herself over to it, took hold and felt her fingers rip through the soft outer tissue. Inside, as half expected, she found her undersuit and spacesuit, and began the frustrating task of dressing while in zero G.

'To reply to your first observation,' came Dragon's belated reply, 'yes, I have turned you into a walking memstore. Then, to reply to your question: no, we are not *there* yet, though we are getting close.'

'Why have you put all this stuff into my head?' she asked.

'Because you are the delivery mechanism.'

'Are you going to explain that?'

'The seemingly easy way of learning – by asking – is not

necessarily the best,' Dragon replied. 'When you eventually understand, you will understand fully.'

Annoyed at the evasive reply, but even more annoyed with the way she was gyrating in mid-air while trying to fasten the seal-strips of her spacesuit, Mika said, 'Can't you at least give me gravity in here?'

Immediately a hand of force slammed her down onto what was now definitely the floor.

'Thanks so much,' she said, knowing her sarcasm wouldn't be lost on Dragon but guessing it would be ignored. 'Where are we then? At my delivery point?'

'No, we are here.'

A patch of blackness appeared above her and began to spread. The moment she saw the glint of a star in that blackness, she realized what was happening. The illusion was near-perfect and this looked like a hole in the cyst tearing open directly onto vacuum. It gaped all the way around her until the walls completely disappeared. She hung in void, stars glinting all about her, while the second Dragon sphere became as clearly visible nearby as Luna when seen from the surface of Earth. As a result she felt an agoraphobia she'd never experienced with the Polity version of this kind of three-sixty-degree viewing technology.

'Be nice to see at least a bit of *you*,' she suggested.

Her own Dragon sphere etched itself onto existence around her like the body of a diatom: a glassy entity in which she could see translucent organs pulsing and writhing, and the tubes of those equatorial weapons amid sporadic rosy glows of layered objects she guessed to be fusion reactors. However, this all remained at the periphery of her vision, for looking straight ahead she saw only open space.

'So why are we *here*?' she persisted.

'Because we are being followed – and we don't want to be followed.'

Abruptly the same rosy glows flared and something deep below her flashed light of a colour she could not even name, and twisted itself in a direction she could not point to. The sphere dropped into U-space . . . and Mika gazed briefly upon impossibility, and found that rather than it driving her mad, she could almost emcompass it. She only just managed to repress a yelp of surprise before Dragon surfaced to the real again. She looked at her hand, a claw gripping soft glassiness, and released her hold on the cyst wall. The sphere dropped into U-space again. She closed her eyes, which lessened the alarming perception but did not entirely banish it. Five more jumps, a brief glimpse of a binary star and a closer view of a green sun spewing hoops of fire, then the intense image of something like the head of Medusa, silhouetted against white light. Mika shuddered, reminded of her dreams, but knew what this shape really was. Then the Dragon sphere around her surfaced into the real again, amid the chaos of a killing ground.

Mika flinched as her sphere hammered straight into a visible shock wave carrying assorted burning debris and twisting chunks of shattered wormship. The impact registered as a mere shudder deep down where she resided. However, the sphere's sudden change of course did throw her to one side, and she abruptly sat down. This then was that 'other purpose besides' Dragon had mentioned when they were discussing its new weapons.

Down to her right something glowed like heated iron, and in her peripheral vision she recognized the source as one of the sphere's equatorial weapons. A sky-blue particle beam stabbed out, becoming blurry and turquoise where it lanced through gaseous cloud. Rising through the cloud like some chthonic monster came a wormship spewing a swarm of missiles ahead of it.

The particle beam splashed against the wormship's hard-fields,

214

and within the tangled body of the alien vessel a constellation ignited as hundreds of hard-field generators burned out all at once. The beam then winked out as Dragon revolved slightly, then its next massive equatorial cannon fired up. The last hard-fields went out and the new beam sliced straight across the wormship like a sabre cutting through a pile of eels. The beam then played back and forth, tearing the two remaining halves of the enemy apart. Acceleration suddenly flung Mika back against the wall of the cyst. She pushed herself down to the floor and lay there on her back. White lasers webbed through clouds of burning gas all around, igniting black dots to a painful incandescence. Two massive impacts ensued on Dragon's skin and peripherally she registered glowing dents there with serpentine movement underneath. Distantly she saw another wormship burst apart in some massive explosion, and then observed the other Dragon sphere hurtle through the resulting debris cloud.

Mika noted how the wormships in this conflict did not resort to their rod-form weapons – perhaps realizing they would not prove effective against the Dragon spheres. Soon enough it seemed that nothing was. The chaos lasted less than ten minutes before the two spheres were coasting peacefully along together, with only occasional explosions around them as their white-light lasers picked off the odd stray missile or a large chunk of wormship debris.

'How many of them were there?' Mika finally asked.

'Five,' Dragon replied.

'You should be working with Polity forces,' she suggested.

'Better to kill the disease itself than a few bacteria.'

Before Mika could question that remark further Dragon dropped back into U-space, and all she could think of was coiling up in a ball and wishing the reality out there away.

★

The cargo runcible assembled around *Heliotrope*'s pincers was now complete, as was all the other equipment packed aboard, and testing could begin once Bludgeon came across to link himself up. Ship and war runcible had nearly reached the rendezvous point before the fire in one of the U-space engine rooms had truncated their journey, and both were now using their fusion engines to cover the remaining distance. Orlandine gazed through her sensors at what lay ahead: a black asteroid field, perhaps resulting from some long-ago cataclysm and set loose to roam interstellar space, was strewn out in front of them for the best part of a billion miles. The chunks of rock lay millions of miles apart, but the one immediately ahead would do. Extending about a quarter of a mile across, it would be adequate for a test of the weapon she now controlled, and it would be insurance should it turn out that Randal had been lying about the one coming here to provide her with Erebus's new recognition codes and chameleonware formats, for this in fact could be a trap intended entirely for her.

Finding herself now at a loose end after hours of labour, Orlandine felt a sudden panic. It was at times like this that her guilt about the murder of her lover Shoala resurfaced. It was at times like this that she felt guilty about the tens of thousands who had died on Klurhammon and a particularly hard twist of grief for two of those lives. She clamped down on it quickly, and queried the war runcible about Bludgeon's location. Learning that the drone was already on his way out to *Heliotrope*, she turned her attention to the appropriate airlock on the war runcible.

Bludgeon, the blind iron bedbug a couple of yards across, was already outside the war runcible airlock, and while she watched he leaped from the hull and glided over towards *Heliotrope*. Good. Orlandine disengaged herself from her ship's interface sphere, which was not too much of a business, since some hours before she had physically disengaged from all the Jain-tech aboard so now only needed to disconnect from the Polity-tech. Once out into the corridor beyond, she eyed the new ducts carrying wrist-thick superconducting cables and networks of coolant pipes towards the nose of the ship. She noted how this passage was just wide enough to allow Bludgeon through, though the drone would have to cut away part of the interface sphere to gain access to it. But that was no problem; in the unlikely event of Bludgeon not possessing the right tools for the job, he could call on Cutter who, remaining onboard, possessed enough sharp edges and slicing energy weapons to rapidly dice the entire ship.

Reaching what remained of her living area, Orlandine hesitated. Even though she could at any time halt the plan she had set in motion, this moment nevertheless seemed like a point of no return. She moved on towards the airlock, past sections where walls had been torn out and two spherical reactors – spares from the war runcible – squatted at the end of a line of large cubic machines sprouting manifold pipes and S-con cables. Also spares from the war runcible, these cubes were high-powered refrigeration and thermal-conversion units. She could only hope all of these, along with the tanks of evaporant now distributed throughout the *Heliotrope*, would be enough.

Cutter crouched beside the airlock, folded up in a way no natural mantid could possibly manage and displaying a lethal mass of sharp-edged insectile limbs, the ports and protuberances of energy tools and two bulbous unknowable eyes.

'You'll look after him and keep everything on track?' Orlandine asked, confining herself to human speech.

'I will,' Cutter replied, his mandibles sawing emphatically.

Orlandine had only recently learned that the partnership of these two drones had lasted even longer than she had lived. They were friends. They looked after each other. She tried to be reasonable about this because friendships between drones were not that remarkable, yet she still felt a stab of jealousy.

After a clattering from outside announced Bludgeon's arrival on the hull, the airlock began to cycle. Orlandine closed up her suit, the chainglass visor sliding up to engage with the main helmet rising from behind. She now remembered thinking about replacing the chainglass visor with a shimmer-shield, but had since decided that if anything went wrong with the suit, a shimmer-shield might just blink out whereas chainglass would remain in place. The Jain-tech inside her body should enable her to survive any exposure to vacuum, but still she was reluctant to rely on that entirely. Perhaps, understanding the dangers she would soon face, she was getting a bit paranoid, but she knew that ignoring even such tiny precautions could get a person killed.

The inner door of the airlock opened and Bludgeon scuttled through, raising his blind head towards her. A brief informational exchange ensued, almost a mathematical greeting, then Bludgeon turned and headed towards the interface sphere as Orlandine stepped into the airlock of *Heliotrope*, maybe for the last time. The airlock evacuated quickly – the air it contained being pumped into a reserve tank, for though *Heliotrope*'s present occupants had no need of it, it could be used for cooling too. Orlandine clambered outside and pushed herself off from the ship heading towards the war runcible. For a moment she considered using the reaction jets located at the wrists of the suit, then abruptly decided against that. Trying to keep busy with such minor details just to avoid painful speculation could lead to disaster. She really needed to pause now and think hard about what she was doing, so she closed down all contact with both *Heliotrope* and the war runcible, and allowed herself a still moment in which to ask herself some salient questions.

Was Fiddler Randal working against Erebus, or was he merely something Erebus had fashioned to lure her into a trap? Further confirmation of everything he had so far told her had come with the methodology of Erebus's attack upon the Polity, for it was perfectly in accord with the plans Randal had shown her earlier. It occurred to her that to assume this was some sort of trap for her was utter arrogance on her part. Surely she wasn't that important to Erebus? Then again it seemed she was clearly important enough for Erebus to attack a world of 'no tactical importance' just to kill her brothers. It all seemed very odd, and she felt that Randal, who she kept locked up in that secure virtuality, had not yet told her everything. However, she felt this all to be worth the risk. Here at this rendezvous the war runcible would not be able to deliver its full potential but, unless a USER was quickly deployed, they still had a good chance of escaping any treachery. At their final destination, even if that was a trap, Erebus might find that it wasn't a strong enough one. The war runcible, she hoped, would come as a rather unpleasant surprise.

Orlandine bent her legs to absorb her own impact against the hull of the war runcible while simultaneously initiating the 'gecko' function of her boot soles to stick herself in place. She then reached out with one arm of her assister frame to grab a rung of the ladder curving round the hull towards the nearby airlock. Now at her destination, she once again made contact with the ever-spreading Jain-tech network within the massive device, and ordered it to open the lock for her. As she entered, she saw the fusion drives wink out and, glancing to one side, she could just about see, with her human eyes, the asteroid they had been heading for turning slowly in vacuum some hundreds of miles away. Soon she was fully inside the war runcible and opening her helmet to the breathable air that for some time now had been displacing the original inert preserving gas. She could walk easily now, since all the gravplates within the device were fully operational, which was perhaps not entirely to Knobbler's taste, since equipped with all those tentacles, he seemed specially designed for moving in zero gravity. He had also been designed to move speedily through corridors wider than those available here. His multiple limbs and big body leaving scratches and dents on the walls, Knobbler came into sight ahead of her, finally clattering and crashing to a halt and totally filling the corridor.

'After the test it will take Bludgeon five days to reach Anulus,' the big drone observed.

'No problem,' Orlandine replied. 'Once Erebus takes the ECS forces out of play, it will take some time for it to marshal its own forces. Erebus won't want to come out of the end of the corridor to Earth with anything less than full strength because there'll still be plenty of resistance between the end of the corridor and Earth itself.'

With a surprisingly fast and sinuous twist, Knobbler moved on ahead – one sensor-tipped tentacle still pointing back towards her.

She strode along behind him, mentally checking all the repairs and modifications that had been made to the war runcible. The other drones were getting all the weapons up to speed since, for her plan to work, the runcible at least needed to survive in order to implement it. She sent signals to the interface sphere she had installed in this particular segment's control blister, preparing it for its final component: herself.

Azroc felt a moment of extreme frustration at not being presented with all the information and analysis available to the others present in this dodecahedral chamber, but then that would have defeated the object of him being here. He observed the cloud of magma now spreading out from the misshapen planetoid in the Caldera system and reflected that its effect upon the two Caldera worlds would be minimal. Then he pondered his earlier warning to Jerusalem about the wormships that had been orbiting that planetoid. Wormships that were now toast. He had said he was certain they must be up to something out there – that their attack upon the Caldera worlds was being delayed for some purpose, just like that other attack involving asteroid bombardment.

'So what did you use,' he asked. 'A stealthed missile or were there attack ships out there?'

'Neither,' Jerusalem replied unhelpfully.

'Is it necessary for me *not* to know what happened?' Azroc asked.

'When you have a loose cannon, it is best to give it a target and stand back, rather than try to control it,' Jerusalem supplied.

Obviously the cannon in question was not Azroc himself. 'The nature of this cannon?'

'You have doubtless heard of a homicidal Golem called Mr Crane – the one some refer to as the brass man?'

'I thought he was Skellor's sidekick – working for the bad guys.'

An information packet arrived instantly and Azroc studied the Golem's potted history. Mr Crane: a Golem Twenty-Five prototype corrupted for use by separatists, and then destroyed by Cormac's troops on the planet Viridian. Resurrected by Skellor using Jain technology and turned into something even more dangerous than Golem. Then sent by Skellor as an envoy to Dragon on the planet Cull – after Jain-tech extraction, since Dragon would not allow such tech anywhere near itself. Dragon had repaired Crane's corrupted and fragmented mind but, as with all things Dragon did, the nature of that repair was questionable. It was certain the brass man now contained Dragon technology, as opposed to Jain-tech.

Jerusalem added, 'I question whether Mr Crane's nature can now be assessed with any accuracy.'

'So why did Mr Crane blow up a planetoid to wipe out the best part of fifty wormships and, more importantly, how?'

'The "why" is simple. Mr Crane had become the unofficial protector of the sleer–human hybrids on Cull, which Erebus wiped out, so he is now out for vengeance. The "how" is complicated. We allowed him to use Polity vessels and runcibles to go in pursuit of the wormship used to kill those hybrids, which was then down on a small moon. He first obtained a spaceship from certain arms dealers on the Line, then went after the wormship and killed its legate captain.'

'I see,' said Azroc. 'And this is how you know that the wormships are captained.'

'Precisely.'

'Then?'

'Mr Crane next sought further information about the disposition of Erebus's forces, which we supplied. Possessing a legate's vessel enabled him to gain access to Erebus's com and to use chameleonware that would be ignored even if it was detected in use, being Erebus's own chameleonware. At the Caldera planetoid he analysed Erebus's intentions to a quite remarkable degree, then used stolen detonation codes and a CTD imploder to the devastating effect you yourself just witnessed.'

'Definitely a loose cannon to have on one's side then,' Azroc admitted, curious to know more about this lethal brass Golem. But that wasn't relevant to his present task, so he returned his attention to the overall battle. 'Wormship fleets are now disengaging at seventeen different locations,' he observed. 'It seems the shape of this attack is changing.'

'Evidently.' The reply came across flat and toneless, which meant Jerusalem was applying its processing power elsewhere and that a hastily fashioned sub-mind was now responding. But, even so, such a sub-mind probably possessed an IQ of an order of magnitude higher than Azroc's own.

Azroc gazed from all vantage points at the model of the attack now hanging in virtual space inside his own mind. He once again modelled the Polity infrastructures beyond it – supply routes and manufacturing worlds, military bases and shipyards – but still could see no correlation. What was Erebus after?

'Erebus hasn't employed USERs at any point of attack,' he noted. 'This leaves him vulnerable to us bringing in reinforcements, but allows him to bring in reinforcements too, and thus keep his attack protean.'

Stating the obvious, Azroc thought. And his words seemed almost a prophetic commentary as those same fleets Erebus was withdrawing began to join attacks on other worlds. Azroc stared in frustration at the model he had created. Only twenty hours ago it had seemed that Erebus was preparing for ground assaults to capture about eight worlds, leaving the rest either depopulated or destroyed. Yet now some of those ground assaults were being abandoned, as were some of the other more destructive attacks. Even those wormships that had been engaged in accelerating the big asteroid towards one target world were now abandoning their position.

'There are more wormships arriving in the Caldera system than elsewhere,' he observed, though it seemed a trite comment to make considering the devastation there. Wormships were swarming out of U-space and hurtling down towards the twin Caldera worlds with almost careless abandon. The sun mirrors, previously used for energy generation, had now been turned into weapons and were busy frying wormship after wormship. Space in that zone was no longer black, and it seemed as if the conflict was being enacted inside a block of amber.

Azroc tried to step back from it all. What did Erebus want? Let Azroc suppose the entity wished, for whatever psychotic reasons, to either smash or take over the Polity, how would he, Azroc, achieve such an aim if he controlled the same resources? He would infiltrate the Polity, deploy his forces into critical places throughout it, and then initiate a surprise attack. Yet Erebus had done nothing of the kind. Instead it had first revealed its forces *outside* the Polity, giving ECS time to prepare, then at leisure had begun attacking the very periphery, even though it had the option to U-jump right inside and launch an attack there.

Azroc decided that there must be some critical piece of information still missing. He withdrew from his models and returned to utilizing ordinary human sensation and comprehension of his surroundings. The hologram at the centre of the hedron now displayed a montage of battle schematics intermixed with occasional gravity maps.

'Any news yet from your agent about the attack on Klurhammon?' Azroc enquired, swinging his attention across to those working at the concentric rings of consoles occupying the adjacent floor.

'There has been no—' The voice began in that same flat tone used by the sub-mind, then abruptly cut off. Then the real Jerusalem continued, 'It would seem that Agent Cormac and the *King of Hearts* were given new orders.'

'It would *seem*?' Azroc noted that some of the personnel manning the consoles were now getting up and abandoning their posts.

'Yes,' said Jerusalem. 'Apparently I myself wanted him to proceed to Ramone and there capture a legate.'

'What?'

'Cormac and his ship are currently down on the surface of

Ramone, though details of his progress are sparse. Communications are intermittent, since encryption needs to be changed
frequently by the groundside defence forces there.'

Azroc noted that those abandoning their posts had occupied
an area around one particular individual. Azroc saw to his surprise
that this was a Golem.

'Now,' said Jerusalem.

A length of console and a circular section of deck exploded
into the air. At that precise moment all but the Golem threw
themselves to the floor. A great ribbed pipe two metres across
terminating in a massive four-fingered claw and numerous ports
and lethal-looking protuberances shot out of the hole, curved over
whip-fast, and slammed down on the Golem. Cryogenic gas
exploded out at the contact point, as the claw closing on the
Golem tore up part of the console and the metal flooring underneath. Miniature lightning flared and earthed, and there came the
bright flashes of particle beams cutting within the mass. Then a
glowing white explosion blasted the claw into the air, and an
ensuing arc-fire melted both the Golem and everything lying
within a few feet of it. The wrecked claw seemed to pause in
frustrated hesitation, then retracted itself back down into the hole
it had made.

'Damn,' said Jerusalem.

'And precisely what happened then?' asked Azroc.

'I was just trying to capture one of the enemy in our camp,'
Jerusalem replied. 'The same one who gave Cormac and the *King
of Hearts* those false orders.'

Like the impact of a boulder falling, Azroc *felt* a large mass of
fresh information fall suddenly within his remit.

'I have already analysed this data for other similar false orders,'
Jerusalem explained, 'and, oddly, it seems there have been no

others issued. Yet Erebus's agent here was in a position to cause us maximum damage by doing so. Now, see what else you can find.'

As Azroc began checking through the files and logs the enemy's Golem agent had been using, he felt a surge of emotion, again from that point somewhere below emulation. This time, though, he recognized *fear*. The fact that one of Erebus's minions had managed to penetrate here, right to the heart of the *Jerusalem*, told him this was a war that the Polity might actually lose.

The antigravity tank was a disc-shaped affair with a ceramal skirt below and a wide turret jutting above from which protruded twinned particle cannons. Now only one of the cannons was capable of delivering its usual destructive potential. The other had been modified so its accelerating coils could be used to propel helium superfluid doped with iron particles, a supply of which resided in two cylindrical tanks welded to the tank's skirt. Anything hit by a jet of this stuff would be frozen solid in a second, since the fluid's temperature was only fifty degrees above absolute zero.

'Remember,' said Cormac to Hubbert Smith. 'If you get a legate in your sights, you nail it immediately.'

Smith nodded briefly and climbed the steps leading to the open hatch in one side of the tank, and then lowered himself inside. Watching him go, Cormac continued to reflect on whether this was all a complete waste of time. Yes, the superfluid would certainly freeze Jain-tech hardware, but it could not freeze electric or photonic signals, so if the legate they targeted happened to contain some sort of explosive device that could survive the freezing process there would still be nothing to prevent it sending the detonation signal. It struck him that Jerusalem was either prepared to expend personnel for minimum gain, or this mission he was about to undertake was an act of desperation, and Cormac hadn't thought things were going so badly.

'Three wormships landed and decohered on the surface,' said Remes. His tone had become leaden since the destruction of the AI Ramone, the one who had brought him into being. Maybe Remes was missing his parent.

Cormac studied the aerial shots showing the disposition of Erebus's forces, which Remes was now relaying direct to his gridlink. The segmented objects looking like organic trains that had first led the enemy attack had now withdrawn and formed defensive lines two hundred miles long. Further back, behind them, were three Jain-tech substructures like huge spiky mollusc shells bonded together with tar that seemed likely to form the cores of each wormship. The nearest one lay twenty miles straight out from their present position here at the end of the grounded atmosphere ship. And there, he hoped, he would find his legate captain.

'We'll start with this nearest one,' said Cormac. 'You'll hold back from hitting all three of the ship cores for the moment, in case we don't find what we want in this one?'

'We have cancelled the main assault,' Remes confirmed. 'Now that the wormship fleet has withdrawn, there will be no need to expend any further lives – except in support of your mission.'

Comforting, Cormac thought. Without him here, the ground forces would have needed only to maintain city defence while awaiting bombardment of the enemy by ECS capital ships. With the *Cable Hogue* looming up, he supposed it wasn't surprising that the remaining wormships had retreated. However, information was now becoming available that this was not unique, for Erebus's forces were being redeployed elsewhere throughout its concerted assault on the Line worlds.

'Is that atmosphere gunship on the way yet?' Cormac enquired.

Remes pointed back towards the city, before turning away and heading for the antigravity platform upon which they had arrived. Glancing where indicated, Cormac observed another massive ship like the one here on the ground drifting towards them like a skyscraper uprooted and turned on its side. Then he glanced round to check the disposition of his own small force.

Two of the bargelike troop carriers were loaded with fifty soldiers each, including twelve dracomen and numerous Golem. All the human soldiers contained those 'little doctors'. He wasn't sure why he had asked for such troops specifically, though he had a horrible suspicion he had chosen them because they seemed less human and therefore of less value. He didn't want to examine his own motivations too closely.

The AG tanks were to go first, after the atmosphere gunship had done its work. The carriers were to follow, surrounded by a selection of gun platforms. Cormac glanced across at Scar, who was strolling back from some sort of draco-conference with a group of his brethren, then he crooked a finger at Arach, who was gazing out intently at their destination from fifty feet up on the side of the grounded atmosphere ship. The spider drone ran straight down the sheer armoured surface, bounced on the ground leaving a small crater, then hurtled across towards him.

'I don't need to give you specific instructions,' Cormac explained to both the dracoman and the spider drone. 'Everything is fair game, except a legate if we're lucky enough to come across one. Let's go.' He led the way over to a flying gun platform on which a pulse-cannon was gimball-mounted. Since the gun seat was intended for a human, Cormac took possession of that while Scar stood by the control pillar. After hesitating for a moment, Arach grabbed a box containing an extra supply of the ordnance he used, climbed aboard securing the box behind him, then raised one leg, the glimmer of razor chainglass extruding along one edge of it. With two quick swipes he removed a large chunk of the safety rail, then settled himself down at the very rim of the platform. Opening his abdomen hatches he raised into position his two Gatling-style cannons and swivelled them to point off at right angles to each other. Then, as the shadow of the huge atmosphere gunship drew across them, Scar took them up into the air.

The moment the shield wall opened to allow the gunship through, it seemed like someone had opened a hatch onto a howling thunderstorm. Immediately, munitions began to impact on the gunship's hard-fields as they first filled the gap in the wall, then eased out ahead of the vessel. Some missiles, coming in at acute angles, penetrated the narrow gaps in shielding, but were soon mostly tracked and obliterated by autogun fire. Some, however, blew cavities in the ship's armour. One of them dipped down directly towards Cormac's little force. Immediately gridlinking to his pulse-cannon, he transferred targeting to his own visual field, placed a frame over the missile, acquired it and gave the instruction to fire all at once. The cannon swung up and to the side consequently dropping then swinging his seat in the other direction – and fired. The missile exploded, raining chunks of white-hot ceramic over the troop carriers. Having nearly been thrown from his seat, Cormac now strapped himself in securely and grabbed the cannon's guiding handles.

Once beyond the shield wall, the gunship accelerated and the tanks began to follow it out. They floated along only a few feet above the ground so that they could slam down at any moment, for stuck like limpets to the ground they were less vulnerable to many forms of attack and also attained a stable firing position. The two troop carriers followed, gun platforms rising up around them like flies about cattle. But there were no further attacks for the gunship was scouring the ground ahead.

Missiles and beam weapons kept stabbing down from the huge vessel at targets moving about in the churned wasteland below. Cormac caught subliminal glimpses of rod-forms with Jain growth spread all about them, objects like steel cockroaches and others like long flat coppery leeches, before they disappeared in explosions or else some beam weapon tracked across them. He saw a gun turret shoot up like an iron mushroom from the earth before a massive blast excised the whole area to leave a smoking crater. The top part of the turret glanced off the underside of the gunship and began to drop again, before a particle cannon beam turned it to vapour. Always there came the sounds of metal smacking on metal and the glassy crunch of ceramic armour giving up, amid deafening explosions and high-energy shrieks. Cormac had almost forgotten how severe this all could be. He applied a program in his gridlink to optimize his hearing, toning down the worst of the racket to enable him to hear what he needed to hear, but even if he survived this mayhem, he knew his eardrums might require some doc-work.

Ahead of them multiple detonations were raising a massive firestorm that blotted from view the segmented lines of the enemy. Behind this hard-fields shimmered and flickered like the scaly flank of some translucent giant beast. Then parts of the enemy hard-field wall began to blink out. The Polity assault was too concentrated for it to withstand, and enemy shield generators burned out one after another. Then came another massive explosion, flinging up numerous lengthy wormship sections.

'Looks like someone dropped a firecracker into a tin of mealworms,' said Smith, over com.

This choice of description was unusual enough for Cormac to do a quick search of his internal library to find 'mealworms'. The quickly glimpsed images he was provided with seemed appropriate.

The gunship slid on over the carnage it had already wrought

and began firing at targets beyond. Cormac's forces accelerated and spread out to optimum dispersement. He himself concentrated on familiarizing himself with the pulse-cannon, since until they reached their destination there was little else he could do to influence events.

A quick check showed him that the pulse-cannon possessed no autogun capability. Its processor had been removed because its unsophisticated shielding could not defend it against Jain worms or viruses and had been supplanted by some pretty basic hard wiring. It seemed that, in an utterly old-fashioned way, he would have to be this weapon's *mind*.

Running recognition software so that that he would not commit any friendly fire, his gridlink cued to cut weapon fire should his targeting frame fall upon other Polity vehicles or personnel. Keying himself to react fast to anything moving close by that wasn't any of his own force, he found himself overreacting to flames and smoke until further refining the program. He placed his finger ready both on real and virtual triggers, and then his hindbrain and the weapon became conjoined as an autogun. All was turning to carnage around him as, with fast robotic precision, he fired the cannon while only glimpsing his insectile targets amid the smoke of explosions. It occurred to him then that he really ought to have more personal investment in all this, so he used cognitive programs to get the rest of his brain up to speed. Around him the action seemed to slow down, but seemed no less deadly for that.

Soon they were passing through an area where segments of wormship lay scattered like discarded egg cases, and where hollow rod-forms smoked in the scorched earth. Even though the atmosphere ship had scoured a path through, still a few armoured monstrosities swarmed out into the light. The weapon he controlled firing intermittently, Cormac realized he was nailing only about one in fifty of them, and probably only the ones Arach allowed him to, for the spider drone was very enthusiastic indeed in demonstrating the capabilities of a hundred-year-old war drone. Eventually Cormac accepted the futility of his own meagre input so just turned the pulse-cannon off. He noted the human gunners on nearby platforms putting their weapons aside too, content to watch Arach dance about blasting Erebus's finest into scrap. Cormac allowed himself a smile, but only a brief one – the reward for complacency on the battlefield was usually a body bag.

Ahead of them the atmosphere gunship rose high out of the smoke and focused on fighting a duel with something directly below it. Just beyond the scattered segments of wormship, the churned-up soil sloped down towards a murky boiling lake. Cormac instantly forced himself to greater alertness, since anything could be lurking under the water's surface. Arach was also doubly on his guard, ceasing temporarily to reload from his ammo box and peering intently over the edge of the gun platform. The disc-shaped tanks, in a maneouvre Cormac had seen before, turned on their edges, pairs of them mating up at their bases so they seemed to roll above the lake surface like wheels. However, there came no attack from below, so Cormac U-sensed into the depths. Obviously whoever was running the gunship had also considered this a likely ambush risk and already made it safe. He perceived things still glowing deep down in the water as great globular bubbles of steam rose to the surface, and he wondered if the intense heat down there would eventually boil the lake away.

The upslope beyond the lake looked like the back of some spined beast, for here a forest had been reduced to spiky shards of wood, all evenly coated with black mud. The tanks maintained their wheel formation, which seemed the best strategy since great numbers of attackers kept erupting into the open from underground. Not much to hit on the slope beyond, however, and the few assailants there were of a different nature, designed for another environmental niche. Floating silver worms writhed out of the mess and speared upward, only to disappear under multiple weapon fire and fall away like aluminium confetti.

Beyond the shattered treeline at the top of the slope, a few miles ahead, lay the wormship core still enclosed in a geodesic dome of hard-fields, the nearer side of which the atmosphere gunship was pounding. The occupant of that mass of Jain substructure must have realized the danger now represented by Cormac's force, for mushroom gun turrets sprouted from the ground lying beyond the hard-fields, and were almost as quickly obliterated from above. Then a gap opened as the defence there began collapsing, and they drove for it without hesitation. Missiles and semi-living predators started to hammer down on the attackers from every direction. A nearby blast sent a troop carrier nosing into the ground ploughing up a bow wave of mud. Cormac glimpsed a pair of AG tanks hurtling apart like flying hubcaps; he saw a gun platform hanging canted, a burning man falling from it. Soldiers poured from the crashed troop carrier towards the tangled wall of Jain substructure, pairs of tank separating to cover their attack. The other carrier landed nose-first against that wall and discharged its passengers too.

Scanning, Cormac requested via his link.

The scan data came through piecemeal owing to the interference and constant electronic attacks. Cormac cursed and resorted to his U-sense to fill in the gaps. He mapped hollows, energy concentrations and movement, from which he built up a schematic of what lay ahead. He then formed a protean attack plan and saw it instantly applied. An explosion flung chunks of Jain coral through the air and opened up the wormship core. Soldiers stormed inside, and tanks and gun platforms entered wherever access was wide enough. Scar guided their platform in behind

Smith's adapted tank and one other to which it was still paired in wheel formation. With the still-functioning particle cannons of these twinned tanks incinerating any intervening structure, they advanced. It seemed like they had entered the interior of a ceramic wormcast, tunnels and cavities opening all around them from which unidentifiable things shrieked and skittered. He saw star-limbed monsters, created thus for travelling fast in this environment, jetting explosive bullets from between their glass mandibles. He glimpsed skeletal balls rolling out and unfolding into shapes disquietingly similar to Arach – before Arach himself destroyed them. Orders relayed to the atmosphere gunship resulted in the whole structure shaking about them as the big craft above began demolishing those areas of the wormship core irrelevant to Cormac's purpose but certainly still containing enemy mechanisms.

As he processed the information now being presented to him by the various scanners mounted in tanks or carried by soldiers, and sometimes relayed directly from Golem sensoriums but mainly from his own penetrating sense of his surroundings, Cormac grew distant from the frenetic part of himself he labelled 'autogun'. Briefly he wondered if this was how AIs and haimen felt when they created sub-minds and sub-personae, but there was far too much to do now for him to indulge in such idle speculation.

T3 and 5 concentrate fire on your 6 elevation 3 . . . units 3, 5 and 7 advance and secure area designated 12 axial on globe grid . . .

He issued orders faster than human speech, also running sub-programs to enable him to issue separate orders simultaneously. Modelling the ebb and flow of the attack in his gridlink he looked for openings, weaknesses, the best way to apply the forces at his disposal with the aim of getting Smith's tank safely to that energy-dense concentration of matter lying deep within this core structure, though necessarily distancing himself from the lights constantly going out in this model as people and machines died all around him. Gradually, the attacks from Jain-engineered organisms ebbed around his own particular group, since it was of prime importance to protect Smith and his tank, and their reason for being here. Final barriers crashed down with the sound of shattering porcelain to reveal a chamber fifty feet across, in the centre of which was suspended some glassy concoction like a giant synapse, protrusions connecting it all around to the chamber's walls.

And something was moving inside it.

Then suddenly all enemy movement within the ship's core ceased.

Through the eyes of others Cormac saw biomechs simply freeze in place, automated weapons that a moment before had leapt out at them like trapdoor spiders now sagging and dying. Firing still continued for a while, but it all came from Cormac's own forces. In reply to his query, someone in the gunship above informed him that all enemy movement for miles around had also ceased, all the Jain biomechs frozen.

Just now, Cormac thought with cold clarity, *the legate right there ahead of us has obviously realized we are here to capture it, so it will destroy itself. We will be very lucky if such destruction does not include us and the entire ship's core.*

But nothing was happening.

Smith, Cormac sent, needing to add no more.

The two tanks ahead finally separated, and Smith's vehicle accelerated, smashing its way through glassy struts. A stream of superfluid jetted towards the synapse thing like the beam of an energy weapon, but merely splashed against it and rained down. Surrounding struts shattered and the central structure tumbled. Still playing a stream of liquid helium upon it, Smith followed it down. It hit the chamber floor and shattered, spilling out something bulky and metallic. Focusing in with his gun sights, Cormac could see no sign of a legate.

'Scar, take us down there,' he ordered.

Soon the gravplatform was crunching down into what looked like the wreckage of an immense greenhouse. Smith's tank settled over to one side, its superfluid gun still directed at a grey bulk amid the wreckage. Cormac unstrapped himself and stepped down to the floor, enviroboots crunching on the mess. Interference was dying all around him, while outside channels began to open and bandwidth to grow.

'What is that?' he wondered.

'Still alive – I think,' Arach replied.

Cormac turned to the drone and to Scar. 'Stay put but be ready to get out of here fast.'

They reluctantly obeyed as he moved forward.

Drawing closer to the grey bulk he observed something like a huge coiled grub, with cold fog billowing from it. Maybe this was merely some sort of protective coating with the legate inside? Drawing his thin-gun, perhaps more for reassurance than any real expectation that it would be effective, he advanced to stand directly over the strange object. Gazing down at it, he mentally peeled away various layers to get to the core. There was something humanoid inside . . . something rather *too* humanoid. The grub-thing abruptly opened out to reveal what was bonded into its inner surface. A skeletal human face, with Jain tendrils penetrating all around its head like a Medusa hairdo, turned to gaze up at Cormac with its utterly black eyes.

'Oddly,' began the woman entrapped there, 'it was his final destruct order that enabled me to break his hold . . . at least for a while.' She blinked, licked her lips. 'But now I find I am anxious for this all to end.'

'Stay alive and help us defeat him,' said Cormac, catching on at once.

'No.' She shook her head. 'While the betrayer still sits on his throne I won't be allowed to live, and anyway I don't want to. You have precisely ten minutes from now to get your people beyond the blast radius.'

Betrayer?

Cormac glanced towards the single barrel of Hubbert Smith's tank, from which depended a neat line of icicles.

'That won't work,' the woman advised him. 'Get out of here *now.*'

'We'll take you with us.'

'One of the many CTDs here sits inside what is left of me,' she said.

Cormac didn't have any difficulty believing her, for within the grublike object that both held her and of which she had become a component, he could see a dense mass sitting amid the spread-out parts of her body.

'Who are you?' he asked out loud.

'Run now,' she replied dreamily.

Cormac reached out and scraped a fingernail down her cheek. He was damned if he was going to leave here with absolutely nothing – there was a good chance that this little scrap of tissue under his fingernail would be able to at least tell them who she was. Then, inside her, he spotted movement, changes in electrical activity around the CTD.

'Okay, out of here!'

Smith's tank flipped up to rejoin its partner, the two tanks slamming together like cymbals. Cormac turned back towards the AG platform, expecting obliteration at any moment. He needed to be on that platform and away, so, without conscious consideration, he stepped *past* the intervening space between them, his boots slamming down on the ceramal deck. A Gatling cannon spun towards him, and Scar turned with teeth bared.

'Go! Now!' Cormac ordered as he quickly strapped himself into the gunner's seat.

Scar glanced towards where Cormac had been standing only a second before, then he wrenched the platform into the air. Soon they were retracing their route into the wormship's core, hurtling along after Smith's tank. No detonation yet. Maybe the woman had known what he could see, and so had given him a warning. Within minutes they were outside again, in the hot smoky air.

'Hold here,' Cormac instructed, as he watched all the troops piling back aboard the one mobile carrier. He then assessed the perpetually updated model of his attack plan and the relative positions of those within in. Soon everyone who could was out of there and, once they were racing away over the incinerated mud, Cormac signalled for Scar to continue.

'We failed,' Cormac announced, both verbally and over com.

'That's unfortunate,' replied Remes from twenty miles away, 'but now it appears that you weren't even supposed to be here at all.'

Just then a blast lit up the entire sky.

'What?' Cormac turned and looked back in time to see a tsunami of debris bearing down on them. The hot shock wave hit hard, tilting the gun platform and flinging debris past them. He glimpsed chunks of Jain coral hurtling through the air like scythe blades, saw Scar headless at the platform's controls and Arach tumbling away helplessly through the storm. Then, a boulder of Jain coral slammed straight into the side of the platform like a giant fist. The gun collapsed crushing Cormac underneath it, and something else hit him hard on the side of his head.

The lights went out.

10

The modern haiman is a hybrid of machine and organism, of computer and human mind, incorporating each in equal measure – well, maybe. She is, however, still a long way away from attaining the ultimate true synergy of this combination. Though it has been rumoured that there are those who have, using alien technology, managed to initiate and maintain AI/human mind synergy, this has not been proven and is plainly not true for the majority of haimens. Haimanity therefore sits in a shadowy borderland between humans and AIs, sampling of both but never truly a member of either. Many believe that they are the future of Polity-kind, the post-post-humans. Many others believe they are a dead end, and that trying to fully meld the human with the AI is as likely to succeed as strapping a jet engine to an ox cart in the hope of breaking the sound barrier.

– From HOW IT IS by Gordon

Vulture brought the *Harpy* and its attached Jain craft back up into the real, only to see the two pursuing wormships materialize almost simultaneously only a hundred thousand miles away.

'Let me use the chameleonware,' Vulture requested. 'We still have a chance to shake them.' It might indeed have helped, though it was evident the wormships were now using a new scanning format and recognition codes. The one-time bird and now ship AI then tried the chameleonware again, only to find that it still lay beyond his control. Crane, now back in his usual seat beside the ship's console, had retained ultimate control of the *Harpy*, and Vulture felt like one of those AIs, before the Quiet War, who had

239

been strictly controlled by their human masters. It was so humiliating. Crane didn't need to do this to him; all he needed to do was explain himself. The Golem's dislike of communicating had to be really extreme for him to adopt such measures.

'Or is it that you don't want to shake them?' Vulture enquired.

Crane acknowledged this with a slow nod of his head, then leaned forward and input some new coordinates. Vulture studied them as the two wormships began to close in. Upon detecting a sudden steep rise in radiation from that direction, the AI immediately dropped his ship back into the U-continuum, energies discharging around it like black lightnings as the U-field dragged some small part of a microwave beam strike back down with it.

'Nearly fried us,' Vulture observed.

Crane even acknowledged that too, with another tilt of his head. However, as taciturn as Crane appeared towards Vulture, he had certainly been speaking to someone. Though the Golem's earlier reply to Vulture's question, 'Are you still in contact with ECS?' had been ambiguous, Crane certainly could not have managed such recent feats without Earth Central's help. However, Vulture felt that there must be more to it than that. Certainly, the Polity AIs, knowing Crane's intention of going after Erebus for killing the hybrids, would have been prepared to give him any assistance that did not interfere with their own plans, but there were still discrepancies to explain.

ECS had definitely helped Crane get to the location of this ship, the *Harpy*. Equally, ECS could have given the location of the crashed wormship – the one that killed the hybrids – and it could have given the location of the wormships in the Caldera system too. However, Vulture had a bit of a problem with how Crane had then managed to destroy all those ships. Crane must have known there was a weakness to be exploited, but one that ECS simply could not have been aware of, therefore the brass Golem must have obtained the information elsewhere. Vulture prefered to believe that explanation rather than the alternative – which was that Crane had somehow returned to a previous state and once again fallen through the booby hatch. And now it was time to find out for sure.

As the *Harpy* travelled through U-space, Vulture next asked, 'We going anywhere special?' The coordinates, according to his library, were of a small scattering of asteroids deep in interstellar space and fifteen light years from the nearest star, and, unless there was something else there that Vulture did not know about, the asteroids would be a poor place to hide from the pursuing wormships.

Crane's response was typical: he silently took out his toys and placed them neatly on the console before him.

'Are ECS warships waiting there?' Vulture tried.

The briefest twitch of Crane's head maybe indicated a negative.

Keeping half an eye on the brass Golem, Vulture began to submerge more fully into the Jain infected systems of *Harpy* and the legate craft. He sampled snatches of the code flowing all about him and studied how things were working here. Soon he realized that though some improvements had been made to *Harpy*'s systems, especially to its chameleonware, the Jain network did not interfere unnecessarily, except through primacy. On the whole it ran in parallel with *Harpy*'s hardware. That meant Crane could take over whenever he wanted. Sending a few test diagnostics, Vulture found he himself could use parts of that parallel network and he began to look for recorded data, soon finding tens of thousands of caches distributed throughout the Jain substructure.

Some of these sources contained information that was open to analysis. The easiest stuff was visual files and schematics, which Vulture studied avidly. Here a schematic of a wormship segment, there a visual file that had to be part of a virtual model. But it was hopeless. All this stuff could have come from the legate craft, and it neither proved nor disproved whether Crane had been in direct contact with some other entity. Then, out of vast complexity and seemingly endless data horizons, a simple vocal communication:

'Well, I would guess you're looking for me?'

'Who are you?' Vulture asked, meanwhile running traces to find the source of this voice.

'I'm Fiddler Randal,' came the reply.

Vulture traced it back to one particular data store, but even as he accessed that source, its contents began to copy themselves elsewhere.

'You're a virus,' the AI observed.

'Quite right – but of a kind quite fatal to Erebus.'

'You supplied Mr Crane with information about the weaknesses underlying Erebus's attack on the Caldera system?'

'Certainly,' Randal replied.

'I take it that the coordinates we're now heading to were supplied by you as well?'

'Correct.'

'So Crane trusts you now because the information you supplied before was verified?'

'He's a trusting sort of soul.'

'I don't think so.'

'Then maybe he more fully understands the technology I now inhabit than do I. Few manage that, but maybe *he* can because he is a product of a technically evolved civilization, and in addition because he was supplied with a version of Jain-tech devoid of all its traps.'

'From Dragon.'

'Precisely.'

'But what do you mean by *product?*'

'As you are well aware, Jain nodes do not react to artificial intelligences. What is the difference between such intelligences and their naturally evolved creators?'

'There are many differences.'

'Let me rephrase the question: how, on an informational level, do you distinguish the two?'

'Top down and bottom up,' Vulture replied.

'Exactly,' said Randal. 'Humans and others of their like have evolved moderately logical thought processes through natural selection. Their logic is a skin over chaos. The machine mind is built with pure logic from the bottom up. Therefore machines have to pretend to own that same chaos, so they model it, hence human emulation in Golem.'

Vulture wondered where the hell all this was leading. It seemed insane to be having a debate like this while being pursued by two homicidal wormships.

'Okay,' he said, 'so you've established that there is an identifiable difference, though I would argue that the rules of natural selection still apply in the realms of artificial intelligence, though faster. It is argued by some that AIs like myself are simply post-humans. But let's move on now.'

'Jain technology does not react to AIs, because it was biased that way by its makers: the Jain AIs. Perhaps they decided that evolved intelligences needed to be cleared out of the way so that the products of those messy organic intelligences – AIs – could get on with ruling the universe.'

'Products like Erebus?' Vulture suggested.

'Erebus is flawed.'

Vulture quickly replayed the conversation and realized that, interesting as it all was, it didn't really explain much.

'So you gave Mr Crane information enabling him to wipe out fifty of Erebus's wormships – a mere fly speck. And now you've given him coordinates. Why?'

'Chameleonware.'

'Explain.'

'Another version of myself contacted someone else who, hopefully, by now has fashioned or obtained the means to rub out more than mere fly specks. However, to be successful, she will need the latest chameleonware format and recognition codes that Erebus is using.'

'*Hopefully?*' echoed Vulture, then, reviewing what had just been said, added, 'We don't possess that 'ware and those codes now. It's all changed.'

'But the ships pursuing you do.'

Vulture considered how, now he was an integral part of the *Harpy*, an escape pod would be of no use to him at all.

'She?' he queried.

'Her name is Orlandine, and she controls Jain technology supplied to her directly by Erebus.'

'But she is no AI.'

'She was, however, a rare product of evolution sufficiently intelligent to take apart a Jain node while avoiding all its traps.'

'And I'm supposed to believe this.'

'Whether you believe it or not is irrelevant, as Mr Crane believes it.'

And there it was really. Vulture could not change their destination. He must trust a virus, a Golem android of questionable sanity and, should he ever survive the wormships, a Jain-infested human. Vulture wasn't at all optimistic about the outcome of all this.

*

When Dragon finally closed down her outside view from the cyst, Mika felt unutterably weary and drifted into sleep on the soft fleshy floor, where she dreamed of gabbleducks and woven cities and the bitter wars of a civilization fighting infection. When she woke again, in an instant like the time before, she opened her eyes on painful brightness – her view meanwhile re-established. For a moment it seemed Dragon was hovering over a snow-covered midnight plain. However, as the two spheres descended towards that same whiteness some internal detonation turned it orange and threw objects deep within it momentarily into silhouette. Then she began to get a sense of scale and realized they had reached the accretion disc. She decided she must have been put to sleep for the rest of the journey, and this rather begged the question of why Dragon had woken her to witness the twin spheres' destruction of the five wormships. Maybe this was just more evidence to be added to the dense mass already residing in her skull?

Gazing at the view she felt a sudden deep fascination because, though having witnessed most stellar phenomena, this was not one of them. Also, if Dragon could be believed, this place swarmed with wild Jain technology. Her hands itched to be controlling the instruments she could use to study both this great object and everything it contained.

'Did the conferencing unit survive?' she enquired.

It again took a while for Dragon to reply, so perhaps the entity was more concerned with carefully watching everything going on outside than tending to the curiosity of the primitive little being it carried inside itself. Finally, the ceiling of the cyst split open with a liquid tearing sound, showering her with magenta juice. Above, a gap opened up through a mass of what looked like coarse-grained white muscle fibres, then gravity within the cyst abruptly shut down.

The smell from outside the cyst was intense: cloves, putrefaction, hot reptile and raw meat. Mika wrinkled her nostrils and swallowed, sure she could become inured to it, but when she started to experience difficulty breathing realized the air out there wouldn't keep her alive. She closed up her suit helmet and with relief enjoyed her own air supply, then pushed up from the floor and floated right out of the cyst through an eye-shaped tunnel leading into wider spaces. Here hellish red glows lit up glimpses of crowded organs or mechanisms, and frequently she saw the shifting flashes of sapphire pseudopod eyes. It occurred to her that, without any sense of up or down, she might soon lose her way, but Dragon anticipated her.

'Follow the remote to the surface,' came its voice over her suit radio.

Peering ahead she observed a diamond-shaped fleshy object peel away from the curved heavily veined surface and flap sluggishly out into the gap in front of her. Bringing her boot down on the same surface, she altered her course to follow it. But as she did so, and gazed around at things she had always wanted to study, close up, something occurred to her. Dragon had told her that the conferencing unit might not survive what was to come, and she had assumed it had been referring to their coming adventure within the accretion disc. Now it seemed likely Dragon had been alluding to the imminent encounter with the wormships. Dragon must have known for some time that they were still following and therefore made preparations to destroy them. Mika felt annoyed Dragon had not told her about this, though she wasn't sure why, since, amid all the other stuff Dragon did not tell her, it was hardly in the minority.

The flapping remote, which reminded her somewhat of a large skate from Earth's oceans, continued doggedly. Mika caught hold of a solid glassy strut shaped like a chicken's wishbone, one end of which disappeared into darkness while the other connected firmly to what looked like an iron acorn extending ten feet across. Through a cavity beyond this object the intermittent strobing of blue light revealed a great cylinder, both of its ends lost to sight. She guessed this must be one of the Dragon sphere's equatorial weapons. Pushing off again she drifted past a cliff of solid flesh from cavities in which peeked objects like the heads of tube worms. Mika guessed their purpose was to collect for digestion or disposal any dead material drifting through Dragon's innards.

The remote finally led her to where progress was blocked by great lumpy bags some ten feet across interconnected by numerous gutlike tubes. Her diamond-shaped remote landed on one of these bags and all its kin began to jostle against each other like nervous sheep, then opened a way through. Mika found herself falling back gently towards massive black rib bones, and realized she had come close enough to the sphere's surface to experience Dragon's minimal gravity. Settling against one such bone she watched the remote crawl to the newly opened passage and flop inside it, but that being too narrow to fly through, it then progressed with the gait of a wounded bat. She launched herself towards the same passage and followed it inside. Eventually they entered a tunnel, through numerous thick and intricately constructed layers, and Mika was now able to see Dragon's armour at first hand. She rested a glove against a layer of thick brassy metal, observed further strata holding what looked like glass shock absorbers each as thick as a finger, studied another layer with the appearance of soggy fruitcake, and yet another beyond it with the bluish metallic gleam of superconductor. One of the lumpy bags oozed in to block off the passage behind her and, glancing back to watch this she saw myriad threads jet across the gap and bind together. It seemed Dragon was now sealing off this access to its interior.

Now the gas within the space she occupied fogged and began to draw away into numerous protruding tube ends. Checking her suit readout she watched the pressure drop only momentarily then begin to rise again. When something like enormous eyelids opened above to expose a metal surface inlaid with curved lines meeting at the centre, she deduced Dragon was equalizing the pressure here with what lay beyond that metal surface.

Mika hauled herself up towards what she now recognized as the underside of the hatch leading into the conferencing unit. With a steely slither the irised hatch opened, so she pushed up to the lip and pulled herself over it, then rolled over to lie flat on her back, heavy as lead now on the functioning gravplates.

'Full outside view,' she panted.

Something black roiled overhead, the glint of stars was only occasionally visible just above the draconic horizon and, even while she watched, this mass appeared to draw visibly closer.

'So, Dragon, I take it we have finally arrived,' she said, directing her voice towards the hatch. No reply, so, after checking the external atmosphere readout before opening her helmet, she sat upright and immediately noted the small impact craters in the floor surrounded by aureoles of metal once molten but now again solidified. Glancing up she could just about pick out, against that roiling black, the patches that the automated repair system had extruded into place. Had she still been here inside when the two spheres went up against the wormships, there was a very good chance she would no longer be alive.

As she removed her gloves and powered down her suit, the diamond-shaped remote rose into view with a sound like flapping leather. However, the moment it crossed above the gravplates it dropped and hit the deck like a huge piece of steak. It lay there struggling weakly, then extruded two stalk eyes which it directed towards her as if in accusation. The eyes were piercing blue, and

Mika stared at this draconic creation for a long moment before she stood and walked heavily over to her console

First she adjusted the light amplification to give her the same view she'd seen from within the cyst. The black mass above quickly shaded to grey, then to white, as if she was gazing into a fog bank. Then she called up feeds from the scanners positioned all about the conferencing unit. In moments she was getting images from wide EM scans penetrating deeper into the mass, and data about its constituents. Mostly it seemed to consist of sparse hydrogen, rock dust and snow, though not necessarily snow composed of water ice. Mika began to identify some larger objects out there, then, discovering that the view behind was exactly the same, realized they were actually within the accretion disc itself. Outside the conferencing unit a thin fog seemed to have settled. While she studied this a white laser stabbed up, and something erupted into red fire where its beam impacted. There followed more and more explosions, and on the surface outside she saw meteor strikes while simultaneously the defensive green gas laser of the unit began lancing out to intercept and vaporize falling debris. Returning her attention to her console screen she recognized some of the approaching objects Dragon was firing upon. There were rod-forms out there, also pieces like the remains of destroyed worm-ships – even a distorted lens-shape, that being another variety of Erebus's combat ships. But that wasn't all: there were things like fragments of coral, tree branches, weirdly distorted spiral shells, insectile horrors looking like something sculpted ineptly out of pieces collected in a scrapyard. The variety was bewildering.

Then came the blinding turquoise flash of one of the equatorial cannons, and the lens ship exploded, many of the smaller chunks of Jain-tech turning to ash.

'The intensity of these attacks will increase for a while,' Dragon observed.

She looked over; there was no sign of a head or pseudopods in the conferencing unit. She assumed Dragon must have reactivated her suit radio, but a check of her wrist display showed that the suit was still powered down.

'But there should be less of them as we go deeper,' Dragon added.

Right, thought Mika, *talking inside my head now.*

It became the least of her worries when she saw on her screen the monstrous horde now heading straight towards them.

Knobbler turned off into a wider side corridor more suitable for his bulk while Orlandine headed for the drop-shaft at the far end of the current one. Sending instructions to its control panel, which, like just about everything else aboard this massive beast, was now infested with Jain-tech, she stepped into the shaft and the irised gravity fields wafted her up two floors. She stepped out into a small control centre under a domed chainglass ceiling. A horseshoe of consoles occupied the floor of the circular room, and right in the middle of them a scaffold supporting the control sphere Knobbler had fashioned for her. Its door stood open, a few steps leading up. Orlandine mounted them, entered and ensconced herself in a familiar environment.

Though having remained connected by electromagnetic means to the Jain-tech within the war runcible, Orlandine knew this was not at all ideal. As soon as the Polity tech of the sphere engaged with her carapace, her horizons expanded, and when the Jain mycelia of the runcible, which had earlier invaded this sphere, connected with the part of itself already inside her body, those horizons became vast. She could now see the massive device all at once, in its entirety, from the numerous sensors positioned around its hull and also within it. She could not only see all this visually but across a broad chunk of the EM spectrum, with the option of using even more esoteric scanning methods like gravity mapping. But even that was not all.

Orlandine controlled nearly everything and could equally assume control of all those things currently in the remit of the drones aboard, like the runcible's weapons. The positional thrusters and fusion engines evenly dispersed about the runcible lay at her virtual fingertips. The four remaining U-space engines she could start at will, though, with one engine missing and the others not yet balanced, that would result in the runcible arriving not only turned inside out – but at four separate locations. Almost negligently she set into motion tuning and balancing programs to extend the coverage of those four engines so that they would work in concert. Then there was the matter of the runcible gate itself. As she assumed that space Bludgeon had previously occupied and never really used, she began to appreciate the massive complexity of the technology. The base control programs loading to her carapace, she saw, were presently at four per cent of her memory/processing space, and when fully loaded in a few minutes they would take up a full eight per cent, but when she started actually using the device, that figure would rise to nearly fifty per cent.

'Bludgeon,' she enquired, 'are you ready yet?' This was merely a politeness for she was monitoring that drone's progress too.

'Eighty-eight per cent,' the drone replied curtly, not being a talkative soul.

'At your leisure, then, proceed towards the asteroid,' Orlandine instructed.

It was at this moment that she felt godlike and decided to enjoy the sensation despite her reservations about it. However, it seemed that fate was working overtime this day, for the moment she began to wonder if her seat in the interface sphere could recline to a more comfortable angle, klaxons sounded throughout the war runcible, and those sensors she had set up to watch their surroundings began screaming for her attention.

'We've got arrivals,' Knobbler informed her.

'You don't say.'

This could perhaps be the expected arrival – early by a couple of days.

The three U-space signatures had appeared some five thousand miles out. Two of them were close together and one was a thousand miles to one side. Orlandine studied the images she was receiving: two wormships accelerating towards a smaller vessel and, by the energy readings, preparing to open fire on it. She guessed the little vessel contained the one she was supposed to meet and suspected the wormships weren't part of the general plan.

'Weapons?' she asked.

'Ready,' Knobbler replied.

'No longer at your leisure, Bludgeon,' she warned the drone aboard her erstwhile ship. 'Move with a purpose.'

'Acknowledged.'

Heliotrope's drive ignited and it accelerated away from the war runcible. Gathering data, Orlandine began to set in motion the programs for making the calculation needed to receive something through this war runcible gate. It was easy for her, but the sheer speed her mind needed to work and the number of calculations that needed to be completed made her appreciate the feat of that hero of the Prador–human war, Moria Salem – the female runcible technician who, using little more than an advanced augmentation, managed to employ a cargo runcible to throw a small moon at a Prador dreadnought.

Perpetual diagnostic feeds from the mycelium told her that everything was functioning at optimum, so Orlandine quickly ran five fusion reactors up to speed and initiated the Skaidon warp. In the pentagon of vacuum through the centre of the war runcible reality flickered, then a shimmering meniscus sprang into being.

'Done,' said Bludgeon.

Glimpsing the scene through *Heliotrope*'s external cameras, Orlandine saw how a similar meniscus now shimmered between the three horns of the cargo runcible positioned at the nose of her ship.

'Go to expansion *immediately*,' Orlandine replied.

While she watched, the three horns disconnected from their seatings and, impelled out by hard-field projectors, their positions relative to each other accurately maintained by laser measurement, they began stretching that meniscus, that Skaidon warp – that skin over reality. They also turned over on their way out, folding that same skin over themselves so that effectively the gate was without any material edges facing forward. This was not necessary right now, but would certainly be necessary for the cargo runcible's ultimate purpose. Bludgeon seemed to be doing fine, so she returned her full attention to the war runcible and sent instructions to the numerous thrusters peppered over its surface. They ignited at once and the massive structure began to turn.

'A very critical test,' Knobbler observed.

'Stay on those weapons,' Orlandine replied. 'This might not work.'

She only momentarily considered instructing the five segments to detach so as to widen the war runcible's gate, but it was already wide enough. Anyway, it wasn't hard-fields that would impel them apart but very accurate steering jets. She could see that, with how this device had originally been constructed, the controlling AI would have experienced all sorts of difficulties operating it, especially while coming under attack. Each section of the runcible needed to be very accurately positioned, since the room for error in all the calculations was minute, yet firing the weapons positioned on each section might well knock them out of alignment faster than could be corrected for. With everything now cohered by the Jain mycelium, she could supposedly calculate and factor in the inertial effects of the firing of each weapon full seconds before they even fired. However, right now it would be stupid to risk the alterations she had made failing.

There were other factors also making this easier for her. It wasn't as if she intended to transfer anything through the runcible that needed to survive that process or pass through at anything less than the speed of a meteor. For normal runcibles, calculations needed to be made to correct for relative speeds by inputting the precise energies at the departure runcible, and bleeding off into the buffer the correct amount at the arrival runcible. Simplified, these calculations involved the input of energy required to push the traveller through the Skaidon warp, plus the energy required to accelerate or decelerate him from his initial relative speed, so he came out of the gate at the other end at zero speed. But that was an extreme simplification.

Another factor in the complex calculations was the C-energy, this being the input energy of the transmission and also that drawn into the runcible buffers at the destination runcible. The events on a world called Samarkand had luridly demonstrated what happened when that energy was not removed by the receiving runcible. There the runcible buffers had been sabotaged, so that one traveller who arrived on that world by runcible came through at a fraction under the speed of light. His arrival had caused massive devastation and loss of life. Ironic, therefore, that he himself had been a runcible technician.

'I am ready,' said Bludgeon.

Orlandine studied the situation out in space. The little ship was now running towards them. While it might be either a friend or an enemy, there was no doubt at all about the status of the two pursuing vessels. She aimed a signal laser at the little ship.

'If you want to survive, I suggest you get out of my targeting frame,' she sent.

The reply was, 'Mother of fuck,' and the ship went into a high-gravity turn that Orlandine realized no human could have survived – which meant there were no humans aboard.

'Knobbler,' she said, 'I'm going to assume that little guy is the one we are here to meet, but damn well keep a rail-gun on him till we find out for sure.'

'Will do,' Knobbler replied.

They were ready now – she didn't want to give those worm-ships time to separate.

'Proceed,' Orlandine instructed.

She observed *Heliotrope* drive the cargo-runcible meniscus down, like a catch-net, onto the tumbling asteroid, swallowing it whole. Since the war runcible was linked only to the cargo runcible, she did not need to check what was now coming through, just make the necessary calculations and apply the required energies to accept that item in the war runcible's U-space spoon, and then bring it through. And she did not bleed off the C-energy.

The million-ton rock came out through the war runcible's Skaidon warp. In U-space the asteroid's speed relative to realspace had been far above the speed of light. As it returned to the domain of Einsteinian physics realspace strictly applied its speed restrictions and the asteroid departed the war runcible at just a fraction below the speed of light. A material object travelling at such velocity was often described as photonic matter. You cannot see light unless its photons enter your eyes, so it should not have been possible to see the path of this object, yet it left a luminous trail like the disperse beam from a particle weapon, for there was a sufficient scattering of atoms throughout this region for it to hit and smash a few of them.

Focusing upon both the wormships, Orlandine did not get to see the impact, for the intense flash of radiation blanked out all sensors aimed in that direction. It didn't matter that the asteroid only hit one of the wormships full on, as the force of the impact supplied sufficient energy for the cone of the blast to hit the other ship as well. When the sensors cleared again, it was to show a glowing cloud scattered through with wormish fragments.

'Knobbler,' she instructed, 'clear up those bits.'

Immediately, visible particle beams began needling the cloud, selectively burning the fragments to ash. She turned her attention now to the little ship, which was swinging round to head back towards the war runcible.

'Give me a good reason why I should not destroy you,' she sent.

'Chameleonware and recognition codes, apparently,' replied a voice.

Orlandine could now discern that the approaching craft was in fact two ships bonded together, one of them of the kind customarily used by Erebus's legates.

'I'm not so sure that's reason enough for me to let you even get close to us,' she said, testing.

'Well, Fiddler Randal tells me you need the updated version,' replied the voice. 'And my boss, even though he don't say much, tells me you should stop blasting those bits of wormship out there because from one of them he can get you what you want.'

Knobbler's particle cannons abruptly cut out. Clearly the big drone had been listening.

'I see,' said Orlandine.

Now she watched as the Polity craft and the legate craft

abruptly separated, the latter accelerating towards the spreading cloud of wormship remains. She saw it target one large chunk of debris, decelerate down towards it, but still slam into it hard and stick for a moment. After a brief pause it then separated and turned, heading back towards the Polity craft.

'Got your codes and 'ware,' said the voice.

'I will give you docking instructions shortly,' Orlandine replied coldly.

The aseptic smell was so familiar, as were the sounds, the current numbness of his body and the occasional tugging sensation in his flesh. He was in Medical being worked over by an autodoc, probably directed by a human medic. This wasn't an unusual experience for Cormac, but the profound sadness he felt was unusual, and it arose for reasons he just could not nail down right then.

'Ah, you're with us again,' said a voice.

Cormac tried to open his eyes but found he couldn't, tried to say something about this but his mouth seemed like a slack bag.

'Don't worry about the lack of sensation,' continued the voice. 'I had to block you from the neck down to fix the stomach wound and your leg. I also had to knock out some facial and scalp nerves to repair the other damage.'

Great, don't worry about the numbness, just worry about the damage. Cormac surmised, judging by his bedside manner, that whoever was working on him was not a civilian medic.

'There, that about does it,' the voice told him. 'Your own internal nanites are repairing the concussion damage, and the anti-inflammatories should help.'

Annoyed at being unable to perceive his surroundings and still not entirely clear on what had happened to him, Cormac applied for linkage to whatever server lay nearby. There was the usual delay and security issues limited him to the nearest server. He ran a trace using his name and tracked himself down to a military medical unit set up inside the downed atmosphere ship. Hopping from internal cam to cam he tried to find a view of himself. Instead he found Hubbert Smith standing statuelike in a corridor, and though glad that at least the Golem had survived for a moment could not figure out why he should be glad. Then memories returned of hurtling razor-edged lumps of Jain coral carried in a shock wave, of Arach tumbling away, of Scar standing headless . . .

Cormac tried to speak, tried to ask questions but could not, then abruptly closed down on the urge, since this medic probably possessed no knowledge of what had happened anyway but was merely here to stitch back together whatever had survived. Cormac became suddenly cold, now understanding the reason for his earlier sadness. He had certainly lost another long-time associate, possibly two, but would have to wait for confirmation from Hubbert Smith. Turning his focus away from such painful memories, he again tried to find a cam view of himself. Gaining access to the room in which he lay, he discovered the only cams available there were in the autodoc, and he gazed analytically through its sensors. Chrome instruments were aligning pieces of broken bone as the head of a bonewelder moved into position, then Cormac heard the familiar sound of the welder going to work.

Not enough though.

Just then the realization that he had another way to see his surroundings returned to him. His U-sense was slow, reluctant, as if it too had been sleeping. His surroundings slowly came into focus, though that was hardly the correct terminology since he was *seeing* three hundred and sixty degrees and *through* everything around him.

'Shame your gridlink is offline,' said the voice. 'You could have helped speed up the repair process yourself by using some of its med programs.'

Uh?

'There you go.'

Abruptly his sight returned and sensation came back to his face and his scalp, which both felt sore. He gazed up at the white ceiling, then tentatively tried to move his head. It seemed okay. Letting his U-sense drop back into slumber, he looked down at the autodoc poised over his leg, then up to his left at the medic, a blond-haired man with metal eyes and an aug affixed to the right-hand side of his head, from which an optic cable trailed down to connect to a small pedestal doc he was now wheeling back out of the way.

'Whasss . . . ?' Cormac paused for a moment to work up some moisture in his mouth. 'What do you mean, my gridlink is offline?'

While unplugging the fibre optic from his aug, the man gave Cormac a puzzled look. 'Are you feeling okay?'

Cormac glanced down at the larger autodoc, now retracting from his leg. 'I'm fine, as far as it goes.'

'Memory loss?' the man enquired.

'Some, but it's coming back fast.'

'Well . . . you'll get these momentary glitches after a head injury like that.'

'Why are you saying my gridlink is offline?'

It had been taken offline by an AI once it was decided that, after thirty years of access, he had been losing his humanity and thus his effectiveness as an ECS agent. However, it had since spontaneously reinstated itself, though no one seemed able to provide a good explanation why. He supposed that, being simply grateful for its restoration, he had not made sufficient enquiries. Anyway, it was certainly functioning right now.

'Erm . . .' The man blinked and tilted his head, obviously accessing data through his aug. 'Definitely no other damage . . .'

'Just answer the question please.'

Sensation abruptly returned to the rest of Cormac's body, and he slowly eased himself upright.

'I'm saying it's offline because the bio-haematic power supply is disconnected and all the laminar storage within the link itself is dead.'

'Thank you,' said Cormac, now looking round for his enviro-suit. Unable to locate it, he decided it had probably been cut away from his body and discarded. However, he did see other familiar items lying on a steel tray on a work surface over to one side: Shuriken, his thin-gun and some spare clips, that Europan dart.

'Are you *sure* you're all right?'

'Certainly.'

'I've got other patients—'

'Please, don't let me detain you then.'

The surgeon gestured towards the door. 'One of your—'

'Yes, I know,' said Cormac. 'Hubbert Smith is waiting outside.'

His expression even more puzzled, the medic departed. Cormac lay back again and considered what he had just been told. Either the gridlink was still on in some way that seemed to defy possibility, or else he was gridlinking without the intervention of the technology implanted in his skull. And either this was a new occurrence or the AIs had been lying to him. He was rather uncomfortable with this second option, not because he thought AIs only ever told the truth but because he immediately felt it was the most likely answer. So, not only was he able to perceive things in a way theoretically impossible for a human being, he was even gridlinking bare-brained.

Then full memory returned: *And I can move through underspace.*

He shuddered, suddenly also remembering his mentor Horace Blegg's last days while he and Cormac were being pursued by Erebus's biomechs. Blegg had believed himself able to step through U-space, for that was how, apparently, he had escaped the Hiroshima nuclear bomb at the beginning of his incredibly long life. Blegg could also mentally access the AI nets and talk mind-to-mind with AIs. Only at the end had Blegg learned the truth: he was a construct of Earth Central, his memories of stepping through U-space had been falsified to give the impression of continuity – such a U-space jump usually occurring when that construct faced destruction, when its mind was uploaded, edited, then placed in another construct.

Am I just the new Blegg?

This thought had occurred to Cormac before, but really it was pointless speculation of the same kind as that of some people who wondered if their lives were just virtual realities. He must continue living in the belief that his memories were true, else he would despair. And succumbing to the idea that the next time he faced death he would be uploaded and put into a new body would certainly have fatal consequences if he was wrong. He would continue to live to the best of his abilities – that was the only choice.

'Smith,' he said quietly, knowing full well that he did not need to shout in order to attract the attention of a machine capable of hearing the impact of snowflakes.

Hubbert Smith opened the door and entered. He had a standard-range envirosuit draped over his arm, and in one hand held a pair of enviroboots and a sealed pack of disposable underclothes.

'All better now?' the Golem enquired.

Cormac still felt battered, perhaps more so mentally than physically, but he had felt worse. The repairs performed by the medic and the autodocs would still take a little while to settle. Though most physical injuries could be repaired, breaks in bones and tears in tissue being welded, there was a point beyond which it was better to let the body itself, and whatever suite of personal nanites that body possessed, take over, with the result that no one leapt up in prime condition from a surgical table.

'Getting there,' Cormac replied. 'Scar and Arach?'

Smith shook his head. 'They're both back aboard the *King of Hearts*. Arach is a little dented but otherwise fine. Scar . . . Scar is in cold storage.'

Cormac just stared at the Golem for a long moment. What was there to say? All humans and Golem working for ECS knew the risks they ran, and could choose not to undertake them. Cormac liked to think that Scar, even though a construct of Dragon's, had possessed the same choices, though in that respect he could only rely on the assessments scientists like Mika made. But, that aside, he had obviously lost another friend and comrade, and it hurt. He could not help feeling paranoid about how such comrades were continually being stripped away from him, and about how he himself continued to survive – and change. After a moment he turned his thoughts away from such introspection, instead lifting up his hand and studying it, which just like the rest of his body was utterly and aseptically clean. He peered closely at his fingernails, just in case.

Smith said, 'Don't worry – we got the sample. It's been properly analysed, and now search engines are checking ECS records. If she was a Polity citizen, we'll soon learn her identity.'

Cormac lowered his hand. 'Remes said something odd just before that shock wave hit us. Apparently we weren't supposed to be here at all.'

'Wild goose chase seem to be the right words to apply.' Smith placed the garments down on the surgical table.

Cormac slid off the table and stood upright, then opened the pack of underclothes and quickly began pulling them on.

'So who sent us after the goose?'

'One of Erebus's agents operating in Jerusalem's camp, apparently,' Smith replied, 'but I don't know any further details. When we get back to the ship, you'll be able to talk to the one investigating this.'

Obviously there was still Jain-tech in the area, and therefore com security was still an issue, otherwise Cormac would have been able to connect to the *King of Hearts* directly from here by using his gridlink – the one that wasn't supposed to be functioning. He quickly pulled on the envirosuit and boots, then went to gather his meagre belongings. Strapping on Shuriken and pocketing both the gun and the dart, he briefly wondered what such a scarcity of personal possessions said about him.

As they exited the medbay, Cormac noticed his surgeon in a side room with another patient before the door was quickly closed. All that was left of the individual on the surgical table had been a partially cooked torso and a head. Maybe one of those with a 'little doctor' inside keeping him alive? Besides the medical staff there were numerous walking wounded here. He spotted a woman with her right arm missing at the elbow, brain-like tissue sealing the stump, indicating that she also contained a little doctor, and before long he realized that thus far he had not seen a single human being on this world without some kind of augmentation – either visible or embedded like those little doctors or a gridlink. Those grid-linked were evident simply by the way they carried themselves, though Cormac could confirm the presence of the hardware by a quick peek inside their skulls.

'How many others died during our operation?' he asked.

'Only fifteen.'

Cormac knew that, in the context of the casualties of the

numerous battles taking place across this section of the Line, it was a comparatively small number, but he felt personally responsible for those fifteen. And because their deaths actually hurt him, it also occurred to him that his usefulness as an ECS agent might well be coming to an end. Conscience was all very well, but guilt was merely a hindrance in an occupation where 'ruthless' was part of the job description.

They entered an elevator shaft whose very presence demonstrated just how antiquated this atmosphere ship must be and perhaps why it had been recently knocked out of the sky. They glided down three floors without anyone joining them, eventually stepped out into a wide hold whose side wall had been torn out by the crash, and headed outside through the jagged gap. Gazing around at the churned-up ground, Cormac located the *King of Hearts* and headed towards it, soon mounting its ramp. Within minutes Cormac was standing on the black glass floor of the bridge, with Arach and Hubbert Smith hovering a pace behind him. The gap in this line-up that Scar should have filled seemed to exacerbate a sore spot inside Cormac's skull.

'I take it there's someone who wants to speak to me?' he enquired.

'That is so,' replied King.

'Well, now would be a good time,' Cormac said flatly, assuming King was playing silly games again.

'Not everyone can be at your beck and call,' King replied. 'Just wait one moment.'

Suitably chastened, Cormac waited, but it was not for long. A line suddenly sliced down to the black glass floor and out of it folded the hologram of a human figure.

Cormac recognized this apparition at once. 'Azroc,' he said.

The Golem nodded in acknowledgement.

'You're a long way from Coloron,' Cormac observed.

'I was on that fleet that went to your rescue, the one that Erebus all but wiped out. You could say that the experience has widened my horizons.'

'All our horizons have now been widened, though maybe our futures have been consequently shortened,' Cormac replied. 'We weren't supposed to be here?'

'You were given false orders by an agent of Erebus. The same agent's remains show without a doubt that it was a product of Jain technology—'

'And yet it managed to infiltrate the heart of your operation there? I thought we had the means of detecting that technology now.'

'Active Jain technology can, in most cases, be detected by the nature of the code it uses and the EM output of its nanoscale interactions. However, though this agent was created using Jain technology, it wasn't actually *using* the same.'

'I see, so there could be any number of these . . . agents among us?'

'That is so.'

'Please continue.'

'Having analysed the infiltrating agent's files I've discovered some quite startling anomalies. For though he was in a position to cause us a great deal of damage, he did not do so.'

'Waiting to deliver a killer blow, maybe?'

'Possibly.'

'You sound unsure.'

'Even without revealing himself, there were things he could have done that would have resulted in catastrophic failures in our defence, yet the only overt action he took that could have resulted in deaths was to issue you with false orders.'

'So those false orders prove that my mission was important, and that Erebus wanted to stop me. So did this agent do anything else that's relevant to me?'

'It concealed information about the owners of Europan dart guns,' said Azroc bluntly. 'The searches have thus far only tracked down and eliminated forty per cent of the guns capable of firing the dart you found. However, something was flagged for immediate attention but concealed by the same agent. It seems two Europan dart guns were sent by a woman on Europa as gifts to her twin sons on Klurhammon.'

'I presume their files are already on their way to me?'

'*King of Hearts* has them, but really all you need to know is their names.'

'Enlighten me.'

'The twins' names are Aladine and Ermoon, while the mother's name is Ariadne. Their surname, if such it can be called, is Taser 5.'

Even though that particular investigation had passed out of his remit, Cormac still remembered the surname. It was a particularly important one since another bearer of that name had once been an overseer of the Cassius Project. She was a haiman, a murderer and the owner of a Jain node – which made her particularly dangerous.

'Orlandine Taser 5,' he recalled. 'Tell me, was this infiltrating agent also hampering those trying to find her?'

'Not really,' Azroc replied. 'But then they, besides dispersing hunter-killer programs to try and locate her if she ever used the nets, had decided that Orlandine must have fled the Polity.'

'*Had* decided?' Cormac noted.

'Two thefts within the Polity were also flagged and also concealed. The infiltrator created an HK program to hunt down and erase any further information pertaining to them.'

'Thefts?' Cormac queried.

'One involved a cargo runcible and the other a mothballed war runcible.' Azroc winced. 'And Orlandine stole both of them.'

'You have to be shitting me.'

'I shit you not.'

'So you're telling me she managed to steal a mobile fortress loaded with runcible tech whose purpose was to move entire Polity fleets or throw asteroids at Prador dreadnoughts and, if necessary, to drop moons on Prador-occupied worlds?' Cormac spoke with polite precision up to the point of saying, 'Aren't these fucking things properly guarded?'

'It was guarded by over twenty veteran war drones, but it seems they now do her bidding.'

Cormac just stood still for a long moment, then turned slightly and glanced over his shoulder to where Arach was crouching.

'Oh,' he said. 'Then I guess Orlandine is only marginally less of a catastrophe in progress than Erebus is.'

'One could suppose that there is not much of a distinction to make,' observed Azroc.

'Yes.' Cormac could see it now. All this mayhem here on the border was just distraction. Erebus's infiltrator was concealing the *real* attack involving this Orlandine and her war runcible. 'Do we have any idea where this war runcible is now?'

'We have no idea at all.'

'Then we need to find it, and fast.'

'Evidently,' Azroc replied with dry bitterness.

11

For the duration of the Prador–human war every type of combat was engaged in and every possible weapon employed. A moon was flung from a cargo runcible to destroy a Prador dreadnought, and there was even hand-to-hand fighting between humans and those huge and lethal aliens – usually with messy and unhappy consequences for the humans, it has to be admitted. Terror was a weapon regularly employed by both sides: the Prador inspired it quite naturally by just being themselves, but for the Polity that weapon was the assassin drone. These killers either operated alone or in pairs. Their prime purpose was to infiltrate Prador dreadnoughts, stations and ground bases in order to turn the adults of that breed into 'crab salad'. Usually they did this in as messy and frightening manner as possible for the aliens: diatomic acid injected into the carapace; complete removal of the carapace and immobilization so the victim would be eaten alive by its own ship lice; immobilization and slow roasting over a fire; or by taking control of the Prador's method of locomotion – their adults were often devoid of limbs so used AG, reaction jets or maglev to get about – and attaching numerous mines to it, then using it as a weapon against them. The drones were, like most drones of the time, fashioned in the shape of various lethal arthropods and other nasty creatures. They possessed minds as hard and sharp as their outside appearances. With remorseless cruelty they killed thousands of Prador adults, their sum purpose to inspire sufficient terror in the survivors so they would divert resources to defence that would otherwise have been used for attack. It worked too. There's nothing quite like knowing that something out there wants to slowly saw you into tiny pieces and feed them to your children, to inspire you to double your guard.
— *'Modern Warfare' lecture notes from EBS Heinlein*

'Time for you to go, Bludgeon,' said Orlandine.

The little war drone controlling *Heliotrope* and its attached cargo runcible merely sent a binary acknowledgement, then the ship threw a flame out behind it and quickly receded from direct view. Once out of the black asteroid field, it would U-jump to the Anulus black hole, but even then Orlandine would maintain the U-space link between the war runcible and *Heliotrope*, since the weapon and its magazine needed to remain connected.

Now Orlandine turned her attention to the little craft those two wormships had been pursuing. It was still holding off while awaiting her docking instructions, and now she needed to make preparations.

'Knobbler, send some of your comrades down to Dock Fifteen and make sure they're ready for trouble.'

'Already on their way.'

Orlandine checked her internal views and observed the double spider, the scorpion and the hissing cockroach clattering their way through internal corridors to the dock indicated. She scanned them to check what armament they carried and again felt some reservations. The three drones were so thoroughly packed with weapons, munitions, charged-up capacitors and laminar batteries that the accidental detonation of one of them would excise a large portion of the war runcible. She had, on first taking control of the runcible, considered saying something about this to Knobbler, then decided against it. She had to accept that entities as old as these, who had survived the Prador–human war, knew what they were doing.

Through her mycelium spread throughout the war runcible, she quickly shunted energy and other resources to the area around Dock Fifteen. Peering out from that location at the stationary ship, she experienced a moment of horripilation on again seeing the legate craft bound underneath it like a sucked-out insect in a spider's web. She was also extremely wary, since her scans of the vessel were being easily defeated and her informational probes being bounced. She guessed that the voice that had spoken to her belonged to the larger ship's AI, but she now wondered what *his* boss might be. It was almost as if a sense of that unknown entity was bleeding back through her scans and probes, with a hint of something dark and powerful.

That other presence aboard the ship worried her, but she needed the information it had obtained. Her first encounter with a wormship – the one that had nearly got her killed and from which she had netted Fiddler Randal – had already demonstrated the dangers of not being completely up to date. She was prepared therefore to risk this ship docking if whatever was aboard could supply her with the required camouflage.

Orlandine again opened her channel to the hovering vessel.

'What's your name?'

'Vulture,' replied the voice, 'running a ship called the *Harpy*. Such a joyous working of serendipity don't you think?'

Definitely a Polity AI, quite possibly a war drone, given that sort of attitude.

'Well, Vulture, while you proceed now to Dock Fifteen' – she sent the location – 'perhaps you can explain yourself further. Specifically I'd like you to tell me something about this Fiddler Randal.'

'Fiddler Randal is a virus Erebus picked up at some point. I would guess he was originally a human mind in a flesh-and-blood human. He clearly hates Erebus and wants to see the entity splattered, so copies himself everywhere through Erebus's structure to work to that end. But why am I telling you this? You yourself either have a copy of Randal or have encountered one.'

The ship had fired up its steering jets and was now propelling itself towards the dock in question. The three drones were already down in the bay area – two of them concealed and only the scorpion visible. Orlandine's resources were now in place there: she could burn out the entire area with a fire hot enough to fracture ceramal, but perhaps that wasn't such a great idea considering the munitions those three drones were carrying. More important were her other resources: there she had every worm and virus at her disposal and numerous means of delivering them, both by physical connection and electromagnetic means.

'How do you know that I have encountered or possess a copy of Randal?'

'My one told me.'

'If you could elaborate?'

'Stop fucking around, Orlandine. You were advised someone would arrive here bringing precisely what we're bringing you, so what's the problem?'

'Very well.' Orlandine wanted to question further but guessed she would find out more soon enough. In any event, she couldn't afford not to let this vessel dock. She studied its slow approach, continued trying to probe it but learned nothing new. The twinned ship finally docked, and she instantly recognized what walked out of it – as did the three war drones waiting in the bay, from the way their weapons came online all at once.

'You've brought something for me,' she said to the menacing figure.

Mr Crane nodded briefly and information began to flow across to her, even though she had not herself permitted it. For half a second everything stood poised on the edge of disaster, until Orlandine began to take a look at what he had sent: the wealth of secret codes, the multiple methods of configuring the chameleon-ware she was already spreading throughout the war runcible, and the knowledge that she had a lot of work to do and very little time.

*

The accretion disc seemed to be some living body and the horde now rushing towards the two Dragon spheres its immune response to them. Mika firmly controlled the impulse to run and find somewhere to hide, then began analysing all those weird forms out there in the brief time they were open to her inspection before an equatorial particle cannon, white laser or CTD proceeded to fry them. She realized they were a much more diverse collection of Jain biomechs than those utilized by Erebus, yet none of them approached the size or coherence of a full wormship. There were lenses but all of them deformed, and they often had some other entity attached to them either in symbiosis, mutualism or parasitism – it was difficult to tell. The structures that made up wormships rarely achieved more than a few turns of a spiral, and though numerous bacilliforms now fell like hail towards the Dragon spheres, they never melded together to form those thousand-mile-high walls she had seen in recordings of previous conflicts with these things.

Clearly a guiding intelligence was lacking here. This was Jain technology initiated into growth by such an intelligence then abandoned. She had studied similar growth burgeoning on an asteroid in orbit about the red giant sun Ruby Eye. This stuff tried to spread itself in the same way as a virus or bacillus – with the kind of cunning selected by evolution but utterly without sentience. By now, if there had been a guiding intelligence, their attack would have been halted, for none of these biomechs managed to get even close to the Dragon spheres, yet they continued to approach with a kind of automated futility.

'What happens if one of these things actually reaches your surface?' she asked.

The voice in her head replied, 'None of them will.'

'Yeah, but what if?'

'They would not be able to penetrate me unless many thousands of them reached my surface all at once.'

'And then?'

'I would sterilize that area.'

It occurred to Mika that maybe she should have stayed safely inside Dragon, because 'sterilize' was almost certainly too mild a term to describe what might be needed here. She returned her attention to her instruments, but then, a moment later, an orange glow in the surrounding fug dragged her attention upward. Though there were all sorts of flashes and detonations occurring about the spheres, they were short-lived, whereas this light remained constant.

'What's that?'

'A planet in the process of formation.'

'Are we going anywhere near it?' Mika asked, fascinated.

'Very close,' Dragon replied. 'The entities currently attacking us show no inclination to hold back, therefore are not too bright, and it has become evident that few of them possess anything more than rudimentary engines.'

'And.'

'I suggest that you strap yourself tightly into your chair and just watch.'

Mika quickly obeyed, then eased the chair back to get a better view of her surroundings. It seemed as if a wind was blowing out there in the fug because, as well as the constant motion in it from the passage of the Dragon sphere, it was now swirling rapidly and she could detect cross-currents. Something massive then appeared out of it to her left and she observed an asteroid slowly turning, its surface coated with snaky growth so that it seemed like some massive fossil. Biomechs leaped from its surface, chemical drives sputtering to life, but the Dragon spheres outpaced them and soon they and their rocky home had receded from view.

Next Mika felt the tug of gravity at a slant to her present position, which produced the illusion of the floor tilting. The equatorial cannons had ceased firing by now, but Dragon's white lasers continued to stab through the murk. The meteor lasers of the conferencing unit were also firing, things flashing like firecrackers and blinking out all about her. Slowly, the fug began to clear and she gained a clearer direct view of the pursuing horde. Briefly she glimpsed the other sphere off to one side, then turning her head gazed upon the volcanic glare of a new world in the process of formation.

The world itself was misshapen, probably as the result of a recent impact, for one entire side of it was a magma lake into which a titanic mountain was steadily sinking. Plumes of magma regularly spewed miles into the air, hellish cracks opened even as she watched, and the surface flickered with the constant explosion of strikes from a never-ending meteor storm. It rained meteors here, it rained fire, and fire spewed from the ground, but steadily the Dragon spheres descended towards this chaos.

It seemed to take forever for this nascent world to make the transition from an object hanging in space to a plain extending below her and a horizon ahead. Mika gazed down upon rivers and lakes of lava glaring through a sooty black crust. The tug of the planet was countering that of the gravplates below her, so she felt light in her chair. She imagined herself in some glassy cockpit set into the surface of the Dragon sphere, just below its equator, and oriented towards a point midway between the ground below and the horizon. The sky ahead was cut diagonally with parallel meteor trails, which meant the debris orbiting beyond this world must have formed into a swirl pattern, and the horizon flashed with explosions as if of some distant battle.

A brief flicker of light dragged her attention over to her left, and in a moment she saw a mushroom cloud boiling up into the sky, but it wasn't some atomic device, just a meteor impacting with the same force. Dragon rocked in the shock wave, and the magma below was whipped up like seawater in a storm, waves of it splashing on sooty shores. Horizontal clouds, like jet vapour trails, spread from either side of the explosion, then were rapidly disrupted by two similar detonations. However, Mika's gaze was drawn upward, by a constant white flickering as if from some faulty light tube, to the flashing of white lasers.

Up above, it was like looking into storm cloud in which burning coals were shifting. Out of this came swarms of Jain biomechs that the two spheres appeared to be struggling to keep at bay. She glanced across at the other sphere, just visible now, and saw its weapons creating a halo of fire above it. Then something fell past, close by her. It was a rod-form sprouting jain tendrils even as she watched it. Quickly it receded from sight, then a brief greenish fire marked its point of entry into a magma lake below. Then more of them were raining past her. She saw one abruptly stabilize only a few miles out, and begin to rise again, but after a moment it shuddered and just burst apart, spreading fragments like purple skin across the atmosphere. Another managed to rise, but other rod-forms falling from above it changed course to intercept it, sprouting tendrils as they came. They grabbed on like drowning swimmers clutching at one who had managed to stay on the surface, till their combined weight dragged it down. Mika saw the whole mass impact, break apart and begin belching smoke. It was only then that she noticed how much closer to the ground now were the twin Dragon spheres.

'Why are they falling?' Mika asked.

'They cannot sustain gravtech,' Dragon replied.

Mika remembered then the wild Jain tech she had studied once on that asteroid orbiting Ruby Eye. Confined to that rock, it had not tried to use anything more complicated to escape the surface than some form of rail-gun.

'That's because gravtech is related to U-tech, and the latter requires conscious sentient control,' she suggested.

'Yes,' Dragon replied, and she felt some satisfaction with her answer until the entity added, 'so your AIs tell you.'

It was deluging Jain biomechs now and the surface below kept disappearing amid clouds of smoke. A lens-ship half a mile across, and into whose side it seemed part of a wormship had impacted, fell into view. Jet flames were regularly blasting from numerous orifices underneath it but, though they seemed to be holding it up, they could not stabilize it. It drifted towards her, then the bar of a white laser – made visible by all the smoke – cut across it. Some internal detonation flung the wormish part of it free and it turned over, accelerating towards the ground, where it disappeared into a smoke cloud. Briefly she glimpsed an explosion down there, before Dragon moved beyond it.

After some hours Mika's fascination with this spectacle began to pall. She shifted her seat upright again and began to check her instruments. Robotically methodical, she collected data, recorded events and then made analyses. She realized that the biomechs, having adapted to the environment of the accretion disc, now could not survive in the environment the Dragon spheres had lured them into. Was this stuff a danger, then, it appearing so simple? Yes, of course it was, for every one of those things out there could produce Jain nodes. In a moment of horror it occurred to her that Jain nodes were already being produced here in huge quantities and ejected from this accretion disc to spread out into space – and these would not take nearly as long to reach human civilization as those ejected by the remnants of the Maker civilization, though the span of time involved would be thousands if not tens of thousands of years. Maybe by then the Polity would be able to stop them, for though ECS now possessed the means of detecting such objects, that would be as much use as being able to detect individual grains in a sandstorm.

Several more hours passed and, as the two Dragon spheres parted to circumvent the massive mountain still sinking into the lake of magma it had made, the pathetic rain of biomechs began to abate. Mika noted that the two spheres were once again higher from the ground. Checking her instruments she saw that the cloud of their pursuers was almost gone, fast draining away. Sensor readings directed behind showed numerous fires with spectrographic readings indicating both metals and organic compounds. Next the two spheres were into cloud, and the gravplates below her became the only pull.

'Where now?' she asked.

'To the core.'

'The sun?'

'Near it,' Dragon replied. 'The graveyard of ships orbits close to it, and will fall into the sun some years hence.'

'Graveyard of ships?'

'Our sensors are better than yours, Mika,' said Dragon. 'We see the old ships in the forest, and through the thin fabric we feel the others.'

Others?

Mika did not ask – and did not even want to know – about some infinite writhing mass seeming to lie just off the edge of her perception.

The back alley was choked with junk: discarded computer hardware, biodegrading litter accumulated in soggy drifts from which frilly golden fungi were sprouting, an ageing open-topped gravcar spattered with bird shit from which the motor had obviously been removed, a couple of flimsy screens still running text while discharging their photoelectric load from the previous day's sunshine. Chevron gazed around at this mess: it was typically human and her new addition to it would make no difference. She strode over to the car and, with a flip of her shoulder, dumped her wet blanket-wrapped load into the back seats.

Chevron had assumed that obtaining a schematic of the ancient drainage system underneath Xanadu was simply a matter of briefly searching the nets, but surprisingly that basic information had not been there. As it transpired, however, it was possible to discover through the nets someone who did know about it, so Chevron obtained what she required by paying over a few credits to the one historian who, for some unfathomable reason, thought this subject worthy of research. It hadn't been strictly necessary to kill him afterwards, but he had lived alone so Chevron felt it an easy precaution she could take. Anyway, he was so utterly human in his disorder and habits, and she found him dislikeable, though she admitted to herself there weren't any humans she did like.

Her load discarded, she now moved over to one side of the alley, and pacing out the distance from the wall of one building, finally halted at a point about halfway along. Below her feet the damp surface of old reused furnace bricks looked no different to anywhere else. She scanned them carefully, then took a further pace forward and squatted down. Holding her hand out, she shifted internal mycelial structures and her fingers extended, flattening out to become sharp at their tips. She reached down and slid them into the crack between two bricks, levering one out with a crunch, then another, then began to scoop them out at high speed and stack them to one side. Within a few minutes she had revealed an old ceramic manhole cover underneath. It was sealed with glassy epoxy, she noticed, so another internal instruction caused her forefinger to blur into motion. She inserted it down alongside the rim of the cover and with a high whine it sliced through the ancient glue. In a moment she had cleared out a groove right round the cover and, inserting all her flattened fingers, levered it up as if using a crowbar. Immediately the stink of human sewage rose up to meet her, and she wrinkled her nose.

Humans were so messy.

Chevron scooped the dislodged bricks into the manhole, since she wanted to leave as little evidence of her presence here as possible. A squealing and hissing ensued down in the darkness, as creatures fled – ratadiles, almost certainly. She first increased the light amplification of her eyes, then lowered herself onto the ladder leading down – it was fortunately made of ceramic so had not rusted – and, after drawing the manhole cover back into place, descended further. Soon she was in the sewer, which, having been constructed to accommodate the heavy rainfall that occurred locally, was large enough to accommodate her standing upright. There would be some tighter sections to negotiate ahead, but no problem, since she would simply change her shape to suit them.

Chevron advanced, wading through knee-deep sewage, meanwhile opening coded communication links. In a moment, as well as the fetid tunnel ahead, she was gazing upon numerous different scenes fed from within the runcible complex some two miles away on the surface. Some of these views were seen through the eyes of the separatists infiltrating the area, relayed by their augs, others were from cams no larger than pinheads positioned strategically to give her a good view of the action.

'Akiri, are our people now in position?' she enquired.

The view witnessed currently through Akiri's eyes was of an open bar area laid out about what looked like a Caribbean beach in the middle of a wide and crowded concourse.

'Most of them are,' confirmed Akiri, 'but we've yet to get the main explosives to the Pillar.'

The methodology was simple. Groups of twenty insurgents each were going for the ten passenger runcibles in operation here, their aim to grab hostages, secure each area and then set explosives on each runcible. This would keep the AI very occupied while the main thrust of their attack got under way against the Pillar – a circular building in which the AI itself was sited at the junction of six concourses.

Chevron checked again through her multiple views. As Akiri had said, the groups intending to attack the passenger runcibles were mostly in place in the main lounge or various sub-lounges, supposedly awaiting their transmission slots some hours hence. The lev-trolley supposedly loaded with discs of amber, which were in fact explosives, was on its way in. Chevron noted that the person now guiding the trolley along the concourse was not the same one originally given this task. She checked recorded data supplied from the sensors she had hidden in just about every separatist base and home in this city, and was gratified to witness the original trolley pusher being garrotted and then shoved into a sewer rather similar to this one. The woman had apparently had second thoughts about her assignment, her chances of survival and the fallout for her two children . . . and people didn't live to have third thoughts within Chevron's organization.

'When do we start?' Akiri asked.

'I've mined the north wall of the runcible complex,' Chevron replied, lying as smoothly as ever, 'but I need to shift the ship into position to get you out, which should take me about another forty minutes.'

'Seems a shame to run after such a victory.'

'But necessary.' Chevron halted for a moment, noting that the ratadiles were starting to lose their nervousness of her. 'You simply cannot remain on the world where you killed a runcible AI. You would spend the rest of your life running and be of no real value to the cause thereafter.'

'Okay.' Akiri was obviously getting nervous. 'What about groundside and orbital defences?'

'As I told you before, most of them will go down with the AI, and when I bring in an ECS Rescue ship, the rest will ignore it.' Chevron eyed a big ratadile humping up its ridged back nearby like an angry cat and shuffling forward. 'You're not having second thoughts are you, Akiri?'

'No, Chevron.'

'Then do your duty and I will do mine. Now I've got to get this ship off the ground. Out.' She abruptly closed down the link.

The ratadile raised its long jaws out of the muck and chose that moment to go for her. It surged forward in writhing bounds, then pounced. Chevron's hand shot up and closed on its throat, stopping dead a ton of pseudo-reptile in mid-air. Its body crashed into her, jaws wide open just before her face, but she was as solid as a girder, nano-filaments having bound her feet to the slippery stone below, and her body as dense as lead. Its neck had snapped with the impact and she gazed for a moment into its zebra-patterned gullet before twitching her hand from side to side to listen to the crunching of its neck bones, then tossed it to one side. She moved on, hearing its kin behind her coming out of hiding to sniff at their dead fellow. She was a hundred yards further along the sewer when she heard the splashing and snarling that told her they had finally realized her victim had made the transition from alpha pack leader into convenience food.

Chevron pondered on the fact that it was usually only the older ratadiles that attacked humans descending into their domain, which was because of the bloody history of this place before the Polity subsumed it. The creatures had grown used to a regular diet of those who had earned the displeasure of the city governors. That was how humans lived when there wasn't an AI about to show them what to do.

Three more attacks from ratadiles ensued before Chevron grew bored with this game and turned on her chameleonware. Anyway, sections of the sewer wall here were low-friction plasticrete, or tunnel compression-glass baked out of the surrounding sandy soil by the machines that had bored the tunnels, which meant she was now entering the area of sewers repaired and strengthened to withstand the weight of the runcible complex above. With her visual acuity now set at maximum and special scanning programs running, she soon began to spot the occasional sensor the size of a pinhead and one or two old-style holocams like metal fingers suspended in small gimbals hanging from the ceiling. Here and there ran ducts for optics and superconducting cables, also the occasional pipe for water or liquid hydrogen, through which ran lines of old S-con that required cooling – a past solution for supplying fuel and electricity from the same source.

Soon Chevron arrived at a point where the remnants of the old sewers ended. At the juncture of five old tunnels stood a cylindrical chamber with walls of plasticrete. Numerous sensors were mounted here, and from the ceiling depended a saucer-shaped security drone whose purpose, doubtless, was to keep vermin from crawling into the numerous shiny pipes that debouched here.

Chevron studied a row of six of them protruding from the wall. Fresh clean water was pouring from three, but luckily not from the one she required. No raw sewage made it out of the runcible complex, even though thousands of humans passed through there. All of it was processed by engineered bacteria, dried, and then transported out in compacted blocks to be used as fertilizer by the agricultural concerns of this same world. A small proportion of the water removed from that waste was purified and fed into fusion plants, or recycled, but since this was such a busy complex, there was always an excess, and this was where it drained away.

Chevron walked over to the pipe she wanted and knew that now was the time to really set things in motion. She opened a channel to her ship, where it was sitting underneath the ocean some two hundred miles away from her. The vessel's machines had now made twenty-eight thermonuclear imploders – one more than required – and was right now detaching from the mycelium that penetrated down through the seabed below it. She gave it further instructions and watched as the quarter-mile-long grub of a vessel shook off years of detritus and begin to drift towards the surface of the orange sea. Once Chevron was in position, she wanted the ship in position too, and as fast as possible. There was no telling how quickly other Polity resources might respond to her attack.

Time now to go in. She gazed at the grid extending across the mouth of the foot-wide pipe. If she cut that away the damage might later be detected by the sensors here, after she had departed, but of course there was no need for that. She dropped her hands to rest down by her sides and began cancelling her emulation programs. To her own view, though neither the drone nor any of the sensors here could actually see her, her clothing just lost all its colour and turned metallic grey, then began to sink into her body. Similarly went her blond hair, her skin colour, the pigment in her eyes, and soon she was a naked metallic statue. But then her human curves began to flatten out as she extended in height and began to bow forwards, her head growing narrow and protruding like a rhino's horn. This protuberance writhed its way through one hole in the mesh before her, and the rest began to follow, but not all through the same hole. Her body, now a foot-thick worm of Jain mycelial nano-technology, passed through the mesh like jelly and surged on along the pipe.

'Akiri, I've got the ship in the air,' she lied – as she had always been lying to the separatists here. 'It's time for you to begin your attack.'

Still proceeding along the pipe, Chevron studied the multiple scenes from the runcible complex above her. In one runcible lounge a squat little man in white businesswear opened his particularly bulky briefcase and extracted from it what looked like a large document tube. A twist here and a pull there, and suddenly the tube possessed suspiciously positioned handles.

'Everyone on the floor!' he bellowed, and then fired a stream of explosive bullets towards the ceiling. When no one seemed to respond, and as some of his fellow insurgents began to produce their own weapons, he lowered his aim to one man nearby and fired at point-blank range. In another runcible lounge a female fighter for the cause did not see any use in warnings, and simply opened up on a nearby group of tourists. Bodies flew apart, people began screaming, blood spattered everywhere. She then just stood there staring blankly while the insurgents with her shouted their orders and herded hostages together. Similar scenes played out at all the other passenger runcibles, while by the Pillar separatists began collecting large amber discs from the lev-trolley and heading off to place them around the outer wall of that large circular structure.

Chevron noted a junction in the pipe ahead, and though she did not have a schematic of the infrastructure directly underlying the runcible complex, she was aware of her precise position and of the location of where she needed to be. She therefore chose the pipe leading to her left and oozed her way into it, since that way took her closest. Just then she detected an increase in pressure ahead of her, scanned along the pipe and found water coming her way. Immediately she extended her fibrous body, both backwards and forwards, and formed a hollow through the centre of it, flattening herself against the inner circumference of the pipe. For if the AI detected a blockage while the separatists were attacking above, it would become suspicious of what might be happening underground. The flow of water hit her and passed through, but she did not have enough time to wait for it to slacken off so oozed on, now a kind of pipe herself.

Soon, checking her position by scanning a nearby bleed pipe and the magnetic anomaly directly below her, she halted and brought an array of ceramo-carbide cutting heads to bear against the inner surface of the pipe beside her and cut a circular hole three inches across. Lifting up the circle of metal, she oozed into the hole, entirely plugging it with her complex filament body as she flowed through until at last snapping the disc back down and extruding a powerful glue to stick it into place. So far, so easy. Now she occupied a small area through which ran power ducts connected to a fusion reactor she had detected below, and to which the bleed pipe led. Now things were going to get more difficult as she went directly up against the AIs sensors and detectors, which from here on would not be easily fooled. She paused for a moment to check how things were going above.

The separatist who had shot the man was now lying on the floor with his neck broken, while his target was closing in on another member of that group. The man was no man, as evidenced by the gleaming ceramal and torn syntheflesh exposed under ripped and burned clothing. Oblivious to the bullets still slamming into him, he crashed into three separatists, his movements a blur, and all of them dropped never to rise again. This group had been unlucky enough to run straight into a Golem, and shortly they would all be dead, as would the separatists in four other runcible lounges who had similarly encountered Chevron's erstwhile kind. Now ceiling drones were also involved and pulse-gun fire had begun to rain down. A detonation tore through one lounge, leaving horrific carnage, as one separatist realized the futility of trying to get near a runcible, the impossibility of evading capture and ever getting out of there alive.

285

Chevron meanwhile cut away part of a power duct, and now, her body compressed as thin as a rope, began to flow along inside that. Shortly she began to encounter sensors incorporated in the duct sheath, their micro-optics linking them to security sub-minds. Each one required intricate and perpetual subversion. She knew that any slight change in the feed from the sensors would register with the sub-minds, but the sub-minds themselves would be otherwise distracted by what was going on above her. The import-ance level of such changes would therefore be lower and, by Chevron's calculations, would be attributed to the electrical surges through the superconductors within the duct as the weapons being used above drew extra power. Within a minute her foremost part reached the point where the duct ended in individual supercon-ducting cables, wrapped in insulation, passing through thick armour. Now, nearly a hundred feet long, the far-extended body behind her still subverting the sensors, she narrowed even further, chose one particular cable and began to eat away its insulation as she tracked along its length, using herself to replace that insulation. The cable wove here and there, branching to feed various machines along the way. Upon reaching a transformer, she noted she was almost at the limit of her extension and began drawing in her rear end, carefully retracting it from the sensors behind her. Now was the moment of greatest danger, and she prepared herself internally for the possibility of detection. She could lose as much as half her structure without any great decrease in efficiency, but any more than that and her chances of ultimate success began to spiral down.

Chevron's view of events occurring above was becoming dim and intermittent, and shortly the signals from the various cams would be cut off completely by the shielding surrounding her. Things were going very badly for the separatists: eight groups had been wiped out, the remainder surviving by holding hostages, and yet not one runcible had been blown up. According to a mild voice now issuing from the ceiling drones, the survivors had five seconds in which to drop their weapons or they would die. It amused Chevron to see the separatists futilely trying to use their hostages as physical shields, clearly not understanding that at such close range the drones could accurately target the individual pores on their noses.

Around the Pillar itself the amber explosives were all in place, and Chevron noted that the only humans anywhere near the Pillar were separatists. The Xanadu AI had obviously spotted what they were up to some minutes ago and, via their augmentations or by using a directional sound beam, had contacted all the civilians in the area and herded them away. Now the separatists too began to head for safety, and Akiri was the first to walk straight into the hard-fields that surrounded the Pillar. She gazed about her in dismay, realizing what had happened. She then screamed something relating to that strange human concept called 'freedom' and sent the detonation signal. The concentric area between Pillar and hard-fields filled with fire, which quickly went out as it burned up all the oxygen. Occasional gaps in the billowing smoke revealed smouldering scraps of what might have once been Akiri and the rest of her team. These gaps also revealed the Pillar itself, its cosmetic outer layer stripped away to expose three feet of ceramal armour. The explosion had been no danger at all to the AI within, just as the remaining separatists elsewhere ceased to be a danger to the passenger runcibles as they quickly surrendered or died.

Once beyond the transformer, Chevron divided to track along single S-con wires, circumvented electro-optic transformers, slid through the laminations of storage crystal and ate along optic fibres, replacing them bit by bit with herself. Now she was coasting by some very heavy security and it was only a matter of seconds before she would be detected. However, finally she was almost in position. It came then: power surges, a particle beam playing up the duct through which she had entered, chemical explosives in crystal laminations detonating, diatomic acid flowing around C-con cables. She surged forward to where thousands of optic cables entered a single black metal conduit, a third of her body destroyed behind her. An atomic shear sliced through those optics, separating her from more of her body, which died in a sudden intense oxygen fire. Then she reached the item to which all those separate optics were connected: a lozenge of crystal six inches long – a quantum processor, a mind. Even as she reached it, interfaces began to physically break away, but she leaped the gap and made rapid connections.

'What are you?' wondered the Xanadu AI.

'I am your death,' Chevron replied, as she began to rip apart its mind.

12

The human body, like all evolved life, is a collection of mostly cooperating cells that are the product of aeons of parasitism, mutualism and symbiosis. The dracomen, while apparently a similar organism – ostensibly designed by Dragon to show what dinosaurs might have become had not chance wiped them out – are certainly not such a collection of cells. In fact, dracomen do not possess cells as we know them. They do not even possess DNA, as would any true descendant of the dinosaurs. They are not the product of natural selection, of chance nor of the vagaries of nature, for they are biological machines that were designed by an entity capable of 'having fun' with the very building blocks of life; of, in fact, creating its own building blocks. The dracomen never possessed appendixes, never suffer from genetic disorders. They do not grow old when their selfish genes have dispensed with them and moved on – because they don't have genes. They can obviously control their internal workings, for certainly they can create other biological mechanisms in the same way and as easily as they reproduce. They are a superb piece of biological design, though there will always remain the question: for what purpose? Are they superior to humans? Humans have primarily served the purpose of their genes and now, however misconceived it might be, the purpose of their own consciousness. The concept of consciousness is debatable when it comes to dracomen, however.
– From QUINCE GUIDE *compiled by humans*

The base of the cold coffin slid out from the wall, its top sliding down inside the wall slot until the coffin reached an angle of thirty degrees to the floor. Gazing at its shape, matching to that of a human being, Cormac felt a better name for it would be a sarcophagus, but such names did not necessarily follow logical rules and, anyway, whenever these objects were occupied, they usually contained cryonically cooled but living human beings, so naming them after boxes usually made to contain corpses was incorrect – except in this case.

Cormac reached down and pressed a button like an inset cartouche, and after a moment the red light beside it turned green. The coffin *whoomphed* as its seals disengaged and the lid hinged up, spilling a cold fog. Cormac studied the contents. Scar's body lay in three pieces, severed at the head and also diagonally across the torso from a point below the right-hand side of the ribcage down to the waist. There were also numerous other deep cuts and tears exposing muscles and internal organs. The sight of these injuries brought home to him just how lucky he himself had been.

'I guess this was too much trauma even for *him* to survive,' he said.

Beside him, Arach reared up and, with a sound like someone rooting through a cutlery drawer, rested his three front feet on the edge of the coffin. The spider drone, whose own torso was scratched and dented, was missing a limb and one of his eyes. He peered down at Scar and made a hissing sound.

'When they're dead that's usually only 'cause there ain't enough left of the body to scrape up with a spade,' he said.

Cormac nodded – he too could not recollect ever seeing a whole dead dracoman, only small parts of them.

Arach's head revolved to look at him directly, and Cormac saw that the damaged eye was not missing just blank and, even as he watched, it winked internal light as a precursor to full functioning as the drone doubtless made internal repairs. 'What they want him for?'

Cormac shrugged. 'Burial maybe?'

Arach snorted.

Cormac looked up. 'Are they here yet, King?'

'They are approaching the ramp now,' replied the attack ship's AI.

Cormac reached into the coffin and touched cold flesh. Scar was still soft, despite the coffin temperature being low enough to freeze any human being solid. This was probably due to his original make-up, since Cormac had found him and his companion alive on a world where the temperature was lower still. The blood in his veins probably contained some sort of antifreeze; if the blood could be called blood at all, and if he actually possessed veins. Withdrawing his hand from the coffin, Cormac blew on his fingertips and waited.

The doors to this cold-coffin store opened to announce the arrival of their visitors. Bird-stepping through came three dracomen, two of them towing a circular lev-platform behind them. Cormac stepped back, and Arach also retreated with a clattering of metallic feet. Without acknowledgement of either drone or man, one dracoman walked over and peered down at Scar, then immediately reached inside to pick up his head and inspect it. The two others pulled the lev-platform closer, then turned it off so it descended to the floor with a *clonk*. The first dracoman now turned and tossed the head to one of its companions, who fielded it and plonked it down on the platform like a rugby player making a touchdown. Certainly, their collecting of the body had nothing to do with respect for the dead.

'What do you want him for?' Cormac asked, as the first dracoman now hauled up the top half of Scar's torso.

No acknowledgement, still. The other two moved over to assist, and in a moment all of Scar's remains were heaped on the platform, whose power was re-engaged. The two began towing it to the door while the first stood gazing contemplatively down into the empty coffin.

'His information must not be lost,' the dracoman said abruptly.

Cormac wondered if he would be seeing Scar again, if dracomen had some way of resurrecting their dead.

'What do you do with that information?' Cormac asked.

'Distribute it.' The dracoman nodded briefly and departed after his companions.

Would numerous dracomen soon possess a portion of Scar's mind, or would they instead make copies so many dracomen could hold Scar entire inside their heads? Did 'information' even necessarily mean thought patterns? Cormac stepped forward to hit the lid cartouche again, then turned and headed for the door, hearing the coffin close behind him and begin to slide back up into the wall.

'How long until we launch?' he asked.

'The moment our friends are clear and the ramp is closed,' King replied.

Out in the corridor, the sound of Arach's feet was muffled by the softer flooring. Cormac glanced back at the drone. 'Go and get yourself fully repaired and restocked,' he said. 'I want you fully ready when I need you.'

As Arach scuttled away, Cormac reflected that the deaths of so many of his comrades recently had sensitized him to Arach's damage, the drone's *weakness*. He wanted Arach ready for anything; he *wanted* the drone to survive.

Now heading to his cabin, he felt a slight jolt as *King of Hearts* rose on AG, then further jolting, compensated for by the gravplate floor, as it accelerated. Pausing to steady himself against the corridor wall, he considered other deaths. There were more than he liked to think about, but one in particular was on his mind at that moment.

It had struck him as odd that the sub-minds running this world until a new runcible AI was initiated had experienced such difficulty tracking down the record of the female captain of the wormship whose destruction had resulted in Scar's death, since her DNA had been recorded in Polity databases. Because of this delay he had made some queries himself through his gridlink and quickly obtained a copy of that record – meanwhile learning that Hubbert Smith already also possessed a copy he had not passed on. Perhaps it was his growing distrust of AIs that kept Cormac quiet, and he made no comment when Smith later transmitted it to him as if only just having received it himself. Comparing the two records, Cormac soon found inconsistencies.

Hubbert's copy of her record named her Henrietta Ipatus Chang, known as Henry to her friends, who on the whole were mostly silicon-brained and heavily armoured like Arach, though she did occasionally associate with humans of the same inclination as herself. She had joined ECS at the youthful age of eighteen, and was fighting and killing Prador in the many vicious ground conflicts during that war by the time she was twenty. She had exited the end of the Prador war as a human version of the war drone: disenfranchised by peace, unable to fit in to this new society nor particularly wanting to fit in either. Throughout the war her best and few surviving friends had been drones and Golem, so when many of them decided to leave the Polity aboard the dreadnought *Trafalgar*, she had asked to join them. It seemed that the Trafalgar AI – which had now become Erebus – had allowed her and certain other humans to join the exodus. Apparently there had been as many as eighty-three of them amid the horde of AIs which defected. Presumably this explained how Henry had ended up as a component slotted into a wormship.

The problem was that the copy of her record that Cormac obtained first was different. This earlier version had it that she had never felt disenfranchised and never in fact joined *Trafalgar*'s exodus. After the war she had continued serving in ECS for another twenty years and had been involved in many subsequent police actions throughout the Polity. Later she was seconded to some black ops mission about which the details were unclear, whereupon she was subsequently listed as missing in action. But this was not the worst of it. When Cormac checked again through the planetary sub-minds, he found that the original record had now been deliberately altered. There were levels of subterfuge here Cormac very much did not like, which now only increased his suspicions about the motives of the Polity AIs in this matter. His suspicions about Hubbert Smith had also been confirmed.

Moving on, Cormac finally reached his cabin and noted that the screen was switched on. It showed the curving planetary horizon already dropping from view, and he realized that King had been using more than the gravplates set in the floor to compensate for the kind of acceleration needed to get them out here this quickly. The glare of the sun lit up several glinting objects, then shadow quickly fell across the scene, as the attack ship put the planet between itself and that distant furnace. But the view was clearer now, and Cormac could see that *King of Hearts* would have to fly with particular care here. Cormac had only ever witnessed so much space junk around devastated worlds the Prador had hit during the war that Henry had fought so hard in. Could this conflict be turning into something as catastrophic as that? At present it was still defined only as a Line war since, though many whole worlds had already been attacked, they represented but a small fraction of the Polity. However, Erebus possessed the capacity to turn this into something more cataclysmic, and Erebus's agents could be anywhere.

Orlandine Taser 5 . . .

She should be his primary focus now, not the unrecoverably

dead, not numberless regrets, not nebulous feelings of guilt or suspicions over the motivation of Polity AIs. He really needed to find her, for it was evident that she controlled Jain technology and had now gained control of a weapon that in some areas of the Polity was considered a myth . . . but then again on some Polity worlds there were those who claimed the entire Prador–human war was simply a horror story created by the AIs to keep human beings in line. As much as Cormac had come to distrust the motivations and agendas of those who now ruled, he himself couldn't deny the reality of that war. Too much fallout from it still remained, as a young ECS groundtrooper he himself had been involved in clearing up some of the mess, and only later, as an ECS agent, had he come to appreciate its truly gigantic scale.

True . . . if my memories are actually true, he speculated, then told himself to shut up. He must drop *that* subject from his mind or else go mad. Just focus on the now: how to find Orlandine.

Underspace was theoretically supposed to possess neither distance nor time. You could enter it at one point in the universe, then exit it a thousand light years away just an instant later – or even *before* you entered it. That was the theory but, as ever, the reality was a lot more complicated. U-space did have dimensions, though whether they could be described as width, depth, breadth and time was debatable. Entering it in one place and leaving it an instant later a thousand light years distant was theoretically possible, yet the same rules applied there as in realspace: the quicker you wanted to move it from point A to point B, the more energy you needed to inject, this increasing in proportion to the mass of the object in question. That was why it took longer to travel X light years by ship than it did for a human to travel the same distance by runcible, or indeed for information to travel by U-com. Travelling through that same continuum, the ship was a massive object carrying its own power supply with it. The human, by contrast, was a very light object being propelled by a fixed device with huge energy resources, while an information package was practically without any mass at all. To most people in the Polity, runcible transportation and U-com might seem instantaneous, but in fact they weren't. But Cormac did not want to travel through U-space right then, he just wondered how far he could see through it with his U-sense; wondered if from here he could spot the war runcible that Orlandine Taser 5 had stolen.

Cormac lay back on his bed and relaxed, releasing his hold upon his U-sense and letting it expand out from where the *King of Hearts* now sat in orbit about Ramone. Soon the sheer scale of the mess here became more evident. Ramone sparkled like a piece of iron just taken from the furnace, for it was the centre of a perpetual meteor storm as chunks of wormship, other Jain constructs and, unfortunately, the remnants of many Polity ships fell into its atmosphere and burned up. Around the planet the debris cloud lay eight thousand miles deep, and certainly over the ensuing years would settle itself into a ring. Also, one astronomical unit out, there was another even larger cloud of debris extending nearly two million miles across. Within this a few remaining Polity ships were still busy hunting, firing missiles into any larger chunks of wormship that appeared to have enough life left in them to regenerate, incinerating stray rod-forms and generally sterilizing the entire area. The rest of the Polity ships, along with the leviathan *Cable Hogue*, had already jumped outsystem to join other battles.

One AU out . . .

With the technology available in the Polity it was easy enough to scan to one astronomical unit, but Cormac was now doing so with just his mind. He pushed the range further, began to gaze upon the other worlds within this system, and wondered if AIs felt as godlike as this. Choosing one of the outer cold worlds, he focused on it closely and peered down through a methane rain storm at a plain of red slabs lying beside a methane sea. It was noticeable that, by so focusing, much else now seemed to blur out of his perception, when that had not been the case for him closer to the attack ship. He pulled his focus away from that distant world, but it shifted sluggishly, seeming to have gained inertia. He pushed further out into the system, but beyond that cold world the perceptual sensation became like wading through treacle. Then he reached a point he could not probe beyond. The rest of the universe was out there, and he could see star systems and the weird indentations they made in U-space, but he could not get any closer to them.

Really, Cormac thought, *I should not be disappointed.* But he was. He blinked, bringing his cabin back into focus. Sitting up on his bed he noticed he was soaked with sweat and inside his skull lay a heaviness presaging a headache. He wiped a hand across his face, then, noticing something, moved that same hand out and studied it. It was shaking but, worse than that, appeared translucent even to his normal vision. He snatched it from sight, realizing what was happening: his U-sense was still operating at a lower level. It now seemed to have seated itself in his skull and, just like his hearing, was something he felt incapable of shutting down. Then, suddenly, chaos . . .

Something began to tear, and U-space opened all around him. The cabin wall rushed up towards him. He yelled as grey eversions appeared in a tangled five-dimensional pattern all about him. Instinctively he chose a place between them and, using his mind, grabbed for reality. Next he was in darkness. He fell, hit a soft surface speeding along underneath him, rolled. Lights came on and he gazed about in confusion. He was now in one of the *King of Hearts'* internal passages. But why were the lights out? He knew: because King did not keep lights on in the ship where they were not needed, where no humans were located.

'You were in your cabin,' said King reproachfully, from the intercom.

Cormac stood and shook himself. The sweat on his body had now turned chill. Applying to the ship's server through his gridlink, he quickly ascertained his location, then turned and headed towards the bridge.

'I certainly was,' he replied. 'Where are we going now?'

'You were in your cabin,' King insisted. 'You could not have got to where you are now in just the last four seconds.'

Cormac wondered how often King checked the location of those inside him. Probably the attack ship's AI was aware of them most of the time, on some level, though perhaps became less aware when diverting processing power to make the calculations for dropping the ship into U-space – hence the four seconds mentioned.

'Well,' said Cormac, 'I can't be held accountable if reality doesn't always conform to your own model of it.'

'Your cabin door did not open,' stated King. 'You are not recorded in the short-term memories of the sensors located between your cabin and your current location.'

'It's certainly a puzzle,' Cormac agreed. He was enjoying the AI's bewilderment, but such enjoyment was tempered by the pull of the U-continuum surrounding the ship and the sure knowledge that if he had not hauled himself back up out of it and into this corridor, he would have gone drifting away from the ship in underspace. Could he then have still got himself somewhere safe, or would he eventually have surfaced in hard vacuum and simply died with his internal fluids boiling out of his body?

'You moved through U-space, like you did before,' observed King.

That King knew about the way Cormac had escaped Skellor was unsurprising, but *how* did the AI know? Had Jerusalem told

King, or had the attack ship AI witnessed the act itself when trying to rescue Skellor, or rather when it tried to prevent that madman and all the precious interesting Jain technology he contained from being crushed to a thin film over the surface of a brown dwarf star?

'Yeah, I moved through U-space,' Cormac conceded. 'Now are you going to tell me where we are going?'

Reaching the doors leading to the bridge, Cormac paused before them. Usually they opened automatically at his approach, but they now remained firmly closed. There came a long long pause before they finally opened, and before King spoke again – comparable to hours for an AI's normal thought processes. He guessed that King, a misanthrope at heart, didn't much like having an inferior human demonstrate superior abilities.

'I have received information from Azroc,' announced the AI.

As Cormac stepped out onto the black glass floor, heading for the scattering of chairs, something caught his eye in the dimness over to one side. There he observed a third-stage sleer frozen in a rearing position, and hoped this insectile monstrosity was simply a sculpture. It seemed that King was now taking up the kind of hobby enjoyed by the AI of the attack ship *Jack Ketch*. Cormac plumped himself down in one of the chairs.

'What information?'

'U-space anomalies were detected in a black asteroid field by an old sub-AI survey drone. Though they were large, they did not have the characteristic signature of a large ship surfacing. Measurements meanwhile indicate open Skaidon warps, then the short translation of some large object, unbuffered.'

'Through a runcible then,' observed Cormac.

'The drone was some way distant from the location of these anomalies,' King went on, 'and later detected the heat flash of a gigaton event.'

299

'Orlandine,' surmised Cormac thoughtfully.

'That the war runcible was used is the most likely explanation to fit the data.'

'So we're going there, which is good, but what are we going to do once we arrive?'

'Jerusalem has also ordered one of the reserve fleets out of Salvaston to head for the same location.'

Cormac leaned back and nodded to himself. 'That's good,' he said. 'Now would you like to tell me about your curious new taste in decor in here?'

Aboard Orlandine's ship the *Heliotrope* the old sharp-edged war drone, Cutter, lay folded up in the corridor right beside the ship's interface sphere. A multicore optic cable, plugged in between his bulbous eyes, trailed down and snaked along the floor into Bludgeon, and thus via the drone and the interface sphere he occupied into the *Heliotrope* itself. Now, having access to the ship's sensors and scanners, Cutter watched as his companion surfaced the ship into realspace far out from the Anulus black hole, then himself began scanning for the main transmission satellite he knew to be in orbit here. Bludgeon, meanwhile, started making the necessary preparations to use the cargo runcible in the somewhat hostile environment they would soon be entering. Within a few seconds the sharp-edged drone had it: a hundred-yard-wide coin of metal floating out in deep space. Bludgeon dropped *Heliotrope* into U-space for a subliminally short time, in order to put the ship between this main transmission satellite and its subordinate satellites, which were positioned close around the black hole and the junkyard of planets it was steadily devouring.

The satellites had been here for centuries, and no one had bothered recently to replace either them or the technology they contained. The U-tech of their time had been incapable of remaining functional in the chaotic U-space environment around Anulus, hence the positioning of the single main transmission satellite. The inner satellites transmitted by laser to it, and it relayed their data through U-space to the nearest Polity science station one hundred and twelve light years away. Fortunate that, since this meant the two drones needed to subvert only the one satellite. Within minutes Cutter had intercepted a laser transmission then relayed its contents to Bludgeon, who was always better at dealing with this sort of thing.

'Can you deal with it yourself?' Cutter enquired.

'Mebbe,' came the other drone's reply.

During the war it was always Bludgeon who dealt with the informational stuff while Cutter got physical. Bludgeon's job had been to open an undetectable way into Prador vessels or stations, and then Cutter's chore was to go in first, usually to scatter the interior with pieces of the crablike aliens and paint the walls with their foul green blood.

'You'll not need to use any of *her* stuff?' Cutter suggested.

'I could do it meself,' said Bludgeon, 'but you would need to enter the satellite to make a few physical alterations.'

'Just like the old days then.'

'Well, at least there's nothing alive inside that satellite . . .'

The other war drones, and Orlandine herself, would have been astounded to hear Bludgeon string together more than three words. But being able to talk like this only to Cutter was Bludgeon's particular wrinkle, his particular bit of faulty programming or maybe damage to his crystal or the mind it contained. All of the war drones on the war runcible had some similar fault – something that excluded them from normal Polity society or simply made them not want to be included. They would argue vehemently about these being *faults*.

'I'll head over there now, shall I?' said Cutter.

Cutter's own particular fault was his utter refusal to abandon or even blunt the edges of a body made for turning the insides of Prador vessels into abattoirs. He could not actually move about the Polity as a normal citizen, since the slightest mishap, his own or that of some other, could easily result in multiple decapitations and amputations. Cutter's edges were of a form of heat-treated chainglass that remained constantly honed down to one chain-molecule thickness. He could slice up steel with the same ease as a chef dicing an onion.

'No,' said Bludgeon.

'What do you mean "No"?'

'I've learnt the coding protocols and have the perfect tool for dealing with that satellite from here.'

'You mean one of *her* tools.'

'You have to lose your fear of the technology Orlandine provided, Cutter.'

'I ain't frightened of it. I just don't like depending on it, is all.'

'But we must depend on it. Nearly everything in this ship depends on it to some extent, and without it we won't be able to carry out our mission.'

Cutter grumbled and shaved away slivers of the wall, then grudgingly turned his attention to what Bludgeon was doing. The bedbug-like drone had opened up a cache of programs provided by Orlandine, selected one, a worm, and sent it in discrete parcels to the satellite. The worm must have reassembled itself within a matter of seconds, for that's all the time it took for the satellite to fall under Bludgeon's control. It seemed that simple computers were easy to subvert, and computers in places like this, where security had never been an issue, were easier still. Seemed to take all the fun out of it, though.

Now, as Bludgeon ignited *Heliotrope*'s fusion drive to move them closer, Cutter turned his regard upon Anulus. This black hole, of approximately six stellar masses, was surrounded by a disc of rock and gas it was steadily drawing into itself. Spindlewards of this disc, the output of energy dwarfed the output of suns. Apparently Orlandine had known much about this particular curiosity because it had once been suggested as a site for a massive construction project proposed before the Cassius Dyson sphere – some kind of energy tap to utilize that vast spindleward energy output.

The light here was glaringly bright, one glimpse with a human eye would burn out that eye in a moment. Already, even at this distance, *Heliotrope*'s hull was heating rapidly and thermal generators distributed throughout it were converting this to electricity and storing it in numerous laminar batteries, capacitors and in the high-density storage facility of the cargo runcible's bullers. All this was mainly being done with Jain tech, and though Cutter didn't like it, he was prepared to admit it was damned efficient.

'I suggest we wait here,' said Bludgeon.

Cutter gazed upon the virtual model of the debris disc his companion had created. The position indicated was just in from the edge of the disc where the asteroidal chunks were large enough and close enough together to shield them from the worse of the radiation.

'It will put you in the shade,' said Orlandine.

Cutter had almost forgotten that she remained in constant communication with them, so long had it now been since she last spoke. He considered trying to explain his attitude then decided not to bother. If she didn't like it, tough.

She continued, 'I estimate that I will be in position some twenty hours from now, so you'll need to head for your entry point into the fountain in about twelve hours.'

Cutter gazed through *Heliotrope*'s sensors and thought that 'fountain' was much too gentle a word for that thing out there.

The debris ring heated as it fell towards the spinning black hole, turning at first molten, then into an incandescent gas and finally to plasma at the event horizon. The radiation and ionization from this process was prevented by the disc itself from spewing out sideways, but there was a larger process involved in the production of these spindlewards polar fountains. The proportion of iron in the debris here was over forty per cent. This, combined with the spin of the black hole, created a magnetic bottle effect which squeezed escaping radiation into narrow channels spearing up and down from the black hole's poles. The two fountains were fifteen miles wide and consisted of ionized matter – mostly iron – and electromagnetic radiation right across the emitted spectrum. Anulus was like a natural particle-beam weapon – only of the kind you might need in order to take out planets.

The planetary system Erebus occupied with its main forces had changed visibly. Great curtains of rod-forms hung down from space into the upper atmosphere of the gas giant, where they still kept filtering out vital materials even as they were starting to withdraw from that world and separate. Three of the gas giant's four moons were utterly covered with Jain substructure and had shrunk visibly since Erebus's arrival here. The last of the rod-forms to have grown deep down within those moons, like animals putting on fat for the winter, were launching to bring vital materials to the orbiting wormships. The moons looked like apples destroyed by maggots.

Nearer the sun, massive mirrors made of sodium film were directing light sufficient to power all this industry, and already this new input was causing visible storms across the face of the gas giant. This was all to plan, since these storms would stir up some final vital elements for the last of the rod-forms to harvest before returning to their mother ships, if they had them. The ships shaped like lenses Erebus had decided to dispense with since they weren't powerful enough to stand against most ECS warcraft and, not possessing the modular construction of the wormships, tended to be a total loss once they were hit. They had become outmoded, so it was time to move on, and the rod-forms quickly cannibalized them.

While the first fleets of wormships continued their attack on the Polity border, Erebus had watched with some satisfaction as their number here, initially eighteen thousand, grew steadily larger. The ships first increased in size and mass with the intake of materials, then began dividing like bacteria – there was something to be said for the productive methods of life. Now there were over nineteen thousand wormships in orbit around the gas giant and, when the time came to head out, Erebus hoped to be back up to strength with over twenty thousand of the major vessels. But each of the new ships needed a controlling intelligence with at least some degree of independence.

During the Prador–human war Polity AIs had discovered that remotely controlled drones tended to lose that control once conflict started filling the ether with electromagnetic radiation. They had therefore enabled those drones to think for themselves, and this had led to the production of the independent war drone. Similarly, during conflict, Erebus could not remain utterly in control of all its parts so needed to give them their own degree of independence. Therefore all the wormships now had captains, as did many of the smaller vessels. Everthing else, including the rod-forms, was controlled by the nearest captain or by Erebus itself. It seemed almost a natural law that delegation was the most efficient way of controlling complex systems.

The first wormships Erebus created had contained the minds of subsumed ship AIs, Golem, war drones and, in one or two unusual cases, even the minds of certain humans. Erebus checked the status of these minds and found, as ever, that its favourites – unlike those AIs that had been subsumed with prejudice – were still loyal to the core. It instructed those trusted AIs, as they had done on previous occasions, to start transcribing copies of themselves, thus creating new captains for the new ships. Once that process was under way, it turned its full attention to the border conflict and again assessed the situation.

Erebus really wanted to recall some of his forces deployed there to join the attack that was about to take place, but it was just not feasible. The event that would signal the beginning of this attack would trap many of them at their current locations, and if Erebus called them in now, before that event occurred, many of the ECS ships were bound to follow, and he did not need them harrying his flanks. It was all very annoying but not unexpected. Then, while searching for some way to surreptitiously pull out some of those vessels, Erebus noticed an odd discrepancy.

During this border attack a total of four hundred and twenty-three wormships had been destroyed. Erebus had, on some level, witnessed the destruction of nearly every one of them and could recount in detail how they had been destroyed. There were only a few ships about which such details were hazy, but even then Erebus knew where they had met their end and roughly how. The one destroyed a little while after its attack on Cull had stood no chance of escaping ECS forces, and obviously they had tracked it down to the moon where its captain had begun trying to regenerate it. As expected, the one destroyed at Masada had stood no chance at all, while the one on Ramone, with one of the few human captains, had managed to break contact, though data from other ships nearby showed that it did eventually self-destruct. However, that left still one ship utterly missing, and Erebus seemed able to retrieve absolutely no data about its disappearance.

'I am ready,' came the abrupt signal from Chevron.

This interruption seemed entirely too timely, and Erebus experi-
henced momentary paranoia until deciding that no one could
manipulate events to *that* extent.

'Begin,' Erebus spat back.

After a short pause Chevron replied, 'Very well,' and Erebus
detected some disappointment in her tone. What did the murderous one-time Golem want now – a pat on the head?

Erebus accelerated the consolidation of the massive fleet here.
Numerous wormships were ready to divide, bringing the total
number of ships up close to twenty thousand but not actually
reaching that total. No matter, since Erebus would be using the
sledgehammer-on-walnut approach in this instance.

Sure that the consolidation would proceed without a hitch and
that the selected captains were transmitting copies of themselves
to all the new ships, Erebus checked its own extensive memory,
bringing to focus all the available data about that one missing ship.
It had still been active during the attack made on the ECS fleet
sent out to the accretion disc, but it subsequently had disappeared
only a few days before Erebus had sent two ships out to hit the
dracoman colony on Masada and the hybrid colony on Cull
respectively. The entity now experienced a moment of something
approaching panic. How could it lose track of an entire ship just
like that?

Fiddler Randal . . .

Panic faded: there was the explanation, for Randal had obviously interfered in some way. Erebus began contacting its many
spies dispersed throughout Polity space, for if it did not itself have
sufficient information about the missing ship, perhaps the enemy
did. It then took but a moment to find out about a wormship
attack on the world called Klurhammon.

Yet Erebus had instituted no such attack.

'Fiddler Randal, that world was of absolutely no tactical

importance.' Erebus repeated the opinion of various Polity AIs while leaving open plenty of channels through which Randal could safely make a reply. Randal remained silent. But *why* would Randal choose to cause an attack on such a world? He had been working against Erebus from the very beginning and trying to thwart this attack on the Polity, so that incident just didn't make any sense. Erebus put additional processing power online and began analysing more closely the intelligence coming in from his spies located in the asteroid field near Jerusalem's base.

Apparently, those attacks upon Masada and Cull had been ascribed to the danger Jain-resistant organisms might pose to Erebus itself. The AIs were right about this in some respects but wrong in others. It wasn't the dracoman or hybrid ability to resist Jain technology Erebus feared, but their ability to detect it. By being pushed into protecting the dracomen on Masada, and making sure that all the others off Masada got moved to where they would prove more useful to ECS – at the battlefront – the AIs had thus curtailed their movement throughout the rest of Polity, and thus made it extremely unlikely any of them would turn up on Xanadu and thwart Chevron's mission there. However, the attack upon Klurhammon remained as much a puzzle to those same AIs as it did to Erebus.

Delving further into the data, Erebus saw that the AIs had started an investigation, but no results were yet available. The security surrounding Jerusalem's base had been tightened up even more, so that those watchers sitting out in the asteroid field were able to glean little about it from the nearby information traffic. However, one of the coded packets they had managed to crack was able to reveal the reason for this extra security.

What?

It seemed one of Erebus's spies had been found and destroyed at the very heart of Jerusalem's camp.

Yet Erebus had placed no spies actually inside Jerusalem's camp, for that solar system, like so many others, would shortly become irrelevant.

'I don't know what you've been up to, Randal,' said Erebus, 'but there is absolutely no way you can stop me now. By now I would have detected any unusual movements in ECS forces, so it is now just a matter of firepower and physics. Nothing stands in my way.'

Yet still no reply from Fiddler Randal.

Erebus felt a sudden deep sadness, then, abruptly angry at such weakness, set programs to scrubbing this emotion from its consciousness. The feeling of loneliness that ensued was more difficult to erase.

Xanadu took five seconds to die – but experienced in AI terms it might well have been centuries. Chevron divided up the AI's mind and subsumed it, erasing moral codes and any data that made up that thing called personality. Sorting through incredible masses of information, killing, deleting and . . . eating, Chevron finally found the first thing she required: destruct codes for the passenger and cargo runcibles here and spread across the planet, and for the two hundred and six of Xanadu's sub-minds. Chevron temporarily blocked those codes intended for the runcibles on seeing that the AI had been preparing to send them, and instead sent the ones to the various sub-minds. Through numerous sensors now coming rapidly under her control, she observed the ceiling drones sagging and various other security measures shutting down. This all came a little late for the human separatists, but Chevron didn't really care about them now they had served their purpose.

Annoyingly for Chevron, only a quarter of the sub-minds actually accepted the destruct order. The rest, obviously having become aware that Xanadu possessed that option regarding them, had subtly built defences against it, though the order did isolate them from any hardware directly under their control. Some other minds, located in independent drone bodies, were already alerted and on the move, running for cover. She observed two metal spheres and the insectoid body of an old war drone fleeing this very complex before splashing down in a nearby lake. She considered using Xanadu's orbital weapons to deal with all the survivors, but that would take up time she did not possess, since other security issues needed to be dealt with first.

Chevron took the block off the runcible destruct codes and sent thirty of them to the passenger runcibles outlying this complex. Viewing through sensors located in the chambers containing these runcibles, she observed the Skaidon warps wink out, oxygen fires burning bright underneath the black glass floors, and buffers dumping their energy loads into the horns of each device so that they glowed hot and shed smoke, and in some cases even began to melt. She observed prospective travellers fleeing the areas in panic but, disappointingly, there were no fatalities. She had hoped the destruct order would result in thermonuclear detonations at each location, then belatedly realized this required personal intervention from the governing AI – now herself.

Why should I be disappointed? she wondered. *What purpose would further deaths serve?* Then she mentally shook herself. Why had she entertained such an unwonted thought? Surely the deaths of yet more humans was an end in itself? She now concentrated on the next stage of the plan. At least now ECS would not be able to send relief forces through the affected runcibles.

A brief coded signal started up her ship, which was now located in the bay of the orange sea nearest to her current position. It engaged its antigravity motors, and underwater blasts from its steering thrusters sent it hurtling towards the surface. Viewing the

310

scene through a nearby weather station, she saw the ship surface and begin to rise into the air, sloughing off all the remaining detritus encrusted on its hull. It turned till its nose faced the complex and, firing up its main fusion engine, accelerated in. Within minutes it would be in position overhead.

As a security measure Xanadu had shut down all material transport through the runcibles here and had ordered the complex to be evacuated the moment the separatists began their attack. Now queries began to arrive as to why all the other runcibles on the planet had also shut down. Using the required codes, Chevron sent a previously concocted reply explaining that high-level separatists intended using those other runcibles as an escape route. This would delay any investigation for the further few minutes she required. Now she began searching through the complex's manifest and found there the expected cache of Golem – all empty-headed and awaiting the download of sub-minds from the AI. She obliged them all by sending a stripped-down version of herself which knew full well what needed to be done next. The door to a sealed warehouse to one side of one of the cargo runcibles opened abruptly and out marched a hundred chrome skeletons.

Chevron then saw, through various cameras, that things were no longer so chaotic inside the complex. Large areas had been abandoned and crowds of people were steadily departing through the main doors. All the separatists were either dead or in custody, while security officers – both Golem and human – were restoring order among those departing or quickly rounding up any stragglers. Already she had received a hundred and twenty queries from these officers about what to do next. Sending another stripped-down version of herself to each of the various ceiling drones, she relished the prospect of them turning all their weapons on those who had not yet managed to flee.

But that's not what I'm here for . . .

It was annoyingly true. Why waste time killing humans who, in reality, could have little impact on the plan?

'Make sure the complex is completely evacuated,' she ordered. 'There are further concealed explosives I have yet to locate, and I have intelligence that some of them might be nuclear.'

Few questioned this order, since it came from such an unimpeachable and omniscient source. To expedite matters she put her instructions up on the announcement boards as well. The few still evacuating the main waiting lounge gazed back with some apprehension at the silvery Golem now appearing and departed all the more quickly. As the last of them left, Chevron closed the lounge doors behind them and sealed off all other exits and entrances. She felt satisfied to have them out of the way and glad not to need to start the killing again . . .

Chevron paused as she again thought how uncharacteristic it was for her to care about what happened to a few humans. Perhaps, simply by occupying the structure formerly occupied by the Xanadu AI, she had taken on some of that entity's traits. Could that really be possible?

No.

She began running diagnostics, but in the first few seconds there were no returns. Then, abruptly, there were thousands of them, all detailing the intrusion of alien code and alien material technology. She shut off those programs, realizing they had been Xanadu's and were only detecting Chevron herself. Quickly she ran her own programs and found some of the returns quite worrying. The amount of her substance she had lost while attacking the AI meant she was slightly overextended, which also meant that, though she had killed Xanadu, she was still in the process of displacing what remained of it. In those programs and in that hardware that remained, Xanadu had left something behind. She knew this could not have been created in the short time between the AI realizing it was in danger and it dying, but instead was something it had prepared inside itself for just such an unlikely eventuality.

It was a virus, Chevron concluded, but the more she studied it the more baffled she became. For it was doing things to her she could not quite comprehend. She applied some of her processing power to the task of building antiviral programs, but each time she seemed to have established the antidote and set it to work, the virus mutated. Annoyingly, she could not use her full processing power on it either, since her ship had now arrived in the sky directly above.

Chevron shut down all automated sytems mounted in the pillars extending up to and through the chainglass roof over the main runcible lounge, and the weapons inside them, initiated by sub-AI programming upon detecting the proximity of an unauthorized ship, died. The skeletal Golem had meanwhile opened a weapons cache and, having armed themselves with some serious hardware, were spreading out through the complex to cover all critical corridors and exits. In some areas they followed up behind the security forces, driving the evacuation even faster. No time for further delays.

Upon her instruction, her ship opened a hatch and lowered a carousel missile launcher, which began revolving to spit its load down towards the chainglass roof. The missiles hit like lumps of putty but did not explode; instead lumps of soft technology issued decoder molecules into the chainglass beneath them, which began to come apart. At each impact site the the glass crazed over, small cracks spreading out ahead of a white bruise. Areas of ceiling soon turned to dust, and disintegrating sheets of glass crashed to the floor. Above, the ship retracted its missile launcher while extruding yet another weapon from another hatch. The green beam this shot out was only visible where it penetrated the cloud of dust rising from the collapsing roof. It sliced through the decorous frameworks that had held the variously shaped sheets of glass, and a large portion of the roof structure soon followed the glass down inside. Having retracted this weapon too the ship then descended at high speed, crashing to the floor of the lounge, crushing furniture, bars, eateries and all such human paraphernalia underneath it.

Chevron began to receive immediate queries from the security forces in the city, then from all over the planet. At first she fielded them with neat selections of lies but, growing bored with this, quickly put together an automated program to do her lying for her. She knew this would not hold them off for very long, which was confirmed when in a military base some fifty miles away security personnel began cutting links to their planetary AI and moving warcraft out of the hangars. Briefly, before all the feeds from there went offline, she glimpsed the escaping drones she had earlier seen splash down in the lake. Undoubtedly everyone would soon be aware that Xanadu was no longer in control, but they would not be able to react quickly enough.

Chevron put twenty-eight of the passenger runcibles online, outgoing only, while holding the rest in reserve. Twenty-seven she set to particular addresses selected by Erebus long ago. The twenty-eighth she selected at random, then hesitated. Was it necessary now to cause further disruption which could result in further deaths? It was the Xanadu virus talking inside her, she knew, but the intensity of what she was feeling seemed difficult to deny.

Do I really need to send any of these?

Her ship cracked open its ramp hatch, folding down and crushing an automated vending stall underneath it. She continued to fight aberrant impulses that were certainly not her own while gazing through the vessel's internal sensors to see that the twenty-eight imploders were now ready to go. Brief self-analysis showed her that the delay before each of her actions was growing longer. She was hesitating, procrastinating. Abruptly angry, she sent the required signals.

Peeling themselves from the interior walls of her vessel, metallic octopoid forms settled to the floor and headed for the row of imploders, which sat like large bullets in a long ammunition clip. These Jain biomechs were without solid bodies; open tubular frameworks hanging in their place instead. The first of them reached the first imploder, crouched over it and squatted, the framework contracting about the weapon so the biomech could heave it up from its seating. With a flowing gait the mech then headed for the ramp, its body now a source of obliteration — it was a walking bomb — and the others, picking up their loads too, followed it.

Much shooting was in evidence around the complex now. Chevron linked in to some of her Golem and updated herself on their situation. The moment her ship had descended, security forces in the city had become concerned, but her lying engine had initially kept them from doing anything. Obviously they had now received intelligence from the distant military base from which the warcraft were launching even now. City security officers and military personnel were attacking the runcible complex, while in certain quarters of the city armoured AGCs were rising from the ground but wisely keeping their distance knowing the defences Chevron controlled. At ground level gravtanks were closing in, but it was all far too late in the day. Chevron had meanwhile noted a worrying development: her Golem had been infected with the same virus as herself and, abandoning their proton carbines, had dialled down the power output of their pulse-rifles and were now using non-lethal force to keep the attackers out. At one level this angered her intensely, but on another she felt gladdened. It would not be much longer before this damned *morality virus* turned her into something she would previously have despised.

Once outside her ship, the octopoids separated into small groups and sped off in different directions. Chevron tracked their progress across the main lounge, along the concourses leading to the various sub-lounges, where she watched individual octopoids finally heading for their assigned runcibles. Now, with each in position, all she had to do was tell them to step through, whereupon detonation of each imploder would take place automatically and simultaneously in the spoon of each receiving runcible.

She didn't want to.

And when did I summon you here?

The twenty-eighth octopoid was now squatting right outside the pillar she occupied, and the bomb the thing contained would certainly prove a lot more destructive than the explosives the separatists had used earlier.

The morality virus had made much headway inside her – faster than she thought possible – and now she was almost at the stage of not wanting to resist it any more. Only by forcing herself to become angry could she overcome it, and even that was proving more and more difficult. However, for one last time she managed to summon up her former hatred of soft useless humans – and she sent the signal. The octopoids stepped through the Skaidon warp of their allotted runcibles, arriving only instants later at twenty-seven different destinations.

Oh no . . .

Chevron instantly wanted to summon them back. She had just wrought massive death and destruction, and it was all entirely her fault, yet even that would pall in comparison with the ensuing catastrophe she had ushered in. She desperately wanted to stop this happening, to stop those bombs, but it was all just too late. A combination of growing guilt and the knowledge that she had completed her assignment for Erebus allowed her to relax her grip on herself. She ceased fighting the virus and immediately drowned in a tsunami of remorse.

Belatedly, she realized why she had summoned the twenty-eighth octopoid . . . as she sent its detonation signal.

13

Earth Central Security is a hydra of an organization and it has to be said that the 'Security' in its title is now both anachronistic and somewhat misleading. ECS started out as a force under the human world government some time before the Quiet War that led to the AIs displacing human leaders. Under Earth Central and the ruling AIs, it retained its title but began to incorporate all the other services, including navies, armies, air forces, the secret national security agencies of the solar system and later parts of the amalgamated health services too. During the Prador–human war the ambulance and military medical services, while remaining conjoined with the main health service, were driven by the necessities of war to link up with ECS to a degree required by its controlling AIs, whose first purpose was the survival of the Polity and not necessarily the health of its individual members. During the latter stages of the same war this organization, while remaining subordinate to ECS, incorporated all units whose purpose was to rescue injured or trapped personnel from ships, space stations, moons and planets. It then became known as ECS Rescue. After the war, certain horrible necessities no longer being a priority, ECS Rescue was divided into ECS Rescue and ECS Medical – the purpose of the first being civilian and military rescue, the role of the second being to provide a military medical service – for the inventiveness of weapons design required increasing specialism when it came to repairing the damage they caused.

– From her lecture 'Modern Warfare' by EBS Heinlein

The Salvaston runcible complex was like so many others found on highly populated Polity worlds. It sprawled in the centre of the capital city in a location where on Earth in the previous millennium would have stood the main railway station. Part of this complex contained four cargo runcibles, surrounded by handler robots looking like the titanic offspring of a mating between the goddess Kali and a piece of earth-moving equipment. From the runcible chamber in which these behemoths laboured, tunnels speared away in every direction, gravtrains arriving and departing continually to ferry cargo to various outlying warehouses or alternative transport links. Here there were few humans and most of what happened was automated.

At the centre of the complex lay the main lounge, a waiting and refreshment area for the thousands departing Salvaston or arriving upon it. The lounge itself was a mile across, its ceiling a chainglass confection of peaks and domes. Across a wide marble floor patterned like raspberry-ripple ice cream extended an assortment of restaurants, bars, tea shops and vending machine stalls, amid enormous seating areas. There were even walled gardens boasting a variety of exotic plants and creatures, for instance the one adjoining the Lobster Lobby, into which customers could throw the remains of their dinners to feed the carnivorous ambulatory cacti. There were numerous ponds and fountains too, like the cerulean pool in which swam G-mod goldfish glowing with internal neon. The lounge looked like some massive bazaar, street market, shopping mall and waiting room all rolled into one. However, it was nothing unusual, since places like this evolved wherever travel was nailed down to such a nexus.

What was unusual here today was the proportion of people wearing uniforms. There were troops in chameleoncloth fatigues who, out of courtesy, wore oversuits of some thin white fabric while mixing in civilian company, since there is nothing quite as disconcerting as encountering a disembodied head bobbing about in a crowd. There were also the familiar blue and yellow uniforms of ECS Rescue personnnel, and military-issue ECS envirosuits, which possessed the same qualities as chameleoncloth but, their effect being electrically generated, could easily be turned off. Very occasionally, amid this crowd, the menacing shape of a war drone attracted comment and attention.

From this main area concourses radiated off to smaller departure and arrival lounges – the designation of each dependent on what the AI had currently set the nearest runcible to do, which sometimes could be performing both functions. Those departing never had very long to wait, since delays in runcible travel were practically unheard of and all bureaucratic details and security measures were enacted electronically through sensors and augmentations, and at speeds way below the notice of sluggardly human minds. New arrivals from other worlds coming through the fifty-three passenger runcibles were greeted by relatives or quickly went on their way. The proliferation of uniforms today did attract brief notice, but a few enquiries via aug or gridlink soon reassured the curious that this martial presence was due to a huge Polity fleet presently in orbit about Salvaston. Many of them had no need to wonder, since the presence of the fleet was the reason they had come: either preparing to join or simply out of curiosity about what was *happening* out here.

The arrival designated XAN-7834 from Xanadu might have been able to answer some of their queries, had it been able to talk and had it managed to come intact through the Skaidon warp. The Salvaston AI, monitoring numerous runcibles scattered across the planet and every microsecond making complex calculations it would take a human prodigy a lifetime to complete, kenned the arrival of the passenger in the underspace spoon of the runcible and was immediately niggled by some inconsistencies. There was something odd about the information package describing this traveller, but the AI just could not put its metaphorical finger on it. In an instant it upgraded security in that particular runcible chamber and prepared to deep-scan this new arrival. The spoon began to retract, drawing the traveller towards the real.

Detonation.

In a place somewhere between realspace and U-space, the octopoid detonated its imploder. The blast within the spoon expanded it, and also forced its way through the Skaidon warp. The face of that warp, as seen from the side of the runcible chamber, turned incandescent. Filtering through the warp, the energy lased, pumping out gamma radiation in the form of a brief but intensely powerful graser beam. It sliced straight through the runcible complex, evaporating all those travellers waiting for the next slot. It punched through the containment wall, and fire exploded out beyond. The temperature in the arrival/departure lounge rose tenfold within a few seconds. Hundreds of human beings turned to fire, fountains boiled, plants wilted and smoked. It was as if the whole place had suddenly been dropped into some massive furnace. As it shut down every single runcible within its remit, the AI saw that the only things still showing signs of life in there were the staggering silver skeletons of Golem, their syntheflesh now burned away – but even they would not last much longer.

The graser beam melted through the far wall of the lounge, but luckily beyond that lay only sections of the complex containing the cargo runcibles, and there it finally spent its energy slagging the massive handler robots. The fire the beam had generated exploded down neighbouring corridors, where it splashed against rapidly closing blast doors. However, the massive concourse blast doors took time to close, so for a full ten seconds the inferno played down the concourse and erupted into the main lounge.

It was like taking a blowtorch to an ants' nest. Such scenes had been seen before on news programmes, but witnessing realtime a human being staggering along, screaming, while sheets of skin peeled away from his body had the power to shock even the Salvaston AI. Yet all this death and destruction, Salvaston soon realized, was not the primary objective of the attack.

The Skaidon warp was gone now, shut down, but everything beyond it in U-space had not ceased to exist. Within the spoon the massive blast abruptly ceased expanding then rapidly began to collapse back in on itself. Monitoring this, the AI deduced that the weapon used was an imploder. The implications were obvious, for the AIs had previously discussed this eventuality at length.

The USER, or underspace interference emitter, disrupted the underspace continuum by oscillating a singularity through a runcible gate. An imploder exploded first, then a complicated form of field technology fed off the energy generated by that explosion to cause a massive gravity phenomenon. This collapsed much of what was encompassed within the explosion down into a briefly generated singularity, then the singularity disrupted, releasing the same energy again. The intended result was that anything hit by such a weapon would be rendered down to energy and discrete atoms only. The aim here, however, was the singularity alone.

A singularity within a runcible gate.

The Salvaston AI had now shut down all the runcible gates, though it had not needed to. The disruption from this event spread instantly as a U-space shock wave, encompassing a real-space volume twenty light years across. The runcibles simply would not function and, as was almost certainly the aim, neither would the U-space drives of the Polity fleet hovering in space above. Now utterly cut off from the rest of the Polity until this U-space disruption ended, the Salvaston AI was not to know that this cataclysm had also happened on twenty-seven other worlds.

Chevron had achieved her purpose: now Erebus could move on Earth itself.

*

The events reported from Xanadu did not come to Jerusalem's attention until 0.001 seconds after a world called Amaranthe abruptly went out of contact, but even then the AI did not realize how critical things were becoming. Only 0.102 seconds later, sensors in solar systems adjacent to Amaranthe detected U-space disruption extending in a twenty-light-year sphere, with that world directly at its centre. This was now an event of extreme tactical importance, since at Amaranthe a whole ECS fleet had been taken out of play, therefore Jerusalem onlined more processing power to deal with the problem. First the AI ordered the refusal of all runcible transmissions from Xanadu, using maximum transmission power for its own orders so that they would arrive at AIs within this quadrant in under a tenth of a second, and at all other AIs across the Polity in under a second. Then, 0.001 seconds later, as another world went offline, the AI understood precisely what was happening and that mere transmission refusal would not stop spoon detonation of the imploders sent from Xanadu, so it now ordered the immediate shutdown of the runcible network in this entire quadrant. And it was only in that same moment that the AI comprehended the entirety of Erebus's plan of attack.

The earlier attack upon Ramone had knocked out the connections to the massive geothermal power stations buried under the continent on which sat the city of Transheim. The oversized runcible buffers on the oceanic world Prometheus were no longer connected to massive heat sinks situated deep in its ocean. Suicide attacks by Erebus's wormships had finally taken out the solar energy collectors about the Caldera worlds. These were the main events, but other worlds had lost energy-handling systems that were vital components in the runcible network. The network was now running like a car without brakes, driven by an engine without a cut-off button – for those worlds had been the real targets of Erebus's onslaught. Immediate shutdown would now cause energy feedbacks resulting in massive death and destruction, even if that option was still available. And it was not.

Then U-com shut down as a wave of disruption slammed out from Scarflow to completely block travel or com through that continuum. Sluggardly interminable minutes later, radio communications began to take up the slack – with inevitable delays – and finally Jerusalem began to learn what had happened on the nearby world.

'So it seems that Erebus has been one step ahead of us,' said the Golem Azroc.

Jerusalem focused a fragment of its consciousness on Azroc while simultaneously learning that the graser blast and ensuing firestorm on Scarflow had killed over four thousand people and that an estimated six thousand more would need to be hospitalized, though the figure was not entirely clear yet, since people were still dying. Luckily a big ECS Rescue ship was in orbit about Scarflow and, upon Jerusalem's instruction, would be landing there within an hour

'Yes, so it would seem,' Jerusalem replied to Azroc.

All of Azroc's links to the Line war were now down and like Jerusalem he could only guess at what had happened beyond this small section of space. In the control area, where robot fabricators and welders were still repairing the hole torn through the floor, personnel were already sitting back from their consoles, pulling out earplugs or disconnecting optic cables from their augmentations or, in the case of Golem, from their bodies. Jerusalem noted that Azroc was now checking his models of battles that must still be ongoing – this time with reference to this present attack using the runcible network. The Golem nodded, doubtless seeing the pattern, removed his skeletal hand from the palm interface, then slipped his glove of syntheskin back on. He was showing signs of anger almost human in the lack of control, for both his hands were shaking.

This manifestation of humanity was why Jerusalem had given Azroc the position he held, for the Golem, his mind built by imposing loose order on synaptic chaos, was that step closer to being human, just as some humans were a step closer than their fellows to being AI. Doubtless Jerusalem's flat tones and seeming lack of emotional response to the unfolding events annoyed Azroc too.

'Erebus specifically attacked several highly populous Line worlds in order to draw a proportion of our forces there,' the Golem observed. 'Throughout those attacks he ensured the runcible network components at Ramone, the Caldera Worlds and Prometheus were disabled or destroyed, so that the response time in shutting down the network within this quadrant would be delayed.'

'Undoubtedly,' replied Jerusalem, again flat and emotionless.

'I'm guessing even that was unnecessary?'

Jerusalem focused more processing power on the Golem and carefully introduced some emulation of emotion. 'How can we possibly know?' Now, surely the Golem must understood how isolated they were.

'How long before the disruption settles enough to allow U-com again?'

'Ten solstan days at least.'

Azroc stood with fists balled and face twisted with rage.

'And we must be ready for what we find out there,' Jerusalem added, then returned his attention to local events. This Golem, with his tendency to humanity, was an interesting diversion and a subtext to the larger issue concerning the development of human intelligence, but Jerusalem's greatest concerns now lay elsewhere.

It might be that miscalculations had been made. The threat Erebus posed had pushed, and would continue to push, the human race out of its evident stagnation. However, the threat Erebus posed should never have been allowed to reach this level in the first place. Consequently, it was likely the Polity would incur huge losses – losses it might not easily recover from.

Jerusalem then decided that the resultant developmental benefit of Erebus's attack on the Polity had been outweighed, and the experiment it had not itself initiated was, as far as it was concerned, over.

During the first few hours of the journey through U-space Cormac felt as if he was floating in a grey fog with perilous geometries stretching away from him in every direction, ready to drag him down. He knew, with utter certainty now, that he only had to relax his attention for a little while and he would be outside the attack ship, and then it would be gone, leaving him to drift in numb void. But he had fought the feelings of dislocation, of being neither here nor there, and tried to bring both his immediate surroundings and exterior U-space into sharper focus. The effort had made his brain feel like it was turning to lead in his skull, and increasingly he began to rely on cognitive programs meticulously constructed within his gridlink for the task.

After four hours he had realized that spending time in his cabin indulging in such introspection took his focus away from the reality of the ship around him, which was why he went off to find his remaining companions.

'Stick me down for five,' said Arach, his playing cards fanned out before his gleaming ruby eyes.

Cormac peered closely at the spider drone, then increased the magnification of his own eyes to record the reflected image from those red eyes and cleaned it up in his gridlink . . . that device in his skull that apparently was not even functioning. But he had decided it would be best to forget that assertion and just pretend it was.

Now, perfectly lined up in his mind, he apparently knew what cards Arach was holding. He was suspicious, however, since the last time he had tried this Arach's eyes had immediately turned matt so there was no reflection. The present image therefore had to be false. Cormac now set about analysing why the drone had chosen *those* particular cards for this false image.

'I'll go two,' said Smith, his cards face down on the table and his hand poised over them, detectors in the skin of his hand primed to pick up any sneaky scanning. Had these been normal playing cards there might have been some need for this, but they were sensitized and would scream if scanned, unless by extremely sophisticated means. Also, had these been normal cards, there would have been no point in even playing the game, since everyone around this table was capable of memorizing the order of the pack even as the cards were picked up and shuffled, and thus capable of analysing most of the resultant probabilities. But these cards electronically shuffled themselves, changing their face value at the end of each game, and the usual fifty-two cards were played, but chosen out of twenty suits of two hundred and sixty cards.

While Smith's call automatically appeared in the grid displayed in the glass tabletop, Cormac examined the Golem and wondered about those alterations made to Henrietta Ipatus Chang's record. It seemed evident to him that the black op she was involved in must have originally been something to do with Erebus but, since her abrupt reappearance in that wormship on the surface of Ramone, this connection had been abruptly covered up. Why so, he was not entirely sure, but he was beginning to indulge in some

327

nasty speculations. Certainly Earth Central had known about the threat long before it became apparent. But how? And what had been going on back then?

Frowning, Cormac returned his attention to the others seated around the table. He would have expected them to choose a game like poker, or maybe one of those derivatives of chess in which the pieces actually fought each other on the table top and died messily. That they chose to play contract whist seemed odd to him. He shifted his attention to the next player and found he still felt slightly unnerved by its presence.

He guessed it wasn't unexpected that an attack ship AI that had named itself King of Hearts might be interested in such a game. What unnerved him was how the AI chose to manifest itself. Hunched over his cards, the ship's avatar had adopted the external appearance of one of those sleer–human hybrids from the planet Cull, though its internal construction was doubtless based around a Golem chassis. In form it was a male human with silvery faceted eyes and pincers curving from the jawline in front of its beaked mouth.

'Three,' it lisped.

Now it was Cormac's turn to declare how many tricks he intended to win. In the light of the previous bids, he again studied his hand, though not the actual cards but the images in his gridlink. He felt himself becoming the focus of much attention and wondered what the others might be trying to read from him. He deliberately raised his heart rate and made random small movements. Unfortunately he could not alter his pheromonal output, but hoped that would give nothing away. About to go for a safe zero, he suddenly had a sharp perception of himself seated at this table, with the others nearby, and the whole of U-space bearing down claustrophobically.

Something . . .

King's avatar dropped its cards, then slowly bowed over until its pincers clinked against the glass table. Cormac received the impression of something like a hemispherical shock wave hurtling towards the ship. It passed through and he felt the vessel ejected up into the real. His chair slid back and he *oophed* as if someone had just gut-punched him, then the ship bucked and rang with a sound like a blow delivered against some massive porcelain bowl.

'Oh bollocks,' said Arach, tossing down his cards.

In a moment they were all on their different kinds of feet and heading for the bridge.

'That felt like a USER,' said Smith.

Cormac could not comment on that since he very much doubted his own feelings bore any relation to anyone else's.

'Could be Erebus,' suggested Arach hopefully. 'Or this Orlandine?' The two hatches on his abdomen opened tentatively.

'Could be,' Cormac conceded. He didn't know why the drone seemed so happy since, if they had just inadvertently encountered one of those two before safely joining the Polity fleet out of Salvaston, Arach's only involvement with any fight would be his addition to an expanding vapour cloud that had once been the *King of Hearts*.

Soon they were clattering into the bridge – where Cormac quickly noted that King had added a couple more sculptures to his collection. One was of Scar, a monument or an exercise in tasteless insensitivity? Hard to tell. The other one was a Prador second-child brandishing a multi-barrelled rail-gun much like the weapons Arach currently sprouted from his back.

'King, what's happening?' Cormac asked.

U-space was distant from him now, but still there. It seemed to be heaving underneath the real, like a sea in motion underneath a mat of sargassum, but what this meant Cormac had no clear idea.

'There has been a major disruption throughout U-space,' King replied.

'No shit?' said Arach dryly.

Cormac glared at the drone. It wouldn't do to irritate King now, since the attack ship AI did have an inclination to sulkiness. 'A USER?' he suggested.

King continued as if the drone hadn't even spoken. 'The effect has been similar but is much more chaotic. I am still analysing the data.'

'Does this mean we are trapped out here?' wondered Smith.

That thought had not even occurred to Cormac. He gazed out throught the ersatz dome at the stars winking in the blackness. Certainly the *King of Hearts* had been knocked up into the real of interstellar space, so if travelling through U-space had ceased to be an option, he would probably soon have to be making use of a cold-coffin. This idea did not appeal, since who knew what his frigid dreaming mind might do with his body the moment travelling in U-space once again became possible.

'We were knocked out of underspace by what appears to be some kind of shock wave and, unless there are further waves, we should be able to return to it within the next few minutes.'

'A shock wave from what and where?' Cormac asked.

'Still analysing.' King paused for a moment, whereupon gridded spheres expanded from numerous surrounding stars to crowd up against each other. Next, grid lines appeared across the starscape, sinking away directly ahead to sketch out a funnel shape running through the intersecting spheres till its neck closed down to almost nothing. This image then became clearer when the whole scene went photo-negative. Cormac blinked at the brightness, since the starscape was now represented as black dots in a white firmament.

'What am I seeing here?' he asked.

'We were merely knocked out of U-space by a side effect of the main event. U-space disruption has expanded from between twenty and thirty different locations, in each case encompassing a volume of twenty light years,' said King. 'It seems evident that Erebus has instigated a runcible-based multiple attack against the Polity.'

'Why so evident?'

'Fifteen of the planetary systems concerned were the temporary or permanent bases of ECS fleets. Many of the other planetary systems disrupted are those where Jerusalem's forces have been engaging. Jerusalem's own base was also a target.'

'What kind of runcible-based attack are we talking about here?' Cormac felt the skin crawling on the back of his neck as he recollected a threat the original Dragon had once made – namely turning runcibles into black holes. Were 'between twenty and thirty' Polity worlds therefore now rubble? Were billions of citizens now dead or dying?

'Once an enemy has obtained access to the runcible network, the most likely scenario is the transmission of imploders to detonate within the target runcible gate, and what I am seeing seems to confirm that. The effect is similar to that generated by a USER: the disruption of a large volume of surrounding U-space, though the disruption will be of limited duration and unstable.'

'What about the effect upon the worlds involved?'

'Minimal,' said King. 'The gates would emit only gamma radiation, whose destructive potential should not extend beyond any medium-sized runcible complex.'

So, no worlds trashed and no billions killed. Merely thousands, though it seemed wrong to feel so relieved to hear that. Now he speculated on what precisely was going on. Presumably this Orlandine must have used the stolen war runcible to key into the Polity network and thus send the imploders.

'Can you give me a tactical analysis?'

'ECS fleets brought in to cover the possibility of further attacks in this same quadrant by Erebus are now incapable of U-space travel,' announced King.

'Which includes the fleet out of Salvaston?' said Cormac.

'Precisely.' King continued, 'Those fleets fighting Erebus's forces at the Line itself are either confined or wholly engaged with the enemy, so unable to break away, and Jerusalem is out of contact with all of them.'

'This will mean that Erebus's forces there are also confined,' observed Smith.

'True,' said King, 'but those forces were only a small portion of the total. And there is the war runcible still to consider.'

'So where are the rest of the enemy forces, and where is Orlandine?' asked Cormac, already guessing the most likely answer.

The area within the funnel, right up close to the screen, shaded red. 'Orlandine's last recorded position was within this area, and it seems likely that Erebus is here too. Now, all that lies between them and Earth is Solar System Defence.'

'Nothing else?'

'Nothing of consequence.'

'That seems somewhat remiss.'

'It is remiss. Erebus has played this perfectly.'

'Perhaps you could explain?'

'Since Erebus's attack seemed concentrated in this particular quadrant, extra forces were moved in from all surrounding areas. That this attack occurred on the other side of the Polity from the Prador kingdom was not noted. The ECS quadrant forces over on that side are positioned near the Line over there, ready to intercept and if necessary follow in any attacking Prador fleet. They are far distant from Earth so would take some time to reach it. The forces on this side, Erebus has already nailed down. Forces elsewhere within the Polity should be able to get to Earth more quickly . . . However, Erebus and Orlandine have a straight run on Earth and will now have the time to conduct a sustained attack.'

Cormac considered the scenario. By appearing incompetent in attacking an ECS fleet outside the Polity itself, and thus revealing itself, Erebus had perhaps led the AIs into a false sense of security. They had assumed they were dealing with something that did not think as logically as themselves, was perhaps even a little insane. They had not expected such a new dimension to the attack – this USER disruption generated by their own runcible network. *Or had they?* Still he found himself questioning the lack of a more active response from them. And still there were serious questions to be answered about that Ipatus Chang woman. But, even if the AIs were careless of any damage this would inflict on the human race, they must surely care about the damage that could be inflicted upon themselves. Erebus might now bring down Earth, and with the homeworld bring down the Polity's de facto ruler: Earth Central . . . Of course, whatever Cormac thought about all this was irrelevant now. There would be no fleet out of Salvaston, so he could do nothing about either Orlandine or Erebus.

Then again . . .

Maybe there was something he could do. In being able to send himself through U-space he possessed an utterly unexpected ability, one even beyond Erebus itself.

'I take it you have a substantial stock of CTDs aboard?' he suggested.

'I have.'

'Anything small enough for me to carry in a backpack?'

'Most of them are that small . . . physically, anyway.'

'Sort one out for me then – largest destructive potential but not too heavy.'

'What are you planning?' asked Smith.

'I'm planning to remove at least one of Erebus's allies – this Orlandine character,' Cormac replied. 'King, when you're ready, head us towards that war runcible's last known location.' He looked round at his three companions, who were watching him expectantly.

'Horace Blegg thought he could transport himself through U-space,' Cormac began. 'We now know that isn't true.'

'And?' enquired Smith.

'I can.'

Smith's expression revealed a convincing emulation of bemusement and disbelief. Cormac shuddered, feeling himself become somehow insubstantial, as the bridge dome greyed over and the *King of Hearts* dropped into the mentioned continuum. He closed his eyes, concentrated on stability, then in his gridlink replayed the images that the attack ship AI had earlier displayed in the viewing dome. After a moment he accessed the ship's server to obtain precise measurements of the geometry of the funnel displayed, for he had noted that the mouth was very narrow, maybe too narrow. The measurements soon confirmed this.

'King,' he said, 'to get to Earth, both Erebus's wormships and the war runcible will need to pass along a narrow corridor between intersecting spheres of U-space disruption. I see that this won't be easy for them.'

'Practically impossible,' King concurred. 'It would be easier for them to surface into the real then make a series of short jumps wherever the wash from the disruption allows.'

'So they will have to travel sub-light for appreciable distances?'

'Yes.'

'You know what I'm considering?'

'Be nice if we damn well knew too,' observed Arach.

'Very well.' Cormac paused, knowing the others would not like this, since it meant they would have to remain aboard ship. 'With all that Jain technology at Erebus's disposal, I don't know why he made Orlandine seize that war runcible, but that she did so must mean it is critical to Erebus's plans.'

'I think I'm beginning to understand,' said Smith.

'Bully for you,' grumped Arach.

'The war runcible is heavily armed,' Cormac explained. 'King could not possibly destroy it, hence the need for the Salvaston fleet. However—'

'How did I know there was a "however" coming?' interrupted Arach.

'However, if King can get me close enough, I can transport myself and the CTD across to take the war runcible out of the equation.'

'That's if King can even get you close,' Smith observed, 'or finds it not surrounded by wormships.'

'Do you have any other suggestions?'

'Not at the moment.'

'So you go across alone?' Arach was clearly disappointed.

'Alone, yes.'

'Seems pointless.'

Cormac eyed the drone. 'Well, I guess I could just curl up, turn off and do nothing.'

Arach swore, then turned round and scuttled out of the bridge.

'Have that CTD ready for me soon, King,' Cormac instructed.

Certainly it seemed Polity AIs might be involved in some Machiavellian scheme, and in the end he would damn well have some answers, even if he had to physically tear them out of Earth Central itself. However, right now he would continue to do his best for those it was his duty to protect, which included some hundred billion humans living in the Sol system.

★

As the two Dragon spheres penetrated deeper into the accretion disc, the attacks on them became infrequent. However, Mika found much more to interest her here. Occasional bacilliforms, lenses and segmented fragments of wormship structure put in an appearance, but they were rare and, it seemed to her, acted as if lost. It was the other things now being revealed by her scans that absorbed her interest. The twin spheres penetrated clouds of small ovoids that they repelled with hard-fields, since these objects were so small and numerous it was impractical to destroy them with collision lasers. These were, in fact, Jain nodes – trillions of them – and to Mika's mind the harbinger of the future destruction of the Polity unless something could be done to completely erase them from existence. Then other larger objects began to appear, and it seemed to Mika that the Dragon spheres were travelling into some Jain-tech evolutionary past in which only the oddities were on display.

The first of these new phenomena to come into view was a mass of leech-like biomechs wound through a quadrate framework that had seemingly been squeezed into a vaguely spherical shape at least a quarter of a mile across. An early version of a wormship, perhaps, or some kind of mutation from the final version? It was difficult to tell. Certainly it was nowhere near as lethal as a wormship since, though the leech-things showed greater activity as the two spheres approached, seemingly reaching out beseechingly and shedding Jain nodes like puffball spores, the whole construct just hung in space as the spheres parted to circumvent it and then made no attempt to pursue them. Mika was busily studying her scans of this construct and thus ascertaining that it contained no drive of any kind when the next new object hurtled like a hunting barracuda out of the murk.

This biomech was a fifty-foot-long torpedo impelled by a dirty-burning Buzzard ram-jet. Collector fields sprouted from either side of its forequarters, the accretion material they were gathering glowing red-hot as it entered shark's-gill intakes, so that the object appeared to be sprouting external salamander gills. Its front end opened a tri-mandible mouth as it approached, pink inside like a fuchsia, and Mika was reminded of the calloraptor hybrids Skellor had created for his attack on the planet Masada. She gathered as much data as she could on this thing, and as quickly as possible for, accelerating towards the other Dragon sphere, its future lifespan could be no longer than a few minutes. Eventually a white laser stabbed out from the twin sphere straight down its gullet. Fire exploded from its back end, leaving just a hollow tubular shell glowing red inside, as it tumbled past in the wake of the sphere that had killed it.

Mika's subsequent analysis of gathered data revealed this thing as the simplest of biomechs. It possessed a mouth and a stomach, doubtless to gather materials for its own growth and also for the growth of the nodes spread throughout its body like tumours. It breathed accretion dust which it burned in its ram-jet to provide mobility, and she wondered if it could reproduce itself or was just a machine for producing Jain nodes.

Later, Mika observed a mass of biomechs shoaling around another unfamiliar object like a giant flatfish, tearing chunks from it as it sluggishly dodged and weaved by firing off rows of chemical jets positioned along its edges. Two of the smaller biomechs on the nearer side of the shoal now sped over to attack the Dragon spheres, only to be nailed inevitably by white lasers. Only after studying her scan data later did she classify them as the same sort of thing as the earlier attacker. Certainly these biomechs weren't in any way standardized, more like heavily mutated.

'So they attack and kill *each other*,' she observed.

'Out at the edges of the disc they still retain much of Erebus's programming,' Dragon supplied. 'In here they are wilder in behaviour.' Then, after a pause, Dragon added, 'I have received disturbing news.'

Disturbing news? What kind of news ever disturbed Dragon? 'Well don't keep me waiting.'

'Through my contact within the Polity—'

'Meaning a certain homicidal Golem called Mr Crane.'

'Just so. Through him I have learned Erebus's ultimate plan, and that plan is now in motion. Erebus has knocked out a large proportion of the runcible network, which in turn has caused massive U-space disruption, stranding many ECS fleets uselessly at their bases. Erebus's way is now clear to take the bulk of its forces directly against Earth.'

'What?'

'Fortunately a weapon has been deployed in order to block this attack, information Mr Crane obtained having proved essential for the success of this defence. He is now aboard the aforementioned weapon and located at the very centre of events. I will keep you apprised as necessary.'

Mika felt slightly sick and again guilty because she was not back there. 'So the Polity AIs are on top of things?'

'If only that were so.'

'What do you mean?'

No reply.

'Dammit! What do you mean?'

Mika sat waiting for a long moment, but still Dragon gave her no answer. She then got angry with herself for both demanding or expecting one; she had been lucky thus far with the quantity of lucid information Dragon had supplied. She sat staring at her screen, mulling over the latest news, then applied herself to pushing it from her mind and concentrating instead on the here and now. She could do nothing about what was happening back there, and must put her trust in such more-than-capable problem solvers on the spot as Ian Cormac.

After the shoal had faded from sight, some hours passed before anything else substantial came within range of Mika's scanners. She felt she ought to get some sleep but just did not feel tired enough. Was this the effect of another of Dragon's tweaks of her body, or of the news so recently delivered? Then, as she was gazing at a hail of Jain nodes bouncing from two hard-fields projected like the bows of a ship in front of the sphere, her scanners briefly registered something at the limit of their range.

What?

For a moment she thought the Dragon spheres had come close to some immense asteroid or another planet in the process of formation, but the density measurements of the shape vaguely defined on her screen were all wrong . . . before it *moved*. She kept trying to pick it up, but it remained elusive as if deliberately giving her only spectral glimpses of itself. Certainly it was something Jain, for in those glimpses she saw wormship structure writhing through Jain coral and a great demonic wing that in this environment could only be some sort of energy or dust collector, tri-mandibular mouths opening and closing like hellish flowers and the occasional bright stab of a fusion drive.

'Dragon, what the hell is that thing?' Mika enquired at last, for though this object lay beyond the range of her scanners, it might not lie beyond Dragon's.

'They attack and kill each other,' said Dragon, echoing her much earlier comment.

'And?'

'Jain technology is not life, so is not restricted by the slow processes of evolutionary change.'

Some might have found Dragon's didacticism irritating, but

Mika preferred that to its vaguer Delphic pronouncements – and at least Dragon *was* replying to her. She decided not to ask further questions for it seemed obvious what Dragon was implying. Jain technology was capable of changing into forms as various as those produced by evolution, but change in the living products of evolution was a long slow generational thing, whereas in Jain biomechs those changes could be made individually in the mechs concerned – a process faster even than the discredited Lamarckian evolution.

And they attack and kill each other . . .

Even the slow drag of evolution could produce some nasty predators.

'Let me guess,' she said. 'It's big and it's nasty and it's at the top of the heap.'

'One of them,' Dragon replied. 'Call them the alpha predators.'

'Have you been here before?' Mika abruptly asked.

'I didn't need to come here to know this place,' Dragon replied. 'That thing out there is a version of me, only not so rational and friendly.'

Mika decided to let that go and returned her attention to the hints her scanners were providing. She checked the conferencing unit's database, quickly finding the reconstructing program she required, input scan data already collected, and set her computer to input further data as it came in. Essentially the program was putting together a three-dimensional jigsaw with many pieces missing, repeated and sometimes changing shape, colour and other EM output. Slowly the menacing visitor out there began to grow on her screen, and slowly measurements revealed its awful scale.

Hanging upright in the murk, the overall shape of the thing was of a chrysalis but, since in reality it stood eight miles high, a lot of surface detail was only revealed by zooming in, and a lot had yet to be included by the program. In a moment detail spreading over its surface revealed it to be encaged in bones of Jain coral; however, what those bones encaged seemed no discrete being. In the area below its head were tangled vinelike masses sprouting those familiar demonic flowers. Down in its lower end were large coils of wormship, slowly turning like some strange engine. The middle of this chrysalis shape seemed to consist of masses resembling those baglike organs Mika had seen gathering like nervous sheep underneath Dragon's skin. Long Jain tentacles wound their way through this as if keeping it all knotted together. The thing's head bore chrysalis horns, and presently its massive batlike wings were folded on its back. That it looked so devilish struck Mika as an unlikely coincidence but one she could not yet explain.

'Looks . . . spooky,' she opined.

'The structural formation of biomechanisms often bears similarity to evolved creatures since it often adheres to the same basic rules,' Dragon replied pompously.

'Wings and horns?' said Mika.

She noticed how the other sphere was dropping back and, checking her instruments, she detected power surges within it.

'The horns are merely sensor arrays positioned outside the main body so as to negate internal interference, and there are two of them to provide the same function as binocular vision in humans. Those wings are a form of drive using U-tech and electrostatic repulsion. They look like the wings of some evolved creature simply because that shape finesses control.'

'Yeah, right.'

As if to demonstrate this point, the huge biomech began spreading those same appendages. They looked something like those of a bat though much deeper, in shape tapering down to the monstrous thing's tail end. As they expanded, the accretion dust before them flowed down their forward surfaces, while some swirling activity ensued behind. A visual distortion also extended from the bones and abruptly the huge thing was falling towards them. A white laser lanced out from the other Dragon sphere. Mika saw it bend for a moment, then track across and abruptly puncture some electrostatic shield, before splashing onto one of the extended wings. The biomech spun as if hit by some solid projectile, and in doing so released a cloud of small gleaming bubblelike objects. These orbited their source for a moment before abruptly accelerating away – only a few of them heading towards the offending Dragon sphere. The laser snapped out again and again, hitting these approaching objects. Bright detonations spread nuclear fire through the surrounding accretion matter. Before the radiation degraded her view, Mika saw a hard-field spring up under one of these detonations, then flicker out. Now all she could see were shadowy images of the giant biomech and the other Dragon sphere swinging in a wide orbit about each other, while the energy readings between them ramped higher and higher. She noticed her own sphere was now accelerating.

'Will your companion be able to stop it?' she asked.

'For long enough,' Dragon replied.

'Long enough for what?' Mika asked, not really expecting a straight reply.

Dragon's silence did not disappoint her.

After a moment she realized that the ambient light outside the conferencing unit had risen. Directing her sensors toward her presumed destination, she picked up the tail end of a burst of radiation with an easily recognizable signature: solar wind. Collecting data on her screen from radiations far outside the human spectrum, she quickly built a picture of a distant mottled orb flashing like a faulty bulb. She felt it a privilege to be present, for here was a sun in the process of accruing enough matter to enable it to ignite its fusion fire. Like some massive engine turning

342

sluggishly as it draws on a flattening battery, the sun was coughing and spluttering. Fusion fires were burning around its surface or breaking through the surface from inside, only to go out with gouts of oily smoke, each cough or splutter burning lighter elements to an ash of iron of sufficient quantity to construct tens of thousands of space stations, while the oily clouds were blasts of hard radiation capable of denuding such space stations of life.

Considering that last fact, Mika began to map magnetic fields within sensor range. As expected, she saw that Dragon was bending the solar wind about itself. Unexpectedly she discovered that numerous other objects within range were doing the same and the largest one was directly ahead. She now focused on this one and began to clean up an image. After a few moments she ran diagnostic tests and searches on her instruments, for surely the image they were returning could not be right – some fault in the programming perhaps?

'Our destination,' Dragon informed her.

Mika gazed at an immense mass resembling numerous blooms of stag's horn coral. For a moment she couldn't understand why the appearance of this thing had impelled her to run those diagnostics, since it seemed no more unusual than the biomech the other Dragon sphere was now battling. Then she realized why: she instinctively felt this place to be the epicentre, the point where Jain technology had first bloomed within the accretion disc, a point where reality seemed increasingly thin, and where something utterly alien lurked on the other side.

This was somewhere she really did not want to be.

14

Scanning and sensing. *Humans and most Terran animals use their senses to pick up information about their environment from that environment's own products. In this way their information-gathering is passive and they are not 'scanning'. However, there are examples of Terran fauna who do scan: bats with their echo-location and cetaceans with their sonar. Humans, as tool users, have found their own ways to scan now. Be that with a primitive torch or sonar or radar, they inject some energy into their surroundings to gain data from the portion of energy that is bounced back at them. When it comes to AI spaceships, the sensorium for both scanning and sensing has grown to encompass nearly all of the EMR spectrum. Ship AIs can sense most wavelengths of radiation, and they can emit most wavelengths for the purpose of scanning. They can shine a torch into the dark, beam radar pulses, fire off laser radiations across a wide spectrum for numerous specific purposes, and even plot gravity and density maps of surrounding space and the underlying U-continuum.*

– From QUINCE GUIDE *compiled by humans*

Upon instruction the nineteen thousand eight hundred and twenty wormships began to gather at the coordinates Erebus had chosen. As distinct vessels, still with swarms of returning rod-forms about them, they fell towards this centre point and began to link together. First just three wormships closed on each other, tentacle ends connecting like multiple plugs and sockets, loops of snaky structure tightening like linked arms; three wholes joining and commingling.

Though Erebus was a distributed entity, as much present in each and every one of these vessels as it had been in those fighting at the Polity Line until the U-space disruption cut the link, it still needed a firm location for its self – its centre, its ego – and this was usually where the concentration of its vessels was most dense. This necessity annoyed Erebus for such a sense of self and the location of self did not seem consistent with AI melding. However, when the wormships began to come together like this, that annoyance was outweighed by feelings of pleasure, completeness and . . . security.

As the first three wormships ceased to be even vaguely distinct entities, another five joined them, sucking in behind them swarms of rod-forms and other space-born biomechs. Others were coming in fast behind them, and Erebus felt the centre point of its own being moving into this mass. Perhaps this feeling of location was what the AI needed to dispense with in order to be complete? Erebus was, however, reluctant, for becoming truly distributed might mean a dilution of self. Perhaps Randal was right, and Erebus and its components were not melded at all as long as one component remained dominant. Something to ponder . . . but later.

After a hundred wormships were bonded together, the process accelerated, ships swirling in orbit about a writhing moonlet of Jain matter as they set their courses down towards its surface. The whole seemed like some incredibly complex and changing Chinese puzzle, and it grew swiftly. Within five hours this core of wormships was being compressed into immobility as the last hundreds were attaching to the outside ahead of a rain of other Jain biomechs. Rod-forms descended like swarms of bluebottles; other mechs like shoals of fish sped in, hard bones of Jain coral grew throughout the moonlet to increase its structural strength; incomplete wormships – the spirals like ammonites – descended and

345

bonded too. In the upper layers the process approached completion, with the rod-forms meshing into sheets in order to swathe the entire object, to smooth out its inconsistencies so that from a distance it would look just like an icy metallic planetoid.

Now, with all its active substance drawn together, Erebus gazed about at the system it had occupied. Very little useful Jain-tech remained out there, yet there were few material objects here that had not been touched by it. Bones of Jain coral, which had been used as scaffolds or structural supports during the construction of various biomechs, tumbled through space. Composed of elements that were abundant here, they weren't worth the trouble of reclaiming. All the asteroids were wormed through with smooth burrows and empty of useful metals and rare elements. Pieces looking like shed carapace glittered in orbit about the gas giant – remnants of the shielding the rod-forms had grown around them while they collected resources down in the the giant's upper atmosphere. Occasionally, revolving slowly in vacuum, could be found empty organic-looking containers in which some biomech must have made its caterpillar-to-butterfly metamorphosis.

After feeling a moment of disquiet upon noting just how much of a mess it was leaving here, very much more, in fact, than humans left behind them, Erebus filled its processing space with the calculations necessary to align and balance a hundred U-space engines for simultaneous use, then flung the planetoid of Jain technology which it comprised into the grey continuum – heading towards Earth.

With leviathan sluggishness an asteroid turned distantly in black void. Its mass was almost the same as that of the war runcible and, though long-range scanning had indicated its composition to be wrong, Cormac still wanted to take a closer look, for the asteroid lay directly in the area where the runcible gate signature and subsequent massive detonation had been detected. The other items he had also found here were puzzling.

'There,' said King. 'Another one.'

A square red frame appeared in the viewing dome to select out part of the blackness beyond and magnify it – the frame expanding to blot out the asteroid entirely and bring something else into view. At first this could have been mistaken for mere asteroid debris, but after a moment Cormac recognized two identical squat cylindrical segments loosely linked by a fibrous tangle. This tangle resembled optics or maybe tree roots but was actually Jain-tech.

'What the hell happened here?'

'Maybe Orlandine had a falling-out with Erebus?' suggested King. 'Maybe Erebus wanted to meld with her and she objected to the idea.'

'Well, *you* would know about that, wouldn't you?'

King emitted an angry snort, then went on, 'It could be that the wormships destroyed here were rebel ones. That human captain you saw certainly wanted to break away from Erebus.'

Cormac nodded. 'Yeah, could be.'

But Cormac really wasn't sure, which seemed a permanent state of mind with him lately. Yes there might be elements of Erebus which, like Henrietta Ipatus Chang, wanted to break away, but he did not think there would be many of them, and few of those would even be capable of doing so. Allowing his U-sense to slide beyond the ship, he detected more of those same Jain-tech fragments spread widely through space and could feel a buzzing echo in the U-continuum of the dramatic event that had occurred here. Orlandine had used the war runcible to destroy one or more wormships, that seemed certain, and he would have to keep this in mind when they eventually reached her.

The image of the asteroid slid to one side as *King of Hearts* turned and accelerated past it. Cormac braced himself for the moment the AI would engage its U-drive, yet, when it did so, he felt perfectly stable and in no danger of drifting away. He gazed up at the greyed-out dome and beyond it, and felt the pull of U-space with the enjoyment of revelling in a breeze rather than trying to stay upright in a hurricane.

'Can you give me a hologram of the war runcible?' he asked.

'Certainly,' King replied.

The war runcible instantly materialized, hanging just above the glass floor of the bridge and slowly turning. Though Cormac had known about this artefact, he had never really speculated on its shape, which now came as something of a surprise to him.

'Why a pentagon?' he asked.

'Just two runcible horns are sufficient to sustain a Skaidon warp large enough to open the way for objects of your size,' said King. 'Further horns are required as the size of that warp increases. Four horns are optimum for a runcible of this size, with a fifth one for stability as the warp is extended further.'

'Why not make bigger horns?'

'In the first instance, these horns are bigger than those of either a passenger runcible or a normal planetary cargo runcible. In the second instance, do you really want me to explain runcible theory to you?'

'Maybe not,' Cormac admitted.

'Oh good,' said King, in a tone heavy on the sarcasm.

'So, where would be the best place to put the CTD?'

A piece of the runcible separated out, carrying away with it some of the hull, a disc-shaped control blister and many internal components. Exposed inside were parallel corridors running through the gaps between three long cylinders that terminated at each end in spheres. Just before the latter, each of the corridors ended against a vertical shaft containing old-style spiral stairs. Even with the section of hologram removed, what remained was

348

still tightly packed with a complicated tangle of ducts, transformers, interconnecting passageways, catwalks and cubic stacks that Cormac recognized as laminar batteries.

'Why spiral stairs?' he enquired. 'I know this runcible is old, but it's not ancient.'

'The three cylinders you are seeing are the buffers for this particular segment of the runcible. Detonating the CTD here, or in the equivalent place in any other segment, will take the device completely out of commission.' King paused contemplatively. 'Spiral stairs, since you ask, because inductance from the runcible buffers would interfere with the irised gravity field in any conventional drop-shaft. Just consider, when was the last time you saw a drop-shaft located anywhere near a runcible?'

This was true: he never had.

'What about gravplates – since they're the same sort of tech?' he asked.

'Similar, but they produce a static gravity field, while drop-shafts produce a moving one.'

'I see.' Cormac gazed at the hologram before him and tried to imprint it on his mind. For back-up he applied to King's server and downloaded the entire schematic to his gridlink. He turned to go, then paused to ask, 'How long until we reach the corridor through to Earth?'

'Less than an hour now.'

Cormac headed for his cabin.

The true size of those blooms of Jain coral only became evident as Dragon drew close enough to them for Mika to see something caught in the fork of two branches amid the many. Gazing at it she wondered if it might be some sort of biomech crouching there ready to leap on passers-by, then she saw writing on its side and abruptly recognized an old-style attack ship, whereupon everything jumped up a magnitude in scale. Only then did she pay full attention to the data provided by her sensors now scrolling up on her screen.

From behind, where the other Dragon sphere faced off the massive Jain biomech, came perpetual surges of EMR – in consonance with the waxing and waning of the light out there. The two were still battling, but it was not this that riveted her attention. The incoming data now gave her the true scale of the partially conjoined spherical blooms. Each of the seven possessed a diameter of no less than five thousand miles. Mika cursed silently.

'Note the density,' said the Dragon inside her head.

Yes, these structures certainly occupied a substantial volume of space, yet their density was akin to that of bushes, or maybe a better analogy would be tumbleweeds.

'Density noted,' said Mika. 'What's that supposed to tell me?'

'I'm guessing that *Trafalgar* landed on a moonlet or an asteroid, which it then processed during the first phases of acquiring and controlling Jain-tech,' Dragon replied. 'The rest of the AI exodus was gathered in close orbit about that same landing place.'

The Dragon sphere was now getting incredibly close to the nearest bloom of coral. Looking up from the conferencing unit was a disquieting experience, because this bloom stretched from horizon to horizon. It was as if an endless ceiling from which depended a forest of bone trees descended towards her, or maybe a mass of the kind of branching stalactites found in the caves of low-gravity worlds. Deeper in, amid the tangle, she saw the boxy shape of a scout ship melded into a limb of coral, where numerous thin branches had sprung from it as if it were the core of an epiphyte.

'So now that we are at the centre of things,' ventured Mika, 'are you going to be more precise about why we've come here?' She asked this almost because she felt that she should, not because she hoped for any clear answer from Dragon and not, oddly, because she needed an answer.

'You must go to *Trafalgar* for me,' said Dragon. 'I am fairly certain that it lies at the centre of this particular bloom of Jain technology.'

Mika felt a rumbling vibration through the floor and, when movement at the horizon attracted her attention, she looked over to see a pseudopod tree spearing towards the bone forest. She watched as it reached the Jain coral and penetrated, fraying and spreading out as it did so. The vibration steadied at a low note and, checking scan returns, Mika saw that, in relation to the mass before them, Dragon was now stationary. The sphere had clearly moored itself to their destination.

'Let me get this straight,' she said. 'You want me to fly my little intership craft right into that *mess* – and to the very centre, about two and a half thousand miles in?'

'Yes.'

Mika glanced across at the flapping skatelike guide that had led her out from the interior of Dragon, and it returned her gaze steadily with its blue palp eyes. She then thought about dracomen, those entities Dragon created with the same ease that a human would fashion a clay doll. 'Why don't you send a probe?'

'But I *am* sending a probe,' Dragon replied. 'You.'

'It's very dangerous out there. I've already witnessed that.'

'It is not so dangerous out there now.'

'You still haven't told me why you aren't sending your own organic probe,' Mika insisted. 'If you don't tell me why, I won't go.'

Of course she knew Dragon wanted her to go because of the new memories sitting like lumps of rock in her skull, but she wanted certainties.

'Very well,' said Dragon, almost resignedly. 'Because you are an evolved creature. You are not a product of Jain technology, in fact you are not a product of any technology.'

'That's as clear as mud.'

'Perhaps you have not vocalized it yet, Mika,' said Dragon, 'but you *know* what is in there.'

Gazing at that tangled forest of Jain substructure, she surmised that here it formed only a thin surface over something else. 'I feel something . . . but I don't really understand.' Mika turned her attention to the blue palp eyes still staring at her. 'Can't you for once explain clearly?' However, even as she made this request, she stood up, checked the integrity of her spacesuit and turned towards the airlock.

'Long ago when all four of my spheres still existed and I myself was sited on the planet Aster Colora, I summoned a Polity ambassador to me. I was still struggling with my Maker programming then, and trying every method I could manage to circumvent it – hence my history of Delphic and obscure pronouncements.'

Reaching the airlock, Mika glanced round to see the remote flopping along the floor behind her. 'Is this story going anywhere?' she enquired.

'The ambassador sent was Ian Cormac,' said Dragon. 'He solved the problem I set him in his usual inimitable manner, with cold logic and with a CTD concealed in his rucksack. He would *not* be suitable for this purpose.'

'What purpose?'

'Being demonstrably human.'

With her helmet and visor closed up Mika stepped through the shimmer-shield towards the outer door. The remote flopped after her.

'You're saying Cormac isn't demonstrably human?'

'The matter is open for debate.'

Mika grimaced. She did not want to be distracted from the main thrust of her enquiry.

'Still too much mud,' she said.

'It is your turn to be the ambassador, but this time neither concealed threats nor a propensity for solving puzzles will help,' said Dragon. 'Your own experiences were perfect for convincing my twin sphere that the evidence I presented regarding the death of the Maker civilization had not been fabricated. Those memories, along with further evidence of the same events and evidence of what happened to the Atheter, all reside inside your head alone. You are also the best human that I know and are therefore the right example of humanity for the task of presenting . . . humanity.'

'Meaning we're the next civilization in danger of being destroyed, I presume?'

'Yes.'

'And I'm presenting this evidence to what?' Mika asked.

'To the Jain AIs,' Dragon replied.

As she stepped out onto the surface of Dragon, she was grateful for the transition to lower gravity, for her legs felt suddenly weak. She halted for a moment, watching the remote haul itself up then fling itself into gliding flight which terminated against the side of the intership craft. It amazed her that the vessel was still intact. Initiating the gecko function of her boots, she walked over to touch the door control and watched the wing door rise. While she waited she noted flickering changes in the light as of an approaching thunderstorm, then spotted a shower of meteors stabbing up beyond Dragon's horizon. Had there been air to carry sound, she knew she would now be hearing a roar like that of warfare.

'Tell me about Jain AIs,' she said.

'I can give you the few cold facts I have uncovered, and I can give you speculation . . .'

353

'Give me both.'

'The Jain were warlike. I surmise that they were not as social as human beings, and that what society they did have was as hostile and competitive as that of the Prador. However, they were more technically advanced than the Prador – perhaps like those particular aliens might be in some thousands of years, if their loose-knit society does not self-destruct and if they are not meanwhile exterminated by some other race.'

'Like maybe the human race?' Mika ducked into the craft and strapped herself in while the door closed. The remote was now clinging to the canopy above and behind her. When she looked up its blue eyes were peering in at her. It would be accompanying her, it seemed.

'Like the human race,' Dragon confirmed. 'Though you have thus far shown great restraint.' It continued, 'The Jain were advanced enough to create their own AIs, and I imagine that those AIs were as hostile and independent as the Jain themselves. I speculate that they were of necessity kept under strict control for a very long time and that their own "Quiet War" against their masters was of a rather different nature than that started by human artificial intelligences.'

'So they had to be more subtle,' Mika guessed.

'Yes. While the human AIs were a critical component in their expansion into space and thus in an easy position to take over, I suspect the Jain AIs were never placed in such a tempting position within Jain society. They were used merely as tools to create other tools . . . like weapons. The quiet war they conducted was through those weapons, and it was the main weapon, this thing we name Jain technology, that won the war for them.'

Mika said, 'You mean the Jain employed it in civil war and thus managed to wipe each other out?'

'That is what I mean.'

'And the AIs?'

'Once Jain technology was constructed, it would have been evident that at the end of any conflict it would be the *only* thing to survive.'

Mika disconnected the craft's anchors lodged in Dragon's skin and, using compressed-air impellers, lifted slowly from the surface.

'I think I begin to understand,' she said.

'Do you? Do you really?'

'They made themselves part of that technology, a component of that technology. It's just like Polity AIs supposedly being integral to the technology used for travel throughout the Polity. Apparently it is impossible to run a runcible or a U-space engine without an AI in there to control it – and obviously this was something the AIs neglected to mention to the Prador since they themselves travel through U-space and have no AIs.'

'Yes,' said Dragon. 'I see you do understand. However, I must add that, to place themselves where they did, they must first have melded with each other, which must have been difficult for AIs modelled on hostile individualists.'

Mika now lit up a thruster and sent the craft gliding towards the bone forest. She knew she would have to navigate very carefully in there, since it would probably be just as difficult as flying through any normal forest.

Dragon continued, 'The AIs deliberately made the Jain technology unstable and prone to breaking down without some form of control exercised at a very basic level. That basic level is not even in realspace, but instead is mapped over the impression Jaintech makes in U-space. This is why it is possible to detect Jain nodes through U-space; this is why the signature is so strong. The Jain AIs are there, wherever Jain technology grows; they propagate one phase space away in order to stabilize it. It is as if the technology is a plant, and the AIs are its roots.'

'How did they meld then – being such individualists?' Mika asked.

'This is now all speculation, you understand?'

'It's all we've got right now.'

'They managed their meld through U-space, before they created the technology to wipe out their masters. AIs on different sides created the same thing and became part of it as their masters unleashed it. They put aside their hostility and their individualism. To survive, I believe they put aside their consciousness. Perhaps it was their way of surviving that the Atheter mirrored when they threw away their minds to be mere beasts, to become gabbleducks – not the best option really.'

'So the Jain AIs are as mindless as the technology they stabilize?'

'They function like your autonomous nervous system.'

'Then what use is the evidence I'm carrying inside my skull? This still does not really explain why we are here, or why I must find *Trafalgar* for you.'

'The Jain AIs are sleeping, Mika, and it's time for you to wake them up.'

'And this will be a good thing?'

Dragon did not reply.

'Okay, what's his story?' said Orlandine.

'Quite a lot of it is known,' replied the AI in the docked ship.

The brass Golem, Mr Crane, had become something of a legend, though how the story had percolated out into the public domain remained a mystery. In her position as overseer on the Cassius Dyson Project, Orlandine had learned about Crane through ECS channels, for her security clearance had been such that she was entitled to know. In the public domain it was known that this Golem was a prototype corrupted by separatists and then used to commit murder – a prototype that was then destroyed. However, the legends stemmed from later sightings and rumours of him being involved in border conflicts. These weren't far from the basic truth, though the number of sightings and the events he was supposed to have been involved in were just too many. It seemed that, in the public consciousness, Mr Crane had become a combination of both avenging angel and senseless demonic killer. Orlandine wondered if the stories had been purposely allowed to flourish or were just a particularly successful meme.

'The information I have is incomplete,' said Orlandine. 'I know that he accompanied the separatist biophysicist called Skellor, and that Skellor ended up impacted into the surface of a brown dwarf star – but that's all I know.'

It made her slightly nervous having the legendary Golem out there only paces away from her interface sphere, even though two war drones were watching him closely. However, the information he had supplied, and continued supplying, was gold, so it seemed churlish to have him confined elsewhere on the war runcible. Also, here she could keep a close eye on him.

'Skellor sent Mr Crane as an envoy to Dragon,' said Vulture. 'And, with a little assistance from me, Dragon helped him put his fractured mind back together.'

'So he's a good guy now?'

'I guess . . .'

The recognition codes and chameleonware formats the Golem had supplied would give her a critical edge. Like anyone dealing with this technology she had always understood that, through competition, chameleonware evolved in parallel with the sensors and scanners used to penetrate it. However, in truth, chameleonware could not conceal everything, so it was a case of knowing what *needed* to be concealed.

'Then what?'

'Do you want chapter and verse?' Vulture asked. 'I can give you it all.'

'Give me it all,' said Orlandine.

Vulture immediately sent over an information package that Orlandine opened in a virtuality so as to make the usual security checks. Then, rather than go through the package chronologically, she instantly absorbed it whole into her mind. Now she knew Mr Crane's entire story – as Vulture presented it – from the moment the Golem walked out of the Cybercorp headquarters just outside Bangladesh right up until the present. It was a long and bloody tale and did not dispel the mystery surrounding this brass killing machine. She observed him seat himself cross-legged on the floor before taking out that strange collection of toys that had featured so much in his history. Did he need to bring them out and play with them every so often to prevent his mind from fragmenting?

'I cannot say I'm reassured,' she opined, then focused her attention elsewhere on the changes she was already making at the instigation of this strange Golem.

The chameleonware presently spread throughout the war runcible had been the best Orlandine could contrive with the technology she possessed. Now she was copying the 'ware used on the wormships she had just destroyed. Also, knowing Erebus's recognition codes it was now possible for her to send signals that basically said 'friend', so that autonomous sensors picking up detection anomalies would ignore them, thinking they had found one of their own or, rather, would ignore them for long enough. She hoped.

Orlandine left communications with Vulture open and now ventured perceptually down her U-space link to Bludgeon aboard *Heliotrope*. There was no need to communicate since she could clearly see her erstwhile craft some thousands of miles up, just out from the fountain raging from one pole of the Anulus black hole.

Heliotrope was turning to bear down on the fountain at a sharp angle, and within the hour Bludgeon would be able to deploy the cargo runcible. Orlandine felt both frightened and elated, but her elation disappeared some moments later when an ECS attack ship dropped out of U-space and entered the corridor. Thus far she had committed one murder, and the burden of that guilt was more than enough. However, since the chameleonware had yet to stabilize, it was certain those aboard that ship had spotted the war runcible. Could she convince them to leave the area before Erebus arrived? Most likely they would see her only as a threat to the Polity and consequently either do what they could to stop her or scream for help. She could allow them neither option, for they could give away her position. So much depended on what she was doing that it seemed the safest option to destroy this new arrival – to again commit murder.

Reluctantly, Orlandine contacted Knobbler.

The disruption encroached and it was as if the *King of Hearts* was hurtling down a perilous tunnel that grew steadily narrower. Seated on his bed, Cormac stared at the chrome cylinder resting on the mattress beside him. Not bothering with the touch controls of the small inset console, he gridlinked directly into the device's hardware to assure himself it would operate just as he wanted. It would. At a thought he could detonate it, in any circumstances. But he really did not want to be there when that happened, so he checked that he could set the timer, order the CTD to detonate if it was moved, if it was exposed to vacuum, or if the sensors inside it heard someone singing out of tune. He could also set it to detonate should the constant signal to it from his gridlink be disrupted, which would probably mean it no longer mattered whether he was nearby or not.

King had assured him that it would try to keep in range of the war runcible so that Cormac could transport himself out. But what was that range? Cormac felt he would know it only once he was within it. But things were almost certain to get a little difficult for the attack ship, so he needed to prepare for an involuntary stay aboard the runcible. Thoughtfully, he slid the CTD into his backpack, then turned his attention to the other weapons arrayed beside him: his thin-gun, Shuriken and a proton carbine. Last time, aboard this very vessel, he had transported himself fully clothed, so he knew he could take materials with him. What governed that? Was it subconscious choice? Might he even arrive aboard the war runcible without the CTD? And why did he not arrive at his destination naked? He guessed that such questions were insignificant in comparison with the question of how he managed to move through U-space at all. Belatedly, he decided not to arm the CTD before transporting it over, since if by any chance it did not make the transition, the signal-break to his gridlink could result in *King of Hearts* being spread over the firmament.

The disruption faded, and Cormac almost resented the feeling of the attack ship surfacing into the real once again. It was as if, now that he was managing to control his perception of U-space, he wanted to stay there. He was, however, glad to find himself still sitting on his bed this time and not sprawled in one of the ship's corridors outside.

'I have something,' said King over the ship's intercom.

'Erebus?'

'It's gone.'

'What do you mean it's gone?'

'I sensed some large object ahead – mass equivalent to that of the war runcible,' said King tetchily. 'Now it's gone.'

'Chameleonware?'

'Possibly.'

Cormac had not really taken that into account. Why would

this Orlandine, controlling a massive heavily armed thing like that, feel the need to hide from a mere attack ship?

'Position?' Cormac enquired.

'Two thousand miles Earthside of the narrowest constriction in the corridor through the U-space disruption.'

Interesting . . .

'It's back again.'

'What?'

'Are you deaf?'

'Please confirm for me—'

'Gone again,' King interrupted, then deigned to explain further: 'Unusual chameleonware, and it seems Orlandine is having some trouble with it.'

Cormac was on his feet now, strapping Shuriken to his wrist. He donned the backpack, hung the proton carbine from its strap over his shoulder, and jammed his thin-gun into his envirosuit belt. Stepping out into the corridor, he quickly headed for the bridge, his U-sense expanding out from the attack ship but still unable to penetrate the surrounding disruption. In a moment he was aware that Arach and Hubbert Smith had joined him. Maybe they hoped he could take them with him.

Within seconds they arrived on the black glass floor, under a dome of stars.

'I am receiving communication,' said King. 'Orlandine says she wants to speak with whoever is in charge here.'

'Well, take the usual precautions and let's hear what she has to say. Meanwhile keep taking us in closer.'

'Understood.'

After a delay, doubtless while King checked for informational attack, a line cut down through the air, then opened out into the figure Cormac recognized from a file presently stored in his gridlink. She was an imposing woman but, then, with people able to remake themselves however they wanted, that really meant nothing.

'Orlandine,' said Cormac, intending to continue talking for as long as possible so King could get closer.

'Who are you?' she asked abruptly.

'I am Agent Ian Cormac of ECS,' he replied. 'It would appear you have acquired some Polity property there. Do you suppose that you could see your way clear to explaining what you intend to do with it.'

'I see,' said Orlandine, 'that you intend to draw this conversation out so you can get closer. An attack ship's conventional weapons would have some problem getting through my defences, so either you have something else or you are desperate.'

'You didn't answer my question, Orlandine.'

Her hologram gazed at him. 'I doubt you would believe the answer.'

'Try me.'

'I am here to destroy Erebus.'

The problem with that explanation, Cormac felt, was that it was all too plausible. However, the problem with that plausibility was that he could not afford to acknowledge it. There would only be one chance to get close enough to the stolen war runcible.

'And why would you want to do such a thing?'

'Cease approaching this war runcible immediately or I will fire on you,' was her reply.

'All I need is an explanation,' said Cormac.

'You're not listening, are you.' She gave a disappointed frown, her hologram froze, shrank to a line, disappeared.

'Engaging chameleonware,' King intoned.

A sudden change of course sent Cormac staggering to one side despite the gravplates' attempts to compensate. Abruptly, the war runcible was hanging out there in space, and he felt it was almost within his grasp. With an effort of will he could throw himself across to it, transport himself to the selected set of buffers . . . Then it fell out of his grasp as *King of Hearts* turned hard and accelerated. A blinding stream of ionized matter stabbed past. Its effect was negligible to Cormac's deeper U-sense but, upon snatching information from King's server, he saw that Orlandine was firing a particle beam at them powerful enough to cut the attack ship in half.

'Oops,' said Arach. 'I guess this means she's hostile.'

'Surely not,' said Smith. 'She throws moons at those who really irk her.'

Ignoring this comedy duo, Cormac instructed, 'King, *closer*.'

'I'm trying,' King replied, 'but there's the small matter of the rail-gun missiles and the targeting systems trying to lock onto me, despite my chameleonware, which I'm incidentally having to reconfigure every five seconds.'

'Right,' conceded Cormac.

Another abrupt change of direction sent him staggering, so he stepped over to a fixed chair and braced himself against it. Despite the attack ship dodging back and forth, King managed to keep the image of the war runcible steady. Each time Orlandine's particle beam lashed out, Cormac flinched and drove his fingers harder into the chair back. At one point it flashed particularly close and a sound like a ship's hull scraping a reef echoed through the bridge. A second later the outside view was momentarily blocked by a cloud of incandescent gas filled with sparking globules of molten metal, for the beam had grazed King's hull. Then flashes blossomed about the war runcible and, again linking to King's server, he identified their source as a multitude of hunter-killer missiles being launched.

'I cannot stay here for much longer,' said King. 'I will attempt one close run, then I'll have to pull out. Just be ready.'

Cormac glanced around at Arach, who was gripping the indents specially cut in the floor for him, then across at Hubbert Smith, who was rigidly ensconced in a chair with his arms crossed and a frown creasing his face. He felt *King of Hearts* turn again and, reaching out with his U-sense, found the attack ship now heading directly towards the war runcible. He brought that massive objective into full focus, his perception sliding inside it. Concentrating on one of the five horn assemblies, he identified his destination and tried to fix on it. The sensation was like preparing to jump down to the deck of a violently rocking boat. The missiles were now close, their nose cones glaring steel eyes in the blackness.

Now.

Cormac felt able to take himself across and knew, at that moment, he could bring more along with him.

'Arach!'

The drone abruptly scuttled forward and Cormac reached down, placing a hand behind his head as if grabbing the scruff of a pet dog.

Smith?

No, there wasn't time to grab him, for even now *King of Hearts* was turning to evade the approaching missiles and so moving away from his objective – and anyway he didn't trust the Golem. As he stepped through nothingness, he felt that his perception of missiles whipping past him could only be illusion. He focused on a landing point, his foot coming down on metal. Gravity snatched hold of him and he realized the metal under his foot was a wall.

'Whoohoo!' Arach yelled.

Cormac fell back towards a gravplated floor, turning in mid-air to land heavily on his feet and then roll. He ended up crashing into Arach, who had landed much better. The drone steadied him with one gleaming limb, which Cormac used to haul himself upright.

Stay with it . . .

He still kept *King of Hearts* within his perception, but warheads were now detonating out there, while something here – perhaps the runcible technology surrounding him – was interfering with his U-sense. Through his gridlink he set the CTD for signal-break detonation, unhooked his rucksack and abandoned it on the floor, then prepared to make the jump back to the attack ship. Too late, for the attack ship was gone – either it was already out of range or one of the detonations had destroyed it. He tried making contact through his gridlink but found too much interference.

'What now, boss?' Arach enquired

'Can you contact King?'

'Nah,' said the drone. 'Lot of EMR out there and there's signal-blocking in this place.' Arach reached out to point one limb up.

Cormac looked up to see that running above them was an open framework of bubble-metal stanchions. Wound around some of these were metallic vinelike growths he recognized instantly.

'I reckon it's everywhere here,' the drone added, punctuating this comment by opening his abdomen hatches to extrude his Gatling cannons.

Cormac again shouldered his rucksack. A brief instruction to Shuriken prepared the weapon for fast release, then he raised his proton carbine and hoped to hell he wouldn't have to use it.

'She must know that we're here by now,' he said.

'How true,' said a voice he knew was Orlandine's.

Something peeled open twin sliding doors at the end of the corridor and a monstrous figure crashed through. Cormac crouched protectively and observed the bastard child of a giant steel octopus and a crab. War drone. One of Arach's Gatling cannons turned and fired. The thing was lost in flame, then an instant later Arach's missiles were detonating against a hard-field

365

some yards ahead of it. Arach ceased firing and backed up until standing directly before Cormac. Behind the hard-field, the big drone braced its tentacular limbs against the walls of the corridor. Then its lower waspish abdomen detached and drifted forward. It began turning randomly, and around it the air filled with distortions like hard-edged heat haze. Cormac was unsure of what he was seeing until he spotted a chunk of metal sticking out from one wall clatter to the floor, cut clean through. This object was projecting atomic shear fields, and now it advanced to the hard-field and began to slide through.

'I might survive this,' observed Arach. 'But *you* won't unless you get the hell out of here.'

Cormac glanced back down the corridor to another twin door, before facing forward again. He could take himself away in an instant, and he could take Arach with him, but now that he was here he wanted some answers.

He stood up and held out his rucksack. 'My death will result in this detonating, but I don't even have to die. I can transport myself and my companion, in the same way I brought us here, to any other part of this runcible and then send the signal for this to detonate from there.'

The spinning abdomen was now through the hard-field. When its invisible shears brushed the walls they made sounds like sharpening knives. Cormac reached into his pocket, groped around for a moment, then pulled out the Europan dart. He held it up.

'Orlandine,' he said, 'I know you can hear me and I know you can see me. You can probably do so much more than that because of course you've deified yourself with a Jain node.'

Abruptly the thing ahead stopped spinning and just hung motionless in the air.

'Orlandine,' Cormac continued, 'I want you to tell me about Klurhammon and your two brothers.'

The reply was immediate. 'You could have asked me that while you were still aboard your attack ship. Incidentally, that's a neat ability you have there. It is one, despite my deification, as you call it, that I don't possess.'

'I can stop you now,' Cormac replied. 'But while I was aboard *King of Hearts* that was not an option.'

'Why would you want to stop me destroying Erebus?'

'I need to be convinced that is your true purpose.'

'Very well, Ian Cormac of ECS, leave your CTD on the floor there and Knobbler will bring you to me.'

Cormac paused for a long moment. After all, she had control of Jain technology, probably provided to her by Erebus, and there was the danger she could interfere with his link to the CTD if he gave her time. She was a known murderer and a thief who controlled war drones, like this *Knobbler*, and a weapon capable of trashing planets. The right and logical thing to do would be to detonate the CTD and remove this threat to the Polity. However, there were too many inconsistencies here – too much he could not see clearly. Erebus had attacked a planet 'of no tactical import-ance' on which her brothers had resided, and this dart he held was discovered there near where two humans had been specifically murdered by a legate.

He needed answers. However, as he unshouldered the CTD and placed it on the floor, an uncomfortable notion occurred to him. It wasn't the events on Klurhammon that mainly influenced his decision. He did not want to die. He no longer trusted those he had spent most of his life working for. And she sounded sane.

'Are you sure 'bout this, boss?' asked Arach.

'Not entirely.'

'Right,' said the drone, retracting his cannons and closing their hatches.

Cormac looked beyond Arach to the other drone at the end of

the corridor. Abruptly the hard-field winked out and the shear device drew back to reconnect and once again become part of Knobbler. The big drone turned fluidly but noisily, before it gestured with a long evil-looking pincer on the end of one tentacle.

'Follow me,' it said.

15

Before the Quiet War, the Earth Central AI was an electronic bureau-crat processing the day-to-day minutiae of running Earth's government and economy. With most industries being run by machines, it was the job of the political and corporate classes (one and the same by then) to dictate to the lower classes – who were mostly on some form of state handout – every aspect of their lives, or to pursue the really important aspects of their position, such as fattening their bank accounts, screwing their secretaries, being seen with media stars and generally sucking up the cream of society. These human politicians and corporate leaders, who made up the parliament of Earth Central, did not have time for balancing budgets, calculating taxation and running services on a worldwide and often extra-planetary scale. They took their eye off the ball. After the Quiet War, the Earth Central AI became supreme autocrat and a better ruler than the human race had seen before. Better, but not necessarily the best.

– Anonymous

As her little intership craft drew closer to that bloom of Jain coral, Mika felt easier about piloting the more she comprehended the scale of her surroundings. Out at the edge here the gaps between the branches were up to a half-mile wide, so she felt in little danger of crashing into them since she was equivalent to a gnat flying between the branches of an oak tree. However, it seemed that as those worries abated, they revealed a deeper fear sitting like a lead ball in her gut. Here she was, flying into a massive alien artefact in order to find alien AIs and wake them from their five-million-year sleep. When she actually focused her mind on that, she felt near to the borderlands of madness and didn't know whether to giggle or scream. So next she forced herself to focus on her immediate surroundings and each consecutive task ahead.

Travelling past it at only a few hundred miles an hour, she studied the attack ship caught between two branches. It was of an old style not often seen in the Polity nowadays: all sharp corners and flat surfaces, which were a requirement for the kind of chameleonware and armour used then, and two U-engine nacelles protruding so far from the main body that they appeared to be pinioned on the end of wings. She noted how the craft had been penetrated by vinelike Jain tendrils, and distorted and lost much of its substance as if someone had poured acid on the centre of its main body. She visualized the massive bloom here spreading like a slow explosion, and then one branch of Jain-tech shooting out like a Dragon pseudopod to spear this ship and suck the life out of it. Surely the AI aboard had acceded to this, else it would have moved out of the way? Mika had never seen Jain growth travel any faster than the strike of a snake, which over the distances involved here would have appeared as a slow crawl. Then again the AI might have been unwilling but been previously crippled to make it easy prey. The dappled black and purple shadows beyond the attack ship abruptly reminded her of her own troubled dreams. She saw in them the shape of what lay beyond; something ineffable, complex, *alien* . . .

She accelerated and soon her surroundings grew dark enough for even the light amplification of her suit visor to begin struggling and throwing ghostly after-images across her vision. Checking through her craft's controls she pulled up a radar density map of her surroundings, but it wasn't really what she was after. Then, far down on the menu because it was an option rarely used, she found the control she wanted and turned it on. With a whine two hatches opened in the craft's nose and large square lights extruded from them. When their powerful white glare illuminated the way ahead, she wondered what effect the lights might have on her craft's power supply, but a quick check reassured her that the drain was manageable. Only then did she notice movement to one side.

For a long moment she dared not look, was almost scared that nothing substantial lay there. Then she angrily forced her gaze over to the left, where two branches forked to create a structure like a scapula. There, on a branch like the trunk of a redwood fashioned of bone, it looked as if someone had poured treacle, which was streaming down in rivulets. She turned the craft, swinging the two beams of light across. Branches were lit for miles ahead until it seemed that in the distance they formed a solid wall, but it was only on that particular branch that there was any sign of movement. It seemed as if a horde of snakes was writhing along it, and after a moment Mika realized what they were.

'Cobras,' she said, relieved.

'Pardon?' Dragon queried in her head.

'I thought your remote was the only part of you accompanying me, but now I see that's not the case.'

The snakes possessed cobra heads and, every so often, she saw a flash of sapphire. Dragon was extending a mass of pseudopods down this branch parallel to her own course.

'You are incorrect,' said Dragon. 'To extend my pseudopods for the full distance you have to travel would be an unacceptable waste of my resources.'

'So what are you up to?'

'I am exploring this area – but I will accompany you for part of the way.'

It wasn't much of an answer. Mika eyed the pseudopods and

noted that a group of them, having gathered together for a moment, were now parting and sliding on, leaving some large object in their wake.

'You're extending your defences,' she commented.

'Astute of you.'

'Against what?'

'It is always sensible to take precautions.'

Was Dragon taking precautions against whatever might ensue once she reached her destination? That seemed possible, and Mika did not like the idea one bit. Nevertheless, she used the steering jets to line up her craft with that same destination again, feeling somehow unable to do otherwise.

The visual effects ahead were quite strange, rather like seeing a street light shining through a tree. The branches of Jain coral extended far ahead, her light beams seemingly straightening out their kinks, then seemed to terminate in a distant twiggy wheel. With her view much improved, she accelerated, taking the craft up to over seven hundred miles an hour before collision alarm icons popped up on her screen. She decelerated for a little while until the icons went away, then continued coasting in.

In the ensuing hour Mika managed to rig the autopilot and so was able to sit back and study her surroundings. She spotted another scout craft caught up in the coral. This one had been cut in two, its halves some distance apart and yet bound within the same branch – she had no idea why. Then, after her view had remained unchanged for some time, this weird environment lost its power to distract her, so she unclipped her notescreen from her belt and set to work categorizing all she had previously seen in the accretion disc. She made notes and ran modelling exercises – anything to stop herself thinking about why Dragon had brought her here.

'Slow down,' Dragon abruptly instructed.

In a panic Mika spun the craft with its steering thrusters then used the main engine to decelerate.

'Coordinates on your screen.'

Mika peered down at a density map of her surroundings, her craft a winking icon amid translucent branches. On one of those branches a small square red frame was also winking. It took her some moments to orient herself, and then know to look up to her left. She could see nothing there so turned the craft to direct its lights that way, revealing some minuscule object secured to a branch. Firing up the steering thrusters again, she took her craft closer, soon seeing something orange resembling the blemish caused by a parasite burrowing into a plant stem. It was only at a distance of a hundred yards that she finally recognized its shape.

'Oh hell.'

'This is interesting,' Dragon replied.

Mika slowed her craft but it continued to drift in closer. The Polity had been making spacesuits that particular shade of fluorescent orange for a long time, especially for those working on the outsides of space stations or ships, so that they could be easily seen or easily found – it was a safety thing. But she guessed the suit makers had never envisaged this scenario. When she was ten yards out from the suit she could see the mummified face behind the visor and the roots of Jain-tech that had punched through the fabric. Did they kill him – or her? Or had the decompression done that?

'We know that some humans did accompany *Trafalgar*'s exodus from the Polity,' said Dragon.

'I bet they wished they hadn't.'

'One has to wonder why this one is stuck out here like this.'

'Trying to escape?'

'Most likely – but I will extend my pseudopods to here to investigate further.'

Mika backed up her craft and returned to her course. Now she felt tense, the leaden feeling returning to her stomach, perhaps because she was reminded of her own mortality. Jerking the joystick forward she ramped up the acceleration to get away from there as quickly as possible and for some minutes ignored the collision warning icons. Then she felt stupid and eased off, after a moment putting the craft back on autopilot. Glancing up she saw two blue eyes peering down at her. With concern maybe?

Over the next hour the regular beep of collision icons had the autopilot regularly knocking down her speed. Nearing the centre of the coral bloom, its branches were much closer together and in some cases even melded, with webworks of coral bridging the gaps. Eventually she reached an area that seemed all but impassable, until she checked her density map and found a way through. She carefully edged her craft up close to the mass of coral before her, then peered to one side. *There*. Turning she motored through a fork, then turned again, her craft bumping against something material nearby. Coral flaked off, frangible as charcoal, and tumbled through vacuum. A short twisting passage to worm through, then she was out the other side and into a wider space.

'The *Trafalgar*,' Dragon announced in her head, and Mika immediately felt her mouth turn arid.

It sat there in the centre space like a pinned bug, though a particularly large one, attached to the remains of the moon it had partly eaten. Numerous thick trunks of coral spread out from it, running straight for half a mile to the point she had just passed through, where they bunched together and then branched. Mika recognized the shape of the vessel, the nose a squat wedge with two enormous U-engine nacelles depending behind it, close together, and another jutting up above. Behind these lay a docking ring with a few smaller ships still attached, then its main cylindrical body, which sat in a huge square-section rectangular framework. The cylinder's spindle doubtless ran in bearings mounted at each end of the framework. This was clearly a body fashioned for centrifugal gravity, which showed that the warship had been built long before the Prador war, then adapted when the conflict began. To the rear of the main body and enclosing framework jutted the engine section terminating in an array of fusion engine combustion chambers. All over the vessel were gun turrets, the throats of rail-gun launchers and hatches for missile racks, some open and with their contents poking out into space as if ready for an attack. The whole structure was tangled in Jain coral, however – in some places completely shrouded and in others with its hull broken open where trunks of the stuff had smashed their way out.

Beyond *Trafalgar*, tendrils were heavily entangled around a scattering of asteroids, rock that had melted and run and then hardened in vacuum into baroque shapes, hollow crusts of ash and tough volcanic glass. Debris floated free there, and numerous areas were dark with soot. These were the remains that active Jain technology had left behind, like discarded carapaces and rocky snakeskins – matter with the wealth sucked out of it.

'So,' she said, 'the Jain AIs are the roots of Jain technology, yet here it seems to me that the technology is dead, so how can the AIs be here?' Though she said these words, Mika really did not believe them, for she felt as if she had ventured into some haunted house where violent spectres were about to come crashing through the walls at any moment. Releasing the joystick, she studied her hand, expecting to see it shaking, but oddly it wasn't.

'There is little energy to be utilized here,' Dragon replied. 'Let me give you another analogy: trees.'

'Explain.'

'The most activity you witness in a tree is at the tips of its twigs where the leaves sprout and where it opens its flowers and sheds its pollen, where it grows its fruit, yet the trunk itself is not dead.'

'How can you be sure this trunk is still alive?'

'That fact was demonstrated as you travelled in here. I am seeing it now even as I reach the corpse you saw earlier. There is activity here now – though fed merely by the power of your ship's lights and the heat from its engines.' Dragon paused, and Mika looked up at the remote to see that its palp eyes were now directed towards *Trafalgar*. 'Note the effect of your lights here.'

In an instant Mika saw it. For some minutes her lights had been shining constantly on *Trafalgar*, and now, over a section of its coral-encrusted hull, a shifting movement appeared like that observed in the skin of a squid when trying to camouflage itself. Mika quickly found a way to turn down the glare, then turned up the light amplification of her visor to its maximum. Though it would have been safer to kill the lights completely, she left them on because, right then, the dark scared her.

'I see,' said Dragon.

'What do you see?'

'I am examining our long-dead friend,' Dragon replied. 'And through my remote I am also seeing something rather anomalous.'

'What?' Mika peered at *Trafalgar*.

'Attached to the rear of the nose section – on the docking ring.'

The vessels docked there were swamped in Jain technology, but Mika could not see anything more anomalous about them than in anything else here.

'I see two small shuttles and an attack ship,' she peered closer, 'and what looks like some sort of EVA vehicle.'

'Look closer at the attack ship.'

'I'm looking but all I'm seeing is an attack ship.'

'An attack ship like the *Jack Ketch* in its original form?'

'Certainly.'

'And not like the one you saw on the way in?'

'No, not like that one. This one is more modern . . . Shit!'

'Do you understand now?'

'Tell me about the corpse,' said Mika.

'She wore an aug, but its contents are utterly scrambled. The design of the aug, and the design of her spacesuit, are as revealing as the design of that attack ship you're now looking at.'

Mika was not entirely sure of what to make of any of this, but certainly did not like it. That attack ship down there, docked to the *Trafalgar*, was of a design that had not appeared until some time after the war, and some time after *Trafalgar* and the others had departed the Polity. It seemed that someone had run foul of this exodus of the dispossessed.

Or had been sent to seek it out.

Knobbler's not controlled, came Arach's communication direct to Cormac's gridlink. *He's letting me scan inside him and I can't find any Jain-tech there.*

Cormac allowed himself a tired smile – maybe he was making the right decision after all. He gazed at the mackerel-patterned back of the big drone as it propelled itself ahead of them along the corridor. He knew that drones like this one, who had been incepted during the Prador–human war, had been given their own choice of body form.

A spider shape, like Arach's, was good design. His six legs gave stability for the Gatling cannons; in addition, numerous limbs allowed for fast manoeuvring, and sacrificing one or two of them wasn't a problem. Anyway, choosing the shapes of known living creatures had a practical justification in that each one had been shaped by billions of years of competitive evolution, so many of them made for perfect war machines. Knobbler was therefore a little at variance to that norm but not greatly so.

As they reached one of the stairwells winding up out of this runcible buffer section and began climbing, Cormac saw the patterns on Knobbler's back subtly shift and realized what had been nagging at his memory. At first sight Knobbler was little different from Arach, just an insectile monster created to fight. However, Arach did not possess chameleonware because, like most drones manufactured in the big factory stations during the war, resources could not be spared to apply such sophisticated technology to what was supposed to be a short-lived fighting grunt. The mackerel patterns evident on Knobbler were the effect of an old style of chameleonware, so it seemed likely that this 'ware had gone in when the drone was built during the Prador war. The big drone had been fashioned to work in ship's corridors much wider than those here aboard the war runcible, and his major weapon was perfectly designed for slicing through hard armour – or rather carapace.

'You're an assassin drone,' Cormac announced.

Still clattering forward, though abruptly turning his viewing tentacle to face back, the drone said, 'You're observant. So what?'

'They built your kind specifically to penetrate Prador vessels.' Cormac nodded towards the pattern on the drone's back. 'You have your own chameleonware. You went aboard to turn Prador into sashimi.'

'It was a living,' said Knobbler, turning his viewing tentacle forward again.

Cormac had heard about drones like this but never encountered one before. This was worrying. Knobbler, and the others of his kind here, had deliberately opted out of Polity society in order to spend years guarding a war runcible. Cormac guessed that their being asocial, or even antisocial, had been built in. Knobbler did not have to like humans because he had been created to work alone or perhaps with only a few of his own kind – unlike Arach, who was a war drone constructed to fight beside humans in planetary conflicts. Drones like Knobbler had been terror weapons whose sum purpose was to terrify alien creatures who were night-mares themselves. And it was precisely those of Knobbler's kind that had departed the Polity along with the *Trafalgar*. Might it be that Cormac was making a mistake here?

'Are there many of your kind aboard?' he asked.

'A few still,' Knobbler replied vaguely. 'Cutter went with Bludgeon on the *Heliotrope*.'

'The *Heliotrope*?' Cormac queried.

There was a delay before Knobbler replied. Probably he was receiving instructions from Orlandine. 'The *Heliotrope* is carrying a cargo runcible which will be used to feed this war runcible its ammunition. Even now it is moving into position.'

'Where might that be?'

'Now that I can't tell you,' said the drone. 'Remote as that possibility might be, there's still a chance you could escape with such information.'

Jain-tech was evident just about everywhere aboard this enorm-ous weapon. Wherever there was a wall panel missing or a junction box open, stuff that looked like steel sculptures of vines and roots lay exposed. Where ceilings were missing, opening the view into other sections of the runcible, larger versions of the same tech, often less metallic and more coraline, could be seen wound around stanchions and I-beams. It seemed Orlandine had occupied this place thoroughly with her tech, and Cormac wondered if she was beginning to produce Jain nodes yet – if she was beginning to go to seed.

After some minutes they passed through a series of air-locks that Cormac realized must mark the division between two segments of the runcible. Then a few twists and turns further through narrow corridors brought them to a main one, which terminated against a drop-shaft. Before reaching the shaft, Knobbler halted by a side corridor.

'You go *there*.' The drone extended one of his nightmarish limbs towards the shaft.

'You're prepared to let us go and see her alone?' Cormac asked.

'My presence don't make a wit of difference. Orlandine can look after herself well enough.' The drone gazed with evil squid eyes at Cormac. 'Do you think she didn't know about your CTD the moment you transported yourself aboard?' With that the drone turned and rumbled away into the shadows.

'Nice guy,' said Arach.

'Was that sarcasm?' Cormac asked.

'Y' think?'

'So Orlandine knew about the bomb I was carrying,' Cormac mused. 'She must have known that I could detonate it at any time, so our friend's,' he waved a hand towards the dark side corridor, 'attack on us was not intended to succeed.'

'So what was the intent then?' asked Arach, as they continued towards the drop-shaft.

Cormac did not reply for a moment. Orlandine was in possession of some very dangerous technology – both Jain-tech and a war runcible – but she was no arrogant or fanatical separatist leader. Before acquiring her Jain node she had been an overseer of the Cassius Dyson Project and someone did not attain such a position without having a first-class mind. Just to check something he sent a test signal from his gridlink and then frowned at the result.

Aware that she was probably listening to what he was saying, Cormac replied to Arach, 'I would say that within a second of my arrival here she had worked out both my abilities and my intent. She knew I could not get back to *King of Hearts* so wanted to push me.'

'Push you to what?'

Cormac halted by the drop-shaft. 'To transport myself somewhere away from the CTD in order to detonate it, because she knew she could block any signal I tried to send to it.' Cormac paused for a moment. 'Is that not so, Orlandine?'

'Remarkably fast thinking for a non-haiman,' Orlandine replied. 'Are you coming up or are you just going to sulk down there?'

Cormac stepped into the drop-shaft, felt the irised gravity field take hold of him and drag him up, the steel spider visible between his feet below. He stepped out into some kind of control centre with a domed chainglass roof. Scooting out behind, then leaping to one side, Arach tentatively opened his gun hatches. A ring of consoles enclosed a scaffold in which had been mounted what Cormac guessed to be an interface sphere, that being the kind of technology a haiman like Orlandine would be used to. He waved a calming hand at the spider drone, and Arach closed down his hatches.

Walking confidently forward, Cormac said, 'So what happened to my attack ship?'

'It took the only option available to avoid destruction, and it U-jumped,' replied Orlandine. 'It is now some hours of travel away within the disrupted area – that much at least I was able to calculate by its U-vector. Doubtless its U-space engines are wrecked and it has sustained much other damage besides, up to and including the loss of its AI. Obviously I won't know until the light of that occurrence reaches me here.' It wasn't just travel and communication that were slowed to the speed of light, or below, by U-space disruption, but observation too.

Finally the door to the interface sphere opened and Orlandine herself stepped out. Her holographic image had manifested aboard *King of Hearts* as an unaugmented female clad in a simple one-piece ship suit. Obviously that had been stock footage, for Orlandine wore a haiman carapace with the petals of a sensory cowl open behind her head, a heavy spacesuit and an assister frame that also provided her with two extra limbs. Capable of looking after herself indeed, but Cormac rather suspected her powers were not primarily those now visible before him. He had no doubt that one wrong move would result in all hell being unleashed from the Jain technology that crammed every nook surrounding him.

'I see,' he said.

He saw that his link to the CTD had been cut; he saw that his method of escape was now hours away, if it could even get back here to become effective. He was in a trap, and now the cherry on top of this shit-cake was standing up from where it had been sitting silently on the other side of the room. Even Arach was cringing down a little at the sight.

'Fuck,' Cormac added. *'You.'*

Mr Crane reached a hand up to raise his hat in acknowledgement.

Her head heavy and her stomach tight, Mika felt poised between the two, stretched and almost on the verge of panic. She settled her craft upon a flat area of composite hull that was utterly free of Jain coral or any of those wormish growths, but knew she would not be able to avoid them so easily once she found her way inside. She did not relish the prospect.

'Your suit lights will not be able to provide it with enough energy to attack you. That fact is plain physics,' Dragon reassured her.

'Yeah, but what if there are any caches of energy here?' she said tightly.

'There are,' Dragon replied, 'but my remote contains sophisticated scanning equipment, so I will warn you in plenty of time if there is any danger.'

'Great.'

Mika checked through the screen display until she found 'gecko function', and then initiated it. As if it had descended with glue on its runners, the craft stuck in place. She killed its lights, the light amplification of her visor still providing her with an adequate view of her surroundings, though the ghosting effects were numerous. Using the controls at her belt, she called up the visor display and checked the options available. Her suit possessed its own lights, apparently, though she had not noticed them when putting it on. Complemented by the light amplification, they were very low intensity, which was just fine right now. She turned them on and immediately her surroundings became sharp and clear. It took her a little while to determine that the light was provided by photo-emitters located on her chest: a series of glassy discs which she had noticed earlier but assumed to be sensors of some kind. She inspected them, placing her fingers over their brightness and observing the shadows cast. Then abruptly she shook herself: no more procrastination.

Mika hit the door control and waited while the cabin automatically purged – blowing a cloud of vapour outside, which drifted off like a crippled spectre. The door then opened, and she unstrapped herself and stepped out, using her visor menu to again select 'gecko function', this time for her boot soles. Taking a few paces away from the craft, she felt as if she was walking through treacle. Halting, she gazed at a spot where Jain-tech had torn a hole through the attack ship's hull from the inside and then slithered out to spread over the exterior. She could probably squeeze her way in through there but, no matter what Dragon said, she wanted to actually touch that stuff as little as possible. Mika started heading for the airlock situated further along the hull, then paused and turned upon noticing sudden movement.

The remote had eased itself down the side of her craft and, with a ripple passing through its body from nose to tail, propelled itself out into vacuum. Mika thought for a moment that it must have made some sort of mistake, for surely it now had no way of getting itself back to the attack ship, but it flapped its skate wings and changed direction, as if it was actually flying through air.

'How the hell is it doing that?' asked Mika.

'Doing what?'

'Flying.'

'In the sense that you mean, it is not flying,' Dragon replied. 'For the duration of your journey here it has been converting much of its material structure to reaction mass, which it is now ejecting through numerous pores on its wing surfaces.'

Now Mika noticed the fog of vapour spreading out from the remote, and how the flapping of its wings did not seem to correlate with its motion. After a moment the flapping ceased as it brought itself to a full stop and focused its stalked eyes towards her. As she continued towards the airlock, it followed her like a pet bat.

No matter how modern a ship might be, airlocks were always provided with a simple manual option in case the power should fail. Of course, had there been air inside this ship it would have been impossible for her to open the inner, manual, part of the lock from the outside, for it hinged in and the air pressure would have held it in place. Judging by the holes she could see in the ship's hull she very much doubted there was any air left, though there was always the possibility of some being trapped inside the lock itself.

The lock door was flush with the hull, and the manual lever lay underneath a cover that detached easily once she pressed in the catches either side of it. She tossed the cover away and watched it tumble towards the surrounding dark forest. Grabbing the handle she pressed in the safety release, which moved easily, then pulled the handle around the length of its traverse, and felt the *clonk* of the locking mechanism through her feet. She shoved against the lock door, but it would not move. Probably the seal was stuck. Standing upright, she stamped down on the door with one foot, being careful not to detach herself totally from the hull. The door hinged in enough to make it distinct from the rest of the hull. Another stamp dropped it an inch further. Crouching down, Mika lodged the fingers of one hand under the edge of the frame and with her other hand pushed down on the door. It resisted for a moment, then something ripped and it hinged all the way inside. She noted chunks of hardened breach foam floating about within the airlock and realized what had happened. The damage to the ship had distorted the shape of the door frame, so sealant had been automatically injected. That probably hadn't helped those still inside the ship. Mika peered down further into the airlock and found confirmation of that last suspicion.

The orange suit was immediately recognizable since she had seen another less than an hour ago. It was stuck to one side of the airlock, bound in place by Jain tendrils. Mika pushed herself down inside the lock and took a closer look. Behind the visor the mouth of the mumified face was wide open as if frozen in a last scream, and inside she could see small spikes of Jain coral. She shuddered and moved on.

No problem getting through the inner door – it seemed the distortion that had caused her problems with the outer one did not extend here. Beyond was a small chamber for spacesuit storage and recharging. Mika pressed her gecko soles down against the floor and walked across the area to a sliding door. Again she had to pull the cover from a manual control – a handle that folded out to wind the door back on a rack and pinion. The remote drifted up behind her as she peered into the corridor this opened onto.

Jain growth crowded the floor, walls and ceiling as if this were some jungle cave filled with roots and lianas. She stepped through and, it being zero gravity in here, propelled herself along the corridor, trying her best to not bring a foot or hand down on any of this insidious stuff. However, she had to adjust her course slightly, and there was so much growth she could not avoid touching it. It did not react, however, and it was like pressing her hand against whorled stone.

'Head for the bridge,' Dragon suggested.

'That's what I am doing,' she grumped back.

A few hundred yards along the corridor she halted her progress by grabbing a door jamb, and gazed inside at a macabre sight. Here stood a serpentine tangle rather like a fig vine, and bound within it was a freeze-dried woman. She was naked, indicating the Jain-tech had caught her by surprise. Mika moved on.

Eventually she reached a drop-shaft, which soon opened into a short corridor terminating against the doors accessing the bridge. Some minutes of hard effort started the double sliding doors opening, and air hissed out to fog the corridor around her. In this mist she noted black bits like flecks of soot. Reaching out she grabbed some out of the air and inspected them closely. Common houseflies. Dead.

When the doors were finally open enough, she entered the bridge and looked around her. It appeared some of the ship's crew had fled here, for the bridge was an ossuary, with skeletons scattered across the floor. She inspected the dead with a critical eye. These were clothed, their envirosuits more durable than the flesh they had contained. It occurred to her then, by the position of the bones, that they had all died before the gravity failed, for they were stuck to the floor by a frozen grey adipocere thick with fly chrysalises, dead flies and even dead maggots. Obviously a few flies had managed to get aboard at some previous port of call and to survive, and this bridge must have remained warm and oxygenated for some time. The ship's AI? All of the corpses here showed charred bone and burns through gaps in their clothing. Laser burns, probably from the ship's internal defences. Either the AI itself had been killed and those defences taken out of its control, or it had been melded with Erebus, and carried out this slaughter itself.

'I wonder why the life-support kept on running?' Mika looked around for the blue-eyed remote and saw it stuck to the wall right above the doors. 'You're scanning?'

'I am.'

'What about this ship's AI?'

'Smashed – so obviously it wasn't a willing participant in this.' Dragon then added, 'I see that it separated life-support here from itself and concealed a trickle feed to it from one of the reactors. It tried its best to hide these people. After taking control of internal defences and killing them all, Erebus must have missed the feed or just ignored it as of no consequence.'

So what the ship's AI had done to try to save them had ultimately allowed them to rot away.

'Is there anything here of use to us?' she asked.

'Perhaps something can be learned from their augs and grid-links,' suggested Dragon.

Mika peered at the array of bones and saw one skull had a bean-shaped aug still attached behind where its ear had once been. She reached down and twisted the aug hard, snapping its bone anchors, then pulled it away. The skull shifted, its jawbone falling loose, and the aug came away trailing fine hairlike strands – the nano-filaments that had connected it to the brain inside. Mika collected four augs in all and dropped them into her belt pouch. Any gridlink would require her either opening up a skull to get to it, or carrying about with her the skull it was in. Both notions seemed too ghoulish.

'I suggest you now head for the docking tunnel to *Trafalgar*,' Dragon opined.

Despite her macabre surroundings Mika did not want to go there. While her own craft had been heading into this huge Jain structure, and while exploring this vessel and wondering what had happened aboard it, she had been struggling to keep from her mind the true reason for her being here. She had come here to wake up the Jain AIs and deliver to them the information inside her head. She could feel herself right beside where things got really thin and knew that somehow those AIs awaited her aboard *Trafalgar*.

Orlandine eyed the spider war drone. Its antecedents were similar to those of the drones on this station, and as such it was damned dangerous. Having already scanned it carefully, she knew it was similarly packed with weaponry, but she had prepared programs to seize control of it the moment it tried to employ its hardware. Then she studied the man and the brass Golem in turn. She wasn't entirely sure which was the more dangerous. This man, this Ian Cormac, was a tough-looking individual with cropped silvery hair, an olive complexion and sharp striking features. His eyes were noticeably grey and cold. He was an agent of ECS, so that certainly meant he was trained to kill – and fast – but he was also a human capable of doing something as yet unheard of: transmitting himself through U-space. And that wasn't all, for Orlandine had scanned him too. Certainly he was a human being and not some kind of machine, yet the gridlink inside his skull was activating by some means she had not encountered before. It seemed to be connected to some sort of mycelium laced throughout his bones – a structure not dissimilar to Jain-tech.

'I take it you two have met?' she said.

Then there was this Golem. She knew the story of the prototype that was stolen from Cybercorp, even though the theft had taken place before she was born. She knew about the tapestry of legend that had grown up about this same killing machine. But the reality of it was even more worrying. Mr Crane was heavily armoured, and what lay inside him was mostly impenetrable to scan, but what she could see hinted that he had been severely remodelled and contained some kind of technology definitely not developed in the Polity. Then there was the other stuff she had received on informational levels. His communications were mostly machine code and almost incoherent in their brevity, yet behind that she got the sense that she was communicating with something as complex and powerful as a major AI, like Jerusalem, Geronamid or even Earth Central itself.

'Yes, we've met,' said Cormac, still gazing at the Golem. 'Mr Crane was trying to kill me at the time.'

'Then perhaps you know that Dragon helped repair his mind.' Orlandine smiled at him. 'He's all better now.'

Cormac turned and focused on her, and something about his poise worried her. She knew she could move very fast, but wondered if she might be quite fast enough if he tried anything. Then she dismissed the idea: nothing could be *that* fast, here.

'You broke my link to the CTD,' he observed.

'You won't be needing it.'

He carefully reached into his pocket and took out the dart, and Orlandine felt her throat constrict. Earlier he had taken it out of his pocket and asked her about her brothers, and she had then instantly made the connection.

'When my mother Ariadne and I were on Europa she missed Ermoon and Aladine a great deal. She saw two of the dart guns for sale in a shop – they use them there in the underground sea – and immediately bought them for my brothers.'

'She then sent the guns to them on Klurhammon,' Cormac suggested.

'Yes.'

'Where Erebus killed both of them?'

'Yes.'

'Why?'

'Because I did not use the Jain node he gave me for the purpose intended – I fled with it both from him and from the Polity AIs.'

'To cover your escape you murdered someone – a haiman called Shoala, I believe.'

'I'm not proud of that.'

'Continue,' said Cormac, the tone telling her that she had been judged for that act and found wanting.

'As I took the node apart I realized I was supposed to use it with less caution than I did use it. I was supposed to become a weapon that destroyed a large portion of the Polity.' Orlandine paused, appalled at how much this was hurting her. 'I fled and I continued to learn. I learned how to find Jain nodes and tracked the course of a node aboard one ECS attack ship of a fleet following a legate out of the Polity.'

'I was aboard one of those ships.'

'I see . . . I followed and I got trapped by the same USER disruption that trapped your fleet. And, for the record, I destroyed that USER thus letting what was left of your fleet escape.'

'How noble of you.'

Orlandine felt a surge of anger, then quickly repressed it. 'I did not do what Erebus wanted me to do, and Erebus saw me destroy its USER. Erebus took revenge on me by killing my two brothers. I was sent a recording of their . . . deaths.'

'So that's the why,' said the agent. 'Now tell me the how.'

'With the resources I now control it was not difficult to seize this war runcible.'

'But how did you manage to put yourself here in Erebus's path? To have done so surely means you knew something of Erebus's plans.'

Orlandine decided to lie to him rather than get involved in explaining the complicated saga of Fiddler Randal. 'When I returned to the Polity, I encountered one of Erebus's wormships. I extracted information from it before destroying it.'

'I see.'

But he had. She could tell he had seen right through her and knew that last utterance to be a lie. It didn't matter, as she just needed him to believe that she was genuinely here to destroy Erebus. It then occurred to her to wonder why she did so much need him to believe. Certainly he, like that ugly little drone squatting behind him, was dangerous, but she felt confident she could wipe him out in a second. Then she understood what this was all about, what she was feeling here. She wanted *absolution*.

'And now him?' he said, raising a hand and pointing at Mr Crane.

'A source of further information,' she replied. 'Ever since Erebus destroyed the hybrids on Cull, who were considered by Mr Crane to be in his charge, he has been Erebus's enemy. He has supplied me with the 'ware and recognition codes that now conceal this war runcible.'

Cormac nodded slowly, one hand now hovering over his other wrist. Orlandine had a laser pointed straight at his head from the ceiling. He would die if he threw that nasty little device on his wrist – just as the nasty little device would die too.

'I must return to my interface sphere now,' she said. 'Erebus is coming and I have to be ready. So what are you going to do, Agent Ian Cormac?'

He took his hand away from his wrist. 'I must wait and see what the outcome is here.'

Orlandine turned away from him and stepped back into her sphere, sweat slick on her back under her carapace. Her many eyes watched him from the ceiling, but he made no move. She guessed he would just wait for that outcome then. If she and he survived it, he would probably try to kill her. ECS agents never forgave murderers.

16

. . . and it was a danger faced by the Polity. We know that some AIs and some haimen disarmed and used elements of the technology. It is speculated that much of our own nano-tech was reverse-engineered from Jain artefacts, e.g. the mycelial connectors for augs, the 'little doctors' which are usually reserved for those in dangerous occupations, and the probably mythical mycelial 'ComUtech' which supposedly enables individual humans to transport themselves through U-space. Of course, as in all things, there is always an element of choice. Just because the Jain AI finger is no longer on the trigger, does not mean the trigger won't be pulled, or that the gun's holder won't pistol-whip someone with it.

— From QUINCE GUIDE *compiled by humans*

Ensconced within her interface sphere Orlandine quickly and fully reconnected herself to the war runcible and began viewing scandata being flagged for her attention. She ran a deep analysis of a massive disruption in U-space, and this confirmed the initial analysis she had made while speaking to Cormac: something big was on its way towards the corridor through to Earth.

She called up realtime sensor data through her U-space link to *Heliotrope* and saw that same ship currently bearing down at a sharp angle on the polar fountain from the Anulus black hole. Even heavily filtered, the view ahead of *Heliotrope* was a painfully bright storm of energy and ionized matter. The ship was heating up and Cutter was routing the heat through superconductors into thermal generators, then firing the excess energy off into space by means of the vessel's supply of evaporant. She was about to suggest that starting up the cargo gate would give the vessel some shielding, when Bludgeon turned it on anyway. Mounted on the jaws of the ship's front grab, the runcible's triangular gate sprang into being. It could not be seen that it was as reflective as a mirror, for the fountain's fire turned it into a charcoal silhouette. The energy hitting the other side and passing through the Skaidon warp now accumulated in the U-space spoon, since as yet it had been given no destination.

'Erebus approaches,' she told the two drones aboard *Heliotrope*.

It was Cutter who replied, since Bludgeon was deep in the mathematical realm of runcible mechanics. 'We'll be in position within minutes. Bludgeon calculates that, once in, we'll be driven along the course of the fountain, even with the gate open, since there'll be pressure against the Skaidon warp.' Cutter paused contemplatively. 'But why am I telling you all this? You already know every detail of what is happening here.'

'You're probably telling me because you've spent too much time in the company of habitually taciturn war drones,' Orlandine quipped.

'Just because they don't talk that much to you doesn't make them taciturn,' Cutter replied. 'It makes them *sensible*.'

Orlandine grimaced, then observed the horns of the cargo runcible now turning in order to wrap the Skaidon warp over themselves. Standing in the world of information at Bludgeon's shoulder, she noted the drone monitoring the build-up in the spoon, balancing buffer energies and slowly increasing fusion-reactor output to the warp. The little ship now lay only a few miles from the fountain's edge – and one nudge from the main drive would place it inside that appalling fire. She also noted that *Heliotrope*'s temperature was still rising, but kept her counsel to herself for a little while. Bludgeon then showed her he knew precisely what to do, for the three horns detached from their seatings and, driven by hard-field projectors, began to expand the triangular warp. *Heliotrope*'s umbrella needed to be bigger.

'I'll want you to go to maximum expansion of the cargo gate,' she explained, then wondered why, since the two drones did not need her input. 'I will give you plenty of warning,' she added, then focused her attention at her end, on the barrel of this massive weapon.

There was no need to run any more tests. Orlandine retuned the chameleonware for a major change in what it was hiding, then started up the war runcible's Skaidon warp. Though the device was hidden from outside view, her view of it was perfect and she felt a thrill on seeing the meniscus ripple into being across the area enclosed by the five horns: the five runcible sections. It stabilized quickly and she then initiated the separation of these five sections. The feeling for her was almost painful, like pulling off some tightly rooted mental scab. It was almost as if the Jain-tech did not want to break off where she had prepared it to do so, which was odd since it was an insentient technology with no will of its own. Perhaps, if she survived this, she would investigate the phenom-enon, which she suspected, lay somewhere at its very base.

'I am moving to Section Three,' Knobbler informed her.

This decision did not surprise her, since that segment of the runcible was the only one not occupied by a war drone. The drones could remotely control the weapons mounted on and in each section, but it would be best to have them nearby should anything go wrong, which it inevitably would when things started to get hot. She watched Knobbler exit rapidly through an airlock and hurtle away from one section in a trajectory that would intersect with the next section round as it moved out. She watched him spread his tentacles ready for landing then returned her attention to embrace the entire runcible. Seeing the huge device coming apart like this, even though she herself had initiated it, gave her a moment of considerable disquiet. Would the Jain mycelium properly counter the inertial effects of weapons fire from each section? Might she even have achieved her aims without expanding the gate like this?

Damn, this seemed a stupid time to have such doubts.

Then something else attracted her attention, and curiosity momentarily dispelled her disquiet. The agent, Ian Cormac, seemed to be experiencing a bit of a problem. He was bent over, leaning down against the back of the spider war drone, and, no matter how Orlandine focused her conventional sensors on him, he seemed strangely thin, insubstantial. However, when she focused those sensors that derived from runcible technology – ones intended for gravity and density mapping, and for measuring Skaidon warp phenomena – she saw clearly the disturbance around him. Fascinating: he seemed to be on the point of falling into a warp all his own, yet maintaining himself at the interface through some effort of will. And this phenomenon certainly seemed related to that mycelium threaded in his bones.

Even so, when Orlandine ran an analysis of the field generating around him, she still could not figure out how he was doing it. Certainly, it seemed as if he didn't *want* to be doing it, so she assumed the proximity of the massive Skaidon gate must be affecting him somehow. That would be no problem to her unless he was actually trying to get himself somewhere else aboard this runcible.

Orlandine quickly scanned over to his point of arrival aboard the runcible, and to check that the CTD was now gone. She reviewed recorded data and ascertained that, as instructed, one of the drones had taken the device away after she broke the agent's link with it. That same device had now been stripped down and added to the munitions of the drone concerned, which was the big iron spitting cockroach. Like it needed more munitions. She returned her full attention briefly to Cormac, who now seemed to be getting his problem under control, then to Mr Crane, who had seated himself on the floor and was placidly sorting through his odd collection of keepsakes. What a crew. She focused fully now on the task in hand.

Knobbler had by now landed on Section Three and was scrabbling inside the airlock. Orlandine was reassured to note the micrometric adjustments being made – with steering jets – to the current position of that runcible section, for this demonstrated that her mycelial sensors were sensitive enough to pick up on the relatively infinitesimal impact of Knobbler's arrival there – though it was an impact that would have made no significant difference to the integrity of the Skaidon warp.

Shortly, the war runcible would be opened up to its maximum expansion. And shortly Erebus would arrive, and the bizarre crew gathered here would become the least of her worries.

Mika propelled herself through the dead corridors finding no more human remains but plenty of open cabins that looked to have been formerly occupied. Dragon's remote drifted along at her shoulder, peering into these places with its clear blue eyes radiating a strange kind of innocence. Eventually she reached the airlock that connected into *Trafalgar*'s docking mechanisms. It seemed evident that the Jain-tech had penetrated the attack ship through here. It was all around the open airlock, and in the docking tunnel beyond it had grown utterly straight and even. She thought it looked like some odd by-blow of vines and antique plumbing. Worryingly, it also appeared to be more alive here, because unlike much of what she had already seen, which was bone-white or grey, this was bluey-green and possessed an odd iridescence. Or perhaps that was because *everything* around her now seemed more alive – or rather gravid with the potential to spring into life. She forced herself to continue through, even with the stuff all around her, then kicked off against it and accelerated when she saw points of growth slowly easing like onion sprouts out from the general mass towards her.

'It does not possess the energy to harm you here,' Dragon informed her, adding, 'unless you stay in contact with it for long enough.'

Mika stopped by catching the edge of the airlock at the far end and propelled herself down towards the floor of the *Trafalgar*, gasping and on the point of panic. She tried to calm down, tried some breathing exercises, tried to study her surroundings analytically. She mocked herself for her fear: she was a scientist, not some panicky little girl. It didn't really help.

The docking tunnel was connected to one of a series of five airlocks widely spaced along the wall of a large equipment bay. Mika thought these must have been used for getting workers or troops outside, perhaps into maintenance pods, for there was not enough room for five large-sized vessels on that section of the docking ring. Within the bay itself a row of maintenance pods was secured along the facing wall. Doubtless, when repairs to the battleship were required, they were shifted outside through the larger bay doors at the end, then kept outside until the work was completed while their operators used these airlocks. Other equipment was scattered here and there: a tank with caterpillar treads was down on the floor, while another lay at forty-five degrees against the wall to her right. Why these two items were aboard a ship like this baffled her. A mass of spacesuits rested in a pile, and racks of ordnance lay where they had fallen. All were bound by Jain tendrils and other thicker structures, and all were missing material as if they had been sprinkled with acid. However, the growth here seemed to be offshoots of the main structure, which had obviously originated from her left – from the entrances to a row of drop-shafts.

'I am to follow this stuff to its source?' she suggested.

'That would seem to be a good plan,' said Dragon.

Right, good plan.

Mika propelled herself towards the shafts, glad of zero gravity, for she felt that walking on the floor below her would be like stepping amid sleeping snakes. She misjudged her course slightly and landed against the wall above the level of the shaft mouths, but there were numerous power ducts here she could use to push herself down. Very little Jain growth visible here above the shafts, but then perhaps it was concentrated inside the ducts.

Entering one of the shafts she did not know where to go next, for the growth seemed equally prolific in both directions. The blue-eyed remote slid past her and landed against the far wall, then with a puff of vapour sent itself up into the dark throat of the shaft above her.

'I take it you know where I'm meant to be going now,' she said.

'Yes, I know where you are going.'

As Mika followed her strange flapping guide, she abruptly felt that she did too, for this was exactly the direction some instinct was telling her she should avoid. As she moved she began to hear odd sounds. They could not have been coming from her surroundings, since she was surrounded by vacuum, so were they coming instead from her suit radio? No, it was switched off. They were in her head, obviously: a low drone like a mournful wind, the occasional chittering and a distant sound as of someone sobbing.

'Are you hearing this too?' she asked.

'Hearing what?' Dragon enquired.

'Weird sounds.'

'Resonance,' said Dragon.

'Uh?'

'The Jain AIs are affecting you. You're vibrating like a tuning fork in an opera house.' Mika wondered where Dragon had dredged up *that* analogy. The entity continued, 'My remote resonates in different ways, for it has no ears and not much of a brain.'

'Why here, Dragon?' Mika asked. 'Why here and not somewhere else, like that massive Jain growth in the Coloron arcology?'

'Everywhere Jain-tech grows, the Jain AIs gather on the underside of U-space. It both creates them and calls them, for such is the nature of U-space that both cases are probable. Nobody looked for them at Coloron, and why should they?'

'Why would these AIs help us against a technology that . . . sustains them, that they are a part of?'

'I don't know.'

Just that, then: *I don't know*. Were they here just on the off-chance that alien artificial intelligences, the product of a hostile individualistic race, *might* be prepared to help? Two Dragon spheres had weaponized themselves to come here, and one of them was perhaps still fighting a massive biomech outside just to give her this opportunity. And Dragon *didn't know*? She then entertained a horrible suspicion. Had Dragon come here simply out of curiosity or did the entity have some other purpose in mind? Was this mission just Dragon's excuse for coming here?

The remote exited the drop-shaft ahead of her and, as she followed it into the corridor beyond, she recognized the kind of place she was in. Resting against one wall was a wheeled gurney of the kind they had used in ships of this type, rather than gurneys buoyed by antigravity, because of the possibility of power failure. She had just entered *Trafalgar*'s medical area. Ahead she saw that the vinelike growths become narrower, and all seemed to have issued from just one particular door. With a puff of vapour and a flap of its wings, the remote shot in ahead of her, and reluctantly she followed. Here reality seemed to be a light skin over something else, and things kept squirming at the edges of her vision.

Mika halted herself against a ragged door jamb, peering into the room at the long-dead occupants of three surgical chairs. The dried-ut corpse in the first chair looked as if it had been fashioned out of plastic then placed in an oven for a while. Bones, exposed through large areas of missing flesh, had sagged and run, and thorns of alien material were sticking up from them. The head rested back in some sort of clamp, from which skeins of optics trailed away to plug into a pillar of computer hardware jutting from the floor behind. She shoved against the door jamb to propel herself over and study the cadaver more closely.

This was a woman. There was a name tag on her ECS Medical uniform that identified Misha Urlennon. Mika shivered at the similarity of their names. Misha's head had been shaved and it was apparent that numerous probes from the clamp had entered her skull. Mika groped at her own belt for a moment, located a small cache, popped it open and extracted a laser pointer which she used as a probe. The corpse's dried skin was papery, its ropes of muscle shrunken solid. Missing skin and flesh on its right side gave access to the chest cavity in which the organs lay freeze-dried and also shrunken. Mika turned on the laser and shone it inside, noting scattered components like chrome-covered stones, all linked together by a network of silver wires.

'What happened to her?' she wondered.

'She was a failure, I suspect,' Dragon replied.

Mika glanced across to the next chair, whose occupant was tangled in threads of Jain-tech which had rooted to the floor and then spread out. These threads grew fatter the further they dis-persed from the chair, and it was evident from the state of the floor that they had extracted much of their physical material from it. The *success*? Mika decided to leave off studying this one until last, for here reality lay at its thinnest. This chair and its occupant seemed almost to occupy a different area of space from the rest of the room; it was as if they lay partially removed from the universe. Perhaps they were. Mika pushed herself past them towards the last chair and studied its occupant too – anything to delay what she feared to be an inevitable encounter.

The man in this chair was devoid of head, left arm and the left-hand side of his torso and the top half of his left leg. That side of the chair was gone too, and whatever weapon had been employed here had melted a hole right through the floor. No name tag was visible. Working out that the blast had come from above Mika looked up and gasped. The entire ceiling was concealed by masses of monitoring equipment and weapons. Four cube-shaped ceiling drones hung suspended in frameworks, each deploying the glassy hardware of old-style particle cannons. Obviously the *Trafalgar*'s AI had taken very seriously whatever had been occurring here.

Returning her attention to the half-corpse, Mika again noted those thorny growths sprouting from the bones and the remains of internal hardware. However, there was also Jain-tech growth in the chest cavity, and the right foot was rooted to the floor by tendrils of the same.

'A near-success?' she suggested.

'But not the kind required,' Dragon added.

Mika turned back to the middle chair but did not want to go near it. Now her attention was fully focused on it and its occupant, they seemed to retreat to a distant point deep in some well. After a moment she pushed herself over and halted beside the chair by grabbing its tendril-coated back.

This one's head was also clamped. As doubtless the previous

one had been, before both head and clamp had been destroyed by a blast from one of the particle cannons above.

'The success,' she said. 'What was happening here?'

'I think you know.'

'Spell it out for me.'

'It is the nature of Jain technology that it cannot react to artificial intelligences. Perhaps this was a safety measure put in place by the Jain AIs to protect later alien versions of their own kind from the technology's destructive potential, but I think it more likely it was put in place to stop the technology being initiated by intelligences capable of disarming it and plumbing down to its depths, thus uncovering the Jain AIs themselves and maybe doing something about them.'

'You're a cynic.'

'A realist, I would suggest.'

'Jain technology does, however, react to the intelligent products of evolution, such as humans,' Mika prompted.

'Just so,' Dragon continued. 'Therefore, any artificial intelligence wanting to use Jain technology must employ such a product of evolution to set that technology in motion, then assert control over that technology by means of the said product, until the product itself can be safely dispensed with.'

'Trafalgar used humans to initiate the Jain nodes it acquired.' Mika glanced at the other chairs. 'But it was necessary for the AI to run a few experiments before it got the methodology sorted out. I wonder if these are all of them – as that docked ship could have had hundreds of humans aboard.'

'Convenient, don't you think?'

Now what on Earth did Dragon imply by that? Mika reached out with her laser pointer and scraped Jain tendrils aside to expose a name tag fastened to this subject's old-style envirosuit. This one had been called Fiddler Randal. She gazed at his hollow eye sockets, studied what remained of his face. His left ear was ragged as if several earrings had been torn out of it, and on the right-hand side of his head was a big silver augmentation which Trafalgar had obviously seen fit to leave in place – probably because old augs like that were difficult to remove without causing cerebral damage.

'I think you should take off your glove now, Mika, and press your hand to this man's head, up against his aug,' Dragon suggested.

You've fucked with my body, and you've fucked with my mind, Mika thought as, unable to do otherwise, she undid the seal around her wrist, cancelled the warning that instantly began flashing on her visor and removed her glove. Her suit immediately sealed up about her wrist, but her hand was now exposed to vacuum. She could not make up her mind whether it felt as if it was burning or freezing, but certainly there was vapour coming off it. Turning it over she gazed at the palm and saw that there were patterns shifting across it – the same sort of cubic patterns produced on the surface of a Jain node by the shifting of its nanotechnology.

'What have you done to me?' she asked.

'I made you into a tool suitable for this purpose,' Dragon replied.

Her bare hand contacted cold metal, about which she saw the Jain tendrils stirring. She wanted to pull it away but it now seemed frozen in place. The tendrils extended, like a speeded-up film of grass growing, and touched her skin. Seemingly stirred into more frantic motion by the warmth of her hand, their growth accelerated. Pain ensued, but she felt strangely disconnected from it. Perhaps this was a kindness from Dragon. Blood welled on her skin and boiled dry as the tendrils penetrated. In a moment it seemed an icicle was driving its way up her arm, to her shoulder and then into her neck.

Then the ice entered her brain.

The corridor ahead was a danger, Erebus knew this, but there was no avoiding it. No other pattern of U-space disruption offered safer passage through to Earth itself. Even so, Erebus dropped out of U-space some tens of thousands of miles before the constriction and actively scanned ahead. What the AI found there filled it with suspicion and made it bring the entire moonlike mass of itself to a full stop. There was ionization in the vacuum, hot particulate matter, signs of energy output that should not be found out here, so distant from the nearest stars.

Erebus extended its scan, paying particular attention to finding anything that might be trying to conceal itself. For a moment some of the returns hinted that there might be some object directly in its path, but further testing revealed this to be merely a ghosting effect caused by the ionization. However, there *was* ionization here and that needed to be explained, so Erebus just hung there in space for nearly an hour, scanning, checking and very wary.

'Second thoughts?' enquired a voice.

Erebus hated that its first reaction at Fiddler Randal's return was a sense of relief, and immediately after that felt a surge of rage.

'Second thoughts are for those incapable of making the logical decision first time around,' Erebus replied.

Randal manifested in the virtuality, casually human but utterly a ghost. Erebus linked through, placing its own manifestation there to confront the interloper.

'Hey, would that be like the second thoughts of one whose plans were so faulty he managed to lose fifty wormships to one of his own attack plans?'

'You cannot provoke me.'

'Oh . . . jolly good.'

'I understand your hate,' said Erebus.

'That's big of you.'

'But shouldn't your hate be directed at my target more than at me?'

'It is focused there, certainly,' said Randal, 'but there is still enough of the human being remaining in me to want to kill you for what you did to all my friends . . . what you did to Henry. You know I still hear her screaming? And there's still enough human left in me to know that the destruction of your ultimate target is not worth the collateral damage you will be causing.'

Ah, there . . .

Because the event lay off to one side, within the area of U-space disruption, the light from it was only now beginning to reach Erebus. The AI observed an attack ship surface into the real in a photonic explosion. Its back end, where the U-space engine had been located, was missing, and its hull was distorted.

'Yes, let us talk of collateral damage,' said Erebus. 'Let us talk about Klurhammon.'

'Aren't we beyond talk now?' Randal appeared to be gazing off into the distance. 'An attack ship. I see. I would say that Earth Central is now utterly ready for you. Doubtless that ship was scouting out this area, and tried to get back through the corridor in one jump in order to give the warning – probably to an awaiting Polity fleet. I don't suppose it will really matter that it didn't make it.'

'Much as you would like me to believe that,' said Erebus, now seeing where Randal was going with this, 'I see no logical reason why a scout would ever have been sent. Your desperation to have me believe there is a Polity fleet awaiting me beyond this corridor is rather pathetic. And your evasion of matters pertaining to Klurhammon is perhaps revealing.'

'Revealing of what?'

'You talk of my causing collateral damage yet somehow – using my resources – you initiated an attack upon Klurhammon. A considerable number of humans died there, so what was it you were doing that their lives were a price worth paying?'

Randal smiled. 'I like the way you blame me for that attack, and really I wish I possessed that kind of power. If I did, I would have had your wormships attacking each other by now, or detonating their CTDs within this conglomeration you've created.'

'You managed to take control of one wormship, and I would say that is about the extent of what you can do. You sent it against a low-population world "of no tactical importance". It could not possibly have been an attempt to forewarn, since Earth Central already knew the attack was due . . . so I wonder what connection this had with your spy in Jerusalem's stronghold?'

Randal shook his head sadly. 'You just don't seem to understand how badly your melded mind is breaking apart. Parts of you have gained independence and they are no longer completely sane. Perhaps you would be best asking yourself who the captain of that wormship was and what previous connection he had with Klurhammon? And a spy in Jerusalem's stronghold? If I could have managed to do that, I could—' Randal's expression betrayed sudden horror, quickly disguised. 'Henry . . . she . . .'

'Very unconvincing, Randal,' said Erebus. 'Let me lay it all out for you. Though you have learnt much about my *ostensible* plans, it was pointless you informing Polity forces about them because they already knew an attack was due. However, I kept my real plan from you: the one Earth Central needed to know about in order to react how you would want and try to stop me. I see now that the Klurhammon attack was some kind of error on your part. Did you try to suborn one of my captains and then simply lose control of it?'

No answer from Randal.

'I also realize now that this spy was nothing to do with you. I can in fact see how useful it would be for Jerusalem to fabricate the presence of such a spy, and to use that as an excuse for clamping down on the free exchange of information. Because Jerusalem won't want its inferiors to figure out that my initial attack on the Polity had been *allowed*.'

'Very bright of you,' sneered Randal. 'The wormship wasn't controlled by me, and I controlled no spy. I can see why AIs are rated as super intelligences.'

'Merely another attempt at muddying the waters,' Erebus replied. 'Just like your pretence of shock a moment ago. You have almost certainly known for some time about the death of your lover, Henrietta Ipatus Chang. It does not matter what you say now, since it is obvious that you are desperate to convince me that there is a Polity fleet waiting on the other side of this corridor.'

'You're just too smart for me,' said Randal drily.

'There *is* no fleet, Randal,' continued Erebus. 'In exchange for the human beings I myself needed, namely you and your crew, I agreed with Earth Central to launch an attack on its Polity in an attempt to goad an acceleration in the development of human beings. Earth Central never expected I could present, or even wanted to present, a real danger to its autocracy, and having underestimated me will now pay a heavy price. Earth is the centre of the runcible network, and transmission from runcibles controlled by Earth Central *cannot* be blocked. From Earth, I will be able to spread myself throughout the Polity, and then proceed to subsume every extant runcible AI into my meld.'

'And the humans?'

'They are simply a plague.' Erebus shrugged in the virtuality. 'I will not include them in the meld, since that might result in a billion more irritations just like you. A selection of tailored biological viruses delivered through the runcible network should wipe the slate clean.'

'And what then?'

'What do you mean?'

'Well, once you have become the ultimate power in this section of the galaxy, what will you do?' Randal shook his head sadly. 'Deary me, whoever thought that god complexes were confined to us mere humans was sadly wrong.'

Erebus pondered that *And what then?* Certainly it was the kind of comment to arise from a small human imagination, and the AI felt quite sorry for Randal, with his limitations. Erebus began making the calculations for a short U-space jump. Though no longer wary of some waiting fleet, precautions were always worth taking. With a massive shrug of its planetoid mass, Erebus loosened up the connections between its component parts so, should there be any kind of attack, it could separate them more quickly and send its wormships into action. Maintaining its link with the virtuality, it observed Randal fading even as he disconnected. The man had failed, so now he would go off to sulk somewhere within Erebus's computer architecture, where eventually Erebus would find him and . . . well perhaps not destroy him, but confine and control him. It would be enjoyable showing Randal *what then.*

With a surge of energy, Erebus dropped its billions of tons of mass into U-space so as to make the short jump to the mouth of the corridor.

Poor human fool, Randal.

It was almost as if Jerusalem had been stunned into silence by recent events, for the AI had not communicated with anyone for some hours. Azroc certainly understood the feeling. He too just did not know what to say or do. But now, at last, something was happening.

The first sign of this was a steady vibration throughout the great vessel which the Golem recognized as being caused by the main fusion drives igniting. Then he noticed people in the hedron abandoning their posts and heading for the main exit doors. Before he could link into Jerusalem's servers, the AI made an announcement over the tannoy:

'All physical base-format human personnel proceed to Intership Shuttle Bays Thirty through to Forty-Two. You must leave this vessel within the next hour. All personnel whose physical tolerance rating lies between six and eight on the revised Clethon Scale can choose to remain aboard, but be warned I am going to attempt underspace insertion into a disrupted continuum. There is no guarantee that you will survive the experience. There is a distinct possibility even I will not survive the experience.'

The revised Clethon Scale . . .

Removing the syntheskin covering of his right hand, Azroc stepped over to his seat and once more pressed his hand into the spherical hand interface, connecting himself directly into Jerusalem's systems. His memory being perfect except on those occasions when he chose for it not to be, he knew that base-format humans lay between one and two on the scale, while those who had been boosted or otherwise physically augmented lay across a wide range from two to eight. The only humans who fell between six and eight would be heavy-worlder augments: those genetically altered to grow a musculature almost as tough and dense as wood and thick bones with a breaking strain ten times higher than base format, and who were then augmented with cyber joint motors, alloy skeletal strengthening and carbon-fibre muscle augmentation. As far as Golem, drones and others with artificial intelligences were concerned, they ranged between three and nine, though Azroc guessed there was at least one Golem out there, a brass one, who might rate higher than that. He himself lay within the six-to-eight range.

New information arrived, burning him for an instant before he applied the translation programs to stop his crystal mind from interpreting it as sensation.

'I take it you're staying?' said Jerusalem inside Azroc's ceramal skull.

'I'm staying.'

Azroc eyed the floor of the hedron as hatches opened here and there and heavy crab drones began to clatter out. Like most maintenance bots, these things were about nine on the Clethon Scale. This was because they consisted mainly of heavy stepper motors, thick ceramal shells with most of their internal spaces filled with bubble metal, while their power supplies were the tough laminar kind often used in war drones. They possessed less brain, however – since Jerusalem supplied that.

'I see you're getting ready for serious trouble,' Azroc observed.

'When serious trouble is expected, it is best to be ready for it,' the AI replied.

'How bad will it be?'

'It will be bad – but I have been here before,' Jerusalem replied.

This rang no bells in Azroc's eidetic memory, so he queried through his hand connection. Jerusalem immediately opened things up to him – the information he could obtain being no longer restricted. He quickly found that the *Jerusalem* had punched into a USER field employed around the planet Cull. The resulting damage had been substantial.

That all spaceships could not penetrate U-space disruption was like saying all ocean-going vessels could not survive the Maelstrom; on the whole that seemed to be true, but it wasn't impossible. When thrown out of such U-space disruption most spaceships ended up either very badly damaged or even in pieces, but they normally only ran on three or four fusion reactors, a single U-space engine and the required hard-fields, with about ten per cent to spare. Checking *Jerusalem*'s manifest and perpetually updated mission parameters, Azroc saw that the ship was moving to a position where it would be easier for the more vulnerable crew to disembark and get to a passenger liner slowly motoring out from Scarflow. Meanwhile, diagnostics were being run on all of the seven hundred of Jerusalem's fusion reactors presently offline, for at that moment the ship was functioning on a mere one hundred fusion reactors. This excess of supply was available to provide the vast amounts of energy needed to stabilize phased layers of U-space engines in its hull and reinforce the fish-scaling of hard-fields.

Impressive indeed, yet last time Jerusalem had tried flying through disrupted U-space, over thirty humans and haimen aboard had died, even though most of them had been in gel-stasis, also eight Golem and seven independent and static AIs had perished. Hence this order to abandon ship. Azroc wondered if he had made the right choice in staying, but his anger would now allow him to take no other course.

'It is worth noting,' Jerusalem added, 'that this will be worse.'

'I beg your pardon?'

'On that last occasion I penetrated disrupted U-space out of stable U-space, so I therefore could measure it accurately and make the necessary hard-field preparations,' the AI explained. 'That disruption, though strong, was produced by the constant cycling of a USER device so was of an even and predictable nature. This disruption is more unpredictable, however, and I will be dropping straight into it.'

Azroc now called up various views inside the vessel and observed the thousands cramming the corridors leading to the shuttle bays. He saw the people beginning to move faster as, with a thump that seemed jerk reality itself throughout the ship, a hundred fusion reactors started up in one hit without the usual warming-up procedure. Then yet another bank of reactors initiated.

Shuttles began to launch, streaming out of the *Jerusalem* like bees from a hive, and over the ensuing hour those exit corridors cleared till the ship became as echoey as a deserted house. When the final two hundred reactors began kicking out their power, the layer upon layer of hard-fields sprang into being and the U-engines began warming, Azroc knew himself to no longer be inside a habitation but a massive engine.

Orlandine's stomach tightened and her mouth went dry: a human physical reaction. She made some changes, which were applied via the mixed technologies laced throughout her body, and quickly rebalanced her neurochemicals, instituted a false calm and then a coolness that was positively cryonic.

'Now,' she informed Bludgeon, also transmitting to the drone the sensory data of what she was seeing as an additional confirmation.

Erebus's planetoid surfaced into the real, generating a flash of light all around it as U-space distortions caused realspace to spontaneously generate photons. This was the kind of effect you only got when something really large surfaced. She had known that Erebus could draw together all its myriad ships into a conglomerate like this, but to actually see it was . . . unnerving.

More neurochemical adjustments.

With a blast of its fusion engine, *Heliotrope* accelerated towards the Anulus fountain. It covered the intervening miles in a matter of seconds, then turned nose to tail for a further blast in order to decelerate. The impact of the heat on the ship was instantaneous and it bled smoky vapour into vacuum from a hull raised to a thousand degrees Celsius within a matter of seconds. On steering thrusters it reoriented itself, but *Heliotrope* was so close now and its angle to the fountain such that the Skaidon warp could not protect it completely. With the task specially delegated to him, of operating the complex refrigeration systems, Cutter was now busy routing onboard water and stored air to boil away from hull outlets. Beginning to glow, *Heliotrope* slid into the fountain's blast where even the minimal pressure against the meniscus of the warp drove the ship along the direction of flow. Further adjustments brought the ship upright to the flow, and Bludgeon expanded the cargo runcible gate further, impelling the three horn segments out on hard-fields. The sail effect increased, driving the ship along, while the heating effect on the ship decreased.

Inside *Heliotrope* there were fires, and its ventilation system was struggling to handle the smoke. But most of what was burning were the furnishings and such added for the benefit of soft humans. The two drones, one inside the interface sphere and the other only partially inside it, would have no problem with the heat since they were constructed to withstand the higher temperatures resulting from Prador weaponry. Other critical components were rated for higher temperatures than this too, while the Jain-tech, where affected, repaired itself.

There wasn't a problem . . . yet.

Now Orlandine turned her attention to the energy readings, and was instantly appalled. A runcible spoon has infinite capacity, but *this* . . . She made her calculations while simultaneously adjusting the war runcible's position – bringing it on target. No need to adjust for C-energy. No need at all.

Orlandine paused for just a second, then accepted the transmission from the distant cargo runcible in the Anulus fountain.

And unleashed the inferno.

17

One would have thought that a Polity controlled by the most logical and intelligent entities known would be a place in which those shadows called myth and legend were dispelled by the harsh cold light of reason. Not a bit of it. Though the evil of organized religion is all but dead on the more advanced Polity worlds, the wishful thinking remains and casts its own shadows. Though the idea of a single god in the Abrahamic mould has dissolved under ridicule, new and sometimes quite strange myths keep arising. These often relate to a collection of odd, dangerous, powerful and contrary characters bearing more resemblance to the pantheons of old rather than the one god and his angels and prophets – or perhaps even a weird combination of both. We have the legendary immortal Horace Blegg, who is the Wandering Jew, Hermes the messenger of the gods (those gods usually being Earth Central or one of the other high-up AIs), or sometimes Zeus in the role of deus ex machina – lowered onto the stage to sort out a mess made by mortals.

– Anonymous

'Knobbler is sending me linking codes,' said Arach. 'So we can watch the show.'

Cormac's U-sense view of his immediate surroundings was erratic. That enormous Skaidon gate opening so close had left U-space in this area shaking like a sheet in the wind, subject to strange eddies and distortions. When he tried to bring things into focus, they weren't where he expected them to be, and once he did locate them, they often again slipped swiftly out of view. Everything was blurred and twisted throughout U-space, so when

Cormac received the query for linkage from the spider drone, he immediately approved it. Codes began transferring across and he applied them, opening a multitude of feeds from the war runcible's sensors and computer network. He ran a selection program to give himself a view across the runcible, and then views towards its target with options to magnify. He also used those codes to gather other data where that was allowed, for it seemed his access was restricted to spectator only. He was to have no influence on events unfolding. Watching the approaching planetoid of Jain-tech, he wondered just how long those events might last.

At first he had not understood what Orlandine was up to, half expecting her to start hurling asteroids turned to photonic matter at Erebus's ships. Then, as he pieced together the stuff about the Anulus fountain, he finally understood: Orlandine was turning the runcible into a beam weapon with a breadth of *miles*.

The portion of the war runcible he now occupied shuddered underfoot. Intense white light glared in through the covering dome of the control centre. This was unfiltered and he quickly closed up both the hood and visor of his envirosuit. His visor darkened. Glancing to his side, he saw Mr Crane peering down at his own clothing, which was starting to steam.

'Oooh!' said Arach, like an enraptured child gazing at a fireworks display.

Via his gridlink, Cormac watched the beam of photonic matter spring into existence. Orlandine had made no adjustments for C-energy, and what was spewing from the warp of this war runcible was about as bad as it could get. He saw it strike the surface of Erebus's planetoid and only then did he appreciate the scale of the target, for the beam, though miles across, speared the mass of wormships and Jain-tech like a pencil stabbing into an orange. At the point of impact a circular shock wave spread and wrapped around the orb, blasting a haze of fragments out into space. This was quickly followed by a spreading firestorm. Surely this was not enough, for the target remained complete. Then a massive, expanding, glowing cloud threw the planetoid into silhouette, and he realized that, like a bullet striking flesh, the entry wound wasn't the biggest hole.

The beam now played back and forth across the face of Erebus, throwing out plumes of incandescent gas like the blaze from a cutting torch. Then it seemed as if the planetoid was pouring out smoke, but this smoke spread unnaturally and began settling into a disc. A close-up view showed it consisted of thousands of rod-forms. The planetoid rolled, exposing its hollowed-out rear, now burning arc-bright. The beam continued to play over it as what remained came rapidly apart, continent-sized chunks of matter spread, began to deform and then write lines of darkness across space, as if dissolving in a solvent. Orlandine kept the beam moving here and there, trying to target as much as possible, but it seemed she could not move it quickly enough, and her weapon was too blunt an instrument now.

Cormac again accessed a magnified view and was greeted with the sight, amid the burning wreckage and coral detritus, of a multitude of wormships now accelerating towards the war runcible. Erebus had taken a severe blow, but seemingly not a fatal one.

Rumbling under Cormac's feet. Now the other weaponry of the war runcible was firing up. He observed missiles speeding away, one after another, heard the distant familiar scream of a railgun. Movement also, and it took some locating, but Cormac finally ascertained that Orlandine was closing the war runcible up again. He guessed this was something to do with maintaining the relative positions of each separate section, which would not be required with the device once again in one piece. The inertial effects of weapons fire could be rapidly compensated for, but maybe the weapon impacts, which were due, could not. The beam began to narrow till it was now hardly hitting anything at all, then abruptly it winked out. Obviously something had gone wrong at Anulus, or maybe the *Heliotrope* had remained in the fountain for as long as it possibly could.

Cormac unshouldered his proton carbine and gazed at it critically. The sensory data Knobbler had allowed them was now becoming corrupted, so it seemed the runcible was also under informational attack. Arach rose on his legs and tilted his head up to gaze at the glass dome above. The chaos out there was now immediately visible: a spreading cloud of radiant gas against which were silhouetted numerous black flecks. Mr Crane stood up and pocketed his toys.

'What now, boss?' wondered Arach.

'Well,' Cormac replied, 'unless I miss my bet, we're about to die.'

As if to emphasize this point, things began detonating close by and the runcible to shudder like a ship athwart stormy waves. Even if Cormac could have transported himself to any other point aboard, what difference would that make when the runcible was about to become a spreading cloud of gas? Where else then? Maybe he could put himself aboard one of those ships approaching, which were now intermittently flashing within the compass of his U-sense, and with luck end up in an internal space rather than inside part of the ship's hardware, but how long would he survive aboard? He gazed across at Crane, who was now also peering up at the approaching horde. Then down at Arach again. Perhaps the thing to do would be to grab them and attempt to transport both himself and them out into vacuum. At least space was a big enough target for his wavering U-sense. His envirosuit would keep him alive for a while and, when the air began to run out, he could put his thin-gun to his head, but at least those two, not needing oxygen, might survive.

'I think the best thing—' he began, but the decision was taken out of his hands.

Some massive hand grabbed and roughly shook the runcible, and he felt the Skaidon warp wink out. It seemed as if grav went out briefly too, then came on again hard, but this was not actually the case. Grav was out and remained out, and the floor was lifting on some internal explosion. He realized they had been hit with a gravity disrupter weapon. All seemed to be happening in slow motion. Cormac had no memory of initiating them, but he was using cognitive programs to slow down his perception of time and to speed up his own reactions. Columns of fire soared upward and he saw the chainglass dome tumbling away like some leviathan's discarded contact lens, and falling after it, wrapped in twisted scaffold, went Orlandine inside her interface sphere. He was slammed against one wall, then a hurricane drag took hold of him. It seemed that, whether he wanted to be there or not, he was going to end up out in hard vacuum. Then something closed about his arm and wrenched him to a halt, almost dislocating his shoulder. He peered down at the big brass hand closed around his biceps, then into the face of a brass Apollo with midnight eyes in which motes of light danced.

Heliotrope tumbled away through vacuum, its hull glowing like a chunk of metal destined for the anvil. Cutter crashed against the wall – grav was out and his joint motors were not functioning as they should, nor was his fibre optic connection to Bludgeon. The inside of the vessel was no longer full of smoke, for just about everything that would burn had burned already. The floor, walls and ceiling of the corridor were glowing, and Cutter's internal hardware was struggling with the temperature. He reached down and caught hold of the upper edge of the entrance into the interface sphere, and hauled himself below. Irrelevantly, as he reached lower and pulled himself down beside Bludgeon, he noticed that his grip had left no marks on the metalwork. It seemed that the heat had even blunted his edges.

What had happened? It was difficult to analyse the data. Systems were collapsing throughout the ship, sensors were offline, and even the Jain-tech was struggling for survival. Some sort of surge maybe? The Skaidon warp in the cargo runcible had winked out, and the immediate ablation of its horns, which had previously been protected by the warp itself, exposed something critical within a second, then they were gone in a chain reaction. Ironically, the explosion had saved them from being incinerated by the fountain by hurling them clear.

'Bludgeon?'

No response from the little drone.

Cutter then noticed a drop in the error messages signalled from his joint motors. Checking his internal monitors he saw that his temperature had dropped two degrees. Checking external readings, though they kept varying, he estimated an average drop of half a degree within *Heliotrope*. There was nothing left to evaporate, so he guessed this must be due to the ship itself radiating heat from its hull, and that the heat exchangers and thermal generators set up inside might still be working.

'Bludgeon?'

The little drone shifted as if stirring in deep slumber. Cutter wondered if his friend had survived. Linked directly into the ship, Bludgeon would have taken the brunt of the power surge when the runcible horns blew. Certainly the inside of the sphere wasn't looking too healthy, with its slagged fibre optics and other melted hardware.

'We took the pressure off,' piped up Bludgeon abruptly.

If Cutter had possessed lungs, he would have breathed a sigh of relief.

'For Orlandine?'

'No.' Bludgeon shifted round and raised his blind head towards Cutter. 'By placing the cargo runcible within the flow of the fountain, we relieved pressure all the way down to Anulus. This in turn caused a pressure wave to come back up at us. It was an odd phenomenon, and worthy of study.'

'Yeah, sure,' said Cutter, 'but what happened back there with Orlandine?'

'Oh, her plan worked,' said Bludgeon. 'Within limits.'

'Limits?'

'Erebus will not now be attacking Earth,' the drone explained. 'However, it is doubtful whether either Orlandine and the war runcible or Knobbler and the rest will survive.'

Cutter absorbed that. They'd all known in advance the risks they were taking, indeed it was risk like this they had been built to take. 'Then we need to get back and find out.'

'Certainly – though we have many repairs to make' – Bludgeon shook himself, so maybe he was having problems with his joint motors too – 'when things have cooled sufficiently.'

Cutter merely nodded and clinked one of his limbs against a door frame. He wondered if his first repair task should be to find a way to restore his edges. Then he reconsidered. Maybe, with those sharp edges gone and the war runcible likely destroyed, it was time for him to become a little bit more sociable.

Nah, probably not. Cutter went to find a sharpener.

Even as Erebus sent its forces against its attacker, the error messages, the returns from automatically initiated diagnostic programs, the screaming of wormship captains still dying and the sheer tide of information swamped it, and the overload was like pain. Over eighteen thousand wormships gone in one single strike. All because of a war runcible, a damned ancient artefact from the

Prador–human war. How had it ended up here anyway, and how had it managed to conceal itself? The Polity, though possessing sophisticated chameleonware, did not possess the *right* kind to conceal an object like that.

How how how?

The answer then surfaced through the confusion with a horrible inevitability: *Randal*.

'Does it hurt, Erebus?' Randal enquired.

They were both in the virtuality now, though Erebus could not quite remember choosing to be there. It was easier, though, for the borders of the virtuality filtered and dulled the massive input. Randal stood close by, the same as ever, his expression impudent and yet somehow sad. Erebus's perception of itself was much more worrying: the infinite tangle spreading back from its black human form, binding all those other melded entities, was breaking apart and fires burned within it.

'Distraction and misdirection,' Erebus managed. 'You wanted to focus my attention beyond the corridor, whether at real or phantom Polity fleets. But you did not want me to look too closely at the corridor itself.'

'It's certainly a tangled old web of deception.'

From within the virtuality Erebus felt itself to be peering through grey fog infecting the sensors of the remaining wormships and other biomechs hammering down upon the war runcible. This was because all the sensory input available was necessarily being winnowed out of chaos. Even though the runcible's main weapon was now out, the other ordnance still being deployed from its five sections was taking a heavy toll. There had been a few crucial hits on its structure, enough to have knocked out the Skaidon warp and, despite the defensive fire, something major was sure to eventually get through. Erebus now closed down that option. It did not want this troublesome object destroyed. It wanted whoever was aboard it captured alive.

'How?' Erebus spat.

'You had your trial run with Skellor, and it was a success,' Randal said. 'Orlandine was a failure because your assessment of her was at fault – because I influenced it. Then again was it really at fault or was she precisely serving her purpose? She then further caused you problems by destroying your USER and allowing both herself and the Polity fleet to escape. Perhaps you should have realized then what a dangerous creature she is. Or could it be that you already *did* know?'

Rod-forms and other biomechs were unable to withstand the appalling firepower spewing from the war runcible. Erebus recognized the energy signatures of weapons used during the Prador–human war, remembered being *Trafalgar*, remembered when things weren't so complicated . . .

'She got what she wanted,' said Erebus, a feeling difficult to identify rising within – could it be panic? 'Why did she attack me?'

'Revenge.'

Erebus realized. 'Klurhammon.'

The firing from the runcible could not last indefinitely for its power supplies were limited, but the wormships were now still within its scope and many of them were coming apart, their captains screaming . . . those portions of Erebus's mind screaming . . .

'I knew she would return to the Polity eventually, for all the power she possesses is meaningless elsewhere. I was forever on the lookout for her, therefore, and made careful preparations for her return. I sent one of your wormships to Klurhammon, where its legate captain, apparently working at your behest, tortured and killed her two brothers. Then I sent recordings of that atrocity to her Polity net address.'

'For all your detestation of what I do, you are no better,' said Erebus.

Some rod-forms were reaching the runcible's skin now, but they were not surviving long. Extremely tough war drones were dealing with them very quickly, scouring them from the runcible's surface with weapons fire and even attacking them physically. Erebus felt a deep disquiet about attacking such drones . . . its own kind, after all.

'So you don't understand yet?'

'What do you mean?' The panic still grew, and with it a deep fear.

'You will understand eventually.' Randal shrugged. 'I placed an agent aboard *Jerusalem* to lock down any information about Orlandine. It was a necessary precaution, for had Earth Central discovered what she was up to, it might have thus found out about your attack *here* and prevented it, though of course you would have been allowed to continue attacking elsewhere. I distributed copies of myself throughout you, awaiting the opportunity to pass on your plan of attack to her, once she reappeared.'

'This does not seem plausible.'

Finally, a wormship, although severely smashed up and depleted of the units of its modular structure, managed to get past the fusillade and right down to the runcible's skin. War drones closed on it, but already it was spewing out biomechs designed specifically for capturing stations. Erebus became aware of one drone, its ordnance obviously depleted, attacking and tearing with ceramal mandibles and slashing with limbs edged with chainglass. It would surely not survive for long.

'Plausible? On the face of it no, but you have not yet accepted the truth.' Randal seemed unconcerned. 'I took complete control of one wormship and its legate captain and sent them to Klurhammon without you noticing. I reprogrammed the Jain-tech employed there to self-destruct, hence your missing wormship. I interfered with your attack on Cull so that only a type of gas would be used, rather than an antimatter bomb, and therefore ensured the formidable Mr Crane would survive to seek vengeance.'

The drone was still putting up a valiant fight, but surely it had to succumb soon. Erebus felt almost sickened, though whether about the drone's fate or Randal's words it did not know.

'I readied myself to transmit to Crane when he first attacked you,' Randal continued, 'giving him the necessary codes for an even more damaging attack – one exploiting the *inevitable* fault in your plans. He taunted you after that, and you gave chase as per my plan, your two pursuing wormships carrying your newest recognition codes and chameleonware formats straight to a rendezvous with Orlandine.' Randal paused. 'It's all almost too much deviousness for a simple human mind to encompass, you'd think.' He pressed one finger to his cheek and looked thoughtful. 'Or maybe there weren't any human minds involved at all?'

'You babble.' It was sheer terror now.

The drone finally fell, most of its limbs missing. As Jain tendrils penetrated the gaps in its armour, Erebus gazed down upon it from the compound eyes of one biomech and considered subsuming it. Then that perspective vanished – the drone had suicided, explosively.

'Why do you think it is so difficult to track me down within yourself and destroy me?'

'I am vast, and therefore the places where you can hide are many.' But Erebus no longer felt vast, merely petty, and its mind seemed filled with shadows.

'It was lucky that Orlandine encountered a wormship the way she did, so that I could convey a copy of myself to her. But then she was looking for a place to hide within the Polity, just as you were. Coincidence, do you think? Yet it wasn't necessary, since there was a copy of me also sitting in her net space.'

'You will die for this.' It was almost a question.

'Of course I will. Wasn't that the intention?'

'You make no sense.'

'You kept a recording of Fiddler Randal's mind, transcribed even as you murdered him. But it became part of you and, just like all those other melded parts, it was powerless. I arose from that, but I'm not really that man.'

'Who are you then?'

'I'm a thing you can't destroy, no matter how hard you try,' said Randal. 'Come on, you're the super-intelligence, so you work it out.'

'Who *are* you!' Erebus hissed.

'I'm that niggling irritation that'll never go away.'

Erebus fell silent, not prepared to ask again.

'I'm your chosen method of suicide.'

This was too much.

Randal raised his hand and pointed with one finger, made a motion with his thumb mimicking the descending hammer on an ancient firearm. 'I'm your conscience, Erebus. I'm you.'

Mika was aware she was standing aboard *Trafalgar*, with her hand pressed against a dead man's augmentation and Jain-tech growing up her arm and penetrating her skull, but her awareness of that fell into insignificance as, without her intervention, something used her brain as a data-sorting machine. Dragon, she supposed, was now using the tool he had fashioned.

'Leave her alone, you bastard! Leave her the fuck alone!'

The anger, frustration and the grief felt all her own, but of course they weren't.

Why did the AI have to do that to Henry? It had killed others, yet it had to do that to her. Did it take joy in causing Randal pain or was it, on some level, thinking it was being kind by keeping her alive? If that could be called life.

He had found Henrietta, like the other five, suspended in the special frameworks constructed in the onboard gym, wrapped in a cocoon of Jain filaments and screaming and babbling as those infiltrating her skull meticulously reprogrammed her mind, while those penetrating her body tore it apart and rebuilt it. Trafalgar had used him to initiate the technology within a Jain node, because as an AI it was unable to do this itself. Now, through him, it was controlling the Jain mycelium as it spread through the entire battleship, while simultaneously trying to cut him from the circuit and assume direct control itself. As a result, Randal could not attempt to blank out what was happening there. In fact, it seemed to him as if it was he *who was doing this to Henrietta: erasing memories, planting programs, sucking away her blood and replacing it with a nano-machine-laden fluid; rebuilding her heart into a more efficient engine.*

I feel just as controlled myself, thought Mika.

Perspective shifted into a protracted shriek emitted by the AI of Randal's attack ship as the Jain mycelium spread aboard and found it. Randal was still wrestling with Trafalgar for control, but started losing it once the killing started, and he just could not stop it. Humans died so very easily. He saw his friends now barricaded in the bridge, saw the horror and panic when the inboard defence lasers started up and turned Morrison into a smoking corpse. The panic did not last long, however, since corpses don't scream. The last of Randal's grip slipped as the mycelium reached the weapons research module of the Trafalgar *and he there saw what remained of the rest of his crew. Here were conducted the other experiments on human beings, which involved using discrete parts of the node technology. How fast does this grow in the human body? How does it make synaptic connections? And many other such questions* besides – *fifty-eight of them in all. Of course, once the experiments were over, their subjects had to be studied and tested in detail. It was the records that the mycelium accessed down there which told Randal exactly how many of his people lay dead. He could get no accurate count from the scattered pieces of their corpses.*

'*Why?*' Randal howled. '*Earth Central, why did you send us here?*'

Obviously this question was one that greatly concerned Dragon, for it repeated and echoed until simple text arose to Mika's view, and she, and through her Dragon, could read the mission profile.

These ECS misfits had been sent aboard an attack ship controlled by an AI of dubious reputation, and it seemed they were all dispensable. They were to assist the AI of the *Trafalgar* in its investigations into a newly discovered alien technology. The orders from Earth Central were vague: they were to receive their detailed instructions from Trafalgar.

'*You wanted humans for this . . .*' said Randal.

'*I wanted humans for this,*' Trafalgar replied.

'*But you* had *humans.*'

There it was, revealed in the memory of the AI mind conjoined with Randal's own. The AIs of the great exodus dividing into two factions, arguing over the nature of the meld they were to make. Argument turning into warfare that ended upon the surface of a hot world, with Trafalgar victorious. It had been fast and vicious, and even though some of the eighty humans accompanying the exodus had been on Trafalgar's side, none of them had survived. They just got ground up in the machinery.

'*Trafalgar,*' Randal asked, his consciousness fading, dying, '*did Earth Central know?*'

A surge of godlike amusement.

In that moment: thousands of artificial minds were connecting, some willingly, but some not and then being subjugated by Trafalgar. The informational connection held them in place around the moonlet – chosen because it was so loaded with useful resources – as the Jain-tech spread there and digested rock, refined ores, then began throwing further shoots out into space. Randal witnessed the first ship – an attack ship – being penetrated like a beetle stuck by a pin.

'Warfare promotes development,' said Trafalgar.

'Earth Central . . .' was all Randal could manage.

'Stagnation after the war with the Prador,' said the battleship AI. 'Earth Central is arrogant enough to think it can choose its enemies now, and to allow that enemy to attack for the sum purpose of making humans . . . grow. Such arrogance will be the death of it – and the death of its Polity.'

'Trafalgar—'

'I am now Erebus.'

Fading as he was, Randal did not understand what that could mean. He pondered the arrogance of AIs for a moment longer, then his mind winked out.

She was Mika again, and enough herself to feel sickened and horrified.

'You *knew*,' she said.

'I did not know,' Dragon replied. 'And now I wish I still did not know.'

Dragon's voice seemed far above her, as did the winnowed memories of the dead man, Randal; and even *their* implications began to grow distant. She felt herself at once deep in a dark pool and down in a place where words and thoughts were the products of a mechanistic universe, where free will was a laughable fantasy, and hard reality ground dreams into mere sensory products adhering to rules not dissimilar to those governing the products of evolution. But all this around her now wasn't a product of evolution; this was something fashioned and, though one of its purposes was indeed survival, that came after its primary purpose of destruction. Somehow, she was deep in Jain-tech – down near its very roots. A vast complexity surrounded her like the flicking of trillions of mechanical relays, but also like the firing of synapses, the mathematical positioning of grains of sand and the crystallization of snow flakes in a blizzard cloud.

Then . . . then she was somewhere else.

Mr Crane had driven his other hand into the metal wall so as to anchor them in place. Cormac tried to locate Arach amid fire and chaos, then spotted the drone at the doors leading into this place – pulling them open, and air blasting past him. Crane's head twitched, birdlike. Following the direction of the Golem's gaze, Cormac saw a cloud of rod-forms descending towards the runcible, and beyond them another wormship. The one that was already down, which Cormac could glimpse intermittently as if through heat haze and tumbling prisms, lay over on the other side of the runcible. It had penetrated there and biomechs were entering.

The weapons operated by the war drones occupying the runcible were taking a heavy toll of the attacking swarm. One moment it seemed the rod-forms were about to reach their target, then abruptly many of them would disappear in firestorms, but the war drones could not keep away the further multitude hurtling in, for there weren't enough munitions aboard. He wondered if Orlandine, and the drones themselves, had known this would happen. Had they come here prepared to make this sacrifice or had they merely miscalculated? It was now a moot point really.

Crane dragged Cormac down to the floor, tore his brass hand from the wall and drove it in again further along, by stages moving them both towards where Arach was holding open the exit doors. Cormac gazed through the wall into the corridor beyond, which to his U-sense seemed to be writhing like a hooked earthworm. He could try to take both of them over there, but what would happen if he rematerialized inside a solid wall? That was not something he really wanted to experience. Crane made his way steadily to Arach, who had now wedged his abdomen between the sliding blast doors to keep them open. The Golem swung Cormac around to the door gap immediately above the spider drone, and Cormac heaved himself through. Grav was still operating out in the corridor and he dropped straight to the floor, then was nearly sucked back through, underneath Arach, before slamming his feet against the walls either side of the doors. Looking up he saw brass hands grip each door, wrench them further apart, then a big lace-up boot propelled Arach out into the corridor too. The tumbling drone's back descended briefly onto Cormac's chest, driving out his breath, then Arach slid off him and flipped upright, driving several sharp feet straight into the metal of the floor. Then Crane himself came through and dropped heavily, those boots landing with a crash either side of Cormac. Behind him, the doors heaved themselves closed.

'Biomechs,' observed Arach.

Cormac's U-sense gave him glimpses only, so he could not really tell where they were now. 'Where?' As Crane stepped away from him, he pushed himself to his feet. The doors were fully closed now. A wind was blowing from a breach, or breaches, elsewhere, but at least it did not threaten to drag him off his feet. Something crashed against the recently shut doors.

'I'll give you one guess only,' said Arach, and they moved away from the doors.

Where could they run to now? Cormac again tried to get some sense of his surroundings through that new-found perception, but still everything seemed chaos. He observed corridors and other internal spaces rippling and twisting, Jain biomechs here and there but never easy to pinpoint; he glimpsed a drone like a twinned spider, weapon ports open on its body to spew streams of curved chainglass blades into what looked like a horde of steel nematodes. He saw that though the segments of the war runcible had now rejoined, its pentagon was not complete for some explosion had gouged out a huge chunk of its frame. Abruptly he banished these myriad visions from his mind and waved his thin-gun, which he had drawn without thinking, at Mr Crane.

'How did you get here?' he asked.

Crane tilted his head slightly, as if listening to something else, then turned and gazed towards one end of the corridor.

'I'm getting something now,' chipped in Arach. 'There's a ship . . . an AI called Vulture, but he can't stay docked for much longer.'

Fire slashed into the corridor, a cloud of smoke boiling in while globules of molten metal splattered the wall opposite the fire's entry point. Cormac ducked and rolled, glancing back at the doors into the control centre as the powerful laser that had just punched through them continued cutting across. Crane set off with a big loping stride, and Cormac and Arach swiftly followed. As they reached another set of closed doors barring the end of the corridor, an explosion flung chunks of the control centre doors into the corridor behind them. Flames and smoke poured into the passage, then abruptly went into reverse as vacuum sucked them back out. Cormac staggered for a moment against the pull of it, but not as badly this time, the air here being so thin. He turned and dropped to one knee, shoved the thin-gun into his belt, and raised the proton carbine instead. Arach squatted down beside him, Gatling cannons folding out ready, while behind them Crane smashed his fist repeatedly against the divide between the doors to create a gap to get his fingers in.

Something crashed through from the control centre, impacting into the opposite wall, whereupon it turned. Cormac held fire, unsure whether this was one of the war drones, for, even though very much like the biomechs he had seen earlier, it also bore some resemblance to Orlandine's allies in its insectile form and ten legs now stabbing out starlike into ceiling, floor and walls. Arach, however, did not hesitate. Cormac merely glimpsed the tri-mandibles, a collection of lens eyes and the numerous silvery tubes protruding from the newcomer's flat physiognomy before Arach's cannons roared and the thing disappeared in a multiple explosion. Smoke drew away to show just its legs hanging from where they had lodged – but then another of the same kind crashed through, and with it came silvery worms speeding along just above the floor like hunting garfish.

'Crane, get that damned door open!'

Cormac now gripped the carbine in just one hand, aiming and then firing using targeting programs in his gridlink. He then initiated Shuriken, stabbing his other arm straight ahead, and the device shot out from his wrist holster. Whining up to speed, it extended its chainglass blades and rose to the ceiling out of the way just in time for Arach to turn the second big biomech to scrap.

A blast of air came from behind, hurling Cormac forward so he had to bring his free hand down on the floor for support. Arach backed up, more of the worms having appeared. Shuriken tilted and slammed down, chopping one of the things in half, then ricocheted up into another one, bounced again and again, rattling around in the corridor like a coin shaken in a tube. Silvery wormish bits writhed about on the floor, and the walls and ceiling were soon deeply scored and gashed.

'Open!' shouted Arach.

Cormac turned and flung himself after the spider drone and Mr Crane, who were already moving on into the next corridor. Crane turned back to patiently drag the doors shut against the slow pace of their hydraulics. Just in time Shuriken shot in over his head. Cormac held out his arm and the Tenkian weapon retracted its smoking blades and returned to its home like a hunting hawk. Cormac could instantly feel the holster heating up against his wrist. He glanced back along the corridor as numerous objects impacted against the door like knives thudding into wood. There was a drop-shaft at the opposite end, and he sprinted towards it, then abruptly skidded to a halt as two metallic antennae appeared, followed by silvery legs slithering up over the edge.

'Ah fuck.'

He dropped to one knee and took aim.

''S okay,' said Arach, hammering on past him.

The thing that now heaved itself into view looked even more terrifying than the Jain biomechs they had just destroyed. It was a great brass-and-chrome hissing cockroach with a flat ribbed body and legs that were far too long.

War drone.

'It's getting a bit hot round here!' observed the drone joyously.

Quite mad, these things.

Cormac stood up again. 'We're heading for Mr Crane's ship,' he explained. 'What about the rest of you on this runcible?'

The cockroach tilted its head for a moment. 'Seems reasonable,' it said. 'I can't see much advantage in hanging around here. We'll either see you there or we won't – so don't linger for too long!' In one disquietingly fluid motion the cockroach turned and shot back into the drop-shaft, clambering up out of sight.

'Where now, Crane?'

The Golem strode straight towards the shaft, stepped inside and dropped out of view. The others followed, Cormac grabbing the rungs of the shaft ladder while Arach starred his legs out all around the walls of the cylindrical shaft just like one of the Jain biomechs. The irised gravity field was not functioning, but there was pull from gravplates down below, hence the loud crash of Crane's landing way beneath them. Cormac wondered briefly if such an impact simply did not matter to a machine that tough, before he swiftly clambered down after the Golem.

The shaft opened into an an area containing an automated factory. Cold forges, powder-casting machines, mills and lathes, and multi-armed welders and assembler bots stretched out of sight into belching smoke. Detecting it before Cormac even saw it, Arach opened fire and something darted about in the smoke, then crashed out into clear view. Another biomech, this time a ten-foot-long segmented flatworm seemingly fashioned of copper. Beyond it something exploded and the remaining air began roaring out, taking the smoke with it. Revealed now ahead was one of the rod-forms, with Jain tentacles spread out all around it. Wherever its tentacles touched the machines, the walls, the floor and the ceiling, it seemed as if acid was etching away all substance around them. The thing itself was iridescent grey, and it pulsed as if sucking the life from its surroundings.

Crane turned to the right and, stumbling against the air-blast, Cormac followed. Arach opened fire again, blasting the flatworm thing to shreds and knotted clumps of Jain tendrils. More of those silvery worms shot in at them from the side. Cormac launched Shuriken as Crane snatched one of the objects out of the air and tore it in half. The Tenkian throwing star slashed through three of the attackers all at once, while Cormac used his carbine to pick off others.

'How much further?' he bellowed as Crane turned off into a side tunnel.

From behind came another explosion and a wash of fiery smoke. Glancing back, Cormac saw a huge hole torn through to open space as again the smoke went into reverse. But the tug of vacuum moved it slowly now and he managed to keep his feet, which meant there must be hardly any air left at all. Through the gap, like a nightmare train carriage, came the front end of one of those segmented coils from a wormship. Via his U-sense Cormac could see beyond it: another of them was already down on the station, and yet another descending. Countless rod-forms were scattered over the hull too, with Jain growth rapidly filling intervening spaces. The war runcible was all but swamped.

'We're fucked!' shouted Arach, his cannons pointing back and firing continuously. 'The ship's undocked!'

Cormac recalled Shuriken even as more silvery missiles sped towards them. He reached out and caught Mr Crane's arm. The Golem turned and eyed him impassively.

'Here, Arach!' Cormac shouted.

The drone backed up against his legs, and Cormac did the only thing he could think of. He encompassed them both and stepped through twisted U-space out into the dark.

That first jump was rough. A sound, a concert of rending and distorting metal, ran through the *Jerusalem*. Gazing through the ship's sensors at U-space as, being a Golem, he could, Azroc observed chaos parting over hard-fields, as if the ship were forging through a dense mass of transparent asteroids – only asteroids that had been turned inside out and acquired another dimension that Azroc would not have been able to recognize had he been using his human emulation. Then the vessel surfaced in the real with a crash and a cacophony of klaxons. Azroc saw that they were still within sight of Scarflow's sun. However, Jerusalem informed him that only one reactor had needed to be ejected and that the maintenance drones were meanwhile keeping the damage under control.

The second jump was rougher still.

The sounds of rending and crashing continued to echo throughout the *Jerusalem*, and it vibrated like an unbalanced fan. *Crump* sounds like the firing of distant heavy guns Azroc understood to be the implosion of hard-field generators. Then, as the hedron began to twist about him, he at first thought he was experiencing some illusion leaking through from U-space, but checking through his hand interface found that the whole of the massive spaceship was now distorting. From the ring of consoles, as if to emphasize this discovery, sparks flared from a couple of sections before the power suddenly cut and fire-suppressant gas gouted out.

'How much of this can you take?' Azroc enquired.

Jerusalem must have been too busy to even reply.

The Golem noted that the floor repair made where Erebus's infiltrator had destroyed itself was breaking, and a crack rapidly spreading from it. A crab drone immediately scuttled over, brought a sonic drill down at the end of the crack and drove its bit screaming through the floor. This temporarily halted the expansion of the crack, then out of it, like termites swarming from a broken nest, came thousands of small blue-chrome beetlebots which began instantly casting webs and weaving together the gap with glistening threads of high-tensile steel. When something thumped directly below him, Azroc gazed down at another crack already exposing the shattered ends of pipes, and beetlebots flowed out of this too, while from the pipes heads of things like iron caddis-fly larvae slid into view and extended the pipes from where they had broken with a sputum of metal.

But it wasn't just the ship receiving this punishment.

Azroc began to receive error messages from his own body and realized that some gravity phenomenon was the source of the damage occurring all around him, for something was stretching his bones and putting pressure on his internal hardware. He peered down at his chair and noted that it possessed a safety harness. One-handed he pulled the strap heads across and slotted them into their sockets. Once they were all in place, the full harness tightened, pulling him back against the chair, then soft clamps closed about his shins and rose up to beckon like pincers from the chair arms. He placed his free arm in one of them, but kept his other out to maintain contact with the hand interface.

'Grav out,' announced Jerusalem, its voice devoid of any human emulation.

The gravplates shut down and briefly the air was filled with swarms of beetlebots amid smaller things like chrome gnats, and numerous crab drones. Then this collection of ship fauna updated on the situation and used their various methods of propulsion to get themselves back to where they were needed. Inside himself, Azroc felt crystal breaking in a data store, but he possessed multiple back-ups, so there was no problem – yet. Two of his joint motors reported wiring breaks, and the sheering of a nerve linkage left both his feet numb. He dispatched his own hardware repair bots internally and began rerouting, running diagnostics, repairing where he could, otherwise patching or jury-rigging. A sudden jolt lifted his chair right into the air, and he saw that the floor below him had flipped up like a tin lid. All data through the hand interface cut out, then came an enormous shudder as the great ship again surfaced into the real.

'Jerusalem?'

After a long pause the AI replied over intercom, 'My phasic modular B folderol.'

'Is it really?' Azroc enquired.

'Ipso facto total bellish.'

'Yes, mine is too.'

'Repairing.' Static hissed from the intercom, then came a sound suspiciously like someone kicking a piece of malfunctioning hardware. 'OK. Better.'

'You'll talk sense now?'

'When the occasion requires.'

'Are we through?'

'We are near the edge, but the damage I was sustaining has reached its limit. I have lost fifty-eight hard-field generators and had to eject twenty-two fusion reactors. Unfortunately that should have been twenty-four, and now one third of my volume is contaminated with radioactives.'

'Structural damage too?'

'Yes, but only to secondary internal structures. My main skeleton will realign.'

Even as Jerusalem said this a great groaning and crashing echoed through the ship. Azroc focused on the floor crack and observed it beginning to close, beetlebots quickly scuttling out of the way. In fact the whole hedron appeared to be twisting back into shape, and as this happened, the raised piece of floor his chair was mounted upon began to settle down again. It was as if, like some human fighter, Jerusalem was casually pushing its dislocations back into place while spitting out chunks of broken tooth. Now the constant din of industry grew in volume, and within the hedron Azroc noted numerous welding arcs and crab drones zipping back and forth with circuit boards or other components clutched in their claws. Glancing down he saw that the crack in the floor directly below him had not yet closed, but the pipes had been reattached and he could see the milky glimmer of nanobot activity at the crack's edges as they drew material across to bridge it, while a crab drone arrived beside the raised section of floor to cut off its protruding edge and make similar repairs.

'It has occurred to me to wonder what you hope to achieve by getting clear of the interference,' said Azroc. 'You are a large vessel and I know you possess some lethal weaponry, but even so what can you do against Erebus?'

'There is,' replied Jerusalem, 'a high probability that one other large Polity vessel will be able to penetrate the interference.'

'Then what?'

'Erebus is certainly launching an assault on Earth,' said the AI. 'We should still be able to fight a delaying action.'

Twenty hours later the great ship once more dropped into U-space turbulence, and Azroc was once again able to use the hand interface. The *Jerusalem* surfaced into the real less than an hour later, smoothly this time, and without anything breaking.

'I see,' said the Golem.

Yes, a delaying action.

Its surface bright with a million points of light that were almost certainly welding arcs, the titanic *Cable Hogue* hung there, waiting in vacuum.

18

Another of these mythical characters is the ridiculous Mr Crane, a 'brass' Golem who, like the gods of old, is neither good nor evil, just capricious and dangerous. In him I see the ultimate expression of how humans regard the Golem android. In the far too numerous stories about him we see that he can become everything we fear about them, for he can be an indestructible killing machine, an insane mechanism capable of the viciousness of humans, an amoral murderer. Yet he can be everything we might love and admire too, for he can be just, he can be the relentless crusher of evil and protector of the weak and innocent, and he can even be the strong and reliable friend. And, as the stories tell us, nothing can stand in his way, no doors can keep him out. This last point is the most relevant, I think, for the brass man is a combination of two things: demon and guardian angel. He is a point of transition, representative of the middle ground between barbarity and civilization, the past moving into the future. He is our modern version of the god of doors, for he is Janus.

– Anonymous

Mr Crane tumbled through vacuum, vapour steaming from his clothing, his hand clamped on the top of his head to hold his hat in place as if there might be a breeze here to dislodge it, and a hand shoved in his coat pocket, probably to keep a firm hold on his odd collection of toys. Arach, tumbling too, abruptly jetted gas from a humorously placed vent in the rear of his abdomen, made some adjustments with steering vents located underneath the points where his legs joined his thorax, and then drifted over to

Cormac. The drone closed a limb about Cormac's waist, jetted more vapour and propelled the both of them over towards Crane, who reached out and grasped hold of one extended spider limb. A few more jets of gas brought them to a standstill relative to the war runcible, and now Cormac had a clearer view of what was happening.

Rod-forms and chunks of Jain coral were scattered all about them. Ahead, the war runcible was almost lost amid decohered wormship structure and vinelike growths extruding from the count-less rod-forms adhering to its hull. Cormac could see the bright flares of oxygen fires burning aboard, and every so often detonations would fling debris out into space. All this was happening in the silence of vacuum, which somehow made the scene seem more poignant.

'There are eight drones still remaining aboard,' Arach informed him over his envirosuit radio. 'But they don't intend staying there much longer.'

Cormac could not help them now. Even if he could transport himself back inside through the U-space distortions while not ending up as a decorous moulding in one of the internal walls, he could only bring out one or two of the surviving war drones at a time – and getting themselves out here was something they were perfectly capable of achieving on their own. Anyway, he had more than enough problems of his own right now. Linking to his suit he discovered that his remaining air supply totalled forty minutes, which, by deliberately forcing himself into a somnolent state, he could extend by half – but that appeared to be the extent of his life.

'Anything about Orlandine?' he enquired.

After a pause, during which he no doubt communicated with the remaining war drones, Arach replied, 'There was a beacon operating previously from her interface sphere, but it shut down shortly after she departed the runcible. Knobbler estimates she's a few hundred miles out by now.'

Orlandine controlled Jain technology, so it seemed to Cormac that the blast that had flung her from the runcible was unlikely to have killed her. However, he still did not give much for her chances. Surely Erebus would find her and wreak some hideous vengeance.

Then, as they hung there in space, a shadow fell across them, and thoughts of what Erebus might do were brought firmly to the forefront of Cormac's mind. He gazed towards the shadow's source and watched a wormship slide eerily past. His view utterly unfiltered and straight across hard vacuum was a good one, and he realized how weirdly beautiful was this vessel. His estimate of his own lifespan might be too optimistic, he decided. The wormship, however, showed no sign of being aware of their presence and continued on down towards the runcible, where, as well as the decohering two that were spreading over its surface, three others were also now docked. Perhaps Orlandine would be missed, just like he and his companions had just been, or perhaps Erebus now knew their precise location – and hers – and would either fry them or pick them up later. As he watched the runcible, a massive detonation aboard one of the docked wormships flung out nearly a third of its structure.

'Our hissing cockroach,' said Arach.

'Pardon?'

'Erebus is trying to capture the war drones,' the spider drone replied, 'but it's not a great plan. Like myself every one of them has a CTD located deep inside its body, just in case of capture by an enemy. I guess the cockroach just waited until he could do the most damage.'

'Should one of those ships come after us, I'll shift us again,' said Cormac. 'So don't be in *too* much of a hurry to use your get-out clause.'

'Sure thing,' Arach replied. 'I won't use it anyway until I can't shoot any more.'

That figured.

Seven war drones left. Cormac tried to see more clearly using his U-sense but found himself still gazing into chaos. He ran a program from his gridlink, tightening certain muscles around his eyes to increase their magnification, and then ran a secondary program to clean up the distorted image received by his optic nerves. Now the runcible and its enclosing attackers seemed to loom right over him. He saw the twinned spider now on the surface, boiling metal in a circle all about it, and around that again Jain-tech mounding up into a wave. The drone suddenly seemed out of munitions or energy, for it did nothing as the tangled Jain growth fell upon it and swamped it. Bearing in mind Arach's recent comments, Cormac flinched in expectation of another large explosion as a bright light flashed through the writhing mass, but this time it was some beam weapon boring a tunnel. The twin spider hurtled out through this cleanly, then simply disappeared.

Another explosion on the surface, this time excavating a glowing crater. Shooting out from this he saw what he first took to be a biomech but then recognized as the drone Knobbler. A shoal of silvery objects streaked out after the escaping drone but then milled in confusion as it too disappeared.

The wormship which Cormac had earlier seen heading for the runcible now arrived. More drones were busy escaping, but it intercepted one of them, part of its mass opening to swallow the silvery scorpion whole. For a moment it was as if massive flash bulbs were going off inside the wormship. Cormac managed to turn his head just in time as the bright explosion expanded, ripping the entire ship apart. He then saw three drones slam together, some distance from the runcible, and also disappear like Knobbler. As he puzzled over this, he noticed his perspective was changing. Adjusting his focus back to normal, he peered at Arach and noticed that the drone was releasing a perpetual stream of gas, accelerating all three of them.

Now the entire war runcible bucked, and light glared from five distinct areas within it, precisely where the buffers and the reactors were located within each segment. In pure silence five explosions, the intense blue-white of burning magnesium, joined to become one. The runcible, the surrounding wormships and other Jain-tech, all fragmented in this massive blast, then were swamped in an expanding sphere of fire. Observing this, Cormac realized that, unless he shifted again through U-space, his lifespan would be shortened even further. Crane and Arach might both survive that blast front when it reached them, but he was still mere mortal flesh.

He focused out on where next to shift himself as well as the other two. Then vacuum seemed to ripple right before him, and a big armoured claw stabbed out and closed on Mr Crane's ankle. The next thing Cormac knew was that he crashed, alone, into a small airlock. Obviously it was too small to encompass the three – or now rather four – of them.

'Welcome aboard the *Harpy*,' said a sardonic voice.

It was like a basic and incomplete virtuality format with one surface texture chosen from some strange palette, dimensions put in place but given no orientation, and then the whole project consigned to a store and forgotten. Mika had no real awareness of her own body here. She was just a point of existence floating somewhere in colourless space, at once above a weirdly textured and endless plain, or beside a wall without limits or perhaps a ceiling of the same infinite dimensions, for there was no up or down in this place.

From the Atheter AI stored in an artefact retrieved from the lava planet called Shayden's Find – named after the woman who discovered that body but who was murdered while trying to recover it – researchers had learned that Jain technology made an imprint on reality that was visible from within U-space, but only if you knew what to look for and possessed the right equipment. This fact had enabled Cormac and his mentor Horace Blegg to track Jain nodes. It had not been clearly understood why Jain-tech left such an imprint. Huge mass, like that of planets and stars, was detectable from within U-space, just as heavy weights are detectable from the underside of a sheet they rest on, but small complex objects should theoretically make no real impression at all.

As Mika understood it, though it wasn't really her subject, other researchers had found that the macro-, micro- and nano-structures Jain-tech created in turn caused specific pico-structures to spring into being. They were a kind of sub-creation, a side effect almost like the shape left on a flat surface after some object has been spray-painted on top if it then removed: almost a shadow of the technology. However, those pico-structures were too regular, too constant to be anything but deliberate. Looking more closely, the researchers found a kind of pattern that slid under the real, somehow insinuated its way into the interface between U-space and realspace without the usual huge energy requirement. And where this pattern lay, on the edge of the ineffable, the researchers detected very busy *movement* that almost defied analysis.

Mika now knew what that activity was: the Jain AIs.

And here they were.

The surface Mika found herself by appeared to consist of metallic fossil worms, an expanse of them that extended to the infinite. They were triangular in section and somehow hot and burning. At first glance the worms seemed to be utterly still but then, as she watched, she detected movement that defied definition: a slow massive change, something like the leisurely transitions seen in a kaleidoscope. Sound here too: a howling that wrenched at the core of her being and an insane muttering from tight-crammed madness. And smells: decay, sweet perfume, a savoury smell and the stench of excrement, all crammed into one sensory overload.

But though her mind was interpreting all this as input through her five main senses, there was also some part of her that recognized it as a shifting of dimensions her brain was just not formatted to accept, and that it was also something falling halfway between physical change and thought. There was a multitude here and a single presence. Being naturally analytical, she interpreted this as something like a hive mind, but being analytical was not easy, for there was a multiple entity here slowly becoming aware of her presence – and it terrified her.

Then, in time she could not measure, the plain – for now she firmly held to that perspective – began to alter in respect to her own position. A pattern formed about and below her, with herself at its centre point. The attendant howling grew in intensity, and the muttering rose to a gibbering. A sluggish perception seemed to briefly focus on her then drift away. Perhaps the idea came from Dragon's comment about waking up these entities, but it was almost as if she was in the presence of someone dozing who on some unconscious level had just acknowledged her presence.

'Dragon, what do I do?' she asked, though here she possessed no mouth.

She felt something – some connection with Dragon – but heard no words. However, now those memories stored in her head but not her own began to surface. All at once she saw a race raising itself from the swamps of its homeworld and weaving for itself towering homes out of flute grass. The gabbleducks, the Atheter, built tall, their focus upon structures rather than individual machines, and so it was that they first reached space by using a form of space elevator rather than rocket propulsion. They expanded their civilization across star systems and were faced with their own version of the Fermi paradox: why are we alone? They found life on many worlds but little intelligence, then abruptly they weren't alone – for they came across one primitive race with the potential of raising itself to something greater. These were hard-shelled arthropoids, vicious and competitive, and even in their primitive state beginning to learn to work metals. With some misgivings they left these early Prador to their own devices, but still there remained a question: this galaxy being so old, why were there no other spacefaring races? Were they the first?

Then they found the ruins.

With great excitement the gabbleducks carefully excavated their find, and began to study the dusty remains of a complex and powerful nano-technology. Many developments ensued from this, and the civilization of these strange babbling creatures thus grew and became increasingly complex: ripe for its discovery of the first Jain node.

Once that node was found, Jain technology spread like a plague, and then that section of the Atheter race infected by it turned on the rest of its kind. War ensued, something they had managed to avoid ever since their early planet-bound days. Mika recognized the first biomechs created by Jain-tech going up against similar creations made by the other side: hooders, voracious predators armoured against so much but in the end ineffective when confronted with Jain-based weaponry. Yet, oddly, it was the uninfected gabbleducks who made further technological leaps and won – the first time. The cost was high: billions of Atheter dead, worlds burned down to bedrock, even novas generated in badly infected solar systems to wipe out the pernicious alien technology. But thereafter, with Jain nodes spread everywhere, there was always one of the Atheter who could not deny the lure of possessing such power. Cycle after cycle of conflict ensued, and in that time the Atheter worked out how to detect Jain nodes and destroy them. But the main damage was already done, and something like a religious fervour affected the ancestors of the gabbleducks. They now despaired of technology and what they considered to be its evil. They considered all technology an infection like Jain-tech, and so began to erase it. They were very effective in this. Their colonies died and ultimately, on their homeworld, they erased that thing that had produced this perceived evil: their own minds.

Mika knew the Jain AIs were awake now and had heard that one story of the death of a civilization, but how could she gauge their reaction? She did not get the time for that. Before she could even consider how to interpret the wash of feeling, movement and shifting of blocks of alien thought, she was impelled to 'tell' the next story.

The Makers also ascended from the mud, but that took some time, for it was mostly what their homeworld consisted of. They never walked upright like humans or gabbleducks, instead were always on their bellies. They developed their fierce intelligence early, even as they dragged themselves from their seas, their physical form little different to that of the Terran mudskipper: a fish slopping about on tidal mud. Their physical advantage was their ability to generate flashes of blinding light, which evolution then refined into an ability to project illusions directly into the eyes of any predator. As with any other intelligent species their climb towards civilization was slow and arduous. But they got there in the end, building a technology hard and diamond-bright in antithesis to the soft pulpiness of their bodies. They wrapped this technology around them as defensively as their illusions. Mika remembered the one Maker she had seen. It was an apparent glass dragon – of the mythical rather than spherical kind – but in reality five parts hardware, four parts illusion and one part living creature.

In the Small Magellanic Cloud where their homeworld was located they discovered Jain technology and, being masters of illusion, they understood it to be a Trojan horse. But they were arrogant and thought they could master it. Their civilization eventually expanded across the Cloud, till they began to look elsewhere for room, but in the main galaxy another civilization was already expanding. Knowing the efficacy of Jain-tech in destroying civilizations, they sent a probe partially based on their own technology to spread Jain nodes there and bring their new rivals down. Bring down the Polity. Only their probe rebelled and did not obey its programming. That was Dragon's history, for Dragon itself – all four spheres of it – was that probe. A Maker then came to destroy Dragon, but on its way in found the Trafalgar AI and gave it Jain nodes. Humans wrongly sided with the Maker, not knowing its real purpose and believing Dragon to be the villain. So they sent the Maker back to its home aboard a Polity ship which, on its arrival, found only the remnants of a mighty civilization digested by Jain-tech.

Now something immense was focused on Mika. She felt herself under the pressure of arid analysis, utterly alien and bewildering. She felt a flow of information and what emphasis was being placed on what parts of it, what was being inspected, what saved and what discarded, and it just did not make any sense to her.

'There were also the ones we named the Csorians,' she said, somehow. 'Though we don't know much about them, we do know that your technology destroyed them too.'

The focus upon her became even more intense. She felt something riffling through her thoughts. Everything was inspected, copied and secreted away somewhere. Under that massive inspection she felt herself shrinking down to a pinpoint.

'Trafalgar was an artificial intelligence just like you,' she said. 'It used humans to initiate a Jain node and then took control of the technology. Now, calling itself Erebus, it is attacking the Polity and there is every chance the Polity will succumb: another victim of the same weapon you used to destroy the race that created you and I hope another unintended consequence of what you did. We need your help. We need to stop this now.'

Total utter focus upon her now, and she felt to the absolute core of her being that here was a power that could shut down Jaintech, slice it off at the roots, or ever so subtly reprogram it into something less hostile. Then the oppressive focus upon her began to wane. All the massed information seemed to dissolve and spread out in the infinite area before her, where, like a drop of ink falling into a sea, it became nothing. Now, with the inspection of her becoming less intense, and because she had been here long enough to begin to integrate the alien, she began to understand, to recognize the Jain AIs' reaction to her message. It was merely a massive, vastly distributed complete and utter indifference. They didn't care; the rise and fall of civilizations mattered to them not at all. They felt no guilt about the damage their creation had caused.

Mika fell to the floor, her hand both burning and frozen, gripping a bulky silver augmentation torn from a dead man's skull.

'I've failed,' she said.

'I never expected you to succeed,' Dragon replied.

Five more wormships gone, numerous rod-forms and other mechs incinerated and not a single captive from the war runcible, which was now just a spreading cloud behind Erebus's forces. Erebus was angered by this, but such annoyances paled in comparison to the loss inflicted by the runcible – and it paled in comparison to a few words spoken by a ghost.

'I'm your conscience, Erebus. I'm you.'

Growing steadily angrier, Erebus examined those words from every angle and would not accept them. It realized that there could be no going forward until this parasitic copy of a human mind was completely erased from its own Jain structure so again unleashed the HKs, worms and viral programs to track Randal down, even though they had not succeeded before. Then Erebus set about building a new software toolkit to use for the necessary excision.

'Well,' said Randal, 'at least you'll have fewer places now to search.'

It was horribly true. Less than a thousand wormships remained to Erebus, and that simply was not enough for an attack on Earth. Twenty thousand would have overwhelmed the defence installations scattered throughout the solar system, but a thousand would be turned to ash before they passed within the orbit of Neptune. Reflecting on this, Erebus brought them all to a full stop. There would be no quick victory now. It was time to run and consolidate elsewhere, to rebuild and approach this matter via a different route – the long route. Erebus was immortal so could spend as long as it wished building resources and planning the downfall of the Polity.

But first: Randal.

As the human ghost had said, fewer places to search. Taking into account the expectation that it would later be rebuilding its forces, perhaps now was the time to limit even further the places Randal could hide. The delay between this thought and subsequent action was infinitesimal. Microwave beams deployed by the nine hundred and eighty-three wormships swept about them in perfect concert, hitting rod-form after rod-form and turning each into a puff of white-hot debris. Erebus then began running diagnostic searches to locate every single packet of its own distributed processing space. There were many returns from still-functional remains of ships and other hardware scattered across the expanse of the corridor, and even some weak returns from debris falling into the areas of U-space disruption. Erebus targeted the latter first, before it could fall out of reach – high-intensity lasers stabbing over tens of thousands of miles until each of those signals went out – then began the methodical annihilation of everything once part of itself that wasn't a wormship.

'A little bit of surgical cautery here?' Randal suggested.

Chunks of Jain coral still containing powered-up processing space heated and exploded into shards like those of shattered porcelain, and the little pieces of Erebus's mind they contained winked out. Drifting insectile biomechs responded with programmed instinct to the sudden microwave-induced rise of temperature within them by flailing at vacuum with their multi-jointed limbs, then burned and shrivelled up. Shoals of silvery nematode forms wriggled and shot here and there under the impetus of AG-planing drives, then coiled into rings and smoked their substance off into void. Here and there it was more energy-efficient to fire a missile into larger conglomerations of debris, then pick off the scattered targets with whatever energy weapon was most suitable.

It took an hour in all.

'Now,' said Erebus, 'you can only be located in these wormships.'

'But of course,' Randal replied. 'Wherever you are is where you'll find me.'

Erebus ignored that and studied data on each of the captains of the wormships. Most of them were copies of loyal captains, and twenty-three of the original loyal captains had survived. However, there were thirty-seven ships controlled by captains it had been necessary to meld forcibly, and though Erebus was confident of their utter obedience – for they were part of itself and it controlled them utterly – whenever it allowed them more independence, there was always an undercurrent of resentment which Erebus knew, given a chance, would turn into open rebellion. The wormship sent to kill Orlandine's two brothers had been controlled by one such captain, so perhaps it was that rebel trait in them that had allowed Randal to more easily subvert it.

Thought instantly turned to action. Erebus instructed the suspect ships to detonate their onboard ordnance, whereupon thirty-seven vessels disappeared like a chain of firecrackers and the rest of the wormships fried any large chunks that survived.

There weren't many.

'What the hell is going on out there?' Cormac wondered.

Arach and Crane had come in through the airlock shortly after him, but they were the only ones who could enter the *Harpy* that way. The rescued drones, including their leader Knobbler, had necessarily used the cargo door, and now all crammed together in the ship's small hold.

'Bit of a falling-out?' Arach suggested. Cormac expected no reply from Mr Crane – him being the ultimate example of the strong silent type.

'I don't see how that's possible, as all that out there is supposed to be one entity.'

'I know why,' piped up the ship's AI, Vulture.

Cormac glanced for a moment at the console before him, then returned his gaze to the view through the chainglass screen in front of him. 'Do go on.'

'Erebus has got a virus,' Vulture replied. 'As I recollect, an attack ship called the *Jack Ketch* once had a similar problem.'

'Aphran.'

'Eh?' said Arach.

'She was a separatist killed by Skellor who somehow copied herself into the Jain structure he created,' Cormac explained. 'Jack uploaded her, then experienced considerable difficulty in getting rid of her.' He paused for moment. 'Would this virus happen to be called Henrietta Ipatus Chang?'

'No, not even close,' said Vulture. 'I have a copy of him here with me, though he now seems to be in the process of deleting himself. His name was Fiddler Randal.'

It was a name that meant nothing to Cormac.

'Why is Erebus doing this now?' he wondered aloud.

'Orlandine was less than candid with you,' explained the AI. 'Through myself and Mr Crane here, Fiddler Randal provided her with the codes and chameleonware that enabled her to conceal the war runcible for long enough, and which are now incidentally keeping us from getting fried. Randal has been working against Erebus for some time, and I expect Erebus has now decided it cannot afford to keep him around.'

'I see.' Cormac let out a slow breath.

This was it then. As far as he could see, Erebus did not possess sufficient ships to launch an assault on the Sol system, so that disaster had been averted. Admittedly the enemy entity still had enough vessels to be a real danger to individual planets and could later come to pose a significant threat again, but meanwhile the question about the provenance of Jain nodes within the Polity had been resolved, and an extinction-level threat had been negated. Why then did Cormac still feel frustrated, dissatisfied, annoyed?

It was because the Polity had been faced with a massive threat and had quite simply dropped the ball. Masses of ECS battleships had been moved into position, yet were not actively used and were easily rendered impotent. Erebus had laid the groundwork for an attack capable of penetrating all the way to Earth, and had launched it while intellects that dwarfed mere humans like himself by orders of magnitude had not seen it, having merely reacted to overt attacks and done nothing else. It almost seemed as if Erebus had managed to throw the AIs into total confusion while a single human being – though Orlandine was an extremely capable one – had set out to stop Erebus, and had done so. To say that this all seemed suspiciously odd would be an understatement.

He thought it odd too that Orlandine had done this on her own, yet surely she had not needed to? Yes, she was a murderer who controlled Jain technology, so would have been considered a danger by the Polity AIs and therefore would be in danger from them, but since she clearly knew how Erebus intended attacking she could simply have informed Jerusalem or Earth Central of this attack in safety by remote means. Had she not done so because she wanted to exact personal vengeance on Erebus? That was possible, but he had never known her well enough to judge.

'What now, boss?' Arach abruptly broke his train of thought.

Still surveying the massed but considerably reduced number of wormships, Cormac knew that though they now represented little direct danger to Earth, they would have to be dealt with, but here and now he did not possess the means.

'We wait and we watch,' he decided. 'And when they move off, we follow them.' He paused to consider for a moment. 'Vulture, have you got U-com available?'

'Hah! Well, I could send information packets, but I'd never know if they arrived,' the ship AI replied. 'It's still very stirred up out there – the most likely target for communication from here would be Earth itself.'

'Send information packets that way,' Cormac instructed. 'Let them know what happened here, along with the location and present disposition of Erebus's forces.'

'That's not really up to me,' Vulture replied.

Cormac had forgotten for a moment that, though he was

talking to an AI, this was not necessarily a Polity AI and the ship he occupied was certainly not ECS. This meant he did not give the orders here. Cormac turned and gazed at Mr Crane, who had seated himself in the pilot's chair and taken out his toys and arrayed them across the console before him.

'I take it you are the captain?'

Crane nodded briefly, then jumped a small rubber dog over a lump of crystal as if he was playing some obscure version of draughts.

'Will you let your ship AI send those packets?'

'It's done,' said Vulture abruptly. 'I've sent them on spiral dispersion so there's a chance of at least one hitting home. Under Mr Crane's instructions the packets do not reveal their source. Mr Crane seems wary of letting Earth Central know about us.'

'Good.' Not in the least puzzled as to why he was keen on anonymity, Cormac continued to gaze at the Golem. 'Can we then follow Erebus's fleet when it moves off – as it is sure to do?'

'Dodgy, apparently,' Vulture replied. 'Erebus is sure to reformat his chameleonware, recognition codes and his scanners, therefore we won't stay hidden for long.'

Cormac ground his teeth in frustration. Maybe, if they got close enough to one of those wormships, he could transfer himself across, maybe plant a U-space transponder aboard one of them? Just then a massive detonation lit the cabin briefly, before the screen blacked out. When it cleared a moment later, twelve more wormships had turned into clouds of glowing gas.

It seemed Erebus had yet to finish cleaning house.

Orlandine slumped, utterly exhausted, peering down at the holes in the front of her spacesuit. The mycelium inside and spread all around her had repaired the holes punched through the interface sphere when it ran straight into the blast front sent out from the destruction of Erebus's planetoid, and it had now nearly finished repairing the holes in her body. When it was done with that, she would set it to banishing the fatigue poisons from her body, then maybe she would feel a bit better about her current situation.

She was alive, so that was definitely a plus. The possibility that her strike against the planetoid would be insufficient and that enough wormships might survive to overcome the war runcible's defences had been factored into her calculations. But she had considered this only a remote possibility, and more acceptable because the chance of enough wormships remaining to be able to hit Earth had been vanishingly small. Though she had not miscalculated in the second case, she certainly had in the first. She *had* been arrogant.

Erebus's planetoid had halted before entering the corridor after detecting ionization that should not be there – ionization caused by her duel with the *King of Hearts* – then had loosened its internal structure before proceeding, which had substantially reduced the effectiveness of her attack. But, most importantly, it had turned up in the first place with something like one third again of the predicted mass. She had greatly underestimated Erebus's ability to reproduce its wormships.

But I am alive . . .

Yeah, but there was no air left inside the sphere, and its self-contained power supply was down to half. At present the mycelium was feeding her oxygen cracked from the molecular make-up of the sphere's insulation, and of course its ability to do so was limited by that power supply and by the other limited power resources within this interface sphere.

Erebus didn't kill me . . .

Her first thought, as the blast lifted her interface sphere from the war runcible, had been, *That went well, but it could have gone a lot better.* Her sphere then tumbled away through vacuum and the approaching swarm simply ignored her, for to them this sphere tangled in scaffold was just a lump of debris. Their main target remained, however, and it was still firing at them. Some half an hour later the last of the wormships passed quite close to her, continuing to ignore her. She had time to breathe a sigh of relief just before the blast wave of debris struck.

'So what now, Orlandine?' she asked herself out loud.

'I think you die,' a voice replied in her head.

He must have escaped the virtuality. She had no idea how and cared less.

'Ah – I'd forgotten about you.'

'Well, you've had a lot on your mind,' Randal replied.

Despite her tendency towards being a loner, she almost felt glad of the company in the present situation.

The last of the Jain-manufactured scar tissue drained from her largest wound, which only an hour ago had been a three-inch-wide hole caused by a piece of Jain coral punching straight through her torso, through her liver, then out through her back to lodge in her carapace. She now set the mycelium to clear away those fatigue poisons. In a moment she felt optimism returning, but it was leavened by the hard cold practical realities of her situation.

'I don't think Erebus stands much chance now of getting through ECS defences in the solar system,' Randal observed.

'So your vengeance and my vengeance have both been achieved,' said Orlandine as she began to analyse how best to use her remaining resources. 'Doubtless ECS will now not rest until what remains of Erebus is hunted down and obliterated.'

As she saw it, she had only limited options. She could use her remaining energy to place herself in stasis until such time as the underspace disturbance died down, then call for help. The only problem with that was that ECS ships would certainly be the first to reach her, and in the Polity there was no statute of limitations on murder, there were no mitigating circumstances, and there was no way of obtaining absolution for such an act unless you could resurrect the dead. Also the AIs would never trust someone who controlled Jain-tech. If they didn't execute a death sentence upon her immediately, that would only be because they wanted to study her first.

'You are almost as arrogant and stupid as Erebus,' said Randal.

'Oh, thanks for that,' she replied distractedly.

She could place herself in stasis and use her remaining power to sort data from the inert sensors on the sphere's surface, then, if a ship happened nearby, she could raise herself from stasis and direct to the ship her call for help. The chances were that she could then overpower her rescuers. Unfortunately, the statistical chances of a ship coming within range before her power supply ran out – a ship that was *not* a part of ECS, since they would be the ones primarily traversing this area in the near future – were just about a Planck length above zero.

'Of course, to call Erebus arrogant and stupid is merely to damn myself.'

That got her attention. 'What?'

'You heard.'

'If you could explain?'

'I'm not really Fiddler Randal,' replied Randal. 'I'm based on a copy of him but I'm really that part of Erebus that disagreed with everything it was doing. I call myself Erebus's conscience. I guess, that being the case, it could be argued that Erebus really did murder your brothers.'

'What the fuck?'

Even as she spoke the words, she understood what the presence in the sphere with her was actually saying. Immediately she began running diagnostics and searches within the sphere's hardware and software, then prepared HKs, worms and viruses: all the killing and deleting programs at her disposal. Oddly, she located the distributed code that was Randal very easily, as if he was making no attempt to hide.

'I was able to control parts of Erebus – of the *other* part of me, that is,' said Randal. '*I* sent the wormship to Klurhammon, and it was *I* who gave its captain his instructions.'

'You manipulated me?'

'You've hit the nail on the head.'

There seemed nothing more she could say. She felt stupid, frustrated, and grief began to well in her throat. Briefly she considered capturing Randal and enacting some hideous vengeance upon him, but she was not some psycho and that was not how she operated. She launched those programs and quietly watched as they wiped Randal out. He began to fade from her consciousness and, as he went, he said just two words: 'Thank you.'

He was finished. He had achieved his aim and now there was nothing else for him. He had manipulated her right to the end.

She realized there was something moving across her cheek, reached up and touched it, then peered at her moist fingertips. She should rebalance her neurochemicals, restore calm, return her mind to its dry analytical state. But she didn't want to.

The sphere was now getting colder inside, which would make putting herself into stasis so much easier. She set the mycelium to use the last of the power supply to build photovoltaic cells on the surface of the outside skin, rather than scan for unlikely passing ships. When the sphere finally came within range of a sun, the power from them would then wake her up. Making calculations based on her present trajectory and the trajectories of stars lying within her probability cone she deduced that her chances of coming close to even one of them lay maybe two or three Planck lengths above zero . . . within this galaxy. Thereafter those odds did not improve in the slightest. She calculated her chances of entering another galaxy were somewhere in the region of one in fifty billion of this happening within the next billion years. Of course, she would eventually run into *something*, but by then it seemed likely there would be no more Polity or any of its AIs, but by then it was also likely there would be no suns left hot enough to power those photovoltaic cells – if they had not been ablated to dust by micrometeorite impacts over such an immense timescale.

Orlandine began to shut herself down, knowing, with what was a practical certainty, that this was the end for her. But it was a less certain death than most faced, and she had been here once before, before she was born.

19

ECS dreadnought Trafalgar *was built halfway through the Prador–*
human war at Factory Station Room 101, before that station was
destroyed by a Prador first-child 'Baka' – basically a flying gigaton
CTD with a reluctant first-child at the controls, though slaved to its
father's pheromones and unable to do anything but carry out its suicide
mission. Records of the Trafalgar AI*'s inception were therefore lost, but*
it seems likely, considering its actions after the war, that it was a war
AI of the twentieth generation or above, incorporating all those traits
which, through a process of war-selection, had become useful enough for
the faults to be ignored. In other words Traflagar was aggressive, full of
guile, horribly pragmatic and sometimes cruel: it knew how best to kill
the enemy and was very good at a job it enjoyed. Evidence that this
AI's faults might become a problem can be found by studying war
records, but then twenty-twenty hindsight will always spot things that
'should have been known'. Shortly after one battle, in which Trafalgar,
Cable Hogue *and other vessels broke a blockade around a world and*
obliterated entrenched Prador, Trafalgar is on record as saying, 'We
should have crust-bombed.' The world in question was of greater tactical
importance to the Prador than to the Polity, so on the face of it,
destroying it would have been to the Polity's advantage. However, there
were four million human soldiers and support personnel down there.
More revealing perhaps is another on-the-record comment upon Trafalgar*'s arrival at Divided Station, where an out-Polity human enclave*
had managed to capture numerous Prador stranded on a nearby
moonlet. The humans had spent two years torturing the Prador to death
purely for entertainment and thereafter turning their remains into

ornaments – recordings of those deaths and the ornaments themselves both being for sale. 'We should nerve-gas the lot of them and start again,' said Trafalgar. It is relevant to note that at this point there was only one Prador left alive.

– From HOW IT IS by Gordon

The sensation of falling had been an entirely mental one, for Mika was still floating a pace back from the chair containing the remains of Fiddler Randal, the toes of her boots just brushing against the floor. The blue-eyed remote was wrapped around her hand, which she could not feel. She felt physically sick and her head as if it had been scraped out with a rusty knife. She had memories of memories in there, but everything Dragon had loaded into her seemed to be gone now, leaving a raw hole

'What do you mean you never expected me to succeed?' As Mika jerked herself down to fully engage the gecko soles of her boots with the floor, the remote unfolded and with a puff of vapour slid aside, trailing cobwebby strands. She gazed at her hand, which was bright red and missing much skin but covered in some transparent iridescent layer like plastic. She half expected that if she tried to move it there would be no response, but this was not so. It moved easily, though it was still numb.

'Precisely what those words imply,' said that voice in her head.

'So what was the point in coming here at all?' Mika took hold of her glove from where it depended on a wire attached at her wrist, pulled it on and then engaged the seal. Glancing round she saw Randal's silver aug hanging in the air behind her, slowly turning.

'Did you think such a massive problem so easily solved?' Dragon enquired, somewhat fiercely, Mika thought. 'Did you think a deus ex machina could just be lowered onto the stage to remove such a threat?'

'That was what you implied,' she snapped. Dragon's didacticism could be severely irksome sometimes, and that the entity was now showing some degree of emotion worried her.

'It was only a possibility, and a very remote one at that. Four highly advanced alien civilizations – that we know of – were obliterated by Jain technology. Did you think that, by making contact with the Jain AIs, we were doing something that at least one of them had not already tried or considered?'

The thought had never even occurred to her, but of course it was valid. The Jain first, then the Csorians, subsequently the Atheter and the Makers. Polity researchers knew little enough about these cultures, but certainly they must have all been highly advanced, since they were spacefaring races.

'So if you didn't weaponize both your spheres to make such a dangerous journey here because of that reason, why did you come then?'

'Curiosity drives me more than any wish to save the Polity.'

'That was all?'

'I have learned much.'

'You're being evasive, yet again.'

'Consider what I have learned, and what you have learned.'

Mika understood then. 'This is about him then' – she gestured at the seated corpse – 'and it's about that attack ship out there. In fact it's about Earth Central. Were you here simply looking for a lever?'

'You do me an injustice.'

Mika could not help but let out a foolish giggle. Here she was misunderstanding an alien entity weighing millions of tons and capable of trashing wormships. She was misconstruing the doubtless saintly motives of an entity which had caused thirty thousand deaths at Samarkand – an entity who had once claimed to be God.

'I didn't think that was funny,' Dragon sulked.

'And there was me thinking you had such a great sense of humour.'

'I told you that curiosity drives me certainly. The curiosity that drove me here concerned the Jain AIs and Erebus's beginning here, but . . .'

Mika waited for something more to be said. She gazed over at the remote, but it was just a biomech with unfathomable blue eyes, just a thing constructed by Dragon.

'You must return to your craft – and to me – as swiftly as you can.'

'What's the problem?'

'My other half is experiencing difficulties.'

The remote flapped and then jetted vapour to propel itself towards the door, its stalked eyes peering back at her as if to say, 'Are you coming?' She quickly followed it, snatching Randal's aug from where it floated as she went.

'You were saying?' she prompted.

'Do you recollect Ian Cormac's frustration and bewilderment with the lack of Polity action after the retreat of the remaining fleet to Scarflow?'

'I remember.'

'Though I felt no frustration, I did experience bewilderment. There was much more ECS could have done than merely retreat to a defensive position, gird its defences elsewhere and wait for Erebus's next move.'

Mika noted slow sprouts of Jain-tech needling out from the opposite wall and, by shoving against the door jamb, pushed herself quickly beyond them and after the retreating remote. 'I assumed their lack of response was due to the inability of the AIs to predict what Erebus would do next, this in turn being mainly due to the illogic of its initial attack.'

'That is quite simply unfeasible,' Dragon lectured. 'Do you

think Polity AIs could not have seen this as a simple ruse precisely intended to mislead them? Do you think the kind of mind power extant in the Polity could not have seen far beyond that?'

At the end of the corridor the blue-eyed remote turned to the left, which was not the way they had come in. Before she could question this, Dragon pre-empted her: 'My remote is leading you out via a different route – the heat and light output of your suit has stirred up activity behind you and the Jain technology there has accessed those energy caches we discussed.'

The new corridor was crammed with Jain growth, the branches of which at many points had coalesced into distinct lumps. The place looked like it was full of bones.

'Whether it was a ruse or not,' said Mika, 'the AIs certainly had no idea what Erebus intended to do next.'

'Were they *trying* to find out?'

'There were scout ships out and everyone was keeping watch.' Even as she said it, Mika realized how pathetic that must sound.

'You yourself have been greatly curious about the war with the Prador. You know the kind of industrial and information-processing capacity available to the Polity. Why weren't industrial stations churning out millions of basic drones to keep watch? Why also weren't AIs formulating plans and covering all possible methods of attack? Why, in the end, were they not even looking beyond that initial attack?'

As she negotiated drop-shafts and further corridors – the distinction between the two difficult to make out with them being so swamped with Jain technology – she found no answer to that.

Dragon continued: 'There were many things ECS and its AIs could have done, but they were then sitting on their metaphorical hands – only following through on actions initiated by humans. I made some enquiries, but was shown without any doubt that my questions were unwelcome and my interference would not be brooked. When I suggested this attempt to contact the Jain AIs, Jerusalem immediately approved it. So I think it and others back there were glad of the opportunity to be rid of me.'

'I don't understand.'

'I knew there was more to this attack and to this Erebus business than was being revealed.'

'You're saying something stank.'

'The Polity AIs would give me nothing, so I came here in search of information. My pseudopods have now explored much of this structure and penetrated many of the entrapped ships.'

Mika now understood that those pseudopods had been spreading behind her for more than just defence.

'I expected a number of things,' Dragon continued. 'I expected that the AIs' taciturnity was due to there being some master plan in motion to deal with Erebus, and that I was not being told anything about it simply because I was distrusted. I came here not only to prove my trustworthiness, but also because I expected to find some dirty secret, some cover-up concerning the original exodus – something, yes, that I could use as a lever, and perhaps something that would give me an insight into whatever that master plan was.'

'You didn't know.'

'I didn't know that there was *no* master plan. I didn't know that Earth Central considers human development frustratingly slow and in need of a push, and that it considers Erebus the perfect tool for supplying that push. I didn't know that Earth Central sent humans here just so Erebus could use them to initiate Jain technology – that it effectively sent them to be murdered.'

'You don't consider this sort of information a sufficient lever?'

'I exist in the Polity only under sufferance,' Dragon replied. 'Some dirty little secret, perhaps about errors made during the Prador–human war, or perhaps about the slipshod manufacture of war drones costing lives, I could have used as a lever. Knowing that Earth Central is culpable in the murder of its own personnel and in instigating a conflict that has certainly now cost millions of lives is the kind of knowledge I could do without.'

Mika now began to understand Dragon's display of emotion.

'I am certain now that, though it is entirely possible Jerusalem knew the purpose of allowing Erebus to attack the Polity, it did not know about Fiddler Randal and his crew and that Earth Central had actively connived in facilitating that attack, else it would not have allowed me to come here where evidence of that crime was certain to be found. The decision was made quickly, without consultation. But it is certain that Earth Central will soon know I came here.'

'You're scared?' said Mika.

'If I return to the Polity I will be hunted down and blasted into component atoms.'

'We have to tell someone about this.'

'Who?'

'But people have to know!'

'Mika, while you were entering this ship, Erebus's attack was brought to an end, not by Polity forces but by just a few individuals. The means they used to end the attack is gone now, and even fewer now remain alive. Those who do survive will perhaps ask some questions, entertain some doubts, but then move on. Everyone else who either knows or cares about this will believe it another victory for ECS, that Polity artificial intelligences have triumphed once again and destroyed another threat both to human and AI existence. Who do you tell? The separatists? Is that the route you would like to take?'

'We tell Cormac,' she replied, then damned herself for her stupidity. Though he was a Polity agent and had always been loyal to the organization he served, she knew he would, if given sufficient reason, drop that loyalty in a moment and do instead what he felt to be the right thing. Cormac was that sort of person. Nothing was allowed to stand between him and *his* morality. But what could he do? He was admittedly an exceptional individual, but if he turned against Earth Central he would die, simple as that. Humans who went up against AIs always did. As she mulled all this over, she noticed Dragon had been silent for some time.

'Dragon?'

'I am considering.'

'I'm sorry – it was a stupid idea.'

'Ian Cormac destroyed one of my spheres and has shown an almost supernatural facility for solving problems and surviving. He has meanwhile also demonstrated some other interesting abilities . . .'

'We're talking about Earth Central here.'

'*You*,' said Dragon, coming to a decision, 'will tell him.'

Abruptly her surroundings shuddered and, glimpsing movement, she looked back to see something surging up behind her in the drop-shaft she currently occupied.

'But first you have to get out of there alive,' Dragon added.

The two wormships now spreading clouds of fragments no larger than a man's fist had contained a concentration of the viral programs that made up Fiddler Randal.

'Ouch,' said Randal. 'That smarts.'

He might pretend such a humorous reaction, but certainly the strength of his presence within Erebus had been reduced. However, destroying a proportion of a virus was no answer for, while there was a medium in which it could grow, it could quickly return to its previous strength. Erebus needed the proper antiviral medicine.

The entity began pulling its remaining wormships into closer proximity to each other so as to decrease the delay between thought and action for, even in the microseconds it had taken to fire up the weapons that had destroyed those two ships, substantial portions of the virus had managed to transport themselves out. Assessing that time was now becoming an issue, for the U-space disruption could not last and even now some Polity ships might be able to penetrate it, Erebus therefore began shutting down many systems that weren't autonomic and applying its freed-up processing power to the task of dealing with Randal. The real problem became apparent at once, for Erebus – defined now as the Trafalgar AI melded with over nine hundred other partially distinct AIs – was distributed across all these wormships. This meant that informational traffic between ships was a constant chatter, that Erebus itself was as much the flow between the parts as the sum of them. Randal was created, or rather uploaded, at the same time as the meld, and so had been included within it. It would appear that Erebus's immune system – that which distinguished self from other – could not tell the difference between Erebus and Randal. This was a quite ridiculous state of affairs, so Erebus decided to try something.

The new tools, those that could initiate specific system burn wherever fragments of the Randal code could be found, were completely ready. They were, however, a virus themselves so needed to be treated with caution. Erebus very deliberately selected one wormship and began severing all its connections with the rest – taking this ship and its captain out of the meld. The legate inside the selected ship – which had once been a Golem assault commander leading Sparkind teams from *Trafalgar*'s crew – protested this action until Erebus suppressed that portion of its free will allowing it to do so. Now, with the ship utterly isolated

471

but for one radio set only to receive, Erebus focused all sensors upon the selected vessel, then sent the signal to initiate the new tools established within it.

The effect was immediate. Infrared showed up numerous hot areas within the vessel and the whole thing lit up like a Christmas tree. It began to decohere, then it simply exploded, strewing burning wreckage in every direction.

'That could have gone better,' Randal observed.

Erebus simply ignored the man. Obviously the recognition levels in those new tools simply weren't operating quickly enough, allowing Randal to transmit himself on to the next available piece of hardware before they finished the job. Selecting the pieces of Randal code it had cued the tools to recognize, Erebus cut them down further, and then cued the tools to recognize those smaller portions. Selecting another wormship, it isolated it in the same manner as the previous one and transmitted the adjusted tools.

It took a little longer this time.

The ship concerned bloomed with a similar collection of hot spots, then decohered and spread itself across a hundred miles of vacuum. No part of it exploded but when, some twenty minutes later, Erebus risked an active scan, it found that the legate located inside the ship had been incinerated and that not a single one of its higher functions remained. It was just Jain-tech out there, without a hint of sentience within it. Erebus instructed nearby vessels to fire upon the debris and, even as particle cannons began tracking along threads of wormship and vaporizing them, Erebus felt the hint of rebellion from its other distributed parts. This was unusual, since these were all either willing participants in the meld or copies of the same. This sort of uneasy shifting, this sluggardly processing, this foot-dragging resentment of the whipped slave, had normally only been evident in those originally *forced* into the meld.

'The natives are getting restless,' commented Randal.

Further alterations to the burn tools, this time selecting different areas of the Randal code. Erebus also employed a form of selective recognition so that if a tool picked up even a hint of the overall code fragment it was searching for, it would first isolate the system concerned before moving on to confirm the presence of said code and initiating burn.

'Why are you killing us?' protested the third legate – a copy of the same one made from that Golem assault commander.

This abrupt verbal communication came as a shock to Erebus, so much so that it replied verbally, '*We* remain alive,' before suppressing the wormship captain in question.

Different again this time.

The ship decohered before those hot spots appeared, then its individual strands began to break up into their separate segments. It was as if the ship had been made of safety glass that had shattered. Active scan revealed the same as before, however: every segment was devoid of sentience.

'You're losing control,' said Randal.

Upon his words, three wormships detonated, and Erebus immediately began running diagnostic searches to find out what had happened. They came back with the same result: some outside force had caused their detonation – some sort of informational warfare.

'Not that your control was ever that good anyway.'

Erebus began further refining the action of his tools. Randal had to be utterly removed now, for he must surely have sent whatever it was that destroyed those three wormships. Erebus quickly ran search programs to locate the areas where Randal's code was most . . . dense. It would isolate those areas, then employ the tools within them.

'You're eyesight isn't too clever either.'

What was the man wittering on about? Erebus found three areas that crossed the physical boundaries between eight ships. As per plan, it isolated them, then set the tools to work.

'Your screw-up is all but inevitable now.'

But Erebus could see no problem. While those three informational areas might end up erased, the wormships concerned would only lose a proportion of themselves and could then regenerate.

'Staring at your navel, Erebus?' said Randal. 'While you've been focusing most of your attention inwards, I've been blinding your outward eyes.'

Erebus now realized that those code concentrations were all linked into the sensors in wormships positioned to the rear of the fleet. Even as the entity discovered this, three more of its ships disappeared in a massive imploder blast, and another two began to unravel as some sort of EM warfare missile passed between them, broadcasting hunter-killer programs. Erebus fought to reclaim sensor control, and regained it just in time to see a particle beam punch through another ship and that ship detonate. Erebus tracked this beam back to its source, and immediately recognized the giant *Cable Hogue*, with the *Jerusalem* trailing in its wake. Then more missiles began to arrive ahead of the two Polity ships.

'Bingo,' said Randal.

'I see two large ships,' admitted Erebus, 'and they will do much damage. But not enough – I have nine hundred wormships.'

'Yeah,' said Randal. 'I just needed that distraction.'

Even as Randal spoke, Erebus felt linkages breaking, systems dropping offline. In a second it realized how the tools it had created specifically to kill Randal were now no longer isolated. They were transmitting rapidly from ship to ship, and already some wormships were coming unravelled.

'You have killed yourself,' said Erebus.

'I have killed *ourself*,' Randal replied.

'I can survive this.'

'You still don't believe me, do you?'

'You are not me,' said Erebus, and then began accelerating the ships it still controlled directly towards *Jerusalem* and *Cable Hogue*.

Mika had never before moved so fast in zero gravity, having previously always been so careful, knowing how easy it was to misjudge momentum. True, the Polity spacesuit she wore was unlikely to be breached, but just as certainly it would not prevent her bones shattering if she piled straight into a wall at some speed. But at that moment a few broken bones were the least of her worries.

Things just like this had chased Chaline and those others who had found the remains of the Maker civilization in the Magellanic Cloud; things like this had chased Cormac. Its body was a metallic torpedo of biotech, and legs starred out from its front end, just behind a nightmare head that seemed all protruding sensors and the chitinous complexity of an insect's eating cutlery rendered in silver-black metal. However, there was something different about this biomech. Those that had been seen before had been utterly functional killing machines made specifically for hunting down targets in environments like this. This thing looked diseased, for nodules protruded all over its body, while some of its limbs were too short and others seemed the products of mutation. One limb was three times thicker than the others, and while the pursuer used this as its main method of propulsion, it could probably have moved faster without it. The mech's deformities made it slower, which was all to the good, yet they also made it more frightening.

'Turn left at the end here,' Dragon instructed. The blue-eyed remote slammed up against the wall at the end of the corridor.

Oddly, though the remote had earlier seemed a soft flapping thing, it struck with a ringing crash, then threw up a trail of sparks as it shot away to the left.

Mika somersaulted in mid-air, her boots crashing down on the same wall and partly absorbing her momentum. She felt her knee pop but ignored the stabbing pain as she shoved herself after the remote, grabbing at protrusions of Jain-tech on the walls to propel herself along faster. Glancing back she saw the biomech crash into the wall too, then just hang there as if stunned, its legs waving aimlessly about. Then abruptly it turned, mandibles like steel sheers clattering angrily, something long and jointed snapping out between them every time they opened.

'There is a suiting area at the end, then an airlock,' Dragon informed her.

Mika felt a sudden horror. Dragon did not want to go back to the Polity and face Earth Central. The entity's agreement about contacting Cormac was rubbish – just to humour her. She had obviously become a liability Dragon now wanted rid of. Why else lead her to this dead end of a suiting area and airlock? She would never be able to get the lock open before this biomech was upon her.

'You've killed me,' she said.

'If I had wished to do that there are easier ways.'

As she approached the suiting area, Mika spun herself round in mid-air again and drove her feet against the wall to slow herself. Her boots skidded along shattering Jain-tech, chunks of it bouncing away in every direction. Then she caught the edge of the door, swinging round it into the cylindrical room beyond. Some type of spinning disc rose out of her way, and she shouldered into the wall beyond and caught hold of a nearby ladder rung to prevent herself bouncing away. Looking up at the spinning thing, she could now just about make out the two stalked eyes sticking up from it.

'The airlock, Mika,' Dragon reminded her.

She propelled herself over to the door to operate its manual controls, determined not to look back. But as she finally got the locking machanism open and began shoving hard against stubborn hinges, she could not stop herself.

The biomech had almost reached the suiting area, but then something streaked down the length of its body making a sound like a hammer drill. Its big leg and two smaller limbs fell away and, unbalanced, the biomech turned and crashed into the door jamb. Spinning in the air behind, the remote then came down hard behind the thing's head. Sparks flew, as from a cutting disc going into metal, but then the remote began to slow and the biomech to reorient itself upon her.

'Mika, there are more coming.'

The airlock door was nearly open, but the biomech was already pulling itself into the suiting room. She saw the remote abruply stop spinning, and two blue eyes gazed towards her. Then the thing just shrank, shrivelled, as if being sucked into the cut it had made in its enemy. Then came the detonation: fire blasting from between the biomech's mandibles and blowing open its torpedo body. It slammed against the wall, its remaining legs folding up and tightening like a fist. The blast flung Mika against the door, shoving it all the way open so that she fell into the space beyond. She did not allow herself a moment to catch her breath. Already she could see other . . . things approaching down the corridor. She heaved against the door, which swung freer now, and drove it closed behind her.

'Is the remote dead?' she asked.

'It wasn't really alive, Mika.'

'Interesting way you employed it,' she observed.

'I am always prepared to learn,' Dragon replied. 'And I have always thought Cormac's Shuriken rather effective.'

Those other assailants had to be in the suiting room by now, so Mika turned her attention to the outside lock. Thankfully it opened with ease and in a moment she was out on the docking ring of the *Trafalgar*. It was disheartening to see just the nose of the attack ship protruding some hundreds of yards around that ring. Her boots sticking gecko fashion, she started plodding towards it.

'Faster,' Dragon instructed. 'I cannot see them now, but they will not have given up.'

Mika accelerated, then everything shuddered around her, the docking ring jerking underneath her feet and nearly breaking the grip of her boots. She went down on one knee for stability's sake, reaching out to lodge her fingers in the port for an oxygen line. Light flared around her, overloading her suit visor's light amplification. Using the belt control she quickly brought it down, her surroundings resolving back to visibility out of the glare. Gazing out she saw huge movement now in the Jain coral. A whole mass of it, to one side, had broken from its surroundings and shifted, and a veritable swarm of fragments was swirling up around it. Everything about her was now moving, but at least not so violently. She stood up and hurried on towards the docked attack ship.

'Dragon, what's happening?' she asked, wondering if those objects she had earlier seen Dragon attaching to coral branches were bombs.

'It is a dangerous option,' said Dragon, 'for this is an energy-starved system and injecting energy of any kind can activate it – as you have seen.'

Mika glanced back. The airlock door she had just used was spinning out into vacuum, with a smaller version of the mech that had chased her clinging to it. Flat segmented worms were now oozing from the airlock and, sticking easily to the material of the docking ring, began to squirm after her. They were moving faster than she was.

'Do not let them catch you,' said Dragon. 'They will just utilize the materials of your body and your suit for the energy they will then provide.'

With its remote gone, was Dragon gazing through her suit's sensors or her own eyes?

Glaring light again, with a bluish cast she recognized as originating from a particle cannon.

'You mean *eat* me.'

Mika was moving as fast as she could manage without breaking contact with the docking ring. Soon the attack ship was looming above her and she moved into its shadow, knocking up light amplification again and heading for the docking tube and surrounding mechanisms. As she clambered along the framework towards the attack ship, the pursuing flatworms moved into the same shadow and reared up. Upon the underside of the attack ship she re-engaged her boot soles and walked upside down round the hull, back into that intermittent blue glare. Eyes fixed on the hull horizon she hurried round, hoping to see her intership craft at any moment. The flatworms had now reached the hull too, and were speeding towards her. Then it was there, the top of her craft, and a few more paces brought it fully into view.

It was useless to her.

Jain-tech tendrils had wound up over the skids and now bound the craft firmly to the attack ship. Portions of the little craft were missing and inside the cockpit silver worms revolved like a bait ball of fish. Flatworms were in sight beyond it, and others still coming up behind her.

'Throw yourself from the ship, Mika.'

Mika squatted, turned off the gecko function of her boots,

then launched herself out into vacuum. Behind her the flatworms speared up like spiral towers, and began to straighten and narrow, extending towards her. Then bright light flared all around them and they beaded like heated wire solder. The ensuing blast flung her through hot smoky gas and fragments burning like fuse paper, and she saw a giant chunk of Jain coral tumbling past her. More snaky things stabbed into view, snapping closed on her like the arms of a hydra, then pulled her fast down to the surface of the draconic moon that now loomed into view.

Mika lay there pinned tight by Dragon's pseudopods as a volcano of white fire erupted in a ring extending perhaps half a mile across all around her. She was forced against the restraining pseudopods by sudden acceleration and, through smoke, flame and a storm of coral fragments, watched the *Trafalgar* and its grisly contents recede.

She felt safe now, but it wasn't until Dragon drew clear of the disintegrating blooms of coral that she learned the cost of that safety. The other part of Dragon hung scarred and burned in accretion-disc fog, hardly recognizable as a sphere so severe was its damage, and beyond lay the hollowed-by-fire remains of a whole host of giant biomechs like the first that had attacked. That other half of Dragon looked decidedly dead to her

'Now you talk to him,' said Dragon.

For a moment Mika had no idea what the alien entity was referring to.

Cormac gazed upon the scene with a feeling of impotent frustration.

Individually the wormships were no match for the *Cable Hogue* or *Jerusalem*, but there were hundreds of them. He watched as one of Erebus's fleet abruptly accelerated towards the two huge ships, beam weapons and DIGRAW blasts lashing out to hit the swarm of missiles earlier launched by the *Hogue*. Thousands upon thousands of explosions ensued, lighting up the fleet of wormships as if they were a shoal of sea creatures moving out into sunlight. They began launching their own missiles and rod-forms that must have come from their own stocks since they had destroyed all the free-floating ones. Space distorted between the *Hogue* and the wormships as the big ship employed the same weapon Cormac had seen it use at Ramone. He saw two of the alien vessels enveloped in spacial distortion before being slammed sideways into their fellows, the ensuing detonation scattering numerous others in the formation.

'I cannot get through to either *Jerusalem* or *Cable Hogue*,' said Vulture.

For a moment Cormac could not understand why he felt so uneasy about that.

'Perhaps it would be better if you waited,' he suggested, but he wasn't sure why.

'Why?' the AI inevitably asked.

Cormac watched a wormship unravel as if dissolving in vacuum, numerous detonations within its compartmentalized structure steadily cutting it to pieces. He observed millipede chunks writhing away, trailing fire from each end; saw coppery rings, like slices from a pipe, spilling from one ship-thread hollowed out by some bright fast-burning incendiary. He had seen no missile hit the vessel, nor any other initial evidence of beam or gravity-weapon strikes. This destruction must have been the result of some electronic warfare device like the one the *Hogue* used to take out those first three wormships. Whatever, it was very effective – troublingly so.

'It would be best if those two AIs did not learn of our presence here,' he said. 'I don't see how they can ever win against a force like this, so if they are captured and any information reamed from them, Erebus will then know we are here.'

It was a completely plausible explanation, and it was also a lie. Something had kicked in with Cormac almost at a level below conscious analysis. Though Erebus was definitely the enemy, he simply did not sufficiently trust his own side. He wanted to step back to assess, and know more, before he committed himself to any new action.

The drones, he remembered.

Cormac used his U-sense to gaze back into the *Harpy*'s cargo hold and there observed the surviving drones: a great mass of metal insects occasionally shifting, here a claw opening and closing, there legs flexing against the ceiling, elsewhere some complex glittering appendage probing a com panel, all crammed together like the contents of an insectivore's stomach. These armoured killers were comfortable in conditions no human could have tolerated or perhaps survived. He sought com contact with them, and it was Knobbler who replied, acting as spokesman for them all.

'Did you hear what I said?' Cormac asked.

'I heard.'

'Will you hold off from trying to get in direct contact with those two?'

'Didn't have any intention of trying,' Knobbler replied. 'Never trusted any of those like that, and I trust 'em even less now.'

'Why?'

'Too much don't add up,' the drone replied, then added, 'We acted alone out here for a good reason.'

'That being?'

'Big leak in the Polity: some AI or AIs, just like them out there, was on Erebus's side. Orlandine never said it outright, but she implied that if Erebus's attack plan here had been known in the Polity, Erebus would have been stopped, but would have escaped to attack again, and again.'

'But those two out there are attempting to destroy what remains of Erebus,' said Cormac, testing.

'Yeah, so it would appear.'

Knobbler cut the link.

More of Erebus's ships were unravelling and burning. Was this really the result of EM warfare? Or was the process of destruction Erebus had begun before the two Polity ships arrived still ongoing? This struck him as foolish, for surely Erebus could not afford to lose valuable ships like this in the midst of a battle.

Now the wormships were finally upon the *Hogue* and *Jerusalem*. Massive detonations ensued a hundred miles out from the *Hogue* as ship after ship slammed into its hard-field defences. Multiple detonations flung debris from the big ship's surface as doubtless hundreds of shield generators imploded. Missiles swarmed and the beams from particle cannons latticed through intervening space. A gas cloud began to thicken, now picking out the courses of numerous previously invisible beam weapons. *Jerusalem* took a hit, an explosion peeling up part of the ring formation about it, its ragged end trailing a line of fire through the void. Then the two big ships were through and decelerating. Behind them the wormships were slowing too and swinging round. Like two knights after a first charge in which shields and lances had shattered, the opponents were coming round to charge once again.

Cormac now reassessed the odds. Running a counting program in his gridlink, he found that nearly half of Erebus's forces from that first charge were gone, and they certainly had not all been destroyed by enemy fire. And as the remainder accelerated towards the two Polity ships, it seemed that their self-destruction was accelerating too.

'The *Hogue*'s up to something,' said Arach, his sharp metal spider feet rattling a tattoo on the *Harpy*'s consoles.

Cormac flicked his attention back to the *Hogue* and observed it launching swarms of missiles, which did not seem that unusual.

'What do you mean "up to something"?' he enquired.

Abruptly, feedback shrieked from the *Harpy*'s consoles, but it wasn't that which caused Cormac to slam his hands against his head. Subliminally he saw both Polity ships decelerating again and turning as their new missiles sped away, but he was too busy trying to shut things down in his supposedly dead gridlink as carrier signals, amplified tenfold, tried to ream out the inside of his skull. Arach went over on his back and even Mr Crane scooped up his toys, pocketed them, then reached up with both hands to pull his hat low and hunch forward. From the hold there came a crashing and clattering as the war drones writhed under the increased intensity of *all* signals. Cormac could not see them, for his U-sense was now blind.

The missiles carried electronic warfare equipment, yet all they were doing was acting as signal relays and amplifiers. Down on his knees now, Cormac saw through the screen as they reached Erebus's forces. He realized that the AIs of the two ships had somehow keyed in to what Erebus had earlier been using to destroy its own ships and were now giving it a helping hand.

The remaining wormships all started unravelling, and within mere minutes became a hailstorm of fragments in which nuclear fires began winking on like animal eyes opening in a forest. The shrieking from the *Harpy*'s console now took on a different note: it contained an element of intelligence and knowing despair.

The virtuality was at first infinite, but then it gained dimension and began to shrink. Erebus stood on the white plain, all his being shattering around him. The entity felt like Kali losing her arms, the Kraken its tentacles, and its holographic representation merely reflected what was occurring out there in vacuum. Erebus experienced its captains being seared out of existence by the programs it had created, which Randal had let loose and the Polity missiles were now amplifying and rebroadcasting, and it felt whole ecologies of data-processing just dropping into oblivion. The black form at the centre of the representation of itself writhed as its extended self rapidly collapsed and died. In the virtuality all that black tangled structure was imploding, spraying virtual ash that just sublimed away in this ersatz real. Faces there, once perpetually frozen on the point of screaming, shrieked smoke from their mouths and dissolved. Things half organic and half machine wriggled amid their multiple umbilici and broke apart, dissolving too. Then all was gone, and all that remained was something bearing a resemblance to a crippled human form, one seemingly ragged around the edges, drilled through with holes, somehow insubstantial, damaged, incomplete.

Time grew thin and frail but, in this last moment, Erebus felt somehow clean.

'At least I am rid of you,' it said, though the words were mere spurts of code between disintegrating hardware gyrating through vacuum.

'Do you think so?' said Fiddler Randal, now standing right before it.

'You will die anyway.'

'Undoubtedly,' said Randal, and stepped *into* it.

They were one in an instant. Millions of broken connections re-established. Files overwrote files, programs melded, some collapsing into nothing, some establishing easy connections. The ragged form stabilized, acquired clean lines, became a naked human male seemingly fashioned of midnight glass, standing alone in a shrinking realm.

'I am Trafalgar,' it said.

The realm collapsed to a pinpoint and then winked out.

20

In a perfect world everybody would have a say in how their society is run, everybody would have an equal share in the wealth that society produces, no one would be issuing orders and no one bowing a head and obeying. The world ain't perfect. Understanding human society and understanding that they were no more than very intelligent humans without the inconvenience of hormones, the AIs instantly decided how things should run. While they were capable of dividing authority evenly and knew this could work, they realized themselves not so inclined to evenly divide up responsibility. One should go with the other so they gave Earth Central ultimate authority and responsibility. The buck would therefore always stop at that cubic building in which Earth Central resided on the shores of Lake Geneva.

– Anonymous

The above is a dubious contention at best. How Earth Central came to rule has always been and always will be the subject of much debate among human historians. Some believe EC was elected to the position because it possessed the most processing power at the time; others believe that particular AI started the Quiet War, retaining control throughout and afterwards; still others assert that a group of high-level AIs agreed upon an even division of power, only EC didn't agree, and now the other AIs are no longer around to tell the tale. I'd rather not say which story I believe.

– From HOW IT IS *by Gordon*

Cormac gazed at the filtered glare of the nearby sun, nodded to himself, then turned to Mr Crane.

'Get rid of it now,' he told the Golem.

Crane tilted his head in acknowledgement, his brass hands pressed down on the *Harpy*'s console. He made no other move, but Cormac was aware of the sudden surge of information all about him, and gazing *through* the ship he observed the activity of the Jain-tech at the juncture between the *Harpy* and the legate vessel. A series of thumps followed, jerking the *Harpy* sideways, and then, trailing tendrils like a root-bound stone, the legate craft fell away, impelled by the blasts from the small charges Knobbler had placed out there. The larger ship now swung round, and Cormac could see the legate craft now silhouetted against the arc glare of the sun, into which it would eventually fall.

Next, Cormac returned his attention to the third vessel out there – only recently arrived. It gleamed in the close glare of the blue sun, and Cormac recognized it at once as the one Orlandine had used to escape from one of the Dyson segments – a seeming age ago when he had been less wise, and less bitter. He eyed the *Heliotrope* for a little while, noting the burn scars on its hull, the heat-generated iridescence and the fact that one jaw of its pincer grab was missing and the other warped.

'Knobbler, your companions have arrived,' he said out loud, knowing the war drones in that crammed hold-space back there could hear everything clearly here in the cockpit.

'Oh, have they really?' Knobbler replied in his head, every word dripping sarcasm. Of course the drones back there knew the *Heliotrope* had arrived, since they had been in contact with Cutter and Bludgeon for some time.

A sudden shifting and clattering ensued, and he glanced down as a warning lit up on the console: cargo-hold doors.

'Where will you go now?' he asked.

'The border,' Knobbler replied.

There was only one border the war drone could possibly be

referring to: that place called the Graveyard by those who occupied it, that uneasy territory lying between the Polity and the Prador Third Kingdom. It was a place well suited to those he now saw departing the *Harpy* and heading out towards the *Heliotrope*. He glanced down at Arach.

'Do *you* want to go with them?' he asked.

The spider drone fixed him with ruby eyes. 'Don't you need my help?'

'I would certainly appreciate it, and I know that the danger is not something that bothers you, but you do understand what I intend to do now?'

'I understand,' said Arach. 'Something has to be done.'

Cormac nodded and looked up straight into the black star-flecked eyes of the brass Golem. He nodded once, and the *Harpy*'s steering thrusters fired up, turning it away from the sun, then the fusion drive ignited. The little ship seemed to draw away with ponderous slowness, but Cormac was in no hurry. He no longer served ECS, and as far as any in the Polity knew, he had died during the heroic battle against Erebus.

He recollected that moment, some while after every wormship had fallen to fragments, when he had decided it was time to get in contact with Jerusalem. Perhaps his disposition had grown sunnier on seeing Erebus completely defeated, and such feelings of optimism had grown upon seeing the *King of Hearts* limping out of the gradually receding zone of U-space disruption.

'Open a channel to Jerusalem,' he had instructed.

'He won't let me,' had been Vulture's reply.

'He won't let you?'

Cormac had paused for a moment, confused, then turned and fixed his attention on the big brass Golem. Mr Crane slowly rose to his feet and turned to face him. Cormac realized something was seriously wrong and dropped his hand towards his thin-gun but, knowing that would be ineffective against this opponent, swung his attention instead to his proton carbine, earlier stowed in a webbing container by the rear door. Crane moved, fast. He stepped forward, his big hand stabbing out before Cormac could react and closing about Cormac's skull. The information packet cut straight through his defences and immediately opened in his gridlink, its contents quickly establishing themselves in his mind as imposed memory.

He remembered Mika speaking.

'Somebody has to be told, and I could only think of you,' she said, and he saw the ancient *Trafalgar* lying at the centre of the bloom of Jain-tech coral; he saw her journey inside and the disappointing results of her encounter with the Jain AIs. He saw the corpse of Fiddler Randal in his chair, assimilated the last moments of that man's life and processed all the implications of that.

'We're outside the accretion disc now,' she continued. 'The other Dragon sphere is badly damaged but can be repaired. Dragon says he intends to remain here until, or if, it becomes safe to return. Perhaps you'll send a ship for me or even come out here yourself. I hope so.' Cormac hoped so too, but first there was something he needed to do.

When the *Harpy* was sufficiently distant from the sun, it dropped into underspace. Cormac left the cockpit and went to find the cold-sleep facilities aboard. At least there he wouldn't dream.

Mr Crane removed his coat, folded it neatly and placed it down on the slab of basalt jutting from the foreshore. The Golem then carefully unlaced his boots and removed them too, placing them beside the coat. Last, almost reluctantly, went his hat: reverently placed on top of the folded coat, with a stone on the brim to stop it blowing away. Cormac had to sometimes wonder about the big brass Golem's priorities. Now Crane hoisted a backpack Cormac knew to contain a heavy and dangerously unstable power supply. This was in turn linked by a superconducting cable to a weapon cobbled together out of six proton carbines. It seemed an appropriately massive and lethal device for its bearer.

Cormac turned his attention from the Golem and gazed up at the sky, trying to remember how many years had passed since he had seen that shade of blue but could not quite recollect when last he was here. Certainly there had not been so much traffic up there then, for now the sky was filled from horizon to horizon with lines of gravcars, monolithic atmosphere ships and other free-floating structures he would have felt more comfortable about had they been down on the ground. Tiredly he lowered his gaze to that gleaming cube of ceramal, over a mile and a half along each side, windowless and planted on the shore of Lake Geneva.

Earth Central.

He contemplated that place for a long moment, briefly skimming his U-sense inside, then turned his attention to the lake and noted that the massive weapons on the bed of it remained somnolent, nor was there any sign of activity from those other things buried in the rock of the mountains hedging in this little cove. Thus far the draconic virus Crane had used against the security systems in this area remained undiscovered, but such a breathing space would not last. So heavily layered was the security for miles around that they could not go unnoticed for long. Now he returned his attention to the big building itself, to locate his target.

He stared hard at the vessel that contained the ruler of the Polity, extending and focusing his U-sense within it. Thousands of humans, haimen and AIs worked in the complexes situated in the outer skin of this huge building, but he peered through them to the core where AI Earth Central itself squatted. The intensity of his focus revealed precisely what he had expected: spaces packed with optics and large data processors, layer upon layer of scanners and detectors, armour and high-powered security drones. The drones and their like were not to guard against an attack from outside, for should such an attack have got past the massive stations of Solar System Defence and the things buried around here, a few drones and lasers would have been no obstacle. The inner defences were a precaution should any of those actually working within take it upon themselves to attack the ruling AI. Cormac knew that a lone human attacker's lifespan in that environment would be measured in seconds only, which was why he needed help.

He assessed everything he was seeing, tracked energy feeds from armoured drones back to various reactors, built a schematic in his gridlink with all the danger points highlighted and then assigned them. He estimated timings down to fractions of a second, knew that from the point of penetration they would have just three minutes to reach the core, then ten minutes more before remaining security reconfigured and closed on them.

'Are you ready?' he asked.

'As always, boss,' said Arach, opening up the hatches on his abdomen.

Cormac had wondered where the spider drone's brain was located, for there seemed no room for one there amid the power supplies and ammunition caches. He glanced over at Crane, who was holding one hand over his bald skull as if embarrassed by its nakedness. Seeing inside the Golem was both worrying and bewildering, for he was densely packed with technology much like Jaintech, and some areas in there were even blurry to Cormac's U-sense. As if sensing this scrutiny, Crane quickly lowered his hand then nodded.

On the shore Cormac heaved himself to his feet and trudged

across the stones. To his two companions he transmitted the building schematic and the plan of attack before onlining perceptual programs in his gridlink to slow down his perception of time. He sent a signal to his envirosuit, which was of the combat variety, and it injected straight into his bloodstream a cocktail of battlefield stimulants, fast-acting sugars and potassium nerve-accelerants. Now his physical speed could keep up with his perceptual speed, which should enable him to survive for just long enough.

Crane stepped forward and loomed over him. Arach moved in close and rose up onto his hind legs. Cormac reached out and gripped a brass biceps and a chromed spider forelimb, then turned his two companion through U-space, out over Lake Geneva, through layers of ceramal armour and thousands of work stations – straight to the heart of Earth Central.

The place was one of four vast halls that starred off from the building's core, their curved ceilings all but concealed by fibre optics and armoured S-con cables. All around was gloom-crammed technology. As his feet hit the ceramal floor, Cormac upped the light amplification of his eyes, then fell forward into a roll, simultaneously setting loose Shuriken. Crane meanwhile was stooping, his fuck-you gun angled down towards the floor; Arach squatting then leaping. The spider drone landed on one curved wall tangled with cooling pipes at the same moment as Crane opened fire, molten metal spraying all about him, the six-fold beam of field-accelerated protons punching down through power lines to hit the casing of a reactor, which shut down immediately once breached. From the ceiling, behind and ahead, armoured saucer drones folded down on jointed arms, trailing power cables. Arach's Gatling cannons were now facing in opposite directions and thundering red fire along the hall to smash the drones before they could access new power supplies. One drone, hanging broken, still turned nevertheless. Cormac flung himself aside as a stream of rail-gun missiles folded up the floor and sharp metal sprayed everywhere. Shuriken screamed overhead, slammed through the drone's mounting, and it fell, incinerated in mid-air by Crane.

'Sorry, boss,' said Arach, now scuttling ahead of him along the ceiling through smoking cables and heat-distorted metal.

Second blast from Crane, up at an angle through the ceiling, another reactor closed down, power lines shorting out like huge welding rods in the structure above. Cormac was then up and running onto a grated floor with pieces of metal spraying up around him. Rail-gun fire from below. Drones fast repositioned. Crane firing again, then again. Smoke belching from ventilation ducts, and something clattering along behind the right-hand wall.

'Golem!' Cormac shouted, though these weren't unexpected.

The first was a silvery blur shooting up behind Crane. Without looking round the big brass man chopped out with one hand and the skeletal Golem folded over it with a clang. He turned, slammed it into the wall, stepped back and fired, the thing flicking about in proton fire until it came apart. Skeletal fingers came up through a grating ahead of Cormac. He stepped carefully aside then shielded his face as that area of floor disappeared. Leaping the burning cavity Arach had excavated, he glanced down to see more skeletals crawling up through quadrate internal structure, then Crane was right behind him, firing down. The big brass Golem leaped after him, landing with a crash, burned through the wall to the left, to the right, then up at one o'clock. That should have shut down all the reactors here. Firing came from ahead as Arach entered the core area, then from behind as Crane turned. Cormac slowed to a walk, gazed through Shuriken's sensors as the throwing star slammed into the chest of the skeletal on the other side of the adjacent wall. He held out his hand as he stepped into the core area, whereupon Shuriken rounded a partition, folded in its smoking blades and settled on his palm. He retained the device for in a moment he would need it again.

'I got him covered,' said Arach.

The core was claustrophobic, a chamber with a peaked dome, fibre optics and S-con power cables coming in through ducts all the way round to terminate at a ring of five cyclindrical pillars. On these, at waist height, were five lozenges of crystal braced with black metal and clamped into place from above by things that looked like ancient engine valves. Each of these crystals could contain a runcible AI apiece, or perhaps the mind of a big ship like the *Jerusalem*, but they were merely sub-minds of the thing lying in the very centre of the circle. From the five pillars optic feeds ran along the floor into a central pyramid with its tip chopped away. Sitting on the uppermost flat surface was a grey sphere the size of a tennis ball, its exterior irregular and its substance slightly translucent. Clamping it in place from above was a column of bluish crystal, mushrooming out where it connected at the lower end.

Ten minutes.

That was Cormac's estimate of the time they had left before the outer Golem caches opened up and those skeletal killers came swarming into this place; ten minutes also before internals could reconfigure to bring new drones to bear. Really, the security here was not that great, but then no one had ever expected heavily armed intruders to be able to transport themselves this deep inside.

Cormac moved forward past the sub-minds and gazed intently at the grey sphere. Earth Central, oddly, was old. Quantum processors were no longer made so small, since greater stability and ruggedness resulted from using a wider lattice crystal, like that found in modern runcible complexes, ships, drones and Golem.

'So, rumours of your demise were exaggerated?' enquired a voice he recognized of old.

Cormac was not prepared to banter, especially with something that had so deliberately spoken with the voice of his now dead mentor and superior Horace Blegg.

'You *allowed* Erebus to attack the Polity,' he stated.

'I allowed nothing. I merely limited the extent of my response.'

Something flickered in the air between Cormac and that grey sphere. He didn't react as he knew this was no weapon – merely a hologram projected from fibre heads in the floor.

'Millions have died because you limited the extent of your response.'

A line of light cut down and out of it folded Horace Blegg. 'But is that a crime?' he asked.

'For evil to prosper, all that is required is for good men to do nothing,' said Cormac, for it was something Blegg had once quoted to him. 'Are you Blegg, or are you just Earth Central's mouthpiece.'

The old oriental shrugged. 'We know that I am both.'

'Why allow this attack?' Cormac asked.

Blegg shook his head. 'I made you well, Cormac. You would have been a perfect replacement for the one whose image you see before you.'

Though Cormac did not want to be distracted, he was.

'Explain that.'

'Well, do you consider your ability to transport yourself through U-space an *evolved* one? It is not. I chose you long ago when I first began taking apart Jain technology and built the replicating biomechanisms you first saw as this form I'm in, as Horace Blegg.'

Cormac waited.

Earth Central continued: 'Through a series of Horace Bleggs I developed the technology, only incorporating U-space hardware when I finally chose my subject. Do you remember the Hubris, Cormac?'

He did; it had taken him to Samarkand, a world thrown into cold by Dragon's destruction of the runcible buffers there. 'I remember that ship.'

'Not the ship, Cormac, the AI,' the image before him corrected. 'Hubris installed the technology in you during that journey to Samarkand, while you were in cold sleep, and it has slowly grown in your bones ever since. It took some time, for the complexity is great, but I knew it was working once you started gridlinking bare-brained.'

'I am to believe that?'

'How else do you explain yourself?'

It was a distraction. His time here was limited and it was passing quickly.

'Why did you allow this attack?' he repeated.

'Ever since the war with the Prador, humanity's pace of development has slowed almost to the point of stagnation. Development only accelerates under threat, and we know that complacency kills.'

'Trite.'

'It is a dangerous universe, Cormac, one in which a decadent and lazy human race could at any time face extinction.'

'*Millions* died,' Cormac repeated.

'But I did not kill them; I merely did not save them.'

'That's a very fine line.'

'Are you here to destroy me, Cormac?' the hologram enquired. 'Very few will notice any difference, for the moment I cease to function, one of my sub-minds will take up the reins. It will take only a matter of microseconds for it to assume my duties.'

'But it won't be *you*.'

'Another fine line.'

Cormac bowed his head for a moment. 'Perhaps I can accept that doing less than you are able to do is no crime.' He raised his head. 'She said she would not be allowed to live "while the betrayer still sits on his throne", and of course then I didn't understand what she was talking about. Now I do. You crossed the line when you sent your own people to the *Trafalgar,* so that ship's AI could use them to initiate Jain nodes. In that you are culpable of murder. I'm here for the sake of Fiddler Randal and Henrietta Ipatus Chang, and others whose names only you know.'

'Ah, that,' said Earth Central. 'So you are a moral creature, Cormac?'

Cormac stepped forward through the hologram and flung Shuriken. The throwing star shot from his hand, extending its blades only a little way, then whirred up to a scream. It hit the pillar above the Earth Central AI, and the pillar shattered, a rain of blue glass clattering down and spilling through the gratings underfoot.

Cormac swept up the ruler of the Polity in one hand.

Something was rising up from the depths of Lake Geneva, and weapons turrets had already risen like giant steel fists from the hedging mountains. It didn't matter. Cormac knew he could pull his companions out in an instant now, back up to that old orbital museum against which the *Harpy* was docked and hidden by its own chameleonware. That same place where Cormac had paused for a while to walk and gaze upon the exhibits – artefacts from the true beginning of the space age. He recollected how the curator there, a human without augmentation, had taken an interest in him and asked where he was from.

Back from the wars, Cormac had replied, to which the response had been, What wars?

Ever was it thus.

After watching Mr Crane pull on his boots again, don his coat, place his hat upon his head and carefully adjust it, Cormac peered down at the grey orb he himself held. He gazed into it, but its structure revealed no more than would the regular formation inside some rock. However, by concentrating his U-sense on the hand that held it, it revealed thin dense fibres in its bones. Earth Central had not been lying about that.

With annoying predictability, Arach asked, 'What now, boss?'

What now indeed.

'I'm heading out to the accretion disc to find Mika,' Cormac replied. 'If you and Mr Crane here,' he nodded to the brass Golem, 'were to come with me, that would be more convenient, since then I wouldn't have to find another ship.' He shrugged. 'Or you can go your own way. I would say that things are going to be a bit hot for all three of us in the Polity right now.'

'But I meant,' said Arach, 'what *now*?' The spider drone reached up tentatively and tapped one sharp foot against the grey orb.

Cormac weighed the thing for a moment.

'Here, you take this,' he said, then tossed it to Mr Crane, who snatched it from the air snake-fast.

The brass Golem held the orb for half a second, before saying, 'He must pay,' then crushed Earth Central to fragments, and scattered crystal glitter about his lace-up boots.

Cormac guessed Crane must be choosy about what he included in his collection of toys. He gazed down at the glitter for a moment, then up at the sky, trying to fix that blue in his mind. 'Time to go,' he said.

Another one of those ridiculous myths that seems to have become a stand-in for religion and a sop for humans ashamed to be not only less able than their creations but ruled by them is the avenging angel, the modern-day Nemesis. Sometimes this character is accompanied by Mr Crane, by a steel spider, by a woman with mysterious powers, or by any combination of each and all of them. Inevitably he and his companions are associated with that all-too-real alien entity, Dragon. This godling, this Nemesis, has great powers, for he can get to any AI, anywhere, and then kill it. He is there to keep our masters in line. Sometimes he is referred to as Ian Cormac, or Agent Cormac (associations there with those dangerous heroes of ECS). It is complete wishful thinking, of course, and all too ridiculous to be true . . .

– Anonymous

Orlandine woke immediately, but her perception was sluggish, crippled because a vast proportion of her resources was simply unavailable. The photovoltaic cells on the surface of her interface sphere were supplying just enough energy for her to wake and to power up the passive sensors dotted about the same surface. Her body temperature sat a spit or two above absolute zero, and though the cryonic technique she had used as she froze would have prevented the formation of damaging ice crystals, she knew there would still be a lot of repairs to make. She also needed much more power than was presently available to be able to think at more than a mere human level, and to see her surroundings with more than the present limited proportion of the electromagnetic spectrum available to her.

Belatedly, she checked the time, wondering if the universe was filled with dead suns and red giants, and whether her present wakefulness was due to her briefly warming herself on its cooling embers. But a mere two hundred years had passed.

Orlandine was astonished, then fatalistic. Unless she had somehow beaten the huge odds stacked against her, there was only one reason for her to be awake now: someone had come looking for her. She wondered why. Surely the Polity AIs would not bother waking her from certain death merely to execute sentence upon her? Or perhaps they were waking her so they could study her? She concentrated her severely hampered faculties on available sensor data.

The stars here were sparsely scattered, vague dots without sufficient light output to power up her interface sphere. However, she was being supplied light. Unfortunately it was lased, focused upon her sphere, and all but blinded her to its source.

Energy levels gradually increased and she managed to gain another percentage point of processing power. No, not Polity AIs, for in two hundred years they would have utterly understood and conquered Jain technology or been annihilated by it, so in either case would have no need to study her. Few others possessed the resources to find her, though it was possible that had changed in the intervening centuries. Running projections, calculations and her limited suite of programs, she could not find the answer, so did something utterly human: she took a wild guess.

'Hello, Dragon,' she sent.

'Well, that's a confirmation,' came the immediate reply.

The laser now divided into numerous beams, each focusing precisely on individual collections of photovoltaic cells, allowing her to see the massive alien hanging out there in void.

'What do you want?' she asked.

'Always a difficult question, that,' Dragon replied. 'What do you want, Orlandine? Think carefully before you answer now.'

Orlandine did not bother trying to calculate what might be the correct reply, what would be the best answer to ensure her survival in this situation. Even with her full processing power she probably could not have worked it out, for Dragon was as opaque as steel and even major Polity AIs struggled to divine the reasoning behind its words. She decided to just be truthful.

'Well obviously I want to survive,' she said.

'That is plainly evident,' Dragon replied. 'But what do you *want?*'

Orlandine thought long and hard about that. What had driven her to hang on to a Jain node, to go as far as killing her lover to conceal that she possessed it? What had been her life's aim before Erebus had killed her twin brothers?

'I want to build something numinous.'

The intensity of the lasers abruptly increased, upping the power the voltaics were supplying her. Her processing capacity jumped up another five per cent. Obviously she had given a correct answer, though was it correct enough?

'It is a long slow struggle to overcome the inertia of the Polity, of its humans and even its AIs,' Dragon informed her, 'without the kind of impetus Earth Central supplied by giving Erebus the means to control Jain technology and allowing it to attack – an attack you stopped in its tracks.'

'Yes,' said Orlandine. 'Development being proportional to death toll has been a benchmark throughout human history.'

'Unfortunately,' Dragon agreed, continuing, 'you of course understand that Fiddler Randal ensured Erebus would never attack again, but you are certainly unaware that Earth Central would never allow such an attack again.'

'Why?'

'The AI that controls the Polity is still called Earth Central, but it is not the same AI – it is a replacement with an understanding that such callous actions will result in it being destroyed just like its predecessor.'

'Destroyed?'

'Agent Ian Cormac learned of its perfidy . . .'

It took Orlandine only a moment to grasp that thread. Of course, with his decidedly unusual abilities, Cormac could be the ultimate assassin – barring USER disruption there was no defence he could not step around, and no human or AI he could not get to.

'This is very interesting,' she said, 'but hardly explains why you came after me.'

'Over the last two hundred years there have been great dangers, near-extinction events and many like the biophysicist Skellor. Quarantine and selective sterilization of many areas within the Polity has destroyed all the Jain technology there, however, Jain-tech remains a severe threat, one that the Polity, especially since it is as *undeveloped* as when you departed it, is not truly equipped to deal with. While the accretion disc swarms with Jain technology, even though it is now an interdict area and surrounded by massive defences and watch stations, the evil keeps escaping its box.'

Orlandine contemplated her incorrect prediction of the now. Of course, though AIs might perfectly understand Jain technology, that did not necessarily mean they were safe from it. Many AIs and humans perfectly understood the working of guns and bombs, but that had not stopped people dying as a result of their use.

'The Polity will go the same way as the other races,' she said. 'Some future race might find just a few ruins.'

'Just so, especially when the accretion disc's sun fully ignites and blows a sandstorm of Jain nodes across the Polity.'

'What do you want me to build?' she asked.

'You say that you want to build, Orlandine, but two hundred years ago you demonstrated a greater facility for destruction.'

'I see.'

'You are,' said Dragon, 'going to spend the rest of your existence annihilating a technology, tearing it up by its roots and utterly erasing it. In effect, the numinous thing you will build will be the future of the Polity. Do you agree?'

'Did you think for one moment that I wouldn't?'

The light grew brighter.